COLD
REVENGE

LEE WEEKS

**SIMON &
SCHUSTER**

London · New York · Sydney · Toronto · New Delhi

A CBS COMPANY

First published in Great Britain by Simon & Schuster UK Ltd, 2017
A CBS COMPANY

1 3 5 7 9 10 8 6 4 2

Simon & Schuster UK Ltd
1st Floor
222 Gray's Inn Road
London WC1X 8HB

www.simonandschuster.co.uk

Simon & Schuster Australia, Sydney
Simon & Schuster India, New Delhi

A CIP catalogue record for this book
is available from the British Library

Paperback ISBN: 978-1-4711-5321-1
.eBook ISBN: 978-1-4711-5322-8

Printed and bound by
CPI Group (UK) Ltd, Croydon, CR0 4YY

MIX
Paper from
responsible sources
FSC® C020471

Simon & Schuster UK Ltd are committed to sourcing paper
that is made from wood grown in sustainable forests and support the Forest
Stewardship Council, the leading international forest certification organisation.
Our books displaying the FSC logo are printed on FSC certified paper.

For Michael James Evans
Esgyn ar adenydd cân
(Rise on the wings of song)

Prologue

Jess the springer spaniel's whole body wagged in excitement as she dived in and out of the debris washed up with the floodwater on the bank of the River Lea. Philip Greenaway was glad he'd worn his Wellingtons for his walk in the Lee Valley Park. The mud was thicker than he'd thought it would be; the river had burst its banks and black silt spewed up over the grassy verge.

'That's it,' he muttered to himself, as the first signs of a new deluge of rain landed in heavy drops on his mac and bounced off the fast-flowing river. 'We're done, Jess,' he called out in the dog's direction, shouting above the noise of the roaring water. She popped out to look at him and then turned back and stepped further onto the platform of debris, burying her head into the water so that three quarters of her body was no longer visible.

Philip was anxious now; he knew the dog was resting her weight on the carpet of broken twigs and floating debris at the edge of the river bank.

'Jess!' he called, more insistent this time, approaching the water's edge. His feet sank through the skin of vegetation and lodged in the mud beneath. Steadying himself, he lifted one foot free, found firmer ground, then moved the other, and gingerly edged sideways towards the dog. She was just feet away when the river surged and filled his boots with icy water, tipping him backwards and seating him in the freezing water up to his waist, and he felt his body start sliding with the current. He grabbed at the branches of a fallen tree, whilst making a desperate attempt to get hold of Jess's collar. Just managing to hook his finger beneath it, he pulled her back towards him as he lifted his feet and tried to propel himself backwards to the bank. And it was then that he saw the arm, waving as it dipped and rose in the racing water, and, as the weeds parted in the dog's wake, a woman's head surfaced from the debris, her white eyes looking skyward, her neck cut open, head thrown back, and the weeds catching around her face.

Chapter 1

Detective Chief Inspector Dan Carter stood on the bank of the churned-up River Lea as the water sped past below him.

'Thanks, Mr Greenaway, sorry to keep you.' Philip Greenaway was wrapped in a foil blanket, standing forlornly and staring out at the river, watching the team of search officers scouring the opposite bank. The day had never really got light; more rain was on its way in the October storms that were bringing the first snow of the winter to the UK.

'Are you a regular walker here?'

'Yes, most days, but I wouldn't have seen her if Jess hadn't disturbed all the floating stuff at the edge of the river. The woman was tucked in beneath a fallen tree.'

His dog was on a lead now; she sat impatiently waiting for her master to stop talking and resume walking.

Carter was looking upstream. 'I'm just working out where she could have gone in? This place is just a maze of lakes and waterways, isn't it? Do you know it well?' Carter already knew a fair bit about Greenaway from the police check. He knew he was a retired civil servant whose wife had died five years before and he had never had so much as a speeding ticket.

'Yes, I'm a volunteer here in the summer. She has to have gone in in the hundred feet of river above here, as beyond that there is the navigation channel, and she can't have got through that.'

'And is this place open twenty-four/seven?'

'Not now in the winter months, the car park closes at seven-thirty.'

'Thank you, that's really helpful. Are you okay? You will get a call from Victim Support, so don't hesitate to ask for counselling – we all need a bit of that now and again.' Carter smiled.

'Thank you, I'm okay, just cold and wet. But at least I'm not dead and dumped in the river, hey?'

Carter waited whilst his partner, Detective Sergeant Ebony Willis, walked back down the bank towards him.

'Mr Greenaway,' she said, as she drew close, 'can I just ask, is that car park, up there on the right, the closest one? It's called Meadowsweet.'

'Yes, it is, I usually park there.' Greenaway was staring into the river, in shock. 'We've had a few drownings over the years. The water is very cold and people come up here on a hot day and think it's a good idea to take a dip. But she didn't look like one of those to me; she was . . .' He paused as his recollections took him back to the face in the water. 'She was injured, her neck . . . and her arm . . . it was almost as if she was waving at me, it was really odd.' He looked from one detective to the other. Willis stared back but her eyes were watching the officers on the bank opposite as they edged closer to the water and prodded the debris with sticks. One of them looked up at her and shook his head.

Carter nodded his agreement with a concerned smile. 'Thank you again for your help. We have your details and you have our number in case you need to get in touch. I'm sure you'll be relieved to hear you can get off home now.'

'Not with this one.' He looked down at his dog and smiled. 'She still needs a walk.' He handed back the foil blanket and went off up the pathway, away from the scene, being dragged along by the dog.

'No chance of divers going anywhere near the water today,' Carter said, 'way too dangerous.' He was older than Willis by ten years, a few months from turning forty, half-Italian, the son of a London cabbie. His nose had been broken many times when he was a budding East End boxer but it had ended up looking almost straight, if a little flatter than it started out, minus its cartilage. His hair was greying in dramatic style with silver buzz-cut sides and thick black hair left long on top.

Willis nodded her agreement before turning and indicating the way she had come. 'The car park is not monitored; there's no CCTV. It would be pretty easy to access the park after hours. I've been looking at possible sites where she went in.' She and Carter had worked together for the last six years, since Willis joined Major Investigation Team 17, based in Archway. MIT 17 was one of four teams responsible for murders and major incidents north of the Thames. 'You want to take a look?'

'Yeah, we'll take a walk up there in a minute. I want to take a look at her again before she's taken to the morgue. The park will be anxious for us to reopen this section ASAP.'

They walked up the bank towards the forensic tent on the grass verge above the path. Willis was taller by an inch than Carter, with caramel-coloured skin from her mixed-race parentage. Broad-shouldered and athletic-looking, she always wore the same combination of shirt and black trousers for work; out of work, the black trousers became blue jeans and the shirt became a T-shirt of any kind that looked clean. Carter liked his clothes flamboyant; he liked his designer labels. Carter and Willis had grown up very differently: Carter had been part of a big loving family and Willis had spent a lot of her childhood in children's homes, and for her, they were the good times. But they both understood the one thing that really mattered to them – they had each other's backs.

Inside the white and blue forensic tent, the photographer was just finishing; he came out as they went in. The woman from the river was lying on a plastic sheet, on her back, the signs of decomposition in the curling back of her lips and the bloating of her abdomen that had forced her rise to the surface. Her skin was lifting glove-like from her arms where her jacket had torn. She was fully clothed in a denim mini skirt and vest top under a burgundy satin bomber jacket. The skin was mottled grey, the flesh blistered and cratered on her exposed legs. Her black hair was still half-tangled inside a pink scrunch band on top of her head and her head was nearly detached from the body; the vertebrae on one side of her neck, the edge of the jaw bone and the corner of the collarbone were all visible.

Willis pulled on some gloves and knelt on the plastic sheet, before carefully lifting and turning the woman's head to the left side. The spine protruded now, pale grey, the flesh eroded, worn away by the pounding water.

'Stab wounds to the neck area.'

Carter let her get on with it; this was her thing. Some

people merely recorded the things they saw, as they put their toe in the water, checked the temperature and decided just to watch from the sidelines, but Willis dived straight in. She'd been through such a lot in her life that she could take a great deal of pain from others, and she could empathise on another level than him.

'All on her right side. There's extensive damage from the river, the debris has exaggerated the wound – opened it up.' She looked down over the body. 'As for the other injuries,' Willis examined the wounds on the victim's arm, 'it's hard to tell whether the lacerations on her were made before she died. When she's cleaned up for the post-mortem, things should be clearer.'

'How long had she been in the water?' asked Carter.

'A month, no more, maybe less. I put her age at mid to late thirties.' Willis opened the woman's mouth. 'Methadone, heroin user, wrecked teeth.'

Carter was getting ready to leave the tent, which was making him feel claustrophobic. He knew Willis loved stepping inside a forensic tent, the white glow, the captured nearness to the deceased, the first smell of their body, the things they brought with them from their last minutes of life. One time she told Carter that being inside the forensic tent made her feel like she was a child, hiding under the sheets, that it was her safe place. The irony wasn't lost on either of them.

'We'll probably be able to lift a print from the couple of remaining fingers,' said Willis, raising the hand. From the elbow down, where the sleeve of the jacket ended, the skin on the arms had lifted and was ready to come away on its own. 'She has needle marks,' continued Willis. 'I would say, looking at the state of her body, that she has been living this life for many years. There are tattoos,' she continued, as she turned the arms outwards.

Carter nodded as he stared at the face. There was something bugging him; did he know her? Was it one of the hundreds of women he'd come across in his twenty years as a copper?

'On her left wrist, I think it says *ignite the fire*, and there is a chain on her right wrist, both in red ink,' she said as she leaned across the body.

He squatted down beside Willis. 'She's familiar to me.'

Willis unzipped the woman's jacket pocket and looked inside. 'Two condoms, bank card with the name of Millie Stephens. Ring a bell?' She looked at Carter and waited as he took out his phone and looked up some information.

He read from the screen. 'Jimmy Douglas? Remember him?' he asked.

'The man who went on trial for the murder of schoolgirl Heather Phillips in 2000?'

'That's the one – they never found the body but they found her DNA in his van. He had a band of loyal followers the press dubbed his disciples. Each of them was tattooed with a red chain to bind them and with his motto – *ignite the fire*. There were seven of them altogether. Millie here was one.'

Chapter 2

Saturday 20 May 2000

Jimmy Douglas sat on the floor of his lounge, and swigged back his bottle of beer as his girlfriend Nicola came in from the garden, floating in in an Indian-print maxi skirt and cropped T-shirt with a Smiley logo.

'The sun's at the back now,' she said as she went through to the kitchen. 'It's reached the patio.' They lived in a bungalow at the edge of a farm. It was the first building on the lane to Hawthorn Farm, just outside Chesham. They'd been there for eighteen months.

Douglas drank his beer and watched her move around the place; she was nervous and excited. It was Saturday and Douglas always took the weekends off. He was away working most of the week, selling his equine products. He had built up a good network across the country and, when he wasn't doing that, he had a sideline going in drugs: ecstasy and weed mainly. He knew all the farmhands and pick-up points where he could buy it for a good price and sell it for more. Nicola sold a good deal of it from the bungalow when they held parties. Raves were banned now, but they could still hold a ticket-only bash on the eight-and-a-half acres that came with the bungalow. They knew how to keep it discreet and Douglas never kept large amounts at the bungalow.

She came in with another beer, lifted her skirt and straddled Douglas as he sat on the floor. He held on to her voluptuous bottom and slid her further up onto his lap. He untucked her T-shirt and pulled it up over her breasts; she wasn't wearing a bra. She laughed as he examined her.

'Has the farmer been over?'

'Of course.'

Nicola raised her bottle to her lips and looked sideways at Douglas, grinning, the beer dribbling down her chin. She laughed as Douglas leaned forwards to lick her face.

'Is he in love with you?'

'Truscott? No way, he's got his beady little eye on the young ones at the stables. He comes down here to get some relief when it all gets too much for him.'

Douglas laughed and their hips rocked together as he sat back and studied her. She wasn't the prettiest of women, as her face always looked a little pissed off, her mouth wide and downturned, her nose a little too long and too big, but her eyes were a pretty brown and her neck was long and white, like a swan's. Douglas loved the way his hand could encircle her whole neck, the way his thumb could press on one side of her trachea and he could watch her almost pass out. He loved the way she was ruled by her senses. Douglas knew he had both the brains and the looks to choose a partner who suited him intellectually but no one would understand his love of pain as she did.

'Tell me, who is in the yard?' asked Douglas. 'Are they up for a night of it?'

'Millie is, there's a few of them for definite; I said we will

have a barbecue this evening. I said they can bring friends.'
Nicola held her beer bottle to her lips, paused before drinking and rolled her eyes skyward. She was jittery, Douglas could feel it. The thrill of the corruption and conquest made her wet. But what he thought was really clever about Nicola was that she could wrap it all up in a cloak of nurturing maternal concern. Jimmy could charm their pants off, but Nicola could offer to wash them, both with the same aim. Douglas had a couple of girls in mind at the moment, but one was an ongoing project.

He'd watched Heather Phillips since the day they first came to look around the bungalow on Hawthorn Farm with the prospect of renting it, on a late afternoon in autumn. They had pulled over to allow a school minibus to park and unload its passengers. A lone girl had got off, not turning to say goodbye, just muttering her thanks under her breath as the door closed behind her. She glanced up at the waiting car and her eyes met Douglas's. Douglas watched her and he saw such beauty in her sadness; she was on the cusp of adulthood, she was a flower waiting to open its petals, waiting to be introduced to the world – his world.

Nicola was sitting in the passenger seat, beside him. They'd been together for six months then, still testing one another out, but already they had gone further than Douglas ever dreamt he would. He had found a partner who understood him, who shared his fantasies, who could take them to the next level. She had looked at him and smiled. They knew they wanted the bungalow at Hawthorn Farm even before they saw it and Nicola knew how to seal a deal.

'Did you say the place comes furnished?' Douglas had asked. The farmer, Truscott, eyed them suspiciously and looked in danger of deciding they weren't suitable tenants.

'The beds can stay but I have others coming to look at the place. It's going to be twelve hundred a month plus bills. Have you got the money? You doing well for Champion?' Champion was the name of the premium horse feed supplement company that Douglas worked for.

'I'm their number-one salesman, Mr Truscott. I make sure I work hard. I can pay the rent, don't worry. Plus, I can help out on the farm when you need; I can turn my hand to most things. My family owned a farm in Ireland,' he lied. 'We had a stud farm.'

Douglas had been brought up by his gran after his mother left him. His gran couldn't cope with him, his behaviour wasn't right for such a young boy and she couldn't handle his darkness. At the age of seven, he lured a five-year-old boy into the woods and tortured him to death. The authorities said it was just a children's game gone wrong.

'Why did you do it, Jimmy?' his gran asked him.

'Just to see what it felt like.'

'And her?' Truscott asked.

Nicola had gone before them into one of the bedrooms and had climbed onto the bed, pretending to test it out. She lay back, her skirt rode up and Truscott watched, goggle-eyed.

'This place has a great feel to it, I can see me fitting right in,' said Nicola. 'I'll have plenty to do, growing my own herbs, making jam. Maybe I can help in your house, Mr Truscott? I can lend a hand too sometimes?' Nicola was bra-less under her T-shirt.

Douglas smiled. 'It will be nice to know she has someone to look out for her just a few minutes' walk away when I'm not here.'

Nicola winked and smiled at Truscott.

'I apologise, Mr Truscott, my girlfriend is a bit of a flirt.'

'No need,' he laughed, over-eager. 'She's a lovely girl.'

Nicola rested on her elbows and smiled at him as she parted her legs a fraction more. Truscott nervously looked at Douglas. Douglas smiled back encouragingly.

'Would you like to kiss my girlfriend, Mr Truscott?'

'I wouldn't dream of it, I mean, she's a lovely girl, but she's spoken for.'

'Go ahead. I'd like you to.'

Nicola slid to the edge of the bed and beckoned him forwards.

'Come and kneel here and kiss me properly,' she said.

Truscott approached cautiously and knelt in front of her. She opened her legs and he stared at her black satin knickers and his breath rasped as he reached his callused farmer's hands to stroke the soft wet satin. He made an odd sound in his throat, like a whimper, as he hooked his finger beneath the crotch and pulled it to one side. Nicola had stopped smiling; her breath was short and passionate and her heels were raised, her legs starting to have the faintest tremble as she rested back on her forearms and watched his watery blue eyes stare up at her gratefully.

Truscott didn't dare move, he looked so frightened that the dream would end, his cock bulging in his trousers. Nicola arched her back as she held on to his head and didn't let go. She wrapped her thighs around his head and held him vice-like and he pushed deeper with his mouth. As she orgasmed she released him and pushed him backwards so that he fell on the floor. Douglas stepped forwards to stop Truscott as he tried to scramble onto the bed and onto Nicola with his trousers catching around his knees. Douglas was smiling as he held up his hands and said, 'Enough for now,' whilst Nicola lay back laughing. Truscott sat back and began to chuckle.

'When do you want to move in?' he had asked.

Now Douglas toyed with the idea of unzipping his flies but he knew the time to make sure they'd have company tonight was fast slipping away.

'Maybe you should get over there,' he said, 'tell them we're going to go for it tonight.' He closed his eyes, tipping his head back to rest on the edge of the chair behind him. He felt the cold of the beer bottle against his chest. Life was good.

'Is Heather in the yard today?' he asked, taking a drink of cold beer.

'Yes, she's been running after the little kids on their ponies all day.'

'You could offer to give her a bath,' Douglas smiled.

'I could, and you could lick her dry.'

'And take both of you at once, one on my cock, one on my mouth?'

'Softly, softly, gentle with baby.' Nicola leaned forwards and whispered in a child's voice into Douglas's face.

He grabbed her throat and then relaxed, smiling, laughing as he slipped his hand to nestle between her warm thighs. 'Patience will be rewarded.' She smiled.

Chapter 3

Millie Stephens' body had been removed from the bank of
the River Lea and was now laid out on a stainless steel dissecting table in the mortuary of the Whittington Hospital
in Archway. It was just a five-minute walk from Fletcher
House, the building where Carter and Willis worked, a
place that held four of the capital's Major Investigation
Teams. Dr Jo Harding was in charge of the pathology
department. She was in her mid-fifties, ultra-slim, blonde-
haired, and with a touch of Scandinavian class about her
in her cheekbones and her fine, make-up-free features.
She was tireless in her approach to professionalism in her
work, but she didn't take it home with her though. When
the hours were done she liked to party hard and was well-
known in the police department that she worked with for
having a voracious sexual appetite that was no respecter of
marital status. But recently, she'd found love with another
woman, an artist from Dartmoor, and she was more con-
tented than she'd ever been.

She was reading through the GP's notes on Millie and
looked up through her visor as she watched the detectives
approach, suited up for helping with the post-mortem.
Willis was going to be the one helping physically, if needed;

Carter would be there to observe. They would stay for the bulk of it, but not all. There were many hours of painstaking work ahead, tissue analysis and sample collection, and they had their own workload to contend with.

Mark, the diener, worked alongside Dr Harding and did a lot of the hands-on work. It was his job to wash, weigh, document and do most of the cutting open of the corpses. It was also his job to sew them back up and get them looking presentable for their families. He had already prepared Millie's body and removed her clothes, to send to the laboratory. He had washed her hair and sifted the wash water before sending it for analysis. She lay naked in the quiet of the dissecting room. Her body was close to being emaciated. Her bones were hardly covered by flesh and her ribs were arched high.

'Good morning, DCI Carter, DS Willis,' Harding said. Mark nodded and smiled their way. 'You have brought me an interesting cadaver this morning,' she continued with a wry smile. 'There is some history to Millie Stephens?'

'We try to keep your work interesting.' Carter smiled.

'Pity she ended up here, but pretty inevitable considering where she came from,' Harding replied.

Mark handed the diagram of Millie's body, with all her injuries noted on it, across to Harding. 'The injuries caused by a weapon and pre-mortem are highlighted,' he said. Carter came to stand next to Harding and look at the diagram. Willis glanced at it and then went around to the other side where Mark was taking measurements from a wound on Millie's leg.

'We have the GP's notes here for Millie,' said Harding. 'She is thirty-three. She's a registered heroin user. There are several injection sites that look to have ulcerated.' She looked up as she said that, and Mark confirmed it with a nod, as he finished measuring one that had been cleaned out by the bottom-feeders in the river and now was three inches in length and down to the bone.

'How long has she been dead, Doctor?' Carter asked.

'Between two and three weeks.'

'These look like defensive wounds?' asked Willis, directing her question at Harding, as she bent to get an eye-level look at the victim's forearms. 'It was impossible to tell when she was straight from the river, but you can see now that the cuts are clean. She fought back hard.'

'Yes, the same short-bladed knife was used to cut her on several places on her body,' answered Harding, 'including her arms, as well as at least five knife wounds into the side of the neck, from back to front, close proximity to one another, which is why they opened up the side of her neck. They cut through the trachea and that's likely to be the cause of death.'

'Any thoughts about the type of weapon, the dimensions?' Willis asked Mark.

'Yes, two point two inches blade length,' he answered. 'It has a hilt on the underside of the knife, and three holes in the blade that left a pattern in some of the wounds. We see this type many times, it's available in many retailers. There is the impression of the hilt; it's left bruising below two of the deeper stab wounds.'

'We'll take a cast from where it inserted into her neck here,' said Harding, 'where it struck the vertebrae. This wasn't the only weapon used on her. There are injuries at the back of the skull, but we'll know more about those when we've removed the scalp.'

'Is there evidence of a sexual motive?' asked Carter.

'No evidence of tearing of the tissue or bruising,' answered Harding.

After a nod from the doctor that she was ready for him to proceed, Mark made a Y incision from each shoulder to the sternum and then, with gentle precise cuts, down to the pubis. He made small cuts through the tiny layer of fat on the abdomen. The smell was pushing Carter a few steps back.

'Millie here missed her guru Douglas coming out of prison. What's he been like inside?' Mark asked, pausing as he began cutting out the blocks of organs.

'He's been a model prisoner, as you would expect,' said Willis. 'He's also used the time to study everything that was offered to him. When he got transferred to Wandsworth, which is now a training prison, he became a chef.'

'The tattoos on her wrists must have meant something to her, she chose not to have them removed,' Harding said, as she looked again at Millie's arms. 'A lot was made of these tattoos at the time.'

'Nicola Stone did the tattooing, apparently,' answered Willis, who had been binge-reading about the case since they found Millie. 'Douglas was represented by the central large link, his disciples by the red links either side, and every new disciple was marked by a new link. They were chained together in secrecy, all seven of them.'

'And *ignite the fire*?' Harding looked at the other wrist. 'Carter, were you around at the time?' She turned to him.

'I was a rookie, I wasn't assigned to the case. Also, this was Thames Valley Police, not the MET, although it spread to other forces, all connecting Douglas up to disappearances of adults connected to the farms he visited. All of them were in their teens and early twenties. They were all vulnerable in some way.'

'I read about it,' said Mark. 'Douglas had this weird mantra he lived by, it was all about igniting the inner fire in someone, opening their eyes to the pleasure in pain, and then he had another line which went something like: *There is no life more exciting than one close to death.* Now he's a chef ... very strange.'

'He was a student of the Marquis de Sade,' said Harding.

'No idea who that is,' said Carter, shaking his head.

'Really?' Jo Harding looked at him curiously. 'Never heard of S and M? Course you have. I can't imagine you missing out on anything, Chief Inspector. The Marquis de Sade popularised it, wrote about it in the eighteenth century, the tapping into pain for pleasure. He was the master of it. Douglas would have seemed like an amateur next to him.' Harding examined the womb on a separate dissection tray. 'No actual births but she has evidence of having been pregnant.' She looked at Mark, who nodded his agreement as he studied the inside of her pelvic cavity and cut away samples of tissue. He took blood samples, bagged and labelled them.

Harding finished handling and dissecting the organs and continued her examination of Millie Stephens' body. Carter and Willis came to stand behind Mark, who was waiting, scalpel poised, to start cutting around the scalp.

'Two sites at the back of her skull,' he said, turning the head, which was resting on a metal plinth, just to raise it enough for examination. 'A here and another, B, here,' he went on, as the hair and flesh on the scalp had become enmeshed with bone and concaved in two places in her skull. 'Neat small areas, made by two different weapons delivered with the same force, probably same weight. Some type of hammer on A, the other a sort of curved claw pick at B.' He began cutting across the top of the head from ear to ear and, using a scalpel, dug away at the membrane that attached it to the skull, until the top section of scalp was free. Then he placed it over Millie's face before freeing the rest of it to make it possible to examine the skull more easily. Harding leaned closer to shine a light directly on the breaks in the skull.

'Contusions, made before death. Site A has a blunt force trauma,' Harding said, 'site B has extended cracking spreading out from the wound. This has travelled much further into the brain. Definitely, wound B would have been enough to kill her. It must have left her unconscious at least.'

Willis stayed at the head of the table to watch, whilst Carter stayed a few feet away as Mark sawed through the section of skull and cut through the membrane.

'We'll dredge the river to see if we can find the weapons.'

'It's going to be hard to get public sympathy for this murder, isn't it?' said Harding.

'Yes,' answered Carter. 'It shouldn't be, though it's always difficult when it's a prostitute, but one that helped cover up the murder of a schoolgirl? Yeah, you're right – it will be tricky.'

Chapter 4

Saturday 20 May 2000

Heather was cleaning up the yard after a busy day of pony club. All the kids had been picked up now and it was over for another week. She was watching Millie grow more anxious as it got near to finishing time. Heather got on with her work whilst watching Millie trying desperately to catch the farmhand's eye. It wasn't working, Gavin was focused on wheeling the muck from the stables and tipping it onto the manure pile. Gavin, the oldest of the farmhands, was muscled and mouthy and he belched and spat but Millie idolised him; Heather really didn't understand why. Millie's dad mended farm machinery and he was the same rough, hard-working type as Gavin, so maybe that was the reason. Her dad, however, was a nice man; Gavin wasn't. Mr Stephens had brought Millie up on his own since her mother died when she was four. Millie was headed for a degree in agriculture and was starting university in October. She had been looking forward to it, having worked hard for her exams, and had seemed happy and excited. But that had all changed when she had become obsessed with Gavin. Now, all Millie wanted to do was hang around the farm, making her father angry when he came to pick her up and she didn't want to go. He looked disappointed with her. Heather recognised that look very well. It was the same one her own father gave to her every day, but Millie had never said her father hit her; she never had to hide her bruises or lie about how she got them like Heather did.

Heather brushed the dirty water, straw and muck into the drainage channels at the side of the yard with firm hard pushes of the bristle brush. She was wiry and strong, but still had a lot of filling out left to do. She was a slip of a girl with bony hips and fried-egg breasts and long shapeless pins of legs. Heather was tall for her age, at five nine, although she walked with her shoulders a little rounded and her eyes on the ground, but when she did look up she had dark eyes, a wide mouth, full lips and the expression of an innocent Italian beauty. Heather would be sixteen in September.

Millie was sighing and mooching and Heather knew there were still tasks to be done. She wanted to say something to Millie to make her feel better but she couldn't think of anything that might help. So, Heather carried on with her tasks and now she took over Millie's as well. She still had Murphy to bed down for the evening; all the other ponies were in their stables or rugged up and out in the fields. It was a light evening, now the days were stretching into the start of summer, but it was still cold as the sunset neared. She was just beginning to feel the chill after the hot day as she wound the hose back on its reel, waiting for her friend Ash to come and see her before she had to head home; he lived in a van with his mum, on the edge of the farm.

She looked up as Nicola walked into the yard in her long skirt and Smiley top and came over to give Heather a hug. Gavin had stopped his work to greet her, and so had the other stable girl, Yvonne. Yvonne was a watcher, she didn't say much to anyone. Millie had come out from the feed store.

'How is my beautiful Heather, still hard at work?' She smoothed Heather's hair and kissed her.

Heather's uncle, the farm owner, Trevor Truscott, came by on his way into the house.

'You'd better be getting home, Heather.' Truscott's eyes were on Nicola and the two exchanged a smile. 'I don't want your dad ringing me.'

Truscott didn't wait for a reply but went into the house via the back door and the boot room. Heather heard him shout out to his wife to see if she was there. She was a riding instructor. There was little love between the two any more. Everyone knew she was in love with her ex-husband who had recently moved back into the area and the two had been seen parked up in lay-bys.

Nicola smoothed Murphy's neck and threaded her fingers through his mane.

'Who's a lucky horse, then?' He twitched as she pulled. 'You know, Heather, if you ever need me, I will be there for you. You understand what I'm saying?'

'Yes, thank you, Nicola.' Heather didn't ever tell anyone about her problems at home but Nicola must know of them from Truscott. He knew them because they slept together. 'I will stand by you, no matter what. I won't let anyone hurt you.'

Heather looked down, embarrassed, and resumed grooming Murphy with long slow brushes of his glossy flanks. Every time she looked up at Nicola she had the image of Nicola in bed with her uncle. Millie said Nicola had sex with everyone, including Gavin. Millie said it didn't mean anything, it was just sex and Gavin was just ticking women off his list. Heather stayed clear of Gavin. She hated the thought of him near her, of him thinking she might ever be one of those on his list.

'We're having a barbecue tonight, why don't you try to come?' Nicola addressed Heather. 'Just for an hour or so?'

Heather shook her head. 'Sorry, I have to go in a minute.'

'Heather's got her exams coming up, haven't you?' said Millie, moving around to stand next to Heather as if protecting her. 'But I'm coming.'

'Good, it's the first one of the season, going to make it a good one. Gavin's coming, aren't you, Gav?' Nicola called over to Gavin who was moving bales of straw across for the horse's beds. 'Yvonne's coming too.'

Gavin grinned and nodded, his eyes on Nicola, and Heather could almost feel Millie's sadness as she stood beside her.

'Okay, well, you know where I am,' said Nicola, as she walked away. 'You look after yourself, don't work too hard, and shout if you need me. Millie, I'll see you later, honey.'

Nicola turned and walked across to the others who were getting ready to stop work. They watched as she kissed Gavin on the cheek and teased him about his hair, whispered in his ear. She hugged Yvonne.

Heather looked at her watch. It was twenty to seven and she had to be home by seven. It was only a five-minute jog but she didn't dare be late. She was hanging on for Ash, but he seemed to know it, and appeared from the lane, running, out of breath.

'Sorry, I tried to get away but Mum was being difficult.' His eyes were full of worry.

'That's okay.'

'Stay with me for a while.' Ash smiled.

'I can't, I have to go home,' she said. 'My father said I have to be in by seven.'

'On Saturday night?'

'I know, but it's been worse since he saw us together.'

'We weren't doing anything.'

'I have to go, Ash, I'll try to come tomorrow.'

'Heather, I've got my wages, do you want to go into town tomorrow?'

'I'll try. It all depends; I may not be allowed out tomorrow. I'll try my best, promise. Will you put Murphy in his stable for me, put his rug on?' Heather leaned her head against Murphy's smooth and shiny neck as she watched Ash. Ash never looked at her weirdly like grown men did, he never made jokes about things she didn't understand, never talked about sex the way everyone in the yard did. Heather felt safe with Ash. She blamed herself for the fact that men whistled at her as she passed in her school uniform, or waggled their tongues at her as they leered out of car windows. She thought it was something in her that they saw and, although she didn't understand it, she could see that *they* did, and it was trouble. But Ash only looked at her with love and, when the time came, they wanted to be the first for one another.

When she got home her father was raking out the fire in the grate in the sitting room. He looked up at the mantel-piece clock as Heather walked in.

'Cutting it fine; I said seven at the latest.'

Heather had stopped answering her father some time ago

because she knew there was no right answer and to give a wrong answer led to a slap. It was five to seven.

He paused, his fingers covered in soot. 'What do you say?'

'Sorry?' Heather always tried that answer first when prompted.

He stood and strode across and smacked her across the face. Heather toppled backwards.

'Don't you give me that tone. Go and get bathed and then you can help your mother with the tea.' Heather was grateful to be dismissed. 'But, Heather.' He called her back. 'I've told your uncle if he wants you to keep helping at the farm he has to send that boy and his hippy mother packing. I don't want any daughter of mine associating with gypsies, travellers, or whatever you call them. Do you hear me? Take those clothes off outside the back door, don't be traipsing straw everywhere. I've told you before about it. Do you want another one?' He held up his fist.

She stood her ground. 'There was no towel for me to use, I can't strip outside.'

'In the scullery, not outside, you know what I mean.' He glared at her. 'What's been going on at that farm? You're changing, and not for the better. Take off your clothes in the scullery and go and bathe. Do it now.'

Heather went back through the kitchen into the scullery where the washing was done. She had forgotten to strip off in her haste to get up to her room; now she pulled off her breeches and T-shirt and stood barefoot on the cold flagstone floor in her knickers and tried to cover herself as her father walked in carrying the coal scuttle. He stopped and looked at her and waved her away dismissively. 'Get up those stairs, like I said.' Heather felt his eyes watch as she passed.

She went into the bathroom and ran the bath. She lay in the steamy water and dipped her head beneath, feeling the warm water tickle her scalp as it closed up over her ears and all other sound was muted. She thought of Ash, and a surge of adrenaline fluttered up into her throat and she almost giggled, then panicked as she lifted her head out of the water and listened to see if anyone heard. She wasn't allowed to lock the door. Heather kept one eye on it as she ran her fingers across her breasts and touched her erect nipples. Her breasts were sore, the bra had left its imprint around her back. Her fingers slid down between her thighs.

She froze, listening to footsteps outside.

'Get out of that bath, your mother needs you.'

She finished washing her hair and cleaning the bath and then wrapped a towel around herself and went to her room and stared out of her window, pressing her burning cheek against the glass. From there she could see the farm and the roof of the bungalow and she could look across to the right and see the top of the farrier's house. She couldn't quite see Ash's van but she knew he was there. Heather started to cry silently; she felt such sadness deep inside, knowing her relationship with her parents would only get worse, and she had been thinking it through now for so long. She would leave a note when she ran away and it would tell of the way her father administered his punishments, the way he seemed to enjoy it and the way her mother hid her bruises. But would she ever actually get away?

Heather sensed a burning in her stomach and low down in her pelvis and it ached in her back. The feeling was so unfamiliar that she didn't know what was happening to her body until she felt the warm tickle of blood running down her legs. She'd been told about this in school: it was her first period. Not knowing what else to do, she stuffed toilet paper into her knickers, dressed, and went downstairs to her mother in the kitchen.

'I'm bleeding.'

Her mother nodded, walked over and gave her an awkward hug and then released her as her father appeared in the doorway.

'Our girl's become a woman,' she said.

Her father looked at her with a look of despair, shook his head, and turned away.

Chapter 5

It was seven p.m. when Willis and Carter got to Millie Stephens' address in Finsbury Park. It was the front basement flat of a large Victorian terrace. The road was synonymous with street workers, and even though the police had tried to limit the kerb-crawlers by introducing chicanes in the road to put them off, there were still men patrolling in their cars when Willis and Carter got there.

A female community support officer was standing by the black railings and the steps leading down to the entrance to Flat 1A. The house had been subdivided again and again over the years and now housed four one-bedroomed flats. Sandford, the crime scene manager, was inside.

'Get suited up and you can come in,' he said. 'Step on the plates.' Transparent stepping plates led from the front door onto cheap stained carpet that someone had made the mistake of buying in the colour fawn and now was multi-ringed with every colour but fawn. The hallway was dark, with no natural light; battery lights were placed around to aid the search. The place smelt of damp and festering rubbish, of neglect.

'There's no sign that she died here: no evidence of a struggle,' Sandford said, as Carter and Willis entered the hallway. 'The bedroom's on the left, she used it for clients by the look of it.' Sandford was in his early fifties now, quiet and methodical, with a soft spot for Willis and her love of all things forensic, but he had little time for Carter who was too brash and cheeky-chappy for his taste. His assistant Dermot, however, shared Carter's love of football and all things flash.

Dermot stood by the bedroom doorway as Willis went in.

'Be really careful where you kneel or what you touch,' he said. 'There are a lot of needles; she wasn't the best at clearing up after herself or her friends.'

There were two wardrobes in alcoves, peeling wallpaper on the walls and a pink plastic chandelier hanging from a rose in the centre of the ceiling of lath and plaster, which had once been beautiful, but was now devoid of anything left of value, cornices all gone although with the addition of stains, leaked from the upstairs flat. Willis walked around to the other side of a double bed, where a full ashtray, a pipe and used strips of foil were on the bedside table. A used sex toy was on the unmade bed. She looked at the table and wondered what Millie had been thinking about before she went out to meet her killer? Who was Millie, beyond someone whose life had started out full of promise and ended up here, on the game in Finsbury Park? Willis squatted to look behind the bed and saw a photo about to slip down the back of the bedside table. It was of Millie and another woman sitting outside a pub, looking happy. So, she did have one friend, at least, thought Willis.

She left the bedroom, photo in hand, and came back into the sitting room, which was integrated with a small kitchenette made up of a microwave, two small hobs with one electric ring and a plastic concertina curtain to separate it from the sitting room.

'The food in the fridge is all from two to three weeks ago,' said Sandford. 'There was a receipt for some milk and tobacco on the table over there, dated the eighteenth of September,' he gestured towards the coffee table which was littered with full ashtrays and drug paraphernalia, 'along with some older receipts. Dermot's made a start on boxing up her paperwork, there're a lot of unpaid bills, including rent demands. We've got no phone, but there is a charger for a Nokia.'

'Yeah, it could be at the bottom of the River Lea,' said Carter. 'We'll search the river as soon as it's safe, for now we'll need to rely on the data from the company.'

Dermot saw the photo in Willis's hand. 'There are some other photos – she has a few of Douglas here, and the other people back in the day.' Dermot handed her a pack of photos from a box of Millie's belongings that were headed back to Fletcher House. 'I've been looking at the case online, I mean, Jesus!'

'He's been Googling every sordid detail about Douglas,' said Sandford, as he continued to swab down the kitchen door.

'I have looked him up, I must admit, as I recognised him in some of the photos,' said Dermot. 'I bet no one's ever seen these before.' He handed them to Willis. 'There's ones from the farm.'

'Better check his pockets, he'll be selling them to the newspapers,' joked Sandford. He was fond of his assistant even if he did talk too much.

Willis went through the photos, one by one, as Carter looked at them with her.

'We have most of the disciples here, don't you think?'

he asked Willis. She was busy scrutinising them. Sandford came to look at them too.

'I recognise those faces from the past,' said Sandford. 'That was a horrible time in history – not only all the farm animals being killed because of the foot and mouth epidemic but then the disappearance of a schoolgirl caught up in some kind of debauchery. Wrong place, wrong time.'

'Not wrong place, wrong time,' said Carter. 'How many paedophiles do we know who just happened to move in near a vulnerable child? They always know what they're doing. Just like Douglas did.'

'Here is one of Douglas with them all, left to right,' said Willis. 'Millie on the end of the sofa, Yvonne Coombes next to her, Douglas, Nicola Stone, Cathy Dwyer, Stephen Perry, there's one missing.'

'Where are they all now?' asked Sandford.

'Nicola Stone is the only one I know about,' said Carter. 'She was given a new identity, and the last I heard she was discovered living in Margate and moved on. But where, I don't know.'

'She was hated more than him,' said Dermot.

'Yes, the public can't understand it when it's a woman involved in violent crimes,' said Sandford.

'She was the only disciple who went to prison for crimes related to Douglas,' said Carter. 'She was done for lying about his whereabouts when he picked up and raped a university student in Bristol. We never got him for Heather Phillips.'

'It just shows you what an important part of Millie's life it was, doesn't it?' said Dermot. 'She still kept all these photos. It seems sad, she looks no more than a child herself, none of them do, even Douglas.'

'Douglas wasn't a child,' said Willis, 'he was thirty-four when this was taken in 2000.' She held up a photo of Douglas sitting in a sun lounger with a beer in his hand. 'All of his disciples, except Nicola Stone, were under twenty-two. Douglas and Stone were parental figures of the wrong kind.'

'Is this where Millie's been since those days?' asked Sandford. He didn't usually make more than basic conversation with Carter. The two men were very different. They had worked together for the last ten years but they had never had a drink together. Sandford was a tall and quietly spoken man with a love for real ale, cricket and woolly jumpers. Carter liked his gold chains chunky, liked the polo ponies to be large when they galloped across his breast pocket.

'She's been in and out of rehab, back living with her dad sometimes,' answered Carter. 'He's still got the same farm machinery business he has always had and she's been sectioned a few times, spent three episodes in the nick for persistent reoffending: drugs, prostitution, shoplifting.'

'I'm in touch with the cold case team who are investigating Heather Phillips' disappearance,' said Willis. 'They say they approached Millie several times over the years in the hope that she might want to make a statement about Douglas and what happened at the time, but she always said "no comment".'

'They all did,' said Carter. 'It wasn't just about Heather, there were other missing people who Douglas had contact with and who may have been seen at the bungalow. But none of his disciples ever talked about their time in the bungalow at Hawthorn Farm.'

Willis handed Carter the photo of Millie with her friend sitting outside a pub. 'This is recent.'

'I recognise that pub,' said Carter. 'It's on Shacklewell Lane, just down the road from here.'

Millie was smiling broadly at the camera and trying to make her friend look up, but she was laughing and turning her face from the camera.

'I think that's Yvonne Coombes with her,' Sandford said.

Chapter 6

Saturday 20 May 2000

Ash put Murphy's rug on him, put him in the stable and then hung around before heading back to his home. In the pit of his stomach he dreaded seeing his mother at the van. They were allowed to stay in Douglas's field. They'd been there nine months now and they were outstaying their welcome. If there was one thing that a life on the road, moving with the travellers, had taught him, it was to know when you'd outstayed your welcome and needed to move on. His mother was pissing everyone off with her rants and her demands and he couldn't talk to her any more. She only had him in the world and now, at sixteen, he had found the roles reversed and he was having to look after his mother. He wasn't so much a carer as a keeper. He'd written to his grandmother and asked her to help. His mother had been a free spirit in the 1980s, a traveller, an artist like her own mother. Her father had been a history professor and they had allowed her free rein in her life. There had been many good years but now things were getting difficult. When his gran replied he'd know what to do.

As he got near to the van he called out, 'Mum?' He saw

her sitting on the chemical toilet at the back of the van. Her head was bowed and she was so still that he thought she'd fallen asleep. He took a few steps towards her and called again. 'Mum?'

'What?' She lifted her head.

'I'm back.' He heard her muttering and felt the horrible leaden weight of sorrow that she was turning into someone who hated him.

Ash turned at the sound of laughter. From where he stood he could see the back of the bungalow and Nicola drinking beer and laughing; the smoke from the barbecue was blowing in her face and she was trying to get away. Ash had come to know a lot about what went on at the bungalow; he sat many nights and listened to the sounds of partying as they carried across the fields.

Ash lit a fire and settled his mum by it, tried to make her comfortable and wrapped her in her red fleece blanket. It was gone ten now, the BBQ was really getting going.

'What can I get you, Mum? Are you hungry?' he asked as she looked up from her thoughts and focused on him. 'Shall we catch a bus into town and get some fish and chips?'

'No, I need a bath, son, will you ask the people in the bungalow for me?'

'It's too busy over there, Mum; they have people there. Let me boil up some water for you, Mum, we'll fill the overhead shower.'

'I can't do it out here any more, I'm too cold.' She started crying. She looked a lot older than her forty-three years. She was so skinny and frail.

'I know, Mum, I'm sorry, but it's too busy at the bungalow.'

She got up. 'I'll ask them if you're too embarrassed.'

'No, Mum, don't.'

She started shouting at him. 'You're useless, you're absolutely useless!'

Ash wanted to cry so badly, he wanted to sit on the floor and sob, now his mother had turned on him. She was aggressive; she was becoming someone else. Sometimes she didn't even know him. He managed to calm her down and she curled up in the van and went to sleep. Ash sat in the darkness by the fire.

He could see the glow from the fire pit at the back of the bungalow on the patio; he heard the laughter. He saw Nicola dancing to some old acid house music and he poked the fire with a stick and sent up showers of sparks. He heard his mum stirring.

'Ash?'

'Yes, Mum, I'm here.' He loved it when he heard the voice of old return and he knew she had come back to him, if even for a little while. He knew she had dementia and that she had often talked about her own father having it. He had died when Ash was ten but he still remembered those times, the good and the bad days.

'Good boy, I do love you, I'm so tired, so hungry, can you get me something to eat, son?'

'Yes, Mum, wait here.'

Ash went across to the bungalow and Douglas watched him approach from his seat in the deckchair by the fire pit. Ash tried a smile; it was always hard to know how things were with Douglas since his mum had become a nuisance. Before then, Ash had gone around the country with him when he delivered his equine products. Ash had loved it; he'd had great times on the other farms, chatting to the farmers, talking to the workers there. Ash had been with him on most of his day trips for work, Douglas liked the company and Ash was happy to help him any way he could. Douglas had been kind to him and his mum. But Douglas's work meant he stayed away most of the week now.

Nicola came out with some chicken drumsticks on a plate.

'Ash, come and have a drink,' Douglas called.

'Thanks, is it all right if I take some over for my mum, I'll buy some more chicken tomorrow.'

Douglas looked at him. 'You take as much as you want, lad, take some over and then come back: I need to talk to you.'

Ash took the chicken over to the van and made sure his mum ate some before she went back to sleep. Then he went across to the bungalow and sat down beside Douglas. Gavin was there and Millie. Gavin was loud and coarse. His mother called him the Troll, but he had a presence about him that was rough and strong and he got girls easily. Millie was getting drunk. Douglas passed him a joint and Ash took it. He was grateful for anything to make him feel happy at the moment. He'd smoked weed ever since he could remember with his mum. It had never seemed to affect her then, now it made her scream and swear.

'What you going to do about your mam?' asked Douglas.

Ash sat cross-legged on the concrete patio, from where there was a sliding glass door into the sitting room.

'I've written to my gran, I'm hoping she can come and get her.'

'What do you think is the matter with her?'

'Too much weed, I don't know.'

More of the farm workers arrived amid the noisy clanking of carrier bags of booze. Nicola had decided to make cocktails. Two of the stable maids, Yvonne and Cathy, were helping her in the kitchen. Yvonne hardly spoke, Cathy never shut up. Yvonne had spent her life in children's homes and had been sent to the area for a new start. The authorities thought the countryside was the place for her and she'd started helping out at the farm and loved it, so now she did it full time and lived in a shared place in the town with Cathy. Yvonne was trying to find her way forward and heal herself. Cathy was self-centred and egotistical with an over-confidence that was brittle and childlike.

Douglas went into the house and came back with a bag of weed, stopping to talk to Tony, a hitchhiker who he had picked up outside Birmingham, who had the vague idea of going to France but was easily sidetracked. Tony sat on a camping chair near the sliding door in the sitting room getting high, getting pissed. He was running away from a bad situation in Glasgow. He'd beaten up his girlfriend and she had brothers. Ash watched Nicola from his seat on the patio; she was getting hyper, he'd seen her that way many times. She partied hard at the weekends when Douglas came back. She hated being alone.

Douglas turned to Ash. 'I need you to come with me tomorrow and help at one of the farms.'

'What are we doing?' Ash asked.

'You remember what we did last time?'

Ash nodded. Douglas had a way of hiding the drugs on farm land, when he delivered his supplies. He got to know the farmers well, knew which fields were left untouched. They even asked him for advice about their crop planting and their animal grazing. Douglas was a phenomenal bull-shitter, Ash knew that much about him. He also knew that accepting all Douglas and Nicola's help with his mum and feeding them both, had to add up to some big favours. He didn't mind, it was just a bit of fun, after all.

'If someone can keep an eye on my mum, then no problem.' Ash was thinking about Heather, but he knew she'd understand. He couldn't even be sure she'd be able to come to the farm tomorrow.

Nicola joined them and handed them beers. 'I'll do that, I'll be here anyway. I expect she wants a bath, doesn't she?'

'Yes, please, Nicola, I'd be so grateful.'

Douglas looked at Ash and smiled, patting him on the arm reassuringly.

Ash drank beer with the hitchhiker, Tony, and with the new girl, Cathy, who talked about herself non-stop and never asked one question about anyone else. By twelve they were all dancing to rave music and getting high. Ash watched as Nicola began dancing with Tony, who was wasted, but he couldn't stop his legs from buckling. The next time he looked into the sitting room Nicola was gone and so was Tony. Ash said goodnight, knowing he had to go back to check on his mum.

At four in the morning, when the dancing had finished and everyone had gone back inside, Ash walked across to see if there was any beer left outside. He couldn't sleep – he was thinking about his mum, about Heather, so many things to worry him. As he approached he heard the sound of Nicola and another woman laughing; it was Cathy or Millie, or both, he thought, and behind their laughter he could hear the grunt and slap and sounds of sex. He'd heard the sounds coming from the bungalow often, but there was another layer in there, it was the sound of someone in fear and pain; it stopped him in his tracks, and he crawled forwards along the patio to the corner of the sliding glass doors and the gap in the curtain.

Nicola was on her back, Tony on top of her and Douglas with his arm around Tony's neck as he was thrusting into him from behind. Tony was fighting hard to get free. His body was jerking in pain, he was trying to scream but Douglas was forcing something into his mouth. Nicola was laughing. Millie was there and Cathy and maybe others that Ash couldn't see. Then Ash saw Douglas grip Tony's head tight in the crook of his arm and twist back and down. Ash heard a loud crack; Tony's body began to shudder and he slumped forwards onto Nicola who squealed with laughter as she tried to push him off. Douglas stood and dragged Tony off her, pulling him by his arm towards the side of the room as Millie started to scream and Nicola carried on laughing.

Chapter 7

They parked up around the corner from the Queen's Head, just off Kingsland High Street at the start of Shacklewell Lane, and walked across to the pub. It was just beginning to get busy as it approached nine. There were a few people sitting around the tables outside and Willis showed them the photo. 'Do you recognise either of these women?' She was met with shakes of the head. A street worker was watching them and walked away before Willis had time to stop her. Willis knew the prostitutes felt harassed by the police; Hackney hadn't got the best record for dealing with the problem.

Inside the pub Willis showed the photo to the landlady who was serving behind the bar. 'This photo was taken outside here wasn't it?' The landlady took the photo and nodded.

'Do you recognise these women?' asked Carter.

She nodded with a pissed-off expression, and then called over 'Cover for me' to one of the staff who was on a break, sitting at one of the tables. 'We'll talk at the back.' She led them past the bar and down to some tables and chairs meant for dining.

'This one,' the woman pointed to the photo, 'I know her; she has a pitch opposite the pub, just on the corner. She is off her head a lot of the time; she's always getting in fights with other girls. The stuff we find outside our front door, you wouldn't believe it; we've even caught her shooting up in our toilets more than once and having a crap between our bins round the side. Feckin' disgusting.'

Willis took out her notebook. 'What's your name, please?'

'Mary O'Sullivan. I manage this place, along with my husband. Although if you see the lazy bastard, remind him of that for me.'

'Can you remember when you last saw either of these women?' Carter smiled.

'This one is the regular.' She pointed at Millie's picture, or Felicity's as she was known on the streets. 'I haven't seen her, not for a couple of weeks. We were just talking about that, because there's a new girl on her pitch now. We said she'd better be careful, Felicity is a fighter. Why, what's happened to her?'

'What about the other woman in the photo? Do you know her name?' asked Willis.

'They call her Donna. I call them all a fucking nuisance. I knew who they were, I'm old enough to remember what they did and Felicity used to brag about it sometimes. She used to try and trade it for a bit of custom, her claim to fame, she'd shagged Jimmy Douglas.'

'Did you see her most days?' asked Carter.

'Yes, not always the same time though, any time she needed the money for her habit, I suppose. They're all hopeless junkies.'

'Did you ever see her with a pimp?' he asked.

'No, she worked with the other one sometimes.' Mary tapped the photo. 'They were good friends because they picked up punters together, or took it in turns, that's pretty unusual for these girls. Most wouldn't think twice about stabbing one another over a customer. Unfortunately my bedroom is at the front and I see a lot whenever I look out.'

'Do you know where Donna lives?' Carter asked, tapping his finger on Yvonne Coombes's face.

'No idea. They are nothing but trouble to me; police do nothing about the girls. They move them on and they come here!' She raised her hands, exasperated.

Willis was taking down what she said but she paused to ask: 'Anyone else come in looking for either of these women?'

'People come in asking for Felicity all the time, she was really popular. Is she dead? I wouldn't be surprised, she was no spring chicken, the streets take it out of you and she'd had quite a life, hadn't she? I hope she managed to die with a bit of drama instead of an overdose.'

'She was thirty-three. Okay, thanks, we'll be in touch. If anyone comes in asking for either woman, please ring the number on the card. If you see Donna, don't alert her, don't repeat what you've heard from us, just ring us straight away without fail, okay? You are not allowed to speak of this to any member of the press.'

'All right, all right.'

They got outside and began crossing the street. 'I want to try the taxi firm here,' said Willis, striding ahead. 'They must know the women, they have a good relationship with the street walkers normally, they look after them.'

Carter caught her up. 'She rattled you a bit, didn't she, Eb?'

'Yes, she did, it's her attitude and the way she said, "is she dead?", like it didn't matter either way to her. One less human being to bother her; one less prostitute to watch from her bedroom window. They should stop persecuting the girls and do more about the kerb-crawlers.'

'You can see it would be a nightmare to have someone crapping in your porch,' said Carter as they got to the pavement outside the cab office. 'Fighting with the other girls? Having sex in your doorway?'

'Yes.' Willis stopped, turning to face him. She knew he was playing devil's advocate; usually it would have been him saying what she said, but Willis felt a huge obligation to try to look after the street workers. 'She also said punters came in looking for the girls, they probably bought a pint whilst they waited.' Something about Millie's case was getting to her. Millie had made some bad decisions but a lot had been made for her, and at eighteen? That was a good age to be steered the wrong way for life.

Willis had only ever trusted one or two people: trusting made her feel vulnerable, it went against self-preservation. But she trusted Carter without hesitation, they had saved one another before and they had each put the other's life before their own.

Willis showed her badge as they entered the minicab office and she held up the photo at the grille. She introduced herself and Carter.

'Do you recognise either or both of these women?' The Cypriot woman behind the counter leaned in to take a better look. 'They may have been working the streets around here?'

'Can I take it inside and show it to my drivers?' Willis passed it beneath the grille. After five minutes two men came out from the back.

'I did see her regularly, most days. This is Felicity,' answered a man of Turkish origin, who was short and dark, with an oversized tan leather jacket, 'but I haven't seen her for a couple of weeks now. Has something happened?'

'We can't discuss that with you at this time.' Carter smiled.

The driver kept looking at the photo. 'The other one is called Donna, she worked with her sometimes but not all the time, just part-time. She comes here for a couple of nights then not again for a few weeks.'

'When did you see Felicity last?' asked Carter.

He thought about it. 'I last seen her working here on a Tuesday, not this last week, or the week before, I didn't work that week and I don't work Mondays.'

'So that would be Tuesday the nineteenth of last month, September?' Carter clarified.

'Yes, definitely, I remember it. It wasn't busy out on the street for us. I remember it was busy for her and I said to her that very thing and she laughed. I think she lived on Queens Drive, I saw her when I drove past, I saw her go in with men. She was a friendly woman – sad she ended up on the streets.'

'Do you know where Donna lives?' asked Carter.

'I have seen her pushing a buggy not far from here, towards Finsbury Park station, she lives down that way. She has a young kid.'

'Okay, thank you, you've been a lot of help,' said Willis. 'If you see Donna again can you ring this number please? My name is on the top, Sergeant Willis.'

'Of course.'

They walked back across the street to Carter's car, his pride and joy: a new BMW SUV in black, tan leather trim: old-school class with a touch of new-school brash.

'We'll make an early start in the morning,' said Carter.

Willis looked across to the pub and saw the landlady staring at her.

Chapter 8

Sunday 21 May 2000

At five in the morning Ash was still lying on his bunk, looking across, through the windscreen of the van, to the bungalow and the patio when he saw the lounge door open and Nicola come out. She glanced across to his van. He watched her walk across with a feeling of dread. When she reached the van she opened the door.

'Douglas needs you.'

'Now?'

Ash felt his voice crack as he didn't dare look at her, and he didn't want to leave his mother with her either.

'Yes, you'd better go, he's waiting.'

Ash nodded but he didn't move for a few seconds. Nicola was watching him and he felt panic. He looked at his mum lying on the bunk across from him.

'Go on, son,' she smiled sleepily, 'I'll be fine.'

'Yes, she'll be fine, don't worry; he needs you right now.'

Ash said nothing as they drove on the quiet roads for forty minutes. The sky was lightening into dawn as they parked up and Ash realised where they were, at Lambs Farm at the beginning of Dunstable Downs. He and Douglas often called in there to share a brew with the farmer, and it was one of the places they'd stashed drugs. Ash said nothing as he stood at the back of the van watching Stephen and Douglas prepare to lay the body out onto a sheet on the ground. Ash couldn't look at it. A glaze had formed across Tony's eyes, his mouth hung open and his teeth, chipped and crossed at the front, looked as if they would leap at Ash and bite into his face accusing him . . .

You saw it and you did nothing!

Stephen stumbled as he lifted the body into the ground. He was wearing flip-flops, shorts and a Black Sabbath T-shirt. The body groaned as it was moved and air escaped.

Douglas handed Ash the shovel. 'Go and dig up the chest, then make it a big enough space for this one. Good lad.'

Ash took the shovel and walked up and across to the corner of the field.

He stopped at the place he recognised as one of five holes he'd dug when he'd travelled the country with Douglas. He dug down half a metre and hauled out the plastic chest and put it to one side as he continued digging out the grave and making it bigger.

After a while he heard the wheels of a crate being pulled up the field towards him. When he stopped and looked up Tony's face was staring at him from between the slats of the crate. Stephen laughed at Ash's expression.

'Get out now, Ash, that'll do, you've done a good job,' said Douglas. 'Go and start digging ten feet up from here, keep it close to the hedge. We need to hide the chest again.'

Ash hopped out of the hole and walked up the field, did as he was told and chose a spot to dig. He'd done that many times, but it was the first time he'd ever put a body in one. He could see that for Stephen and Douglas, it was not the first time at all. He kept his eye on them and watched them tip the cart backwards into the grave. Tony's body, all arms and legs, was dumped in, bottom first. Douglas started filling in the grave on top of him.

By the time they were finished covering the grave with stones and making it look like it had always been there, Ash was ready for the chest. Douglas took out a few bags of pills and packets, and then closed the lid again.

'Stash the stash, Ash,' he grinned.

Stephen tittered. He was still stoned; he was having a hard job standing up without swaying. He lost his balance, toppled over and lay there looking at the sky and laughing.

Chapter 9

Next morning Willis was in work early. Carter had called a meeting for eight a.m. but there had been a development overnight. Willis had seen the headlines when she was on the way to work. The press had already got hold of the story.

Janice the press officer was waiting to talk to her. Janice had poker-straight red hair and sensible shoes that clashed somewhat with the tattoos that extended up her neck in a butterfly. She had the tabloid papers in her hand, their front covers plastered with photos from the time of Douglas and Hawthorn Farm. None of the front pages showed any sympathy for Millie.

Carter joined them. 'Janice, pleasure to meet you.' Carter pulled out a seat for her to sit down. 'We've talked on the phone, haven't we?'

'That's right. I thought I should come into the office as this case is more complicated than we are used to handling and I'd like you to talk through your priorities so we know how to handle the press. There's a lot of Douglas fever in the papers already.' Janice brought up a few headlines on her laptop to show them. *Devil's Disciples, What Happened to Heather?*, plus the usual speculation about how many victims there could be and how Douglas was due out of prison soon and hoping for fame and fortune as a chef. There were photos of Douglas at a work party away from the prison – apparently he got to work in Michelin-starred restaurants as part of his rehabilitation and preparation for coming out.

'Jesus,' said Carter.

'We want to keep this simple,' said Willis. 'It's about one woman and her murder, not about the backstory. Whatever she did in life she deserves justice in death.'

'I'll try to word it like that. What have you got for me to work with?' asked Janice.

'She was motherless from the age of four, her dad brought her up,' said Willis. 'She did really well in her exams and was headed for a great career in farm management when she fell into Douglas's path.'

'That's still about Douglas,' said Janice, taking notes.

'Okay, well, talk about how she is one more statistic of prostitutes dying,' Willis suggested.

'But she is special,' Janice replied, 'she isn't just one more, is she?'

'Okay, let us think about it,' interrupted Carter. 'We're headed into a meeting. We'll be in touch afterwards.'

They walked into the inquiry team office and set up a monitor at the end of one of the six long tables that housed the majority of the thirty-six detectives that made up MIT 17.

Willis addressed the assembled team, showing them the photo of Millie and Yvonne outside the pub on the screen.

'This is Millie Stephens, thirty-three. Her body was found in the river in Lee Valley Park yesterday morning. We believe she was in the water from sometime soon after the nineteenth of September, three weeks ago. If we take a look at the map on the screen, we have a stretch of water along here beneath the two bridges, and that's where we are pretty certain she must have gone in. We have been told that one of the bridges has yielded some results forensically – traces of blood – we're waiting to hear about that. We have yet to recover her phone. The post-mortem has been carried out and we believe she didn't drown; she was dead before she hit the water. We think she died from stab wounds to the neck.'

Willis passed out the diagram of Millie's injuries. 'She was also assaulted with two other weapons.' She pulled up the photos from the post-mortem on screen. 'The hammer used on the blunt force trauma leaves an unusual pattern on impact.' She showed some more photos of the injuries to Millie's skull. 'There are ridges on the head of it, they seem to have caused limited shattering, and have created a small concave in the skull. The other weapon, a claw weapon,' she changed the photo on the screen, 'is two centimetres wide at its base, and was much more invasive. We are looking for all of these weapons still. We are hoping the divers can get into the water in the next few days. Here is a picture of the knife we are looking for.' Willis brought up an image. 'It's a widely used knife, multi-purpose, it can be bought in many outlets, it gives us nothing except this is not a knife that a professional killer would use.'

Willis took a breath. 'She didn't go quietly; she has defensive wounds to her arms and hands. A public appeal for witnesses will go out today.' She paused as they were joined by someone new. 'We have a new profiler to bring into the team today,' she said. 'Chris Maxwell?'

He held up his hand by way of greeting to the rest of the team.

'Take a seat,' said Willis.

Maxwell was a clean-shaven man in his early thirties with good skin and neat features.

'You're French, is that right?' asked Carter. Both men were around five nine, both keen on their presentation, but Maxwell had gone for neutral colours: camel overcoat, dark tan loafers, burgundy turtleneck sweater. Neat blond hair, cut short and parted to the side. He was very much going for a 'Mr Understated' look.

'Dual nationality, I've been working here for two years,' answered Maxwell.

'Was there not enough work in France to keep you busy?' Carter asked with a smile.

'Plenty, I just fancied a change.' He smiled back, confidently. 'I hope I can be of help.'

'Yes, so do we,' said Carter. 'Welcome to MIT 17.'

Willis continued. 'We are building up a picture of a lonely woman, struggling with addiction. Her life still seemed to revolve around her past and Douglas, as all the photos we found in her flat were from that time. The only recent one we identified was that of Millie with Yvonne Coombes. We are searching for an address for Coombes at the moment.'

'Any of the sex workers been able to help us with this? Anyone worried, or heard about someone who might have done this? Or did anything come up on recent attacks on women in the area?' Carter asked Hector, a detective in his early thirties who liked his suits light grey and his shirts cream-coloured or pink. He was a graduate who had found his niche in the ever-expanding and complex world of intelligence: laptops, mobile phones and social media. 'What about the national site for sex workers?'

'There have been two rapes this year, eight violent

attacks,' answered Hector. 'None that involved taking a victim to a park though. They've been warned to stay off the streets until we solve this but that's unlikely to be heeded. We are looking through Millie's phone data and CCTV is being analysed of all the cars that have visited the car park nearest to where she was found going back to the beginning of September.'

'We will step up patrols in the area,' said Carter, 'and get some undercover officers to walk the streets, try to keep the women safe.'

'We don't think she would have gone to the park with a john,' said Willis. 'She had a perfectly good bed at home, just around the corner. This was probably someone she knew, someone she trusted. We can't ignore the fact that people knew who she was in the area. She'd bragged about her past relationship with Jimmy Douglas, whether this was a factor or not, we don't know, but we can't ignore it.'

'We're working our way through known offenders in the area. So far we haven't found one who used both a hammer-type weapon and a knife. But, there is a long list of violent offenders living around there. We might get lucky and be able to match a number from her phone to one of those. Have SOCOs found anything else of interest at her flat?' Hector asked Willis.

'Sandford says he's nearly finished there now. There are many other prints besides hers,' answered Willis.

'Understandable, the place is going to be DNA Central. Chris, what are your thoughts so far?' Carter asked the new analyst.

'This could be two people. Could be two women she works with, women she's pissed off. Perpetrator is not necessarily taller than Millie, who was five six. The blows to the head, as discussed, could have been to knock her to the floor to make killing her easier. Someone who knows the park, who used to live there or still lives there. Someone who knew Millie and who she liked, who had picked her up before or who offered her enough money to make it worth-while – we know she was facing eviction for non-payment of rent. But the messiness of this killing has an amateur feel to it and the person would have thought hard about what weapons to take so we cannot assume this is a person who works with a hammer, or a man, or anything just yet. We need to find the people Millie was close to. My gut instinct is that this is someone she knew well.'

'DC Blackman, what's the feedback from the streets?' asked Willis. Zoe Blackman was not long promoted to MIT 17, having been a policewoman at Archway Police Station next door. Carter had mentored her and she was good friends with Willis.

'I've been talking to some of the girls on the streets and no one liked Millie, mainly because of the fact she bragged about her time with Douglas. She was also really popular with the punters, which didn't make the others take to her very much. But none of them thought it would have been a fellow prostitute who murdered her, not when I said it had actually happened at the park, none of them would go in there. They said they would have stuck her on the streets if they were going to do it.'

'What about her father?' asked Hector. 'I saw that he's been up in front of a court a few times for assault. There was a restraining order against him for attacking Gavin Heathcote outside his father-in-law's pub, the Swan.' He was interrupted by one of his researchers who handed him a note. 'We now have Yvonne Coombes's address.'

Chapter 10

Sunday 21 May 2000

Heather hadn't slept well. The moon, on the wane, still filled her room with light and the scream of foxes mating was sharp and violent in the night, which had brought her fully awake, as had the pain and sweats of her period. She'd crept along the landing at just gone six on the Sunday morning, pausing to wince at every squeaky floorboard as she made her way to the bathroom. She sat on the toilet and filled the bowl with blood.

She heard her father walking about at seven and then he went outside and began chopping wood. After waiting for a safe amount of time she knocked gently on her mother's bedroom door. She hadn't heard her mother get up; normally she would be doing household chores by now.

'Mum, can I come in?' She got no reply, so she opened the door and looked around in the musty gloom. 'It's gone eight, Mum, can I go up to the farm and turn Murphy out?'

'Did you ask your father?' Her mother had her back to her as she answered.

'No.' Heather stood waiting, anticipating refusal,

gearing herself to be disappointed but instead, her mother turned and looked at Heather.

'What about your exams?'

'I'm taking my books with me.' Her mother sighed. 'I'll do it, Mum, honest.'

'I hope you do, Heather, because your father's had enough of your behaviour and it's making my life a misery.'

'I don't understand what I'm doing wrong?'

'Don't give me that! I can see it in your eyes that you're chasing boys. You'd better be careful not to get caught out with their lies. Especially now you've got your monthlies, you get yourself pregnant and you'll be on the streets, my girl.' Her mother rounded on her angrily, then sank back on the bed. 'Do you understand?'

Heather stared at her mother's back, unable to quite believe what she was hearing.

'I don't know why you're saying things like that,' she answered.

'Yes you do – you're brazen, I can see it, it's written all over your face.'

Heather stepped closer to the bed.

'You okay, Mum?' She noticed her mother had bruises on her shoulder.

'Don't bother asking; just make sure you keep your eyes on your work, and don't be a fool, Heather. You mind your own business up there in the farm otherwise you won't be allowed up there any more and I know my brother has plans for you.' She turned around. 'He's told me you will inherit the farm when he's gone, so you play your cards right and get on with him.'

Heather nodded, still struggling to understand why her mother was suddenly telling her all this; it was as if overnight she was supposed to see things as an adult now. She was supposed to understand.

'Tell your dad I said you could go to the farm. Now go, don't answer back and don't say you're sorry – that gets him so angry – just stand up tall and tell him you're going to study.'

Heather nodded. 'It's not right, the way he takes out all his anger on us. We should leave.'

'I'm not leaving this house. I was born here. That's enough moaning about life, you don't know how good you have it. You should be grateful to your dad; we never expected to have another one after Oliver. I wish many a time that we hadn't. It hasn't been easy. I thought having a little girl would bring joy in my life but it's brought nothing but trouble and sorrow. Now you're a woman, Heather, I expect more from you. You want to stay in this house, you try and get on with your father and take some of the pressure off me.'

'He hates me.'

Her mother sighed but didn't answer. Heather slipped out of the bedroom and down the stairs, through the back door and walked across to the gate. Her father stopped working to watch her.

'Where are you going?' he asked.

'To the farm, I'm studying there today. I have all my things in here.' She patted her backpack to emphasise the point. 'Mum says I can. I'm doing really well and Uncle needs me up there to help him today; he asked me to come early.' Heather threw in as much as she could remember and stood tall and looked her father in the eyes.

He looked startled and nodded.

When she reached the farm there was no one in the yard. She took the shortcut across the fields to Ash's van. She knocked gently and then opened the door. Looking inside she saw the mess and the barbecue remnants but no Ash or Elle, his mum. She waited for a few minutes, deciding what to do, before walking on across the field and onto the road and then around to the top of the lane and past the bungalow that way. As she passed, she heard women laughing and recognised Elle's voice. The frosted glass in the bathroom was steamed up but she could make out the naked female forms moving inside.

Heather went straight down the lane and into the farmyard to Murphy's stable and called him. He sauntered over and nestled his soft nose into her hand, looking for a carrot. She gave him one from the feed store and he crunched away on it. She slid her hand beneath his rug and along his neck and winced from the pain in her arm as she raised it. Her father's fingerprints were pressed into the flesh on her upper arm.

Her uncle came out of his back door looking flustered and still pushing his feet into his boots as he stamped on the concrete. He didn't glance up or say hello; instead, he hurried into the feed room and started dishing out the scoops of feed for the horses. After a few minutes, he called her in to help him.

'Give me a hand, Heather, you can sort out the quantities and put in the scoops, I'll read out the amounts to you.'

Heather was aware that he was sitting on the stool watching her, and it was the first time she felt embarrassed by his attention. It felt different from usual. Maybe it was because her hormones were making her over-sensitive.

When they'd finished he smiled at her.

'Thank you, Heather, you're a great help to me.' She smiled back at him. 'You're going to have to watch it with the lads soon, Heather, you're blossoming, aren't you?' he went on, staring at her breasts that were swollen and painful from her period, like two apples beneath her shirt.

She instantly rounded her shoulders and turned away, embarrassed.

'I'm only saying,' he continued, looking at her from his seat. 'Your father will be beating them away from the door. You know, Heather, your aunt, didn't come back last night.'

'Didn't she?' Heather felt her face burning.

'No.' Truscott stood and came across to her. 'I can still get a hug from my favourite niece though, can't I?'

Heather smiled awkwardly but stood still whilst he hugged her and she felt her breasts being painfully squashed against his chest. She was already as tall as him.

'You get on now; I expect you want to ride this morning, don't you? Stay clear of that lad in the van, he's trouble.'

Heather worked all morning mucking out the stables and sweeping the yard, grooming the ponies. She went for a ride across to Saul, the farrier.

Saul was sitting in his garden reading the newspapers. He got up to walk out into the field and meet Heather.

'Shall I put a couple of jumps up for you?'

'That's okay, Murphy and I are both tired, but thanks for the offer.'

Saul patted Murphy, who was taking the opportunity to eat the grass.

'I'm going to sit and study in the yard,' said Heather. 'I've got my exams starting next month. I'm bound to do badly.'

'Try your best.'

'I might not even sit them.' She looked at Saul with a sideways glance.

'Is that on the cards?'

She shrugged. 'It's quiet here today,' she said, changing the subject.

Saul nodded. 'Douglas and two others left early – Ash was one of them. Enjoy your ride,' he said as he went back into his house.

When he'd gone Heather went back out onto the lane leading Murphy. She stopped by the bungalow and saw Nicola in the kitchen, standing by the window staring out. Nicola seemed to be just staring at Heather for ages. She wished Ash didn't have to live next to the bungalow. She wished he didn't owe such a lot to Douglas. He was trapped. They were both trapped.

Saul watched her go. He had seen them leave in Douglas's van early that morning. He hadn't slept well; the lighter evenings were difficult for everyone but for Saul they brought back memories of his wife and daughter and of the joy that spring and summer brought into their lives and how that was all gone now. Now, he preferred the winter months.

He went inside the house and made himself a mug of coffee and went to stand at his sitting-room window. His house was upside down; he'd built it like that to make the most of the views of the surrounding countryside, and he could see for miles. From there he could see Douglas and the others in the bungalow. From his first-floor kitchen window, he saw the farm and Truscott's house. He saw into the yard, just the top of the stables. He saw the manège where the pony club kids did their best to gallop and throw spuds into buckets. He could see Heather's house, her garden, the field at the front where the foxes mated at night. He could see her bedroom window. He had listened to Heather's voice since the first day they brought her home from the hospital and his heart had leapt at her baby cries; he had always loved her. It broke his heart to hear her cry now. It made him die inside to see her lonely at the window. Sound carried through the fields and around the valley; it was amplified. Saul heard the sound of the horses neighing for their food, the sound of Heather's father chopping wood on a Sunday morning and Saul heard Nicola's laughter countless times, vibrating in the air. He knew the sound she made as she came. He watched Truscott go into the bungalow when Douglas's van was gone, and he heard the sound of Truscott's muted roar.

He watched Elle come out of her van naked and wash herself in the sunshine or the rain. She was all skin and bone and red dreadlocks that she had left to go wild and overtake her so they were too heavy and large for her small head.

And Saul saw Ash and Heather, kissing by the hedge, just inside his field. If he switched off the lights, he could watch them embrace and he was slightly jealous of their love and the way it began and grew. It made him just as sad as it did happy, to watch Heather growing up and becoming a woman.

Chapter 11

Willis knocked on the front door of the flat on the fourth floor of Seven Sisters Tower, a rundown estate in Finsbury Park, built in the 70s. New pale blue-and-white cladding had been put on the outside to give it a better appearance, but inside everything was still as shabby. The lift wasn't working and the stairs smelt of wee. The local shop they'd passed had been deserted and vandalised. Teenagers were smoking weed and sitting on the swings in the kiddies' playground.

A television was on inside the flat. A dog barked from one of the other flats as they knocked on the door. A woman answered, her skin showing the ravages of drugs, her eyes dull and her hair scraped back into a ponytail. She had on black leggings and an oversized grey T-shirt. She had a young child on her hip. Willis checked her phone; confirmation that it was Millie's blood on the bridge had just been received, it had seeped through and settled on the underside.

'Yes?' The woman was nervous.

Willis showed her badge. Carter did the same.

'Yvonne Coombes?' asked Willis. 'May we come in for a chat?'

The woman stepped back to allow them to come past

her into the flat. The smell of toast was in the air. The place was clean but needed painting, needed some money spent on it. They followed Yvonne into the kitchen, where she sat down with the little girl on her lap. The child looked full of cold, hot-faced, whingeing as she tried to breathe and suck on a bottle of juice at the same time.

'We've come to talk to you about Millie Stephens.'

'I heard, on the news.' Yvonne looked pale and numb. She cuddled her child and tried to entice her with a dummy instead of the bottle.

Carter answered, 'Millie's body was found in the River Lea yesterday.'

'Was she murdered, like it said on the news?'

'Yes, she was, and we need your help to piece together her last moves so that we can find out who did it.'

She turned away from them. 'I can't help you, I haven't seen Millie for months.'

Carter nodded, smiled. 'Tell us about the last time you did see her.'

'I bumped into her. I didn't know she was a street worker.' She switched the little girl to the other hip to try to settle her.

Carter was waiting with a sympathetic smile on his face. Willis paused in taking notes and looked up at Yvonne.

'I didn't know, I swear.' Yvonne looked from one to the other.

Willis reached into her backpack and took out the photo of Millie and Yvonne outside the pub.

'That's you in the picture with Millie, isn't it? We know you worked the street together sometimes, we have several people who have confirmed it,' she said as she pushed the photo across to Yvonne.

'We also know you've been through some really tough times and you're trying to keep your child now and go straight,' said Carter. 'It's Bonny, isn't it? That's a lovely name.' Yvonne nodded.

'We're not here to make any trouble for you, we just want justice for Millie and to find out who killed her.'

Yvonne looked close to tears as she picked up the photo and looked at it.

'Millie got this man to take the photo as he was walking past and we were having a drink together. How did she die?'

'We believe she went with someone into Lee Valley Park and she was killed there. Is that a place she ever mentioned to you?' asked Carter.

'No way. Millie was really paranoid about getting in the car with punters, she preferred them to come to her flat. If she didn't like the look of someone she'd let them pass. Millie would never have gone to some park for sex or anything else, no matter how much they offered.' Yvonne bounced the child on her lap, chewed the inside of her cheek.

'Who did Millie consider a friend?' asked Carter. 'Would it be someone from the past or present?'

'No one from the present. Millie's life was a mess. She was about to lose her flat because she hadn't paid the rent. She had tried to get money from her dad but he wouldn't give her a penny. She was desperate. Millie had no friends but me and I said I couldn't see her any more. She was just a liability; she even tried to tap me for money. I have to do everything to hang on to Bonny. I can't risk it. Shit . . .' She wiped her eyes on her T-shirt.

'We understand,' said Carter.

'Was this about Douglas?' Yvonne looked at Carter as though she was dreading his answer.

'We don't know, Yvonne. We don't know anything at this point.'

'I told her not to tell people. They didn't need to know. Millie thought the punters would pay more. She told them who I was as well.' Yvonne made it sound as if she had gone along with it.

'That time seemed to be still really important to Millie,' said Carter. 'She had a lot of photos from Hawthorn Farm in her flat, so she obviously looked back fondly on that time?'

'I don't know why she did. It ruined both of us.'

'I see you don't have your tattoos any more, Yvonne?' said Willis.

'No, I don't want anything to do with it.'

'But you have never offered to make a statement about your time in the bungalow, about what might have happened to Heather Phillips?'

'We were advised to say nothing at the time and I never knew what happened to Heather. I was friends with her; I'd never have hurt her. Me and Millie, we always kept an eye out for her. We were victims, Millie and me; our lives were ruined there. Look, I can't talk about this any more,' she said, agitated. 'I'm trying my best to put the past behind me. I'm struggling here. I don't have enough money to keep the heating on for my kid. I am trying really hard. It's just me and Bonny now. I have to make it for her; I can't let her down again. I can't let her go through what I did. I'm going to be a good mum.'

'What about Bonny's father?' asked Willis. 'Do you get any help from him?'

'No, we were never together.'

'When was the last time you saw Millie?' asked Carter, sensing that their time talking to Yvonne was running out. She put the child to lie down on the sofa and started cleaning up the dishes. She was becoming more distracted. She turned to them and he realised she was very scared.

'Are we safe, me and Bonny?'

'Have you ever felt threatened because of your association with Douglas?' asked Willis.

'Many times, in the beginning, but not for a few years now and, with him coming out soon, I thought it would disappear altogether. Have you seen the others? The other disciples?'

'We'll see Gavin. Do you think you know who killed Millie?' asked Carter.

She shook her head. 'All I can tell you is that Millie would never have gone to some park with a punter.'

'Do you think Millie's death had something to do with Douglas?' asked Carter.

'I don't know but she talked a lot about it in the last years or so, about what she thought they owed her.'

'Who?' Carter pushed.

'The others: Gavin, Cathy and Stephen.'

'Did she ever see any of them?'

Yvonne hesitated. 'Look ... she got money out of them sometimes, a handout. When the news breaks about Millie, will we be safe here?'

'People might recognise you, Yvonne,' said Willis, 'but there's nothing we can do about that. We cannot be sure what photos the press will come up with. Do they know your real name around here?'

'No, they call me Donna.'

'You should be okay.' Willis tried to reassure her.

'Do you have addresses for the other disciples?' asked Carter.

'No. I saw them when I was with Millie a couple of times, that's all. I wouldn't go out of my way to see them again. I'm not answering any more questions. I want you to leave now. I have to get to my cleaning job.'

'What about Bonny? Is she going with you?' asked Willis, not meaning to sound accusing.

'Bonny stays with my neighbour, I wouldn't just leave her, you know? I'm a good mother.'

'Of course. I can see you are,' said Willis.

'Keep this card and if you want to talk to either of us, you phone that number,' said Carter.

Yvonne nodded and her eyes filled with tears. 'I've said enough. If they can do that to Millie, they can come for me. I am sorry for everything that happened in those times. I am truly sorry, but I'm not going to be the only one who breaks the chain. I am not going to say anything against anyone from that time.'

'Douglas can't hurt you, Yvonne.'

'You say that because you don't know him.'

Chapter 12

'Never be late for the work party,' the prison guard, Kowalski, growled at the man who was last onto the minibus, waiting to set off for the restaurant out in Kent. The Michelin-starred chef who ran it was generously allowing several prisoners some work experience in his kitchen and in his adjoining grounds and gardens. Douglas had been there for two months now, and he was loving it. Being late was a cardinal sin. It jeopardised everyone else's chances on the bus. Douglas stared at the latecomer.

'Prisoner 513, I'm giving you a final warning,' said Kowalski. 'Shut up and get on this bus or we will not be moving from here today.'

The prisoner mumbled something back in reply. He was having trouble talking, his face was swollen, he had bruising that was livid on his cheekbones; he had black eyes. The other five inmates already on the bus were holding their breath. Talking back to an officer would result in punishment, punishment took time to organise, and they wouldn't make it today. Douglas moved closer to the window to glare at the prisoner. The officer in charge caught Douglas's eye and made a decision to ignore 513's remarks. Douglas smiled at Kowalski.

'On the bus, that's an order.' The man heaved himself up into the vehicle. He'd had a bad night, he'd been in a fight and come off worst. Now his broken tooth was killing him and he had been refused permission to see a dentist that day.

Jimmy Douglas glared at the back of the man's head as he sat down in front of him.

Kowalski got on the bus and the driver pulled the door to. The guard sat down at the front and slid back in the seat, so his back was resting against the window and he was side-on to the prisoners.

It took just over an hour and a half to reach the grounds of the restaurant. After an hour of prepping Douglas went out into the garden to collect the salad leaves and found prisoner 1280 who was on gardening detail. Douglas knew him; he helped him write letters home. The man was illiterate. Now 1280 looked up and watched Douglas approach. It was bad manners to ask what each man was in for; you became a number when you went in, except everyone knew who Douglas was.

'Jimmy? That cunt nearly cost us this, this morning. I don't reckon he's going to be on time tomorrow either. Then we'll all be penalised,' said 1280.

'How would you feel about that, Stitch?' It was not the first time Douglas had called the prisoner by his nickname; he usually did it as a reward when 1280 did something right in exchange for the letter writing. Once, without too much persuasion, 1280 had brought Douglas a SIM card, with credit on it. Now Douglas had four phones he could use. Battery life was a problem, as charging them was very hard. Douglas had brought two of them with him and was charging them off the freezer plugs in the kitchen.

'You just keep your cool, Stitch, you'll be okay.' He was nicknamed Stitch because of the tattoo around his neck. 'If you start something here, that will be the end of your gardening work party. It will be the end for all of us.'

'But if he doesn't get on that bus tomorrow, on time, we'll lose this job and I like it here.'

Stitch had worked his way through the categories of prisons, just the way Douglas had. He was hoping to be released in the next couple of years. Although it was bad form to ask what Stitch had done, it was well known that he had murdered the man he found in bed with his wife, but not instantly – it took ten days and afterwards he murdered his wife.

Douglas's fellow prisoners never thought of him as a murderer or a rapist. They somehow understood that he had been wronged. No one who talked as softly, as sensibly, with so much compassion for his fellow prisoners, could ever have been evil. He had definitely covered up for someone else. He was innocent, like so many banged up.

'I do agree with that, 513 will fuck it up for us, and he has to be stopped but not here and not now.'

'When then?'

'I don't know, I'm not into that kind of violence. You need him to promise you he will never let you down again. Promise you he understands the way you feel, doesn't just dismiss it, as if you mean nothing. He has to understand how important this is to you. This is everything to you right now. All you can do is wait, get him on his own and just reason with him, ask him to give and take here.'

Stitch was listening, eyes on the ground. He accepted what Douglas said and moved off.

*

The governor made an announcement the next morning as he interrupted the chaplain and his morning mass.

'There has been a brutal stabbing and a prisoner is dead. All work parties will carry on as usual. The prison has a duty to fulfil its obligations to outside employers and to present a good impression to the outside world.'

Chapter 13

Sunday 21 May 2000

When Douglas got back from Lambs Farm after burying Tony, Nicola was cooking curry and making sugary-topped lemon cakes and dancing to rave music in the kitchen. Yvonne was on the sofa and Gavin was outside on the patio, Millie was on speed and gabbling away to everyone, but no one was talking about what happened the night before. Yvonne wanted to go home but she wasn't allowed, not until her tattoo was done and that would be when Nicola wanted to do it. Stephen went to crash out on the sofa in the sitting room.

Douglas went in for a shower before going to lie on his bed. He didn't need to see Ash to know he would be in crisis. He would be staring at his wrists, red and swollen from the fresh tattoo, and he would understand that he had turned a corner, crossed a line. Douglas would comfort him later, tell him all the plans he had for him. This had been a massive step up for Ash.

He heard Nicola's laughter. She knew the task of keeping the group together afterwards was down to her. Douglas had done his part, now this was hers and she told them they all had to wait for their tattoos. No one could leave. The old disciples had to have new links added, the new ones, Cathy, Ash and Yvonne, had to have them from scratch. The tattoos took time and Nicola would stagger them throughout the day. If anyone felt sick she would nurse them, or bathe with them or they could cuddle with her on the sofa, but they could not leave until the tattoos were done.

Nicola came out of the kitchen with cakes and fresh coffee and looked around to make sure her brood were all present, but one was missing. She went out onto the patio and looked across to Ash's van. She knew Elle was inside sleeping where she'd left her after she'd tidied the van and washed up. She watched for a few minutes.

'Where's Ash?' she asked Gavin, who was sitting outside in the weak morning sun, looking pale and tired as he rocked in the sun lounger. Yvonne had come out to rest on the other lounger. They had been cleaning up together; they both had hangovers from hell. Yvonne had come out of Stephen's bedroom that morning and walked into a hellish scene and she'd been trying to cope with it ever since. Gavin had never suffered from sensitivity. He had an indifference to all human life that Douglas found refreshing. He had no problem with getting his hands dirty; he'd been on many a journey with Douglas. He'd been as innocent as Ash once.

Yvonne was keeping her eyes shut, hoping to wake up and find out that it had all been a horrible dream. They had told her she was partly responsible for Tony's death, she didn't remember, they said, she'd been off her head, but all of them had seen what happened. Nicola told her she would get Douglas to drive her home when he got up, but for now she gave her a blanket and a cake and she left Gavin to look after her. Nicola gave him a prod with her knee on the chair and he stirred. She put a coffee down beside him, gave him a cake in his hand. Then Nicola went back into the kitchen and turned off the gas ring. She'd accidentally placed a baking tray on top, it was red hot, she was going to have to stay focused. She was the one holding everyone together. She was angry with Ash. As soon as Douglas got up she would tell him Ash had disobeyed.

Inside the sitting room Stephen was up and being his usual brash self. He rented a room at the bungalow and he'd been there for six months, since his parents kicked him out for doing nothing but drugs after finishing university. Stephen was a posh boy, prompting the others to mimic his accent. With his floppy hair, he seemed out of place, as if he'd naively stumbled into a nest of adders and laid down in it enjoying the warmth there. Douglas loved to bounce off him intellectually and was learning all the time from Stephen. He was absorbing him, mimicking his mannerisms, observing his responses. Stephen was trying to entertain Cathy.

Millie was getting smashed; she'd opened a bottle of vodka and was handing it around for shots. She fed it from her mouth into Stephen's to see if Gavin was watching, but he wasn't . . .

'I'm going in to wake Jimmy up,' she said as she danced and laughed her way into the kitchen, 'see if he wants some company in bed.'

Nicola laughed but her eyes were bright with anger as the two women stood facing one another. Millie was pushing her luck.

'Give me a hand first, just move that tray for me a minute.' She nodded towards the baking tray on the cooker.

Millie's scream was delayed. It took two seconds for her brain to register her fingers were burning before she dropped it onto the floor.

'Quickly, quickly,' said Nicola, turning on the tap and pulling Millie's arm to get her hand under the running water, only to see it pour out of the hot tap and the boiling water split the skin and peel it back from Millie's palm and fingers.

'Oh, my God, I am so sorry,' Nicola said. 'I had no idea that it was the hot tap.'

'It's okay.' Millie backed away, trying to laugh, trying not to look at Nicola.

Nicola dressed her hand and wrapped it in white bandages and Millie settled down in the armchair and drank her vodka in silence.

After a few hours Douglas got up and came out to hold council. He would take each of his disciples aside and tell them how to live their lives, he'd tell them how each of them had a touch of greatness.

Chapter 14

'Mr Stephens?' Don Stephens still ran the same farm machinery repair business he'd had for the last thirty years. 'We are here to offer our condolences,' said Carter. Carter and Willis had driven out to Chesham to talk to Millie's father. As well as having an area stacked with machines waiting for attention, the place was half scrapyard and machine graveyard.

'I heard,' he said, leaning over the engine in a tractor. 'I've already had them offered, thanks. A phone call was sufficient.'

Don Stephens was wearing blue oil-smeared overalls. He was a man-mountain. He stood six foot six and was almost as broad with a silver beard and a peaked cap on his head. He looked as if he could have stepped off the set of a thriller set in the Rockies.

'When was the last time you saw your daughter?' Willis asked, keeping her distance from the big man with the wrench in his hand, who carried on looking inside the tractor. The place was strewn with various machines in mid-repair.

'Mr Stephens, stop working please, we need to talk to you,' Carter said.

He stopped, wiped his hands on his overalls and stood tall. His lined face was solid with grief.

'We know this must be very hard,' said Carter. 'Can you tell us the exact date and what the circumstances were?'

At first he looked as though he might resist but his shoulders slumped in defeat and he began to speak. 'It was the weekend, beginning of last month, that was the last time I saw her. She turned up here on her mother's birthday, the second of September. My wife would have been sixty-five. I was just contemplating getting blind drunk and Millie bangs on the door and she's pretending she's just passing, but she's caught the bus up and she wants to stay and, like a fool, I say okay. I start talking to her about her mother and she don't give a shit. She's looking around the room and I realise she's looking for things to steal from me again. She started to get really edgy, feverish, and I knew she was going through withdrawal. Then the pleading started, same as always, and I couldn't bear it, I did what I always do. She only came out here when she was desperate and wanted money for drugs. I caught her trying to steal some things from my workshop to sell, so I changed the locks. That's what she'd become; I had to warn neighbours not to let her in. She'd come around here screaming outside their houses as well as mine. She'd become less than human.

'I'd say, "You can't have it, you need help" and she'd kick off, she didn't want any more rehab, she just wanted heroin. Then I'd have to carry her onto the truck, force her into the seat whilst she's screaming and crying and calling me every name under the sun, and I had to drive her back to north London and dump her at her flat. Sometimes I'd give her money, even though I knew it was pointless, but I hoped she'd at least use some of it for food and rent.'

Willis got out her notebook. 'When you last saw Millie, did she say anything that worried you about who she was meeting?'

'I don't remember her discussing her latest johns with me, no. That's a fucking stupid question.'

'Did you ever hear her talk of a friend; maybe she turned up with someone?' Willis asked, unfazed by him.

'No, she didn't. She knew better than to bring anyone here. I might have a little love left for Millie, but I sure as hell wouldn't have any for her friends.'

'You have had a few assault charges against you before. Were they related to Millie's friends?'

'You know they were. That piece of shit Gavin Heathcote has a lot to answer for. Him and Jimmy Douglas, who if I see, I will kill, believe me,' he said sadly. 'You have no idea what this is like.'

Carter reached out and laid a hand on his shoulder.

'Less of the threats, Don, we don't want to cause you more problems, we are here to help.' Stephens nodded, as he wiped his eyes on the sleeve of his overalls.

'I swear, she was a normal bubbly, healthy, beautiful teenager until she went to work on that farm with that man. Until she got in with the wrong crowd.' Don took a few deep breaths, his anger rising, before he banged the wrench on the side of the tractor. It jumped out of his hands and was lost inside the engine.

'Shit.' He sighed deeply. 'That man Douglas took my daughter and turned her into a stranger, saw something he could warp and destroy and he did. And, in some ways, that Nicola Stone was worse. She saw my daughter needed a mother; her own died when she was four. She saw it and she exploited it.' He shook his head sadly. 'But I always hoped she'd find her way out of the mess in the end. I paid for so much rehab, counselling. She's been back to live with me I don't know how many times and sometimes I thought she'd make it but always she went back to the streets.'

'It's tough, I'm truly sorry. Must be heart-breaking,' said Carter.

'She broke my heart a long time ago. I can hardly hold my head up here any more. People will always know me as the man whose daughter was a bad one. I can start again now, I can put it all behind me and try to remember her as she used to be, not what she became.'

'Mr Stephens, we will let you know when her body is going to be released. Someone will be in touch with you about making arrangements to see her and find out what you want to do about the funeral.'

'I tell you what I want, I want her body strung up on Tower Bridge and I want everyone who passes to know that my beautiful daughter died for the love of drugs and bad company and there was nothing I could do to save her.'

'Come on, big man,' said Carter as he put his arm around Don Stephens' shoulder and held him whilst he sobbed.

Finally they left Don Stephens and drove back into town.

After a few minutes' silence between them, Carter spoke.

'We are going to have to follow up on him. He has all the temper needed to do it. He may have been pushed too far. We can't ignore his record.' Carter glanced across at Willis from the wheel of his BMW SUV, his pride and joy. He was beginning to regret stopping at a garage and buying Willis a pasty as the flakes of pastry had spread further than the extra napkins he'd made sure to pick up. Carter had bought himself a neatly packaged feta and hummus wrap, cut into two portions, easily eaten without fallout, whilst they were driving on the M25. Willis was making him edgy – not even his son Archie was allowed into the car with food. Carter usually managed to contain Willis's messy habits, but wasn't so lucky today. She saw him glancing across and started taking smaller bites as she wiped her mouth of pastry crumbs.

'I agree. But I don't think he'd take a roundabout route with three weapons, do you? If Don Stephens wanted to kill you he could crush you with his bare hands. If he'd swung a hammer at her head it would have been off.'

'What are you looking at?' Carter asked. Willis was reading from a tablet.

'Gavin Heathcote doesn't live far from here. He has a building firm, the Heathcote Roofing Company, in Rickmansworth. I would have thought he'd have changed his name.' She cast a glance at Carter. 'I mean, he must have been hated?'

'In the rest of the country, maybe, but here? I don't think so. Douglas gave parties that were famous around here, he was everyone's friend. I reckon people didn't want to think bad of him, even though they were faced with the facts, they still couldn't help liking him and they probably half-admired the disciples for sticking up for him.'

'I'll give Gavin Heathcote's number a ring. Let's find out where he is and swing by and talk to him.'

Gavin Heathcote's wife, Sandra, had told them where to find her husband. His van was parked outside the Victorian semi-detached latticed in scaffolding in Chesham. Three men were working on the roof when they arrived. Music was blaring out and Heathcote was balancing on the apex, renewing tiles.

They stood on the opposite side of the street and Carter held up his badge. Heathcote swore a lot on his descent. He had on grey tracksuit bottoms and a T-shirt with a list of reasons why beer was better than sex. He shouted up instructions to his mate to take over the tiling.

'Jesus, this better be good.'

'Gavin, can we have a chat?'

'What is this about? I'm not leaving this site; I need to get this roof finished before the rain comes.' Gavin lifted his chin defiantly and glared at the detectives in turn. His square head was pock-marked with evidence of scars and knocks. He had three-day-old mottled stubble on his chin.

They walked across to a green area with a few trees and sat on a bench.

Willis opened her backpack and took out her notebook. 'We've come here to talk to you about Millie Stephens.'

Heathcote shrugged, looking slightly caught out and irritated. 'What do you want me to say? I picked her up a couple of times, that's all, I felt sorry for her, why do you have to hound blokes like me? I already had a letter sent to my house from your lot. I'm already in enough shit with the wife.'

'We're not here to talk to you about kerb-crawling, Mr Heathcote,' said Willis.

'What's this about then?'

'Millie's body was found in the river yesterday morning,' replied Willis.

'That's sad, but why do you come to me about it?'

'This is a murder investigation, so we are looking for

anyone who knew Millie who might know if she was feeling threatened at all. Seems like you knew her pretty well, as much as anyone did?' asked Carter.

'Don't be fucking stupid.' He shook his head and smirked. 'How can you ever really know a junkie who lives that kind of life? I told you, I felt sorry for her, occasionally I bunged her a few bob, that's all.'

'We've just come from her dad's. You were very good friends once, he said. We are hoping you might help to tell us a bit more about her.'

'How can I help, for fuck's sake? Millie was a drug addict, a prozzy – she was never going to have a long life. I'm sad for her but I can't tell you anything about her. Don hates my guts; he blames me for the way she turned out, he thinks we were close once, but we never were. Millie would shag anyone.'

'When was the last time you saw her?' Willis asked as she took notes.

'It must be a couple of months ago now. I met her for a drink.'

'You said you've picked her up more than once?' Carter said.

'The first time was an accident. I saw her when I was on a night out with the lads. We went down Finsbury Park, see if we could get some action. We were just having a laugh in the van. I pulled up to talk to this bird, ask her how much for the four of us, just for a laugh, and it was Millie. I tell you, I was shocked. I hadn't seen her for ten years. I hardly recognised her. I gave her a few quid for nothing.' He looked at Willis to make sure she understood that he hadn't bought any services from Millie. 'I mean you really wouldn't have wanted to, if you know what I mean? She had sores on her legs and arms from injecting. She was a real mess.'

'Worse than the others on the street that you did have sex with?' asked Willis.

He shrugged uninterestedly. 'I accepted the kerb-crawling warning, I haven't done it since.'

'But you said you saw her again, after that?' asked Carter.

'Yes, a couple of times, we had a drink in the pub, for old times' sake. She was a sad case.'

He started rolling a cigarette as he glanced behind to make sure work was continuing on the roof. Radio Hits was blaring out.

'Did you ever take her to a park for a chat? What about Lee Valley Park, do you know it?' Carter asked.

'I know it, been there a few times fishing.'

'When was the last time?' Willis asked.

'I don't know, a couple of months ago, August?'

'Where were you on the nineteenth and twentieth of last month?'

He got out his phone to check his calendar.

'I was on my father-in-law's roof. When I wasn't on it, I was drinking inside it – it's a pub, the Swan in Rickmansworth.'

'Do you have vehicles that you use besides the van?' asked Willis.

'No.'

'Who else do you keep in contact with from those times?' she asked him, as he pulled a lighter from his tracksuit bottoms and shielded the flame from the wind as he lit up.

'I haven't seen anyone for a while.' He looked up at Willis and shrugged.

Willis read off the list of Douglas's disciples.

'I heard Yvonne's got a family,' Gavin said.

'Remind me where she lives?' Carter asked.

'Hackney somewhere, I don't know where, she never invited me round. Why, are you looking for her?'

'We're trying to put together an idea of Millie's life and any friends she might have had, we think she must have known her attacker.'

'Yeah, I tried to give her friendly advice but I gave up, all she wanted was money from me.'

'What advice did you try to give her?' asked Carter.

'Oh, you know, clean up, wake up! You're a long time dead.'

'What about the other disciples, do you keep in touch?' asked Carter, watching Gavin Heathcote closely. He was sniffing all through their conversation, and looking around. He shook his head.

'Cathy Dwyer? Stephen Perry?' asked Willis, reading off the names again.

'No, afraid not. Not since the days of the bungalow and Hawthorn Farm.'

'What do you remember about those times?' asked Carter.

'Lots of parties, lots of sex. Just what you need when you're a young lad, like I was.'

'And Douglas? What do you remember about him?'

'No comment,' he laughed, jokingly, as if it was all a game. 'I tell you what I do remember is the foot and mouth epidemic. Now that was a real event. That really happened. We'd rock up there with our guns and our mallets and we'd get to work and kill every one of those farmers' animals and then they'd pay us and we'd move on to the next one. It was a mad time.'

Carter was nodding, but he was also looking at what Willis had written: *Gavin Heathcote comes alive when he talks about death and killing. These are great memories for him.*

'Must have been a lot of comradeship between you lads?' said Carter.

'Yeah, there was, it would get surreal with us seeing how fast we could bash a lamb's brains in, seeing who could kill the most, but at the same time we had to be respectful of the farmers – they were hanging themselves, sobbing in the fields. We had to come in there like some crack A-team and kill everything they loved and take their money. I made a shed-load of money that spring and summer. Even after Douglas was arrested, we just kept doing it, everyone knew us by then and they had no one else to call. There was a huge shortage of people to do it. We had false gamekeeper papers, we all had shotgun licences and we had a ball.'

'Who's *we*?'

'Me and Stephen, Posh Boy, lived in the bungalow with Douglas and Nicola.'

'I notice you still have the disciples' tattoos on your wrists?' said Willis. 'Why is that?'

'Because I choose to.'

'Many people would have had them removed,' Willis said. 'It still links you to Jimmy Douglas, doesn't it?'

'Maybe I don't have a problem with that.' He glared at Willis with a smirk on his face.

'Even though he's a convicted rapist serving a life sentence?' Willis answered.

'One that's about to come to an end.' Gavin smiled. 'I don't know what he did or didn't do. I know he went to prison for rape, but I don't know whether he did it. Douglas

was a friend to me. We had a good laugh. I wish him well
and I'm looking forward to seeing him again. Yeah, can't
wait.' Gavin rubbed his hands together.

'Gavin meant what he said, didn't he? He really can't wait
for Douglas to get out,' said Carter.

'He hasn't got any nicer over the years. Douglas is
coming out to a hero's welcome, by the sound of it.'

Carter was negotiating the local traffic headed towards
the motorway.

'Scott Tucker, he interviewed the disciples at the time,
it was one of his first cases. I remember he talked to me
about it.'

Willis had gone silent, looking at her notebook. Tucker
was a friend of Carter's, based in Devon, who had been
Willis's on-and-off lover for two years.

'He's up here at the moment. Did you know?' Carter
asked. Willis shook her head, kept her eyes glued to her
tablet. Carter knew when to back off, for a few minutes at
least. 'No way Heathcote would have gone out of his way
to bung Millie a few bob and get nothing back, is there?'
he continued as they joined the M25. The roads were busy.
The rain had started.

Willis shook her head as she looked at her phone. 'No,
I agree. I've got the house-to-house started. Sandford has
found nothing else after the eighteenth for Millie. There's
a copy of the *Evening Standard* paper in her flat.'

'How long is he going to be in there?'

'He's done. The results are in from her phone according
to Hector. We're running a scan for frequent numbers.'

'Tell Hector I want Gavin followed up,' said Carter. 'I
don't trust anything about him.'

'Will do.'

'What's actually happening between you and Tucker?' asked Carter abruptly.

Willis shook her head, moved closer to her screen and exhaled loudly.

'Do you want to talk about it?' Carter pushed, as he always did. He'd told Willis from the first time they worked together, when she was a new DC on the murder squad and he was a renegade DS who thought he had no hope of promotion, that if they were to work together, be partners, they had to talk about everything. They had to know one another's strengths and weaknesses, fears and hopes, they had to have each other's backs, and over the years together that was exactly what they had done. But, for Ebony, opening up was the hardest thing. She hated putting her feelings into words.

'Why is he here now anyway?' frowned Willis, still looking at her tablet.

'He says he hasn't had more than a text telling him you are too busy to talk in the last six months. What is it, Eb? Come on, I can see you're not happy at the moment.'

'It's the distance between us, it means I have to go down there for a few days to make it worthwhile, and that's not working out for me.'

Carter smiled, amused. 'Why, because you have so much else you'd rather be doing? Come on, Eb, he's a good bloke, he's not short of a few women after him. I know you like him, you're just afraid to admit it to yourself.' They were snagged in traffic so Carter continued watching her until she looked up. 'He's staying at mine,' Carter said with a look of expectancy.

Willis nodded. 'How long is he up here for?'

'He hasn't decided.'

'Why did he have to involve you?'

'Because him and me are old friends and so are you and me. It's a . . .' Carter held up his hands and touched thumbs and forefingers together '. . . triangle of love.'

'That's a diamond,' she said, hiding a smile.

'A diamond? Engagement, huh?'

'Shut the . . . up! Anyway, this all comes from a man who's been engaged for six years.'

'Taking my time, it's going to be a big bash, needs planning for. I'm looking for a place to hold it.'

'You're going to be a right Groomzilla, when it does happen.'

'Probably, Eb. You know Tucker is talking future plans, you need to be clear about things; he'll walk otherwise. He wants to move forwards; don't always be holding back, sometimes you need to take risks in relationships.'

Chapter 15

Monday 22 May 2000

Douglas hadn't seen anything of Ash by the time he prepared to leave on Monday morning. So he walked across to Ash's van.

Ash was staring out from his bunk. Douglas stepped inside and sat on the bed next to him.

'Hey, we're good, aren't we? We're friends?'

'Sure.' Ash sat up and tried to sit a little away from Douglas but Douglas only moved closer.

'So what are your plans?'

'See to Mum.'

'Leave it to your gran to do it, you're sixteen, for fuck's sake. You get rid of all this shit and come and live with me and Nicola, we'll look after you and maybe you and me can go into business. I'll cut you into a percentage and I'll get you a job with me, how's that? Proper pals, mates, working together like father and son? Maybe we can cut out all the drugs and make enough to start a stud farm, you can train the horses, how's that? Hey, you like that idea?'

Ash smiled and nodded. There was a faint rekindling of hope in his eyes, just the flicker of an ember.

'Okay, well, I'll be away this week. When I get back on Friday, you make sure your mum is sorted.'

Douglas went to the van and sat there for a few minutes as he looked at the list of deliveries and follow-ups on new clients he had to make that week, deciding what he could get out of it for himself. He had some unfinished business to attend to before his first client later that afternoon. He drove down the motorway, M4, M5, and then headed off on the A39 and through Bridgwater towards the farm in the foothills of the Quantocks, in Somerset. Margery Farm wasn't a place he delivered equine feed to but it was close by one where he did, and he'd struck up a kind of friendship with the farmer.

Douglas pulled off the road just before one and drove down the lanes that led to the dirt tracks at the back of Margery Farm. He pulled into the entrance to a field, opened his glove box, took out keys and unlocked the gate. Douglas had bought the field from the farmer; it was just a couple of acres of stony ground that had been ruined and the farmer used it to dump his old machinery. There were no subsidies for a field where only ragwort and brambles thrived.

He drove in and parked up by an old cattle shed. There were several broken tractors and bits of machinery dotted around, attachments for ploughing and muck-spreading all gone to rust, which had become living sculptures with creeping weeds and bracken. Douglas got out and took a few moments to listen to the silence and to look across the valley from Margery Farm, a place he knew well, to Hill Farm, where all was quiet. He knew that Jones the farmer was so overstretched that Douglas didn't have to worry about being seen; Jones didn't have time to stand gazing across his fields.

Douglas went across and unlocked a metal shipping container that nestled between the cowshed and the stone-wall remnants of an old shepherd's hut. He slipped between the layers of plastic curtain that separated the inside from out and the stagnant air hit him. It was the smell of human, existing in a pod of fear and filth. He flicked on the battery light and looked around. From the corner of the container, a pair of eyes blinked at him from behind the bars of a metal crate. Darren Slater, he was the quiet one, the shy one, the gay one. He was hardly older than Ash; the two of them had got on well. That had been a hook for Douglas. Ash was a lure, even though he didn't know it. Darren was a perfect find for Douglas because he was so strong. In the two weeks he'd been locked up there, he'd managed to endure so much pain that Douglas felt a good deal of admiration and respect for him.

Douglas went across and opened the top of the cage and looped Darren's bound wrists over a hook attached to a chain, and cranked a handle to winch the lad up and out of the cage. Darren was trembling violently, naked, cold and hurting. Douglas stood in front of him and toyed with the idea of letting him live a little longer but then he looked into his eyes and saw that Darren just wanted to die.

At the bungalow, Nicola was in bed with Cathy and Millie. The heat was stifling in the room: the smell of sex and sweat. Nicola scraped out lines of cocaine on a mirror on the bed. It was nearly eight in the evening now and the temperature hadn't dipped below twenty-five degrees. The weather had gone mad with a heat-wave that caught everyone by surprise. Daytime temperatures had hit the mid-thirties.

Cathy got up and opened the door to the sitting room

and walked through to stand at the open patio doors. She looked across at Ash's van and called back to the others, 'Shall we get Ash over for a foursome?'

Nicola laughed. 'Poor Ash, he's not happy with us at the moment.'

'Heather makes him happy,' said Millie, 'they're so cute together.'

'Heather has a lot to learn about life,' said Nicola as she watched Millie snort up more cocaine and then lie back on the bed to allow it to settle down her throat. Then she sat up again.

'I'm going to make us cocktails,' said Millie, jumping off the bed.

'Go on then, not too strong, you have work tomorrow,' said Nicola.

Millie clattered about the kitchen. She put on some music and started singing at the top of her voice.

'You okay, Yvonne?' Nicola asked as she reached over to stroke Yvonne's arm. Yvonne was looking at the ceiling. She nodded but she didn't answer.

'How is your tattoo now?'

'Itchy.'

'Let me see it.' Nicola took her wrists and examined each in turn. 'That's pretty good workmanship, if I say it myself.'

Yvonne sighed and turned her head to stare at the door. Millie was still singing.

'Millie's okay about it,' said Yvonne.

'Because, she understands it for what it was – nothing, he was nothing but a douche bag. You don't need to worry about it any more, it's over, forgotten.'

Yvonne started to cry. 'I try to, but then I keep seeing his face.'

'It's the same with any person who's gone through a trauma. You're still in shock. Come here.' Nicola held Yvonne close. They had had a lot of sex in the bungalow since the events of Saturday. All the women had needed some physical reassurance after it. They all needed Nicola to comfort them, even the ones who didn't ask for it and didn't seem to need it, like Cathy.

'We are your family here, Yvonne, you belong here with us, and we're always going to look after you.'

Millie shouted out from the kitchen.

'Shall we get Gavin round?'

Nicola rolled her eyes as she looked at Yvonne with a smile; Yvonne smiled back and whispered, 'She's so obsessed.'

Yvonne shouted back to Millie, 'This is a girls' love-in, we don't need him. No boys allowed.'

Cathy was still standing naked at the patio doors. She was watching Ash's van.

Nicola came to stand beside her, to run her fingers over her back.

'Incy wincy spider ...' She kissed Cathy's shoulders. Cathy didn't respond, she was still staring at the van. She could see Ash watching her. He was on his phone, his face was lit up. 'What're you looking at?'

'Ash, he's up to something. I think he's scared of us.'

'And so he should be. We are invincible. We are the warrior women.'

Cathy didn't answer. Nicola knew what Cathy thought of her; she thought she was not very bright, she thought she was naive and she knew the only reason Cathy came around when Douglas wasn't there was to leave her mark, to establish her presence, to be what Douglas would want her to be, dominant. She, out of all of them, completely understood what was happening. If only Nicola didn't feel the knives being sharpened, she would share Douglas with Cathy, but she knew that was not what Cathy wanted.

'My beautiful little spider about to mutate into a butterfly, aren't you?' She walked her fingers up Cathy's back and made her shiver.

Cathy turned to look at her with a frown. 'Do you mean a caterpillar? They are the ones that change into butterflies.' Nicola smiled. 'What will happen to Ash?' asked Cathy.

'What do you think should happen?'

'I just wonder if we can trust him. He's seen a lot. I think we should make sure he understands what will happen if he speaks out.'

'You can decide his fate, my little spider.'

Cathy turned and smiled at her.

Chapter 16

Maxwell was busy looking at all the details of the case when Willis and Carter arrived back at the station at nearly three. Hector was with him. They were sharing an office; it was pretty cramped. Also in there were two civilian researchers. There was a small office off the main space which Hector usually used for privacy when he worked, but it had been given over to Maxwell until they could find somewhere better. Hector was looking frazzled.

'What happened with Yvonne?' asked Maxwell.

'Come with us, we're headed for the canteen and we can fill you in there. Hector? All okay?' Carter asked as they were retreating.

Hector gave him a thumbs-up.

The canteen was busy; Tina, Ebony's housemate, was flat-out cleaning up after the lunch service, washing up all the stainless steel vats. They ordered their drinks and took them over to a quiet corner.

'How was it with Yvonne Coombes?' asked Maxwell.

'Yvonne Coombes is now a single parent on methadone,' said Carter. 'I feel for her, she's doing her utmost to try to make it through with her little girl.'

'She was Millie's only friend by the sound of it, and

hadn't seen her for a couple of months,' said Willis. 'We know this was an especially bad time for Millie, broke and without Yvonne to turn to, or her dad.'

'She'd fallen out with everyone, so maybe Millie took some chances she wouldn't normally have taken. She was obviously thinking about the friendship, the photo of them both was by her bed. I'm not ruling out the possibility that she needed money so badly she went into that park with a man,' Carter said.

'She was still bragging about her time with Douglas,' said Maxwell. 'She was never going to make many friends like that.'

'No, probably not,' said Willis, 'but who else did she know? Yvonne might be able to help with that, if I push her.'

'Could still be one of her peers,' suggested Maxwell. 'They have fights all the time, they have stabbings over territory, over punters. This is one step more, that's all.'

'Yes, I agree,' said Carter. 'Except, they'd have had to drag her kicking and screaming into that park.'

'Or doped?' volunteered Maxwell. 'She could have been given a bigger dose of heroin. What was her father like?'

Willis answered, 'He was bitter, angry, frustrated. He's had to put up with a lot, but she was his only child; so mostly he was heartbroken.'

'Could he have tipped over the edge?' asked Maxwell.

'It's something we will need to look into further,' answered Willis. 'He is the kind of person she would have gone to the park with but I don't think it's his way.'

'Gavin Heathcote, a former disciple, who still proudly bears his tattoos and talks about those times with great affection, especially his part in the slaughter of the animals in the foot and mouth epidemic, he needs looking in to more thoroughly – he is capable of killing and he says he has seen Millie a few times. Having met him, I don't see Millie getting anything for nothing. Maybe she became a nuisance, and perhaps Gavin decided enough was enough,' said Carter.

'He has an alibi,' countered Willis. 'It was provided by his wife and backed up by his father-in-law, the landlord of the Swan pub near Gavin's home, who says Gavin was working on the pub roof for two weeks from the fifteenth of September through to the first of October all day, and spent all night drinking in the pub.'

'He works with a team of men, let's find out who they are and ask them.'

'Will do,' answered Willis, taking notes.

'She tapped all the disciples for money, apparently. Did she get to be a massive nuisance?' Carter wondered. 'But, this was no way a professional hit. Two of the ex-disciples have done very well: Stephen Perry and Cathy Dwyer. If I was one of them, and I had the money as they do, and Millie was a nuisance, I would have paid someone to kill her.'

'But, who would you have paid?' asked Maxwell. 'Someone from her own world, like a person who lived or worked on the streets? That's what I would have done. This still could be a professional hit.'

'I agree with the theory of that except,' said Willis, 'if people hated her that much, then they would be queuing up to tell us who did it, and they're not.'

'Sorry we don't have a lot for you to go on at the moment,' Carter said to Maxwell. 'I know you're a facts and figures type.'

'That's okay, I'm looking at known offenders in the area, charting their movements. I'll also pursue any of the working girls who have had charges for assault in the past. I would also like to take the rest of the day to go and do a bit more research on Douglas.'

'Sure, what are you thinking?' asked Carter.

'The farm he took the rape victim Rachel McKinney to, the one he intended to bury her in. I want to get the feel of it.'

'Okay, I have no objection to that,' said Carter, looking Willis's way.

'Why do you want to go there?' asked Willis.

He shrugged. 'Even though I studied the Douglas case, I have never been to see it, and it's really the only solid evidence they ever had against him. I want to understand a little of what it would have been like for Millie and the others, to have known a man like Douglas. Did he dig that grave himself, or did others dig it for him? Were his disciples just as bad as him? Did they take part in the abduction, assault, rape and attempted murder of Rachel? I just want to get a feel for it all.'

'Okay,' said Carter. 'Take a pool car, and you'd better get a move on, it'll be dark in a few hours.'

After Maxwell had left Carter and Willis stayed where they were to talk.

'Is he going to be useful in this, do you think?' asked Willis. 'He is pretty intense.'

'I blame the French side of him,' Carter grinned.

'He is super-sensitive,' said Willis. 'I feel like I'm walking on eggshells around him.'

'Don't. Be yourself, blunt as ever. It's up to him to adjust to us, to fit in, not the other way around. I'm hoping he will be really useful to us in this and I don't mind the way he's jumped right in and wants to go the extra mile.'

Willis brought up photos of Millie and the other disciples on her screen.

'Millie was damaged at the farm and she stayed that way for life. She and Yvonne were warped right at the point when they were as malleable as they were ever going to be in their entire life. Douglas knew that,' she said.

'Yes,' agreed Carter. 'Douglas knew everyone's weaknesses. Except, I don't reckon Gavin was moulded by Douglas, he was merely pushed deep into the mould, but he was already a thug.'

'Agreed,' said Willis. 'But Cathy Dwyer? Stephen Perry? They've done well since their times at Hawthorn Farm and the bungalow. Have they done well because of it or despite it? Did Douglas's lessons make them instead of breaking them?'

Chapter 17

Chris Maxwell signed out a detective's pool car from the desk in Archway station and drove down the M4 and A303 towards Somerset. Two hours down the road and he pulled his car off at the signpost for Hill Farm. He drove for a mile and then stopped to get his bearings.

In the quiet of the early evening, Maxwell got out of the car and stood looking around him. He checked his map, he was in the right place. These were the notes and maps taken from the original investigation. He'd had a look at the farm via Google Earth and it hadn't changed at all in seventeen years since the day she was brought here to die. Except that was summertime and this was a wet and cold October. The field that he needed was just half a mile from the main road but it was enclosed in a patchwork of small fields and high hedges and it rose steeply to a stand of trees that must have been there for at least a hundred years, tall gnarly oaks. The sky was deep blue tinged with magenta.

Maxwell went around to the boot of the car and reached in to take out his boots.

The gate to the field was open. 'Hello?'

He jumped. Turning round he found a man walking towards him on the lane.

'I seen your car lights, what do you want?'

'Mr Jones?' asked Chris.

'Do I know you?'

'I phoned, my name is Chris Maxwell. I am the crime profiler working for the police. I was hoping to have a look around this field?'

'Of course, I have no problem with that. I have to keep an eye out for gypsies thinking they can set up camp wherever they like; you go ahead. Is it about Rachel? Lucky for her I was on this road then.'

'Yes, she was lucky you came along. Have you developed the field since then?'

'No, the place where he dug the grave is still there. Far side, halfway up on the left of this field where the hedge bulges and there's an ash tree growing tall from it. You'll see where it's marked out. I put a piece of corrugated iron over it. I didn't like to get rid of it altogether. Thought you might need another look one day. When I first saw your car, looking so clean, I thought maybe you were here about the Euro subsidies, thought you were snooping. It's all about us leaving the EU now. I don't know what I'll do with all my land; it's not good for planting, there's no money to be made. I don't know what will happen to the farms in this country.'

'Is it all right to park here in the gateway?' Maxwell wanted to get on before the light went.

'Yes, you go ahead, do what you've got to do. It's hundreds of acres, mind, are you going to look at all of it, by yourself? You'll be here for a week.'

'I'm just here to get an overall view of this field and the few next to it.'

'I see. Well, you crack on.' He started to walk away

and then turned back. 'I still find it hard to believe it was Douglas, mind.' Maxwell carried on putting on his thick socks and boots. 'When they came here years ago we had police talk to me about a man that used to deliver feed here, they said he might have killed people. I told them at the time, won't have been Douglas! He was a good chap, you see, nothing was too much trouble for him, he had a nice way about him, do you understand?' Maxwell nodded and continued pulling out his equipment from the boot of the car. 'He always helped me out when I needed it,' continued Jones. 'Ah, well, she'd never have been found. I was on the way back from the pub when I thought I saw headlights on this lane. By the time I calmed her down and got her in the car, he'd scarpered. When I saw her, I thought, Jesus, Mother of God, how is she still alive?' He swung his head from side to side. 'Do you want me to come with you?'

'No need, thank you, it's only a case of walking around the edge of the fields. Am I right in thinking you don't have any livestock in these four fields here off this lane?'

'That's right. Don't worry, no bulls. There's sheep in the next field but they won't hurt you. I'll be off, young fella, leave you to it, get home for my tea.' Jones disappeared up the lane.

Maxwell took out his camera and walked in through the open gate. He stopped to turn and take it in. He wanted to get a feel for it: the quiet, the stillness, they didn't bring peace, they brought tension.

Rachel McKinney was celebrating the end of the first year of her law degree at Bristol University and she intended to pack up the next day and head home to her parents in Plymouth for a long leisurely summer before coming back

in October. She had drunk some shots and become separated from her friends when they moved on without her.
She started making out with a man on the dance floor. But
it had only been a kiss or two and, once she had a good
look at him, she realised he was pretty awful. Her friends
didn't answer her calls so she went looking for them in
the usual bars. Instead of finding them, she ended up in a
private party with some other students she vaguely knew
from the third year. At four in the morning she'd sobered
up enough to realise she didn't want to be there and decided
to get home. She had no idea where she was and no battery
left on her phone as she started walking towards what she
thought was town.

She stuck out her thumb and a van stopped. It had a
horse on the side of it and the inscription 'Champion'. She
looked in through the open passenger window at the sweet-
faced man who sat at the driving wheel, leaning across at
her and smiling.

'Where are you going?'

'Bristol centre.' She didn't notice the woman sitting just
behind him.

'You're in luck, get in.'

Maxwell started walking up close to the hedge in the direction of the grave. He found it where Jones had described
and lifted up the corrugated iron and rested it back against
the hedge. Beneath it, the ground was bald. A slow-worm
slithered away, deep copper-coloured against the red earth.
The grave was protected by a plastic sheet inside and,
although it had mostly collapsed, it wasn't difficult to see
where it had been.

*

Rachel McKinney shivered uncontrollably but she stayed conscious through the drug-induced world of fog and pain and no feeling, and she said to herself: 'Listen ... you are nineteen years old, you are about to die,' and she listened to Douglas and his laboured breathing as he dug the earth, and she heard the sound of the soil as it crumbled and she heard the scraping of the spade and she heard him curse the hardness of the soil and she looked up at the moon and she said to herself: 'You are nineteen and your life ends here, in this place, and no one will ever find you,' and she touched her bare leg and she knew then she was sitting in a field as the grass enclosed her. 'Wake up ... wake up ...' words tried to reach her though nothing, no feelings, no hope, no self-preservation was left.

She turned her head at the rustle of an animal in the hedge and then she looked up and saw the distant fuzzy lights of a car and heard the rumble of its engine.

She looked at Douglas, he was still digging, deep now, she could just see his back as he bent over. Rachel McKinney said to herself: 'You are nineteen, you are not going to die here, get on your feet, for Christ's sake, and run!'

Rachel McKinney pushed herself to her feet in one massive effort and staggered as she ran down the field, trying to make her legs work.

In the minute after Douglas heard the car himself, and realised she had gone, he hopped out of the grave and ran after her. But the lights were stronger now, the engine louder and it was coming towards the crossroads and most likely turning this way. McKinney was too far ahead.

He turned around and ran back to his van, threw his spade in the back, slammed the doors shut and drove.

*

Maxwell stayed exactly where he was for several minutes, then he got out his camera and switched it to video mode and filmed as he walked up to the brow of the field to get a look at the area.

He dictated into his recorder:

'The field rises gently away from the lane. Not overlooked, not easy to see into without entering field, cannot see the lane from where I am standing. Across the valley from here there is another farm, there is a dilapidated cattle shed on the hill in the distance, and old machinery abandoned in a field on Margery Farm.'

Chapter 18

Friday 26 May 2000

Douglas returned home later than usual that Friday night. Before he went into the house he took time to check the back of his van was secure. He had been too tired to deal with Darren's body and had left him in his van all week. He would get it done tomorrow.

Douglas locked up the van and walked in at just before midnight and found Nicola having sex with Gavin in Douglas's bed. He stood over them, watching, and Nicola smiled at him from over the shoulder of Gavin, who was unaware of him, and Douglas watched his naked rump and smiled. He contemplated joining in but he wanted a beer and a smoke after his long day, long week. He went into the sitting room, where a few people were dotted around the floor: Stephen and Cathy were there, and Yvonne. The air was thick with the smell of weed. The French doors were open now as the evenings were light and warm. It was the month before the longest day of the year, the disciples sat around and drank beer and smoked weed and the air was filled with heat and sex and summer. Outside the fire pit had clearly been lit hours ago and the logs on it were white hot. He looked across and saw there was movement in Ash's van.

Douglas sat around the fire pit with the others, smoking weed and drinking beer, before he took Cathy into his bed. He could see it annoyed Nicola but he didn't care. He was keeping this whole way of life going; everyone was there because of him. Cathy sat up in bed afterwards and talked non-stop, about her excitement in life, all the countries she wanted to go to, all the money she wanted to make.

'And you will do it all, I believe you.'

They went out to join the others.

Ash walked over to the bungalow.

'How's your mum?' asked Millie, sitting at Douglas's feet, joint in her hand.

Millie inhaled deeply and then ejected the smoke in a fit of laughter that she couldn't control, it was contagious, and soon they were all laughing. Ash didn't join in. His mother had been sectioned. She'd gone into town and exposed herself and ranted and screamed and been taken away.

'Stop it!' Nicola stood and went across to Ash. 'We don't mean it, Ashy baby.' She tried to kiss him, but he turned away.

Douglas laughed and, as Ash turned to leave, he picked him up bear-hug style and carried him through the sliding doors into the sitting room.

'Nicola, Millie, come on, you owe Ash a birthday present, he's sixteen, he deserves to have a little female attention.'

Ash tried to laugh, tried to get away. His arms were held tight by Douglas as the others came in from the patio to watch.

Nicola came across as Douglas held him tightly, and

began kissing him as he twisted his mouth away. He began fighting harder against Douglas but the grip only increased. Ash was angry now but still trying to show he understood it was a joke. He asked to be let go, he asked again. Douglas kept on ignoring him and laughing and he called Gavin over to help him hold on to Ash. Millie undid his flies and wriggled his jeans down.

She picked up his penis, floppy and small, and began sucking. Ash tried to kick her away but she kept returning and every time his cock grew harder and stronger. Nicola came to suck him and Ash was caught in the agony of embarrassment and sorrow and disgust and unstoppable orgasm.

Ash tried to laugh it off afterwards as he hung about for a beer. When he finally got away, he walked back over to sit in his van. A horrible feeling of doom hovered over him. He curled up on the bunk where his mother slept and he stared out of the window. Douglas's warning was clear. Ash had decided he would phone his gran again and push her to take responsibility for his mum. That he was dispensable to Douglas was obvious, and he was alone, isolated. Ash knew he had to go and get his mum settled and then he had to come back for Heather as soon as he could. Now Ash had nothing left but fear in his heart.

In the morning Douglas slept in. It was late by the time he decided to face the job of disposing of Darren's body.

Douglas came out into the sitting room where Stephen was already up and drinking coffee. Yvonne was in his lap, still sleepy. Stephen and Cathy had slept together on the floor of the sitting room and their mattress and sheets were still spread out. Gavin was still dozing, Cathy sat up and pulled her T-shirt on over her head before searching for her knickers. Douglas could smell them, with their rancid smell of yesterday's sex and sweat and mess and dirt, and he nudged Stephen with his foot.

'Get washed. I need your help.'

Douglas went outside to check on his van and smelt it as soon as he got near. The nights were getting hot. The body was in a bag, swimming in its own juices.

'It stinks.' He turned to see a figure standing behind him. It was Saul the farrier. 'What you got in there?'

'It's not what's in there, it's what's under the van and on the tyre. I went to a slaughterhouse in the week where they were washing the yard, and most of it went over my van.'

'The van looks clean to me.'

Douglas always went through the car wash with it once a week.

'It's underneath,' he said.

Saul nodded but he didn't take his eyes off Douglas.

'When's your next party?' asked Saul.

'Why? Are you coming?' Douglas smiled.

'I don't have to come, I can hear it from where I am, can't I? I was thinking of putting livestock on the fields. I can't do it if your party-goers are going to trespass and worry the sheep.'

'Next party is in a few weeks. We may have a few friends over before that but I'll keep them out of your fields, make sure they don't barbecue any of your sheep.'

'They'd better not, otherwise they will be next in the fire,' Saul said, without a smile.

Douglas watched Saul walk back; he hopped athletically over his gate and strode away up the field. Douglas went back inside the bungalow. Nicola was planning the evening.

It was going to involve plenty of drink and drugs. Douglas didn't want to waste time now. He needed to deal with his problem in the van. He looked at Stephen and called him out.

'We have work to do. We'll take Gavin too.'

'Now?'

'Yes, sooner we go, sooner we get back and enjoy the evening, work has to come first.'

'What is it? Weed? Pills?' Stephen asked.

'Something like that.' He could see by Stephen's face that he knew it was going to be like last time. Stephen and Gavin were the two that Douglas trusted most. Ash accepted everything Douglas asked him to do through fear. Stephen did it for the excitement it gave his over-privileged life. He wanted to bum about his whole life and inherit when it came to it. Gavin was all about the drugs and the drink and the sex, he didn't care what he did to get it.

Cathy was told to go and get Ash. She found him in his van.

'Ash?'

'Leave me alone, please.'

'I just wanted to say don't worry, it's no big deal.' He didn't turn around. 'Don't worry about anything, Ash, the sex thing, it was just a laugh. Don't take any notice, it's just what they do. They think it's funny. They wouldn't mind if someone did it to them, so they don't really get it.'

He turned around and looked at her and realised that Cathy wasn't alone. Douglas was behind the door. Douglas stepped out and put his arm around Cathy's waist.

'How's it going?' Douglas asked.

'I was just telling Ash you need him. And I wanted to see if he was okay,' she answered.

Ash sat up. He was stripped to the waist, his skin brown, his wiry body changing into brawn from the work on the farm.

'He's all right, of course he is, he got sucked off by two women. My God, you'd have to pay a lot of money for that. You should ask Heather if she wants to see how it's done, Ash. Ask her if she wants to watch and learn.' He laughed and Ash turned away.

'I'm only kidding, for feck's sake! I'm sorry, Ash. Thought you'd find it funny. Hey, didn't mean to upset you, little man. I have great plans for all of you. Never doubt that, Ash.'

Douglas laughed and moved Cathy in the direction of the bungalow.

'Ash, get your arse into gear. I need you,' he called back over his shoulder.

Ash had to sit in the back of the van and he couldn't stretch his legs out because the old bag that was tied with string and stretched in places was taking up all the space. The curve of a skull, the shape of a shoulder pushed against the bag as the dead body rocked with the movement of the vehicle.

'Who is it?' asked Ash. Gavin glanced across at Douglas. Douglas looked in the mirror at Ash.

'It was someone who tried to stitch me up over a deal. He pulled a knife on me; I stuck him first.'

Stephen laughed. 'Fuck him!'

'Yeah.' Gavin laughed too.

'Does it matter who it is?' asked Douglas. 'Don't we all stick together? If you or Gavin here have any trouble with anyone, then Stephen and me are going to be at your side and, you remember that, we are chained together, where one link goes we all follow.'

'To hell and back.' Stephen grinned and ended with a whoop out of the window.

'Saul noticed the smell,' said Douglas as the van fell silent.

'He's a fucking queer weirdo,' said Gavin. 'He watches us, you know, at the yard. I've seen him sometimes, at his window upstairs. I reckon he watches us a lot.'

'What do you think, Ash, does he watch us?'

'I think Saul is okay.'

'You think so?' Glances were exchanged between the others.

'I don't know,' Ash said, back-tracking.

'No ... well, we'll see. We may have to stop him spying on us,' Douglas said, glancing across at Gavin.

Ash sat quietly for the rest of the journey. As they blasted down the road the movement of the van caused the body to roll slightly and release more odour. Stephen opened his window right down to get rid of the smell.

Douglas pulled off the main road and took the road back to Lambs Farm.

'Stay here,' Douglas said, as he got out to make sure they were alone.

This wasn't ideal for Douglas, it was still daytime: it was light and hot, but he couldn't wait. Next time, he told himself, he wouldn't sleep on it; it had been an unnecessary risk. He should have buried Darren by himself but he had to be sure everyone was involved.

He opened the back of the van, Ash got out and Douglas handed Stephen and Ash shovels.

Gavin and Douglas slid out the plastic sheet that the

body in the black bin liner was resting on and placed it on the ground. Douglas sent Gavin into the back of the van to unhook a cart from the side. He dropped it off the back of the van and they loaded the body inside the high-sided rectangular trolley used to transport bags of horse feed.

'Stephen, go up there with Ash to dig out the chest.'

Ash knew where he was going, as he was in the same field as last time. The soil gave way easily. They went back down to the van to help bring up the body. The field was steep.

Gavin dragged it up the field, pulling the dead weight behind him as Douglas pushed the cart uphill. They reached the grave and tipped him in from the crate. Douglas reached in and cut through the plastic and Darren's body squelched out from his bin-bag womb.

He ended up on his front. The stench of decomposing flesh was overwhelming. Stephen began to vomit. Gavin and Ash started filling in the grave.

Saul the farrier looked out of his window and saw the flames rise acrid and orange, black soot and firing sparks ripping up into the air with a haze of heat around them. Ash's van was on fire. He watched Truscott come running up the lane, scrabbling across the field, and he saw Nicola and Douglas come out onto their patio and start to walk across. Saul moved to his kitchen and looked over to Heather's house. He could see her at her bedroom window, she was hitting the glass with the palm of her hands until suddenly he saw her father appear and the curtains were pulled shut.

He went back to watch from his sitting-room window. Now the flames were in danger of setting the whole hedge alight. But nothing was going to put this fire out now.

*

'A toast to Ash and his mum,' said Cathy as she poured out shots and handed them around.

'Where is he?' asked Yvonne, staring at the scene, transfixed by the sight of twenty-foot flames, angry, searing into the blue sky, choked by black smoke.

'He's found his freedom.'

'Where has he gone?' Yvonne looked at Cathy.

'Away.'

'What did he say?'

Cathy turned away irritated. 'How the fuck do I know. Toast to Ash,' she raised her glass, 'to his stinky old van, to his mad mother, a toast to them all.'

Chapter 19

In the morning Willis switched off her alarm and sat up in bed. She swung her legs over the side and sat for a moment feeling the itchy cheap carpet beneath her bare feet before she stood and began pulling on her running kit. She had time for a quick run; it would sort her head out for the day. She picked up her trainers and crept downstairs from her top-floor room. She heard her housemate Tina's radio on; she was listening to Radio 2. Willis skipped lightly down the rest of the stairs, opened the front door, slipped on her trainers and began running. The day was glorious; she ran past Mo's convenience store on the corner, past the new Spanish restaurant and the Greek café and across the Green and into the park. She felt free when she ran. She could lift her head and look forward and feel like her feet were flying and she was soaring into the sky, and when her feet felt like lead she could turn her thoughts to things that were troubling her and take her mind off the run. It was therapy, whichever way she looked at it. Halfway around the park she got a call.

'DS Willis?'

'Yes,' she answered, jogging on the spot.

'A woman has been found dead in a flat in Homerton, Sarge.'

'Who found her?'

'The vicar, Sarge. She lives alone.'

'Ring DCI Carter and tell him I'll meet him there.'

'Yes, Sarge.'

Forty minutes later, Willis and Carter stood on one side of the busy road in Hackney looking across at a three-storeyed block of flats behind a high laurel hedge. They could just see the top floor of the building. Between them and the laurel hedge was a hissing stream of traffic.

Willis followed Carter as they dodged across the busy road, past the police car, and then walked up the side street. Cedar Road was lined with London planes losing their leaves.

They stopped at the entrance to Cedar Court, a large, brightly lit porch with dying insects gathering in its corners, chipped-paint mailboxes and a concrete flight of stairs leading to the upper floors. They were met by a community support officer, standing alert and enthused.

Willis and Carter showed their warrant cards.

'Straight through the doors and on your right, ma'am, sir.'

Laptop, a uniformed police constable, was waiting for them at the entrance to flat number six on the lower floor. They knew him from Archway Police Station.

'Remind me who found her?' asked Willis.

'The local vicar, Sarge, he had tried to reach her last evening and didn't get a reply so came round early this morning,' Laptop answered. 'He confirmed her name as Melanie Drummond. A paramedic confirmed death. House-to-house has started. DC Blackman is on it.'

'Good work,' said Carter.

'Where is the vicar now?' asked Willis.

'He asked if he could leave,' answered Laptop, 'he was pretty shaken up. I took his details; I thought that it would be okay.'

Willis didn't comment; she was looking down the row of doors under a covered walkway. To her left there was a fenced area of merging front gardens that had their own gates, their own paths, leading to the lane at the back. A toddler was riding a trike on the path between the strips of grass; the woman with her was keeping an eye on proceedings.

'Did you go inside?' Carter asked Laptop.

Laptop passed Willis and Carter the crime scene log to sign.

Willis walked across to the woman who was now pushing her little girl on the trike.

'Do you speak English?'

The woman nodded.

'Do you live here?'

'Yes.' She pointed to a flat on the second floor with a purple door and a boarded-up window.

'What's your name, please?' Willis took out her notebook to write it down.

'Mrs Aziz.'

'Do you know the lady who lives in that flat, number six?'

Mrs Aziz shook her head. She was layered against the cold. Her black hair and her round face were sheathed in a red cloth arranged around her head and draped over her shoulders, bright against the grey sky.

'Have you had a problem? What about the window?' asked Willis.

The woman shook her head. 'Children do it.'

'How long have you lived here, Mrs Aziz?' asked Willis.

The woman tipped her hand in the air, thinking. 'Maybe year and a half?'

'And you have never spoken to the woman who lived in that flat?'

'Sometimes I see her, say hello, that's all.'

'When was the last time you saw her?'

'Yesterday in the middle of the day. Here. I was in the garden with my daughter.'

'Did you hear any noises coming from the flat in the last few days? Anything strange?'

She shook her head. Her daughter came to stand next to her mum. Her clear brown eyes were sharp and inquisitive.

'Did you see anyone you didn't recognise? Anything not quite right, someone hanging about?' She shook her head in response. 'Thanks for your help, Mrs Aziz. We'll need a statement from you, one of my officers will be calling around in the next few hours.'

She nodded and reached down to lift her daughter onto her hip, watching Willis walk away.

Carter was speaking with Laptop when Willis got back to him.

'What else did the vicar say about her?' she asked.

'That she never socialised, he didn't think she had anyone else in her life, nothing but the church.'

Willis stuffed her jacket into her backpack and left it at Laptop's feet as she prepared to go inside the flat by putting on a forensic suit.

'Did he like her?' asked Carter, getting into his and covering his feet with protective booties.

'He seemed to.'

'Look after that.' Carter handed Laptop his expensive Armani coat. 'Guard it with your life.' Laptop smiled.

As Laptop held the door open for them, Carter squatted down to take a better look at the doorframe. 'No sign of a forced entry,' he said, 'and the key question is why did she open the door? She has a spyhole, so it must be someone she trusted or what they said made some sense to her. She had to have decided to let her guard down.'

Willis pulled up her mask and took the first step inside the small flat and into the hallway. The stillness was heavy in the half-light. Carter stepped inside behind her. Willis's eyes were on the hallway ahead. She'd already made up her mind about the doorframe. Laptop closed the door behind them. They stopped at the bathroom door on the right and Willis nudged it open with her foot.

'She didn't get this far, then,' said Carter as he peered over her shoulder into the neat and tidy bathroom, clean water in the bath and pink shells along its rim. A glass was on the side of the bath.

Willis smelt it. 'Gin.'

Back in the hallway, they took a few steps to the sitting room. There was a large window straight ahead; beyond it was the strip of communal gardens to the front of the block. From somewhere outside there was the sound of a child laughing and still the drone and hiss of the steady stream of traffic on the wet road beyond the hedge. Willis's eyes came to rest on a vase of fresh flowers standing defiantly beautiful, against all odds, on the window ledge. Lilies, their pungent smell had turned into decaying perfume. Carter hung back; he let her do her own thing. Her world was not his, and he was glad of it. In his world things added up or they didn't, in Ebony's they just kept unravelling. She didn't build; she split into atoms and then split again. She didn't observe the tragedy; she lived it with the victim.

He walked into the kitchen. 'No blood in here, but there is a knife missing from the rack.' He returned to the sitting room to stand next to Willis. From where they were standing at the entrance of the room, they could see right into the bedroom and the back of a woman's bare legs, one twisted over the other.

'Things went wrong in here,' said Willis. 'No blood in the hallway, kitchen or bathroom, but furniture knocked over in here.'

The woman's body was lying on its side, turned away from them. Blood had turned the pale blue bedding a deep reddish-brown. Puncture wounds in the woman's back had opened up and bled out whilst she still had blood pumping through her veins. They walked into the bedroom, and Carter went around to the head of the bed.

'Christ . . .' he said as he looked up on the wall. **Heather?** was written there in blood.

'Do you see her wrists?' Carter asked.

Willis nodded. *Ignite the fire* was on one and a red chain on the other.

'This is another disciple.'

'Not just *any* disciple – this is Nicola Stone,' said Carter.

Chapter 20

Inside Flat 6, Sandford had arrived and Dermot was photographing the papers strewn across the floor when they heard Carter and Willis returning after talking to the vicar. A tent was now erected around the front door. Laptop was still on duty. He'd managed to blag a cup of tea from the neighbour.

'Get suited up and come in. Step on the plates,' he said to Carter and Willis as they reached the door. Sandford moved back from the hallway into the sitting room. 'I heard that we have a connection here,' he said.

'Yes, we are sure this is Nicola Stone,' Carter answered.

'We're going to need all of this furniture taken out of here before we can examine this place thoroughly – carpets, curtains, everything has to come out. We're in the process of bagging up,' added Sandford.

They walked into the bedroom where Dermot was still preparing the body to be moved by placing plastic bags over the victim's feet and hands.

'Heather isn't a name you hear any more, is it?' said Dermot, staring at the wall in the bedroom where he was working.

'No,' Sandford answered.

'Heather?' he repeated, as if trying it out. 'Pretty name though. I had a cousin who was called Heather.'

'Was she Scottish?' asked Sandford.

'Yes, she was actually. She was flame-haired and freckly. We used to play together.'

'Sounds like you were in love with her,' said Carter.

'My cousin?'

'Well, it happens,' Carter said. 'Don't knock it till you try it.' He was distracted by the way the letters were written, by the question mark. 'We must get this handwriting analysed.'

Sandford stood next to him. 'We've taken extensive photos; video's been done and downloaded already. You want to take more, help yourself.'

Carter declined. 'Sexual activity?' he asked.

'I can't see any evidence of it,' said Sandford, turning back into the lounge and standing on the plates in the centre of the room. 'The place has been gone through, someone was looking for something. They seemed to have been calmly looking through her correspondence afterwards. They had rubber gloves on by this time; the ridges from the fingers have left an imprint. This person was careful, but not careful enough. I've found a good deal of money here, scattered around the sitting room. It would have been easy for the killer to take, it wasn't concealed.'

Willis went back in to look at the body and the stab wounds in Nicola's back. 'It's not the same knife as Harding described for Millie's injuries,' she said, 'there's no evidence of bruising from a hilt. This knife was thinner.'

'The kitchen is missing a knife,' said Sandford. 'We've only found the prints on the rack so far. I think the perpetrator may have been cut, two blood types here, we're still testing.'

'They didn't intend to kill, maybe?' said Willis. 'They didn't come in here with that intention?'

'Nicola Stone would have been well able to handle herself,' answered Carter. 'She would have used her wits, she might have attacked first.'

'We haven't found the knife. What is going to be the main focus here?' asked Sandford. Carter was the Senior Investigating Officer and everyone in the case took their directives from him.

'Extract all her documents, records, let's find out all we can about Melanie Drummond before people realise it's Nicola Stone. That's where my emphasis is. We will also be making detailed background searches on the residents, and checking CCTV. Someone managed to get in here without busting the door down, that would point to someone she trusted.'

'I've cordoned off the whole street and the lane at the back that leads to the garages,' answered Sandford. 'The area of pathway from here to the entrance will be my focus and will have to be closed for half a day while I bring a team in to help search the route through the garden onto the lane. I need support teams to search the gardens and bins in this area, starting with Cedar Road, searching for any bloody clothing that's been discarded.'

Willis was looking at the walls around her and had already decided that Nicola Stone had never really made this flat her home. There was a small dining table in the corner by the back window and two matching high-backed chairs were tipped over. Not a painting on the walls, not a lampshade that didn't look as if it had been chosen for its cheap ugliness, and yet there was money to do it up. It seemed to Willis that the only prettiness Nicola allowed in her life were the flowers and the shells at the edge of her bath tub. Was it guilt? Probably.

'We'll need the teams to start searching now before it gets dark,' Sandford said. He looked at Willis for a reply.

She nodded. 'We're on it.'

Outside, Blackman joined them. DC Zoe Blackman was a single parent with two boys – her mother helped her out when she could, looking after the children whilst she worked. She had fought very hard to get where she was. Zoe was short and blonde and ferociously competitive when it came to drinking shots. She had the face of a choir-girl but she could arm-wrestle for England.

'I got some useful information from the man at the end of the row, in number eleven,' said Blackman. 'He's on palliative care and the victim used to come and see him every day. He said he saw her yesterday evening at just before six. I think you might like to speak to him?'

Roy was sitting on the edge of his bed when they got there, wearing a threadbare pair of grey tracksuit bottoms and a faded red sweatshirt with a basketball logo. His scruffy room was decorated with photos of Africa: a lioness resting in the shade of a solitary tree, a photo of a house and a cove featuring turquoise seas, icing-sugar sands.

Carter introduced himself and Willis did the same.

'Is that home?' Carter asked, looking at the framed photos.

Roy nodded. 'Have you ever been?' He reached for his oxygen mask and strapped the elastic around his head. Roy's words were punctuated by the need to stop and breathe.

'No, afraid not, but I'd love to one day,' answered Carter. 'Has it been a long time for you?'

'Too long, my friend.'

'Roy, we'll try not to stay long,' said Carter. 'We've come about Melanie Drummond from Flat Six. You told the officer you saw her yesterday?'

'Yes, I did. What is it? Where is she? What has happened to Melanie?'

Willis remained standing. She was used to taking notes that way. Carter sat down in one of the two armchairs that had seen better days. The smell of the ashtray and the sight of cigarette butts made Carter dip into his pocket for another square of nicotine chewing gum; he wished he found the smell of ashtrays repulsive instead of irresistible. Willis was looking out at the back garden, the hedge, through the gaps in the foliage. This was the same view as Nicola Stone had from Flat 6. This flat was identical except that the partition wall to the bedroom had been taken down to allow Roy to live out his days in one twelve-foot space.

'I am very sorry, Roy, I have some sad news,' said Carter. 'Melanie has been killed.' He reached out his hand and put it on Roy's paper-thin-skinned and bulging-veined hands. 'Was she a good friend of yours? Did you know her well?'

'Oh, God . . .' He nodded and dragged in the breath and his eyes bulged as his face turned purple. 'Poor Melanie.' He shook his head mournfully. 'How? Why?' He spoke with the mask on his face. His chest heaved and his lungs made a withering sound as he exhaled.

'She was killed by someone who entered the flat. We don't know why or who yet, Roy, that's why we are piecing together her last movements. You said you saw her yesterday, can you tell us about that please?' Carter put his hand back onto Roy's. 'When you're ready, you take your time.'

Roy took a few minutes to collect himself as he waited for his lungs to stop screaming.

'She popped by, to see if I need anything, the way she always does.' Roy nodded. 'Every day, like clockwork.' His face cracked and he sobbed into the mask.

Willis moved back from the window to look at Roy's shelves, which held few possessions.

He started to cry. His sobs looked to be in danger of killing him as Carter got out of his seat and leaned over him to give him a hug. Roy clung to him as he dragged in a breath.

'Can I get you some medication, Roy? Do you need me to call someone?' asked Carter.

Roy shook his head and released Carter with a smile of gratitude. 'Honestly, I want to help. Give me a few minutes. I'm such a useless old bugger.' When he was ready, he took off the mask.

'How did Melanie seem yesterday?'

'Melanie never said how she felt, she just listened to me moaning on.'

Carter got up to feel if the radiator was on in the room; it wasn't.

'You should have the heating on, Roy. Where's the switch?'

Roy pointed to the kitchen. Carter went in to see, found the boiler and checked the programme. He put it on timer. The boiler fired up.

'What time did Melanie come by yesterday?' asked Carter.

'In the afternoon ... about two. I was waiting for my

carer ... he didn't show up ... Melanie helped me take a bath.'

'What time did she leave you?' Carter asked.

'I fell asleep, but I think about six.' He shook his head, he couldn't talk any more, his lungs were squealing, his body exhausted.

'Can we get you someone or something?' Carter asked.

'You said Melanie came by every day?'

'Yes ... or she called me ...' He jiggled his iPhone in the air to illustrate. 'To see if I needed anything ... from the shop. Not alcohol ... I couldn't ask her for that. Not that, oh God, no!' He shook his head, tried to laugh, started coughing, began dragging in the oxygen again through his mask. He stayed silent for a few minutes.

'Take your time, Roy.'

He took off his mask again to talk. 'She just wanted to be left alone but she had a good heart, she always came to help when I needed her.'

'How long had you known her?'

'Over a year. I don't know exactly. She was a good friend to me. Private person.' He held up his hand to show he needed to wait, to calm. When he was ready he smiled at Carter. 'Bloody cigarettes. We all have our little vices, demons, don't we? Last Chance Saloon, this place is. We're all fuck-ups in this place, all of us on the lower floors anyway.'

'What about Melanie, was she also?' asked Carter.

Roy looked at Carter and nodded. 'She had her secrets; do you know who she is?'

'We believe she is Nicola Stone.'

Roy nodded. 'She told me. I was shocked, at first, but she was good to me.'

'Did she ever talk to you about that time in her life?'

He shook his head. 'She said she had served her time, done her penance.'

'Did she talk about Douglas getting out?'

'The other day, I asked her was she looking forward to seeing him again. She didn't think it was fair that she had to hide away like she did, the public really hated her. All she did was give an alibi to the man she loved.'

Roy waited for a reaction from Carter but he didn't get it. Instead, Carter asked, 'Do you think she could have been in contact with anyone from her past?'

'She talked a lot about them recently, she even showed me some photos of them.'

'Do you have any idea who was in them?'

'She pointed them all out to me, all the people I'd heard about. She said they were people she still felt enormously bonded to. I'm so tired. Sorry, I am so sad and tired.' He lay back on his pillow and shut his eyes.

'We'll be sending along an officer to help you through this, Roy.'

Roy didn't answer.

Outside, the ambulance pulled into Cedar Road. Willis stood at the door of number six as Nicola Stone's body was wheeled out and through to the ambulance that would transport her to the mortuary at the Whittington Hospital. She stayed inside the cover of the tent over the door as she watched Dermot bagging and labelling furniture for removal. He stopped what he was doing and waited for her to ask her question. She always had one, in his experience.

'Was there anything interesting after she'd been moved?'

'We've found more money in the drawers.'

'Anything else personal?'

'Passport, issued two years ago, to Melanie Drummond. None of Nicola Stone's fingerprints remain on file as she was given a new identity but we have a new set to go on now.'

'Anything else, Dermot? Anything missing?'

'The phone is missing.' Dermot handed over a monthly phone bill in a plastic sheath.

'Okay, thanks. I expect it's long gone. We tried it earlier.'

They watched the ambulance drive away, lights flashing, no siren. Willis took out her phone and put out a location search for Nicola's.

Carter looked across at her as she was watching her screen.

'What is it?' he asked.

'Her phone is emitting a signal.'

After an hour and a half's drive, Willis and Carter turned into the lane near Dunstable Downs signposted towards Lambs Farm.

'Who owns this farm, Eb? No animals, no crops, looks deserted.' There were fenced fields on either side of the lane and up ahead of them they could see the austere grey farmhouse, dominated by large cattle sheds to its right. At four o'clock the sky's grey clouds had become so thick they brought on a premature darkness.

'It's been empty a year, it's a probate sale,' Willis answered. 'It comes with over two hundred acres.'

They parked up in the yard. The emptiness of the farm was eerie; from somewhere a loose piece of corrugated roofing rattled and vibrated in the gusts of cold wind. The stable doors left open in the yard swung and banged on their hinges. The evening was fast descending.

'Have we still got it?' asked Carter. Under the gloom of a leaden sky they took out their boots from his SUV and replaced their shoes.

As they finished up and closed the boot, Willis paused, computer tablet in hand, and made sure of the direction. The signal from Nicola Stone's phone was still strong.

Carter looked at her screen and the blinking GPS.

'That's less than five hundred metres.' Carter was not a lover of the countryside. It was too big a space for him to control, too unpredictable. No streetlights to see what was out there.

Willis looked up to get her bearings. 'Down that lane.' She nodded in the direction of a lane leading off from the back of the yard. It was hard to make out anything but shadows in the empty stalls and stables. From the concrete of the yard they walked past an empty cowshed, and past fields on either side until Willis stopped at an open gateway.

She nodded, staring at the screen in her hand and pointed to her left. 'It's this way.'

Carter hesitated, gazing around him as if deciding it was a mistake, but looked at Willis who was walking ahead and joined her. They stayed close to the hedge; the field was grass and weed and bare brown mud.

'We're near now,' said Willis as she stopped and looked at her screen before walking on a few more feet. They looked up to see the sun's low rays on a corner of the field and the glint of something shining there. The wind got up and the first blast of icy air hit their faces as it drove across the field in a curtain of cold, picking up the topsoil and throwing it into the air. Carter turned his face to shelter it.

'I can see a light, it's the phone,' Willis said as they pushed up the field against the wall of icy sleet, the phone blinking at them. The sound of the wind buffeting them drowned out everything else except the beep from Willis's tablet. They walked on the next fifteen feet and the ground became uneven. The darkness descended as the clouds took all light from the field, which had nothing else to feed it but the sun and the moon. Carter switched on his torch and shielded his eyes from the sleet as it whipped around them, turning to hail. They got within feet of the phone when Willis stopped. Carter shone his torch over the ground in front of them.

'The soil has been dug here,' Carter said. 'This is recent.'

Willis reached forwards to pick up the phone and her fingers touched others, bony and pushing up from the ground.

Chapter 21

'Surgery open,' Kowalski said to the queue of prisoners waiting outside Douglas's cell door after breakfast.

'Each person gets fifteen minutes,' said the guard. 'If you're not prepared to wait your turn with good manners then fuck off now and don't waste Mr Douglas's time.'

'Like we have something else to do?' someone muttered, and the queue broke out in a ripple of laughter.

For two hours Douglas worked his way through the line. He found the nearer he got to his release date the more restless he became. It was impossible to forget it. He tried all the mindfulness techniques he knew but none of them gave him the satisfaction of projecting himself forward in time to the day in June when he would walk out of the prison and start his life again.

He'd enjoyed his time in prison. It had given him time to think and it had given him time to grow. Now he was fully formed and he realised in all those years before, the one thing he didn't have was connections. He had been an ignorant good-looking lad from Ireland. He'd used those attributes to the max and they'd taken him to many pleasurable places but now he wanted more, so much more. Gone were his good looks, but very much arrived was his intelligence. He felt he was in his prime because, after all, it may have been the size of his muscles that mattered when he was young, but it would be the size of his wallet as he grew old. He was now capable of anything. Now his disciples had become the people he had always thought they would. Cathy might still bear him a child, thought Douglas. She might be in love with Stephen, but even after all these years she still needed the reassurance of the man with the connections. He found that disappointing. Her potential had never been fully realised because of her stupid pretentions. When Douglas got out he'd make so much money for them both that no amount of prejudice could stand in their way. It was what she'd always wanted. Stephen wouldn't stop them. No one would. Douglas looked across at the man opposite and he asked him, 'What else would you like to say to your wife?'

The man started talking and Douglas listened to how the man was sorry, how he would make it up to her and the kids, and Douglas wrote that, and when it was time to seal it into an envelope, he enclosed a letter of his own, to be posted on by the recipient. He chose the people who trusted their wives. He knew it was all about give and take in prison. Jimmy Douglas always paid his debts, good or bad.

At the end of surgery Douglas closed his cell door to regain some of his peace and prepare for his work party. He looked at his calendar, took it off the wall and turned the months over until he hit June. He saw a photo of a glorious beach in Cornwall: turquoise seas and yellow sand, cliffs that jutted into an Atlantic swell. But then, as he looked closer, he saw a skinny girl up to her ankles in the sea and he felt a stabbing sensation in his heart. A shortness of breath. Was it Heather still haunting him?

*

Cathy Dwyer listened to the music; it calmed her. The candles in the room gave off an erotic ylang-ylang perfume mixed with deep spicy scents from the East. The woman's hands were oiled and as she spread her fingers up the back of Cathy's perfectly toned thighs, Stephen Perry was having his own massage on the next bed.

'Does he know about Millie?' Perry asked as his calf muscles were pummelled by a petite Thai woman with fingers like steel pins.

'Whether he does or doesn't, we keep things light, we talk about positive things. He has a lot to contend with.'

'You're excited about seeing him?' asked Perry.

'Of course. It's been so long.'

'He's going to be some fat old git, been banged up for sixteen years.'

She looked across at Perry. 'You never got it, did you? You never understood why we women couldn't get enough? You're still jealous.'

'Hardly.'

'You should be. It was all about the power for me.'

'Time to leave,' said Kowalski, although there were still many more prisoners to be seen. They would start the next day where they left off. In prison letters had to wait to be written, time stood agonisingly still and all the frustrations in the world didn't make things any easier.

The work party was on time and had a new member in it. Prisoner 66437 dragged his arthritic legs towards the minibus and heaved himself up and into his seat. Douglas was happy to be getting out. All the groundwork over the years was coming to one point. It was nine months till June when he would be released and all his planning, all the covert letters, all the half-thought dreams, would become a reality. Today was an extra-special day because Douglas was meeting someone he'd only ever contacted via others. He was meeting the man who believed in him.

As the walled garden at Gordon Stowe's Michelin-starred restaurant was heading towards winter the majority of the salad was being brought on in the hundred-foot polytunnel. Today they had special guests in for lunch from the catering, restaurant, nightclub and bar business and they had come at special request.

Cathy Dwyer ordered the taster menu. She and Stephen Perry were staying overnight in the hotel spa attached to the old manor house and the three-starred restaurant.

'Can I take a tour of the herb and vegetable garden?'

The maître d' smiled. 'Of course, madame, you and your companion are welcome. Do you know the way?'

'I can find it, thank you.'

Chapter 22

After leaving Lambs Farm Carter and Willis arrived back at Fletcher House just before six p.m. and Carter called a meeting. He addressed his team:

'We have confirmation from the team who were supposed to be protecting her, that the person found dead today, known as Melanie Drummond, is in fact, Nicola Stone. Another of Douglas's disciples dead, which makes two close together, is not a coincidence we can ignore. And now there's the grave, that could be Heather in there. Someone went to a lot of trouble to show us where it was. We'll start the dig in the morning when it's light; conditions are bad now, the wind is up and we could be in danger of losing evidence if we try to begin right away.'

'Nicola Stone's protection team are blaming us, they're spitting blood,' Hector said.

'Yeah, they would say that, but Nicola was obviously getting fed up with hiding away. She planned to come out of the closet when Douglas got out. She was always putting herself at risk,' answered Carter.

Willis turned her monitor around at the end of the table so that everyone could see and started playing the video of Cedar Court recorded by Sandford. It began at first entry into the flat and made sweeps of the hall, bathroom and kitchen before slowly panning across the sitting room and turning into the bedroom where the video ended in an overhead view looking down at Melanie Drummond lying on her side. The image froze.

'She sustained numerous wounds,' explained Willis. 'Post-mortem is going to take place tomorrow.' The rest of the office had fallen quiet as they watched the video. 'Here is a photo of Melanie Drummond aka Nicola Stone, from her passport issued two years ago when she moved to Flat 6, Cedar Close, Homerton.'

Willis held up an enlarged photo of Nicola. 'Aged forty-six. Nicola Stone was a churchgoer, a very private person, who opened the front door in her dressing gown. Why? She had a spyhole. Whoever they were, she trusted them enough to open her door. This attack was haphazard. We do not yet know if the assailant brought a knife with them but we believe Nicola took one out from her own kitchen. Whether she instigated the attack, we don't know.

'If the attacker doesn't live at the flats, they would need to have changed, covered up, very quickly. Plus, the furniture was knocked over, and we think it took the attacker several minutes to subdue her in order to get her incapacitated on the bed. Someone has got to have heard or seen something,' said Willis.

'We located her phone at Lambs Farm, north-west of Watford. The farm is up for a probate sale,' Carter told them.

Chris Maxwell held up his hand to interrupt.

'I checked, it was one of the farms Douglas delivered feed to. I've been to see the farm where Rachel McKinney was taken to be killed by Douglas, and Lambs Farm has many similarities.'

'Hector? What about her phone?' asked Willis.

'We can't find out anything about where she was, location services were only activated after the phone reached Lambs Farm. She had calls to Roy, to the vicar, to the florist, she liked a takeaway or two and she used it for her Internet so her browsing history is being looked at now.'

'We need to keep open minds about this. Yes, it could be a link to Heather Phillips, both Millie's murder and Nicola Stone's. It could be the same perpetrator, but we cannot be sure of anything yet. The backstory is interesting, but someone still had to come in and out of Nicola Stone's flat and they left their DNA. This can be solved with a lot of solid police detection work, so ignore the hype, ignore the Douglas connection for a moment. We have someone taking big risks and that's how we need to catch them.'

'We think the killer must have changed their clothes somewhere,' said Willis. 'And they might be injured. There are officers searching all the hedges, bins and drains along the way. It's back to basics with this investigation. DC Blackman?'

'Anyone can park on the road,' said Blackman. 'There are no parking restrictions. People park to walk to the station. We're leaving leaflets on cars, and talking to the people who are there every day to see if they saw anything strange. Someone may have been sitting in a car waiting for hours before she was killed.'

'What about CCTV?' asked Willis.

'There are cameras outside the station,' answered Hector, 'and outside the Spar shop and the off-licence. We're analysing them now. The garages on the back lane that allows access to the gardens at Cedar Court are used almost exclusively for long-term storage except for a mechanic who rents one of the garages on the end. We are following up alibis and histories of the people living at the flats. But, these flats have a multitude of different people coming and going with no security.'

'Having said that,' added Willis, 'someone must have seen a person hanging about. It takes time to put together a plan like this, surveillance and planning and possible befriending of either the victim or someone close to her.'

'Like Roy,' said Blackman.

'Yes, put a camera and some surveillance outside Roy's. We might have a revenge attack on him and I want to see who comes and goes,' said Carter. 'Roy knows everyone in those flats. DC Blackman, I want you to liaise with the cold-case team handling the Heather Phillips disappearance. We're going to be sharing information with them.'

'Yes, sir.'

'Hector, you talk to the protection team,' said Carter.

'My pleasure, I will enjoy finding out who fucked up.'

'Go carefully, if this is an officer on the take I want him nailed,' said Carter.

'Understood.'

'Chris, expand your thoughts about this farm for us. Did you get the information on the history of it?' asked Carter.

'Yes, at that time it would have been lived in by the previous owner, Pritchard, who died two years ago. I will be interested in seeing the results of the LiDAR, that's the light detection and ranging equipment. We can have a look at what else he may have left in the field, besides the body.'

'Okay, I'll sanction that straight away.'

'With the information I have at my disposal, right now,' continued Maxwell, 'I think I can best help you by reanalysing the farms that fit the same brief as this. I will take this farm, Lambs Farm, as one starting point and where Rachel McKinney's grave was, Hill Farm, as another and work out from there. This will be a combination of both murder investigations, I presume? Plus, looking for more remains that can link to Douglas?'

'The Heather Phillips case is not ours,' said Carter. 'We need to keep that in mind, but we also need to realise that she could be the motive and we will work closely with the team. We may have found her body.'

'And this presents us with opportunities to find out what happened in July 2000,' said Maxwell.

'Were you even out of nappies then?' Carter smiled.

'Yes, I was definitely house-trained, but you're right, I wasn't qualified then. However, I have studied the Douglas case. What about Douglas? Are you going to interview him? It can't be ignored that it is just months until he is due for release,' said Maxwell.

'And we know that Gavin, for one, was looking forward to it,' said Carter. 'It would be good to throw a spanner in the works.' He grinned. 'However, even if we find Heather here, we still need to find sufficient evidence against Douglas to try him for her murder again.'

'And, even if we do find Heather,' said Willis, 'Douglas did not kill Millie Stephens or Nicola Stone.'

'Yes, agreed,' Maxwell said, 'but the killer brought us to Lambs Farm to make that link, past to present.'

'Well, I hope that we kill several birds with one stone, and that, in trying to show us a link to Douglas, the killer is really showing us a link to himself,' Carter replied.

Willis nodded. 'I've been reading all I can on him, and looking at the case files from back then, and it seems Douglas was hardly ever alone; he took someone with him on a lot of his trips to farms in the week. He got lonely, they all say that, there was always someone going with him. It means interviewing everyone again, from last time round.'

'This killer could be a glory hunter who has taken it upon himself to act as a vigilante against Douglas and his disciples,' Hector said.

'If he was a glory hunter, I think he would have come out and told the world by now,' countered Willis. 'I think this was personal between him and the disciples, that's what it feels like to me.'

'His disciples must be a little nervous now, they may feel it's worth opening up to us, if their lives are at risk,' said Maxwell.

'Yes, exactly,' replied Carter. 'They may decide prison is a better option than being carved up like a Christmas turkey.'

'As long as they don't end up in a prison where Douglas is the chef?' Maxwell smiled.

Chapter 23

After the meeting, Carter went in to see his boss, Superintendent Bowie, who was in charge of all the four MIT teams at Fletcher House. His main role was to liaise with those higher up and the press. They knew one another well. Bowie wasn't much liked by the people who served under him. He was the opposite of Carter, who was a man's man to the core. Bowie was work-shy and seemed to sneak his way through life. He had had numerous affairs during his career but always seemed to come out of them unscathed, whereas the women he dated had had their careers halted or been forced to resign. But Carter had time for Bowie – he respected him and he understood him in many ways. Behind the watery blue eyes and the limp blond hair, the ill-fitting suits and the unpolished shoes was a man who had helped crack the biggest paedophile ring Britain had ever known and he did it undercover.

'You've been busy,' said Bowie.

Carter closed the door behind him. 'Yeah, you have no idea.'

'Two disciples dead. Looks like someone is on a vendetta. Can they be linked for certain?' asked Bowie.

'No. It's not the same weapon used. The only thing that links the murders is the histories of the victims.'

'The angle of the wounds, the method is comparable on both victims?'

'Not conclusive. We can't be sure this is the same killer, we have too little to go on. On paper, these are completely different. The first involved a vicious hammer attack on Millie Stephens, followed up by stabbings in her neck, whereas Nicola may have attacked her killer first. We have a blood sample, but it doesn't match anything else we have on record.'

'What is the progress on Millie Stephens?' asked Bowie.

'I'll find out exactly how we're doing in a minute, I'm about to head to a meeting. It wasn't sexual or robbery as her bank card was there. There haven't been any similar attacks on the streets. We have to think this is a personal attack on Millie and not on her lifestyle.'

'Drugs? Pimps?'

'We don't think so. We think it likely the killer must have gone to the park to talk with Millie, probably because Queens Drive where she lives is heavily policed, and there are a lot of kerb crawlers, so someone might have seen. No way is she going to go into a park with someone she doesn't know for thirty quid, that takes her away from the street for an hour longer than needed. She knew this person and similarly Nicola Stone opened the front door to someone she knew or trusted. We haven't found anyone who links them both, in their daily lives. This has to be about the fact they were both disciples.'

'And you have found some human remains?'

'The killer led us there, to Lambs Farm. We start the exhuming tomorrow first thing.'

'We have to assume security was breached for someone to have found Nicola.'

'What are her protection team saying?'

'They're not taking the blame. It was probably a mistake made by the victim herself; she confided in the wrong person, we think, but it's early days.'

'Nicola Stone, Millie Stephens, both were always suspected of knowing more about Heather's disappearance than they admitted to. I spoke to the head of Stones' team ten minutes ago, they are carrying out their own internal inquiry into what happened. He's filled me in on the basics of where she's been since she came out of prison. She's lived in three places. Margate, Bristol and then here in north London.'

'Why was she moved every time? Was she found out?' asked Bowie.

'She was, in two of the places. She's pretty recognisable. She should have had some work done on her face; people have long memories. But she lived on benefits, she didn't exactly live the high life.'

'There will be no prints on record from her,' said Bowie, 'no DNA, and any prison records would have been removed from the database as part of her new secret identity. That should delay the press finding out,' he added. 'Once that happens there will be no stopping it, the floodgates will open and we will have to deal with enormous pressure over the failed Heather Phillips case. If this is a vendetta against anyone around Douglas we'd better get hold of the other disciples we think might be at risk.'

'We're locating them now. We've found Yvonne Coombes, she's a sad case – a methadone addict, struggling to keep her child this time. She says she broke off her friendship with Millie because Millie was out of control. We know that's the case from her father. We're getting mixed messages from Gavin Heathcote. He gave Millie money. I wouldn't be surprised if she became a nuisance to him. We are looking for Cathy Dwyer and the seventh disciple who we presume is a lad called Ash. We don't know what role he had, if any, in the group. We do know he and Heather were close. If that's Heather in the ground then we may find him too.'

'What about Douglas? Are you going to see him?' asked Bowie.

'I think I should wait,' said Carter, 'until we know more.'

'I would go while you have a window of calm, but it's your shout,' said Bowie.

'Calm? You're joking, aren't you!' Carter smiled. 'But, you're right, better to go before the story breaks. I doubt if we will get anything from him, he's up for release. He's not going to tell us anything that could harm that.'

'He's a very difficult person to get your head around,' said Bowie. 'Find someone who's a match for him intellectually, someone he won't run rings around. I think it's worth going to see him now, even to break the news of his girlfriend's murder, see his reaction.'

'Let me think about it,' said Carter. 'Who was the SIO in the Heather Phillips case?'

'Superintendent Davidson, now retired.'

'Not my favourite person,' grimaced Carter.

'No, nor mine, and he made a pig's ear of the whole thing. Douglas played him like a fiddle.'

'I heard he was living in Spain now,' said Carter.

'He was, but he's back here now, he's a widower. Here's his number.' Bowie turned his phone around for Carter to see the screen.

'Okay, I'll ask for a meet ASAP. Didn't know you had him on speed dial?' Carter joked.

'Yeah, good luck with him; he hates you almost as much as he does me.'

When he came out of the meeting, Carter shepherded Willis down the stairs to the first floor and through to Archway Police Station, which adjoined Fletcher House, and into the canteen. Ebony's housemate Tina was working behind the counter, as usual.

'I'll get it,' said Carter, when they got to the counter. 'What do you want?'

'Just a Coke, no ... and a doughnut, with jam and cream,' said Willis as she waved at Tina and headed off to the back of the canteen where she could hear her friend laughing as Carter ordered. She had a habit of laughing loudly at any of Carter's remarks, even when they weren't meant to be humorous.

He carried the tray over, shaking his head. 'Tina finds me irresistibly funny.' He set down the tray, taking his tea before sliding the rest across for Ebony.

'I know, but then, there's no accounting for taste.'

'There's something I want you to do for me,' said Carter as Willis took a big bite of doughnut. She was poised, waiting to hear what he was going to ask and, at the same time, tipping the doughnut to catch the escaping jam which was about to explode out of the bottom.

'I want you to ...' Carter began, and stopped. 'Christ, wait a minute, I can't watch you eat.' He turned away in mock disgust and counted to five before turning back to find her licking the sugar from her fingers and then trying to clean her sticky fingers on the paper napkin. 'I want you to interview Jimmy Douglas. How do you feel about that?'

Willis frowned as she thought it through. She was a big frowner, her forehead was quite mobile.

Carter continued, 'It may be the only chance to catch him off guard, to establish a relationship before the world's press is focused on him again.'

'Yes, I get that.'

'Exactly.' Carter was studying her. She had on the face that was hard to read except he'd worked with her and been friends with her for six years now and he had more chance of understanding her expression than most.

'Okay.'

'What are the first concerns that come to mind? Talk it through with me.'

'I am rubbish at interviewing, that's a concern, did you think about that?'

'Of course I did, and I took that into consideration. This is not trying to wheedle a confession out of some low-life petty criminal; the reports about him say he is way up high on the IQ scale. He can run rings around most people because he studies them, tries to trip them up, tries to get inside their head. I don't see that happening with you.'

She was nodding, drinking her Coke and thinking hard. She wouldn't have asked herself to do it, she would have chosen Hector, or Blackman, anyone who had achieved higher grades in their interviewing than her.

'But, Eb, you don't have to do it. You can say no.'

She put down her Coke. 'I want to do it. Don't you dare give it to anyone else.'

*

On the way out of the car park as Carter headed home for a few hours' sleep, he saw Maxwell coming out of the office. Carter stopped the car.

'How did you get here?' Carter asked, looking around for a car.

'Bus, bike, tube, walk, it varies; today it was the tube.'

'You staying near here?' asked Carter.

'King's Cross; it's okay for now. We'll see how long this case goes on for, how much help I can be.'

'I hope a lot.'

'Yes, of course. It's a mainly scientific process. As long as I get all the information I can do my job and make a difference. If you give me all the information you have on it, I can make a start.'

'Get in, I need to talk to you, I'll give you a lift.'

'That's okay, I can walk.'

'No, I need to talk to you, get in. King's Cross?'

'Thanks, by the station will be great. I need to go to the supermarket inside.' He got in the car.

'Are you living on your own? No girlfriend? Wife?'

'No ...' Maxwell's voice trailed off, he sat looking out of the window as they waited at the end of the road for people to cross.

'What brought you over to the UK originally?' Carter never veered from the forthright approach.

'Well, you know, one of those decisions you make after a break-up.'

'Okay, I get it. It's the best cure – hit the road. Just don't drink and dial, that's my advice, too easy to do these days. The first time you get your heart well and truly mashed is the worst. You will get over it but you'll never forget. I'm still in love with all my exes.' Chris looked across and chuckled. 'Yeah, really,' Carter grinned, 'I miss all of them, in some way.'

'Are you married now?'

'Not married but I've been with my partner Cabrina for about eight years. We have a son, Archie. We've just moved out to Barnet for the schools. I'm finding it difficult to get back in time to see him in the evenings now. It's always a trade-off, I suppose. Ah well, we'll see how it goes, it's always hard to settle at first, isn't it? How long were you with your lass?'

'Three years.'

'That's tough.' Carter glanced over and nodded sympathetically. 'Do you have family over here?'

'No, unfortunately I don't.'

'But you were brought up here, weren't you?'

'I came to school here, yes.'

'What school was that?'

'It's closed down now, it was a small private one in Norfolk.'

'You don't have an accent from there.'

'No? Well that's a shame.'

Carter laughed. 'Do you think you'll like working in MIT 17?'

'So far so good.' Maxwell smiled. 'I am updating the information relating to all those individuals who were questioned as part of the investigation at the time of Douglas's arrest: their addresses, old and new, where they work, where their kids go to school, where they go to the gym. I am going to plot sets of diagrams and see if we get a crossover, old suspects and new. I also thought, if you don't mind, until I am given sufficient information to help more with the Nicola Stone murder, I'd work on possible search sights for Heather's body. I've used data they had in 2001 and I've contacted all the farms that Douglas used to deliver to; the company still exists that he worked for. I've been on the phone to farmers but I'm not getting a lot of help. I've asked each farmer to talk me through each one of his fields that can be accessed fairly easily from the road, within a mile of the road, as we know that the rape victim Rachel McKinney was walked across a field to a pre-dug gravesite. What about McKinney?'

'She's come a long way to find peace with herself. She's still very fragile. She is a single parent now and you get the sense she's doing okay but it's not easy. She still has all the scars from Douglas. I find it unbelievable that he wasn't convicted of attempted murder. But he had the touch of genius to win over a jury that didn't understand what they were hearing. They didn't believe the facts and, because she was barely able to speak during the trial, there was no other side to the story and no evidence that he caused those injuries to her body. He said they had sex in the van, full stop. I've been thinking about what you said earlier on – take a few days to go around looking at the farms of interest, speak to the farmers and see them first hand. Come with us in the morning and look at Lambs Farm and liaise with Mr Sandford, our crime scene manager.'

'Okay.'

'What were the other cases you worked on?' asked Carter.

'One was a serial killer in France, a delivery driver. It was a tough case, he murdered hitchhikers, and we had a hard job tracking him down, but we managed it.'

'What about his victims?' Carter asked.

'He confessed to two but we found four more. It was

always the same with him, he chose sites he knew, always within an hour's drive. They were similar places, same remote areas or near reservoirs. It is a major thing, deciding where to bury a body. A lot is at stake and the killer will be making mental notes everywhere he goes; he'll be storing up co-ordinates, making checklists. It's never a random choice, even if he thinks it is. And when he thinks it is, especially then, he will give himself away.'

'Wow, impressive, clever stuff.' Carter smiled.

Willis opened her front door and heard the sound of the television coupled with Tina's laughter. It took a moment for her to realise Tina was talking to someone and not just laughing at something on the TV.

Shit, thought Willis, she had forgotten she'd invited Tucker for a meal and a drink.

'Sorry, got delayed,' she said as she walked in. She could see by Tina's face and the fact that she had been caught in her dressing gown that it was awkward. 'Shall we go, Scott?'

'Hi, Eb.' He got up from the sofa and walked over, and she gave him a quick hug.

'Teen, we can wait while you get dressed. Do you want to come?' Willis looked at her hopefully.

'Thanks, but I'm okay. I need an early night.'

Willis and Tucker walked to the kebab restaurant around the corner. Tucker was wearing his usual off-duty clothes: dark-blue workman's-type jacket, blue checked shirt, jeans and tan leather Chelsea boots. He was very tall and had a laid-back approach to walking that made him look as if he was leaning back. He looked over at her, smiling.

'I like your hair,' he said.

'It's no different than usual, I've just plaited it, that's all.'

'You look well,' he said with a bashful smile.

'Why did you come up here?' asked Willis.

'I fancied a break. Actually, I'm leaving the force.'

'Really?'

'Yes. They owed me a lot of holiday, so effectively I've already left, although not officially. I'm still a copper for a bit longer, on paper.'

'Really?' Willis stopped and looked at him, absorbing this new information.

'Yes, I'm going into business to produce oak-frame buildings with my mate.'

She walked on, not quite able to take it in, but a part of her was really pleased. 'That's great, it's shocking, but it's great,' she said. She squeezed his arm. 'I'm happy for you.'

'Thanks. I was never going to make it beyond sergeant and I got tired of all the stress. I lost my drive for it. Trouble is I wasn't high enough in rank to just concentrate on the things I did like doing, community projects and liaising with the public.'

The more Scott talked the less attractive he was becoming and Willis felt his chances of staying over were slipping. They'd risen when she thought of him having the drive to leave the force and set out as a carpenter, but they'd plummeted when she imagined he'd rather be at village fetes handing out leaflets on the Green Cross Code. She knew she was being mean but she had reached a phase in her life when she wanted a lot more adventure than she was getting and she was starting to think she needed to be much more proactive. She kept choosing men who were so laid-back they were practically horizontal.

'I'm buying a flat in Torbay.'

Oh God, thought Willis, *he's retiring to the seaside.*

'But I'm really not sure where I'll be working yet; my mate does a lot of work in France and Spain. When he's not building houses, he designs sets for films, adverts, music videos, that kind of thing.'

'Interesting . . . We have a massive case on at the moment, did Carter tell you? I heard you interviewed Douglas's disciples years ago?'

'I did, I also interviewed Douglas.'

'No way! Why didn't you tell me that before? I'm meeting him tomorrow.'

'Because it didn't seem a good topic. I didn't want to spend all evening talking shop, but that's what we've ended up doing anyway, isn't it?'

'No, we haven't. Tell me about Douglas!'

'I was working on the Heather Phillips investigation when I first made it as a detective. He was just someone who worked selling farm feed. I turned up to see if they knew about a missing farmhand from one of the farms on Douglas's rounds. His name had been mentioned a few times, but HOLMES software wasn't used, no one put in the data, so no one connected it all up nationally, or realised we had a potential serial killer on our hands, who still hasn't been done for one murder.'

'What tips can you give me?'

'Stick it out. Be in there for the long haul, arrange to meet him a few times in quick succession, get under his skin. He starts to show his true colours after a while. I read that he's taken every opportunity he could to sit exams, study, he is really clever. He's going to try and manipulate you any way he can. But if anyone can handle him, you can.'

*

After an hour more of chat, they paid and left. Willis looked at her phone.

'Shit, I didn't realise it was so late. Sorry, you can't stay the night, I have a really early start,' she said, as they walked back around towards her house.

'No worries.'

She reached up and gave him a kiss. 'Okay, take care, Scott. Thanks for the chat. It's nice to see you.' She didn't wait around to see the look that she was sure would be on his face as she walked away.

Chapter 24

Maxwell arrived just ahead of Carter and Willis the next morning at Lamb's Farm. He got suited up and went up to introduce himself to Dermot who was standing inside the field, coffee in hand, watching the sky.

'Nice to meet you, the boss is up there.' Dermot pointed to Sandford standing on the brow of the field. Overhead, the drone of the helicopter was diminishing as it flew back to base having completed its survey. At the bottom of the field, four white-suited forensic officers were conducting a line search from the gate and following the hedge.

Maxwell set off up the slope.

'Morning, Mr Sandford, my name is Chris Maxwell.'

'It was a good morning but the cloud's headed back,' he answered with a wry smile.

'How is it going?' asked Maxwell. 'I saw the helicopter as I was driving here. Has the digging started?'

'Yes. Come and see.'

Willis and Carter arrived and, along with Dermot, walked up the field to join them.

Floodlights were illuminating the left-hand corner of the field above the grave. There was the drum of a mobile generator and arc lights gave that corner the look of a film set. A tent, with a soil-sifting station, had been erected nearby. It was an eerie-looking sight – the white tent, with the grave being excavated, and the black hedge behind. The white tarpaulins flapped and billowed like sails in the wind and the stormy clouds settled overhead.

Dermot stopped and stood up for a moment, from the excavation pit, beside the main grave, and stretched his limbs to ease out the cramp from being confined. When he stood, the grave came up to the top of his thighs. He lifted his arms up for a stretch and then paused as a barrage of hail pelted the plastic awning above their heads. The wind suddenly picked up and almost turned it inside out; shouts went up to cover everything that was exposed. SOCOs caught in the middle of the field cowered over buckets of soil and endured the sharp balls of ice bouncing off their backs. When it stopped, after three minutes, the ground was covered in hail. A laugh went up and caught on, before everyone continued where they left off.

Sandford stood looking down at the grave. Dermot went back to kneeling in an extension of the excavation, which allowed for easy access to the remains without causing too much damage. He was sweeping away the earth from a kneecap, which had come to rest against the edge of the grave as the victim went in. Both legs were propped up against the side wall of the grave. The victim was lying mainly on her back, but leaning over to the right. The skull rested on an outstretched right arm as if she had been caught sunbathing, or she was about to turn in her sleep. The other arm reached up, fingers pointing skyward.

'It's definitely a female, isn't it?' said Willis, observing the shape of the pelvis together with the unpronounced brow bone.

'Yes. I think she's been in there a long time – ten years at least – but it's not Heather, she was taller. Also, this woman has had children and she's in her thirties, early forties maybe,' said Sandford.

Maxwell seemed to take time to assimilate that knowledge, looking agitated.

Unlike Maxwell, Sandford was very calm; he was enjoying being out in the fresh air. He was a man who never minded any part of his job but standing in the countryside on a fresh autumn morning was pretty good although he wished his head didn't have a woodpecker inside it from the beer he'd drunk with Dermot the night before. Dermot was watching the helicopter, transfixed. The bringing-in of giant toys like helicopters made Dermot look idiotic with a permanent grin on his face.

'Here she comes again, boys!' he bellowed from the grave and the SOCO team stopped to gaze skyward with appreciation.

The helicopter was flying below a giant cloud of biblical blackness. In seconds it swallowed the sun and hovered over them, threatening to unleash its fury again at any moment.

'Rather them than me,' said Carter, looking up at the belly of the helicopter. 'They're sitting ducks up there, just asking to get fried.'

'The helicopter is able to withstand lightning strikes, it acts as a conductor,' answered Sandford. 'It would be damaged but not badly.'

'A conductor, huh? Great, that's really not very reassuring,' said Carter, shading his eyes and watching the helicopter as it looped around for another sweep of the area.

Dermot walked up to talk to them. 'I bet if you scanned

every farm in the UK, you'd find a fair few bodies. Many times we'll find legitimate graves. You can bury your loved one in your own back garden if you get permission and subject to health and safety issues. Of course if you want to sell the house, it could be tricky . . .'

Willis was watching Maxwell, who hadn't been listening to Dermot.

'Where is the helicopter going?' Maxwell asked, worried.

'It's finished its search now,' answered Sandford as he started walking down the field and the others followed. He went across to his van and sat in the driver's seat with the door open, laptop open on his knees.

'How long does it take before we know if there are any more sites of interest here?' asked Maxwell.

'We expect to get a full report within a couple of hours,' said Sandford. 'We are not asking for a complicated model – we just need to see if there is any historical soil disturbance, any more graves, that kind of thing. The software is pretty simple for that.'

Sandford looked at Chris.

'You're the profiler, what do you do, look for access from the road or a quiet lane, that kind of thing? Why this farm and not one of the others?' he asked.

'I'm interested in somewhere that's a short drive from a main road, but with access along small lanes. On paper, this is similar to the Rachel McKinney field at Hill Farm. This one was also owned and worked by a small farming unit: a husband and wife. It was mainly arable and set-aside land. It was the right size, the same setting with the line of the tall conifers, the way the field slopes upwards and hides behind the tall old hedges. On either side of the lane there are only fields. No house within a mile of the site. The lane is for access for farm vehicles only and even they had no need to come to a field that was set aside for meadow. Okay, I'm going to take a walk around the farm, if I may, get a look at things, and then I'm going to look at a few more farms in the vicinity.'

'He's a funny chap, isn't he? A bit hyperactive,' Dermot remarked as Maxwell walked away.

'He's not used to coming on site,' answered Carter. 'It's all formulas and diagrams for him.'

'I thought he was going to cry when the helicopter started flying away,' said Sandford.

'Well, I don't blame him for that,' said Dermot, 'it was pretty cool.'

Carter walked across with Willis to the gravesite. 'How soon will you know who she is?' he asked.

'We'll finish getting her out and then get a DNA sample from a vertebra, probably. I can see her teeth are in pretty bad shape.'

Inside the grave two other SOCOs, who specialised in removing skeletons that were more than ten years old, were taking it in turns to work from the excavation channel.

'Any idea how she might have died?' asked Carter.

'Your guess is as good as mine,' Sandford said.

'Okay, well, I'm hoping we can narrow it down a little.'

'Yes, of course.' Sandford smiled, pleased that he'd rattled the ever-charming Carter just a little. 'And, if she's in the system, then we'll know who she is within an hour of testing. If she isn't, it's a piece-of-string scenario.'

Carter turned away and addressed Willis. 'Eb, I may as well head back to town, I'm going to talk to Davidson. Will you get a lift back with Chris Maxwell?'

'No problem.' She went to look for the analyst and

eventually found him walking back along the lane. He looked as if he was searching the hedgerows as he went.

'What are you thinking?' she asked, watching him.

'Nothing. Just making sure nothing's been missed. We still haven't found the murder weapons for either murder, have we?'

'You okay?' she asked, watching him wince as he stood up.

'Fine, overdid it with the abdominals last evening,' he smiled, embarrassed. 'I was following this challenge online.'

'Oh, I know. The abs challenge. It's tough,' said Willis, who could talk fitness all day long. 'Which gym do you use?'

'I just work out at home,' Maxwell replied. 'I have everything I need there.'

'Self-motivated, that's good.'

'What about you?' asked Maxwell, sensing he wasn't going to win in any fitness competition against Willis.

'I run a lot, go to the gym as much as I can,' she said with a smile. 'I get seriously depressed if I can't exercise. It's in my DNA.'

'I understand. Some things are just in us.' They walked along the lane together.

'I'm getting a lift back with you when you go, by the way,' said Willis. 'I thought we could go through my approach with Douglas, seeing as you made a study of him. I've been in touch with the governor, they can't speak highly enough of Douglas and all the work he does with the other prisoners.'

'Are you going to tell him about here?' asked Maxwell. 'If you do, don't tell him any details yet. We lose the surprise element otherwise, which means we lose control, and Douglas is all about control.'

'Yeah, I get that about him,' replied Willis. 'It's control over people less bright than himself, or the really young and impressionable like on Hawthorn Farm.'

'And the other farms he visited,' replied Maxwell, getting animated. 'Douglas could be responsible for so many disappearances. He was definitely involved with the disappearance of Darren Slater.'

'It was never proven,' replied Willis.

'Slater was last seen getting into Douglas's van.'

'But who was with him, besides Darren?' Willis had stopped to face Maxwell, interested. She'd decided she liked him. He was eccentric and she wondered if he had a touch of Asperger's about him. It wasn't a problem for her. She liked the way he was so interested in everything to do with the case, so earnest.

'Ash, he was there. I don't know about anyone else,' he answered.

'How do you know that? I've never seen it anywhere. Also, what happened to Ash?' Willis asked.

'I know because I talked to the detective who worked on the case, when I was working towards my degree. I befriended one of them, she helped me with little insights into the case and why they never got Douglas. As for Ash? I think he became one of Douglas's casualties. I think he's probably dead.'

'What about the trail when his mother went into hospital?' asked Willis.

'After she left, the trail went cold. The trouble is we don't have any DNA to match either him or her, not unless we put out an appeal again and then perhaps a relative might come forward. If we do find them in the ground it could take years to identify them.'

'They burned his van, according to statements at the time. Ash left and his mum went into hospital and his van was burned to the ground. That was over a month before Heather disappeared.'

'That's right,' answered Maxwell. 'He was never considered a suspect. But,' he stopped to look across at Willis, 'was he inside the van at the time?'

'Maybe,' she replied. 'He and his mother were easy to lose in the system with him being home-taught and being on the fringes of the traveller community. I'm going to have to go and see Truscott, the owner of Hawthorn Farm, as soon as I can now. I'm really interested in what happened to them. We need to know what became of the seventh disciple. Carter is meeting Davidson now, I wonder how that's going.'

'It would be good to be a fly on the wall, wouldn't it?' said Maxwell. 'Davidson fundamentally failed Heather and all the others. He deserves prosecuting, but it would never happen.'

They noticed Dermot looking for them further down the lane. He beckoned to them to get back.

Sandford was sitting in the driver's seat of his van and drinking coffee when they returned to where the vehicles were parked at the bottom of the field. The dig was still ongoing.

As Willis and Maxwell approached he turned his tablet round to show them the results of the scan.

'We're going to be busy. These are the areas identified by the LiDAR, approximately fifteen to twenty feet apart from one another all within ten feet of the edge of the field and the hedgerow. If we start with the one that's at the top of the field ...' began Sandford.

'We need more equipment,' said Maxwell, looking around

at the radar machine being unloaded from the back of a specialist firm's van and wheeled up the field in front of them.

'No,' answered Sandford, politely, firmly and almost as if talking to a child, 'we don't because we are going to deal with one site at a time.' He looked back at Willis and resumed explaining the process. 'We begin with site one at the top of the field and work our way down. Treat each site individually and we can bring in the dogs if it looks promising before we start digging.'

'It's clay soil, we might struggle to get a good reading,' said Maxwell, looking at the ground.

'We should be able to get a good reading down to fifteen feet,' said Sandford. 'No one's going to have buried a body that deep.'

'Don't be nervous, Chris,' said Dermot. 'You're not used to all this fresh air, are you?' He gave a laugh.

Maxwell looked irritated and confused by the remark at first, but then he relaxed as they watched the ground radar machine being made ready. Alex Copeland, the operator, had just begun.

'Chris? You feeling lucky?' asked Dermot.

Chris frowned at him, not understanding his humour. 'It's not really a case of luck.'

Dermot grinned, nodded; he had decided that Maxwell didn't have a sense of humour. Even Sandford had more of one than Maxwell, and he appeared to be enjoying the lack of understanding.

'Eb, did you research the man?' asked Dermot.

'Douglas?' Willis asked.

Sandford groaned. 'He's been spending all day looking up every detail of Douglas's debauched lifestyle and his weird bunch of disciples.'

'He's definitely scary,' said Willis. 'According to people who have interviewed him over the years, he stares a lot, and he smiles all the time.'

'He's started,' Maxwell interrupted as he set off up the field towards the graves and the radar machine, which had begun to sweep the areas identified.

Copeland diligently manoeuvred the machine in vertical sweeps up and back across the small patch of field, stopping sometimes to mark the ground with a spray of chalk. When he'd finished he unclipped a tablet computer from the handlebars of the machine and brought it across to show them his findings.

'You see this area here, which forms a break and a change in pattern? That's the edge of your site, your walls of the grave. That corresponds to the mapped-out area from the LiDAR scan. It extends down for one metre. This is definitely manmade. Here, where the area turns dark? Here's your void, initial depression as the ground is not level from the top, and here is your second depression, probably where the thorax on your victim decomposed and collapsed. I marked it on the ground with a cross.'

'Okay, we have the dogs standing by to double-check the results. Nothing is a substitute for digging out the graves to make sure, but this gives us a starting point,' Willis said.

After pipes were inserted at intervals into the grave area, a springer spaniel named Izzy, a victim recovery dog, was brought up to the field and walked in a zigzag pattern from the top. When she reached the tubes she went at will, weaving in and out. Suddenly she stopped, wagged her tail furiously and barked at her handler. She stayed absolutely still, her nose an inch away from the top of the tube above the collapsed thorax, just her tail wagging furiously.

Chapter 25

Carter drove to Upper Street in Islington and found a parking space on a side road. Ex-Superintendent Davidson, the senior investigating officer from the Heather Phillips case, was waiting for him inside the restaurant for an early lunch. They shook hands.

'Thanks for agreeing to see me so quickly.'

'It's no problem. Bad weather for golf anyway.'

Carter saw a lonely man in front of him who had decided there had to be give and take if they needed his help. It was worth lunch in the newest and the most expensive restaurant, just to eat moss and dried Bambi. They waited until the waiter took the order. It was one of those niche places that had adopted the term Nordic and involved rare breeds of animals and pickled carrots.

'How can I help you?' Davidson straightened the cutlery in front of him.

'Do you remember the Heather Phillips disappearance?' asked Carter.

'Of course I do. Jimmy bastard Douglas. We were unlucky. On another day we'd have had him for Heather Phillips and a few more besides. We were coping with a difficult time in the country then. The foot and mouth epidemic made our investigation very difficult.'

Carter nodded, trying to keep the cynicism from his eyes as Davidson held his gaze. Carter was thinking – foot and mouth began in February the next year. What were you doing up to that point? *Taking too bloody long.* But Carter knew him from old. He knew what was expected. Davidson was waiting for it. Carter smiled in an 'unlucky, you were robbed' way, but inside he was already rekindling his hate of this man who had always given Carter a hard time when Davidson was his boss and never put him up for promotion – Carter was never 'old school' enough.

'How can I help? What do you need from me?'

'What do you remember about Millie Stephens?'

'She was a dedicated disciple: easily led, a simple girl.'

'You know she's been murdered, her body was washed up on the banks of the River Lea, in the park, and she had stab wounds in her neck. She's been a street prostitute in Finsbury Park for the last fifteen years.'

'So, it could be just another prostitute killed by a john, but you wouldn't be here then, would you?'

'No, Nicola Stone has also been murdered. Douglas is due out soon and she wasn't hard to find.'

Davidson made one of those 'what do you expect?' faces.

'Millie was one of their most successful prodigies – vulnerable, impressionable, they did a really good job on ruining her. She was brainwashed. In the end she was as bad as Nicola Stone. I interviewed her many times and all she said was "no comment" with a smile on her face and sometimes she turned her wrists up to me so that I could observe the chain that bound them, the vow of silence that they had all made. She was very close to Heather. All of the disciples were party to some big secret, even before Heather disappeared. They were this gang who had a link representing each one of them tattooed on their wrists to show their bond. In other words, Douglas conned them all into belonging to a cult they didn't dare leave. With Douglas as the cult leader, they were in it for life. I think they embraced the whole thing, each one of them was evil.'

'Except some of them were easily corrupted and they were unhappy?'

'Right.' Davidson rolled his eyes.

'The night Heather disappeared, she was there at the party in the evening, she left early, if I recall?'

'She planned her escape well. After the note was found we made routine inquiries at the farm but mostly we concentrated on sending alerts to other forces. We were looking for sightings at railway stations. It was the note that threw us off, without that we would have had the place turned upside down and we may have found some trace of her earlier. By the time it escalated to a murder inquiry, it was February and the farms were in lockdown with foot-and-mouth. When we found the blood in Douglas's van I swear none of the disciples looked at all shocked. They sat there, opposite me and just stared and smiled and said "no comment". They may have been young but they were wise enough. Nicola Stone had a way of nurturing all these young ones. I interviewed Nicola Stone many times and she was "no comment" all the way through with a smirk on her face. She was evil.'

'She found God in prison.'

'Well, good luck to the both of them. Where has she been all this time?'

'Moved from one place to another, and most recently she was in Hackney. That's where she was murdered.

Someone wrote Heather with a question mark on the wall, in Nicola's blood.'

'Bloody hell!'

'We still aren't a hundred per cent sure it is the same killer but coincidence doesn't really exist in our job, does it?'

'If I'm honest, I'm surprised it hasn't happened before. She became one of the most hated women in the UK. It's ironic the way they never forgive the women in these cases. But where she was concerned, it was justified.'

Carter looked questioningly at Davidson, wanting to retaliate with a list of accusations of possible missed procedures meaning that they never really uncovered what Nicola Stone was guilty of, but he didn't. Davidson could walk away, he was the ultimate self-server, and if Carter was going to have any luck in getting anything useful he had to flatter the old bastard.

'So, it was the mothering element she brought to the party?' Carter asked. Davidson nodded ruefully, as he opened out his white cloth napkin and shook it to place it neatly on his lap, looking hopeful as the waiter passed with someone else's food.

'Exactly.' He sighed. 'Let me tell you something about Nicola Stone, she was as bad as Douglas. We know where she was all week, while Douglas was away, she was grooming the youngsters at the yard, ready for him when he came back at the weekend.'

'But we don't know what he got up to when he was away, do we?' questioned Carter. 'He delivered all over the country and the farmers loved him.'

'Yes, they bloody loved him!' Davidson waved his fork in the air.

'Loved him enough to let him have a lockup somewhere?'

'Yes, of course we considered that, but we weren't able to get to the farms during the foot and mouth. And before that Heather was just a runaway for the first six months. I have no regrets about the way I handled the case, and there's nothing I would have done differently, no stone left unturned.' He smiled at his joke. 'Sure, I followed the path that I thought would lead us to a conviction against Douglas. I know what you're angling for me to say, you want me to say I was wrong. Well, I still don't believe I was. Douglas was protected and he was loved. None of his disciples would talk. I've never met a man who exerted so much power over others.'

Davidson thanked the waiter for the arrival of his starter of mackerel with wild berries, smoked over newborn lamb's hay.

'No disrespect meant, sir,' said Carter. 'I'm just talking about hindsight, that's all – we all wish we were blessed with it. Who do you think should have been investigated but wasn't?'

'The family,' Davidson said with his knife poised in the air like a baton. Then he scraped the Melba toast with soft butter, piled it high with mackerel and paused to examine it as he raised his eyes to Carter. 'The father was a difficult man, he decided early on that we were not going to find his daughter; I don't think he wanted us to. He was a bully and they'd had Heather late in life, I guessed it wasn't what he'd wanted to be doing at sixty, keeping tabs on a teenager. Got his computer off him.'

'Okay, thanks, anyone else that you would take another look at?'

'There were so many. He had every odd bod for miles

coming to the parties. We managed to get a couple of people to talk about something that had happened to them at the bungalow – sex, rape, violence – but none of them could back up their stories. Look at these people, the ones who made statements against Douglas, see where they have been for the last sixteen years.'

'What about the uncle, Trevor Truscott, or her brother, Ollie?'

'Her brother was at university and nearly finished – there was a nine-year age gap. We didn't see anything in him. He obviously left home as fast as he could and never went back. Truscott had alibis for everything. He is the wife's brother. He said as little as he could get away with. He was up to no good, we knew he was having affairs. Truscott was probably shagging everything that moved on that farm, but it didn't add up to murder.

'He was one of the last people to see Heather, and he was very friendly with Douglas.'

'But Heather liked going to the farm, would she have gone there if the uncle was a threat?'

'Don't forget he made money from Douglas and his raves, they scratched one another's backs. He screwed Nicola Stone for the rent. It was an arrangement that worked.'

'What about other possible victims?' asked Carter.

'We plotted all those missing who fitted the same profile as Heather and the rape victim, what was she called, I forget?'

'Rachel McKinney.'

'That's it. If we could have got her to open up to us, we might have understood more about Douglas, but she was in no fit state. She was just before Heather was abducted, different part of the country, and nothing to connect the two things, until her DNA was found in his van as well as Heather's. By the time it came to court six months later she was a wreck. She might have given us a second site for Douglas. We know he held on to her for five days. He didn't keep her in his van that whole time. Mentally she was jelly, no matter how hard we tried to help her. She wanted to drop the charges, she was so scared when she came to face him in court. Rachel McKinney was cross-examined for days and she just fell apart. He said it was consensual sex and the injuries were nothing to do with him, that he didn't know anything about the grave. There was nothing of his in the grave, no footprint, nothing; it was waterlogged. We think it was dug weeks before he took her there that night. The jury listened to three pages of doctors' reports detailing the injuries on her body – mutilation which included partial flaying of her skin, for God's sake – and they found him guilty of rape, only because of his semen inside her anus, but not guilty of attempted murder and not guilty of grievous bodily harm. There was no proof, no evidence, and she couldn't speak, she couldn't even look at him in court. The prosecution argued that the mutilation was self-inflicted, it was the beginning of a spiral downhill, they said, despite the fact she had been a perfectly bright and healthy girl at university before it happened. The judge handed down a life sentence. I shook his hand. It was sixteen years and no parole. It was the best we could hope for.'

'So that grave could have been meant for someone else, you think?' said Carter.

'Exactly. We made a shortlist of thirty people, both sexes, aged from children up to thirty. Taking the profile from the rape victim and Heather we decided he probably thought that Rachel was younger than she was. She was a slight nineteen-year-old at Bristol uni. The profile we came up with was between twelve and eighteen, slight build. But then we found out that Douglas was bisexual and had had encounters with a few of the farmhands at places he got to know. Have you seen the notes from the investigation?'

'I have, but I wanted to talk to you as soon as I could,' answered Carter.

'Well, you'll find the list of the missing in there. Some may have turned up now. Plus, we didn't have the luxury of the modern forensics, the geo profilers you have now. You could do a lot with this now. You have tools at your disposal that we didn't have then.'

'What happened to Douglas's van, do you know?' asked Carter.

'When we'd done with it, it went to a public auction. At the end of the day, the disciples were sucked in with the drugs and the sex, the non-stop parties. It must have been every teenager's dream, even when it turned into a nightmare. They got away with it, didn't they? None of the disciples, except Nicola, went to prison. All of them have a lot to thank her and Douglas for, they could have landed all these kids in it. I was in no doubt they saw a lot of things going on in that bungalow that they knew weren't right but they never said. So you're looking for someone who wants vengeance on Douglas and his disciples?'

'We think it's possible. This can only harm Douglas's chances of getting out in a few months' time. He's headed for celebrity chef status, he has backing already.'

'Are you going to talk to him?'

'It's being organised. I'm sending DS Ebony Willis, do you remember her?'

'Mixed race? Tall? Mother was a murderer?' Davidson smiled. 'She made sergeant then?'

'Yes, she's well-respected. As you point out, she has a unique perspective on life and human nature.'

'You call that human? She'd better be more than well-respected, she'd better have nerves of steel.'

'She has, and she isn't afraid to face a highly intelligent killer. After all, she had one as a mother.'

'How is her mother?'

'Still in Rampton, she's not going anywhere, not since she cut a woman's baby out of her stomach. That's Belladonna for you, the nurturing kind.'

'One thing I will tell you is that, when we were investigating Douglas and the foot and mouth epidemic was in full swing, you could smell the smoke from the burning carcasses for miles.'

'I remember it well. The whole country remembers it.'

'At the time,' said Davidson, 'I thought to myself, perfect time to get rid of a few bodies.'

Chapter 26

'... This was in the other, we knew it didn't have a body but ...' Dermot lifted the lid of a plastic chest that they had dug out of one of the gravesites. 'Although the chest is in perfect condition, that's the joy and the curse of plastic, never degrades, does it? But the stuff inside has had it. I'm guessing these were someone's stashes of drugs.'

Willis and Maxwell had been there all morning, whilst the graves were dug out and the soil was transported bucket by bucket down to the sifting station at the entrance to the field. One set of human remains had been found so far, but another, lower down in the field, was yet to be excavated, even though it had been positively identified by the dogs. Sandford was sticking to his plan of taking things carefully so as not to cross-contaminate.

'So, he dug holes to put chests of drugs in and then used the hole to bury someone if needed?' Maxwell asked.

'Saved for a rainy day,' agreed Dermot. 'That's pretty smart.'

'Yes, maybe,' said Willis.

'They were dug in pretty much the same timeframe,' said Sandford. 'The palynologist is at work analysing samples but these graves are identical to the structure, size and shape of Rachel McKinney's, the one at Hill Farm. You're looking at the same technique, same tools used to dig them.'

'Seems like when he found a field he liked, he came back to it many times,' Willis said. The wind was getting up, the tarpaulin over the tents billowed. 'We should scan the rest of the fields at Hill Farm.'

Maxwell was deeply engrossed in the dig.

'How many more like this then, Chris?' asked Sandford.

'I'm not sure. From my list? We could easily dig up a hundred fields and get lucky with three,' said Chris.

Sandford nodded. 'I understand. Three would be a significant find, especially if we know once we strike lucky with one grave, there will probably be more.'

'If this is Douglas's work, do we know how many people we could be talking about?' asked Dermot.

'We know he worked for the Champion farm feed company for three and a half years altogether,' answered Willis. 'That certainly would have been his easiest time to kill and bury, with perfect access to burial sites like this, but he could have been killing all his adult life. We need to find someone who saw him do it and who isn't a disciple.'

'How likely is that?' asked Dermot.

'We are working through all the original statements from people who attended the parties at Hawthorn, or were working as farmhands and got invited to the bungalow,' answered Willis. 'A lot of them saw things they weren't comfortable with but nothing conclusive. There were allegations of rape that came out when people were asked about things that might have gone on at the farm, specifically the bungalow, but the SIO, Davidson, concentrated all his lines of inquiry on what he believed would lead to a conviction and that wasn't an account of a rape at a party. As short-sighted as that was by him, we're going to have to go back and re-interview and reinvestigate those allegations.'

'You're putting people through a lot,' Sandford sounded dubious, 'to look for the missing piece of jigsaw?'

'Yes, and more of them need to come forward to support each other. There's a big cloak of silence over Jimmy Douglas.'

'Why?'

'Because he was popular amongst the adults, the farmers, the farmers' wives,' answered Maxwell. 'He was every gay young lad's crush. He knew what people wanted and he gave it to them. They didn't want to see anything bad in him. That's what he enjoys more than anything: controlling others, he is the puppet master.'

'Willis, what about Douglas?' asked Sandford. 'You okay with taking him on? It's a big responsibility.'

'You saying I'm not up to the job?' She smiled at him.

'I would never . . .' Sandford raised his hands, shook his head. 'But are you going to ask him if he forgot to pay his apprentice back in 2000?'

'Carter thinks the same thing.'

Sandford nodded. 'I think this is all about Douglas, revenge on Douglas. Someone wants us to find something in this field that connects straight to Douglas and keeps him inside with a life sentence that means life. Something that puts him right back into a tiny cell with no privileges, and they know him, or knew him, well.'

Dermot called out to them as he stood at the new grave and loaded more soil into a bucket. 'We have something here; it's been put in with the body.'

'It's a plastic photo frame,' said Sandford as he took it out of its bag. 'The photo is destroyed but there're marks, looks like someone's carved "Ash" into the frame.'

'If this is Ash here, Heather could be with him,' said Dermot.

'I don't think that's possible,' said Maxwell.

Dermot looked at him. 'Why not?'

'Because the scan would have shown two bodies and it only showed one.'

'We'll get this chest removed and finish excavation then we can start on the next grave,' said Sandford. 'The last grave shows signs that it may also contain human remains. The woman's skeleton has been removed now and is on its way to be DNA-tested, let's hope we get a result soon.'

Willis got a call and stepped aside to take it.

'Chris, you want to head back up to town now? I can see Douglas today.'

Willis had come to Wandsworth Prison, now transformed into a training establishment for Category C prisoners. The Bad Boys bakery was famous and Jimmy Douglas had spent the last four years excelling as a chef in The Slammer restaurant. It was one of three open to the public to come and dine in.

Willis waited with Officer Kowalski, the guard. He checked her bag, counted in the items. Looking at her curiously he asked, 'What's this about?'

'Thank you,' she said, returning her items to her backpack with a smile that said 'no chance'.

'Okay. You want to take a seat again, Detective Sergeant Willis, he's being brought over from the kitchens. He'll be about twenty minutes.'

'That's fine. He's a chef, I believe?' Willis sat back down to wait.

'Yes, and a fantastic one too. He made me a special meal when it was my thirtieth. Me and my missus came to eat at The Slammer. I've never eaten food like it: braised ducks' hearts, bone marrow stuffed with liver pâté.' He shook his head. 'Incredible.'

Willis was nodding politely. 'Sounds like you know him pretty well?'

'I suppose so, he's been here for the last five years and I've dealt with him most days. You get to know them, there's a bit of mutual respect.'

'Yes, of course, any advice?'

'He's no problem; he's a humble man. He spends a good deal of his time helping the other prisoners, those who have trouble with the basics, like reading and writing. He helps with their letters, and other people come and get his advice about legal stuff they don't understand. He's a useful man to break up arguments. He likes peace and quiet, order, good manners. If something kicks off in here, you'll find him doing his best to calm things down or staying out of trouble in his cell. He accepts every change in routine without question. As long as he can cook and create his dishes, he's happy.'

'What if he couldn't do that?'

'He wouldn't like it but he'd adjust. He has a lot of determination. He can stare at the same spot on the wall for days, I've seen him do it. He can shut his system down. But I hope that's not going to happen.'

'When did you see him do that, stare at the wall?'

'I think it was when his grandmother died and he wasn't allowed out for the funeral. He took it hard. He didn't speak, he just shut down.'

'I see. Do you ever think he feels remorse for what he did to land him in prison?'

'I think he does; sixteen years ago, he made a mistake. He's a different man now.'

'How is he around women?'

'Very respectful. He works with them in the kitchens he goes to, and we've never had any complaints about his behaviour when he's on work placement, quite the opposite. He's charming, people can't praise him enough.' Officer Kowalski was staring at her strangely.

'Is there something you want to ask?' she asked, intrigued. She wondered if they'd met before, yet she knew they hadn't. She had a good memory for faces; she had a way of turning them into objects and animals in her mind. Sometimes they crossed over. This guard had the face of a monitor lizard with constant licking of his lips when he talked.

'No, I don't think so. Jimmy should be back in his cell now, if you'd like to follow me.'

Douglas's pretty boy-band looks had turned pudgy and slack-faced in the last few years but his eyes were just as mesmerising: the colour of still seaweed in a deep ocean. His bald head was perfectly smooth and shiny. His stubby hands stretched out on the desk in front of him – working hands, red fingers. He had a slouchy but clean look in grey tracksuit bottoms and a dark grey T-shirt.

'Did you have a good journey, Detective Sergeant Willis?' he asked, after she had introduced herself. His voice had a feminine lilt along with a Southern Irish accent. 'I hope the roads weren't too busy? If I'd known I was to have a visitor I would have prepared you something nice to eat. You must be peckish?'

'No. I'm fine, thank you.' Willis met his eyes briefly then looked around the walls. 'You've been busy in prison,' she said.

'Yes, as you see, I have used my time wisely.' He swivelled around in his chair to face the certificates on the wall. He had photos of Irish countryside all over his cell, along with a weekly calendar crammed with tiny writing.

Her notes said that he was someone who the psychologists had assessed as having a high IQ with psychopathic tendencies that included narcissism and lack of empathy. He hadn't the capacity to relate to others. It was all about his own ego, his own gratification, even when he tried to package it to look differently. He had prospered in prison, he had worked the system, in prison and out. He could turn his hand to most things in life and charm his way through. Now he had decided to become an expert in fine dining. Even the warden used him for private functions. He was paid a proper wage for his work in The Slammer restaurant.

Douglas continued smiling as he sat back in his chair and tilted his head a little to the left. He waited for Willis to get sorted as she placed her recorder on the desk beside her. She sat on the one chair in the tiny cell: he sat on his bed. Douglas had the luxury of a cell on his own. Willis was thinking next time they would be meeting in an interview room.

'I bet you enjoy Mexican.' Douglas smiled. 'I'd put you down as a fajitas type.'

Willis didn't answer. He was right in a way, but any fast food was her favourite.

'What can I do for you?' Douglas asked politely, a fixed sweet smile on his round face.

'You're a busy man?' Willis indicated the writing neatly crammed into the calendar space for December.

'The winter menu starts in less than a month. I should be in there preparing right now. We are trialling recipes, a new take on an old favourite – oxtail soup. It's all about the stock: it takes several processes to make a fantastic broth. It's not just about boiling bones.' He ended with a question in his eyes.

'Have you always loved cooking?' she asked, still looking at the walls of his cell. He had made a home there. She wondered how he would cope on the outside.

'I can see you are not a foodie. This little cell is not going to be home for much longer. I am looking forward to getting out,' he said, as if reading her mind. 'I most definitely am a food lover. I've always been interested in the provenance of the ingredients we use, where they come from, how they come from the earth, their life cycle. We take so much for granted but the farmer has to plough, to fertilise, to sow his fields, to nurture, to rear and to slaughter. Ultimately, I am interested in how to do justice to the produce. You must come to the restaurant, as my guest. I'm sure I can create a meal that will appeal to you. I do a wonderful buttermilk fried chicken where I stretch the skin and deep-fry it; you won't be disappointed, it's just as good as Kentucky Fried Chicken.' He smiled at her. 'Did you come to talk about my cooking skills? As I said, I need to get back to work. I don't mean to be rude, and whilst I am enjoying your company . . . are you here to tell me about Millie? I saw it on the news.'

'I came to tell you that Nicola Stone and Millie Stephens have been murdered.'

He nodded, frowned as he thought about that fact, and his eyes went to the wall as he considered it.

'Well, thank you for coming, was there anything else?'

Willis sat facing him, staring him out. Douglas smiled as he blinked.

'My dear, you'd make a good poker player. Nothing moves in that face, does it?'

Willis didn't react. She took out a file from her backpack and set it on her knees.

Douglas was still smiling although his mouth had begun to twitch.

Willis showed him the photo.

'The killer wrote this on the wall in Nicola's flat; it was in the bedroom, above her body.'

'How interesting,' he said sarcastically. 'It means nothing to me.'

'We presume this refers to fifteen-year-old Heather Phillips.'

'Not guilty, remember?'

'Not proven, insufficient evidence. But someone doesn't want it forgotten. We don't believe this was a random attack on two of your disciples. In the case of Nicola Stone, they took time to track her down. They knew who she was and they killed her because of it.'

'How do you know it was because of it? It could have been a "five minutes of fame" man? And – if I am allowed to ask – how was it allowed to happen? Who fucked up? I understood she was under police protection.'

'It is under internal investigation.'

He sighed irritably. His mask of congeniality was slipping. Willis had been inside the cell with him now for longer than he'd anticipated. He was becoming agitated. Tucker had prepared her for it; she'd been waiting for it. He couldn't keep smiling for ever. The shock tactic had been a good one. His façade had slipped quickly. He looked flustered, unsettled.

'Someone is trying to hurt you, maybe,' said Willis.

'I saw it on the news that Millie had become a street prostitute and prostitutes die. Am I supposed to feel something? You are talking about people from my past who I barely remember.'

'You must be sad about Nicola; you were in a relationship for a long time. You were a big part of each other's lives.'

'Only seven years. I've been inside here over twice as long. I have a bigger relationship with the food I cook than to any human. If the police didn't leak the information then she must have blabbed. She must have kept in touch with someone she shouldn't have.'

'That's what you think happened?'

'I don't have a crystal ball, Detective. I'm just trying to help you out. You're supposed to be the clever detective.'

'Have you ever kept in touch with anyone that appeared at your trial? Any of your disciples?'

'I'm sure you'd know if I had.'

'Things get into prison that aren't monitored, plus you have been allowed out, unaccompanied, for some time now.' He didn't answer. 'They all stuck by you at the trial. Your disciples are almost all still around.'

'Of course they did because I was not guilty and they knew it.' He smiled, but he leaned across the table, exasperated. 'I was merely one of many who knew Heather. Ask her uncle, he had his grubby little hands on everyone at that farm, all the stable girls had been groped by him at one point. He and Nicola were always at it behind my back. Ask her father, he was a bully of biblical proportions.

It was all punishment and penance with him. Ask him what happened to his daughter. Or Saul, the weird farrier who spied on us all. We used to act out little charades for him on the patio at the back of the bungalow because we knew he was always watching from his first-floor windows. Ask all of those people what happened to Heather. Davidson tried to get me for Heather because he wanted it so badly. He couldn't see anyone else in the equation. He gambled and he absolutely lost. You want to find out what happened to Heather, be my guest. You will never get me for that.'

'We are in the process of searching more than one gravesite at Lambs Farm in Buckinghamshire. Do you know it?' asked Willis.

'Never heard of it.'

'You used to deliver there.'

'I delivered all over the UK.' Douglas was distracted; out, he was running through his memory.

'We have found a grave. In fact we were led there by Nicola's killer. He left her phone on a grave. Since then we have uncovered more in that field. It's a field with trees at the top, secluded, a high hedge, no houses in sight.' Douglas stared at her as if he heard something from the past. 'We will continue searching. If we find something that links to you we will push for a prosecution. If you co-operate with us at this point it will go better for you.'

Slowly his eyes cleared, the clouds lifted, the mist over the green rock pool lifted and he smiled.

'Sergeant, search as much as you like, you will find nothing of mine in there. I have done my time, paid my price; I deserve to come out now. My past is behind me.'

'The past is never really gone.'

He smiled. 'Maybe you're right. You know who I think

murdered Nicola and Millie? This is Heather herself, saying: "Look at me, everyone, I'm alive!"' He laughed. His laughter trickled on until it ended as a sigh. He kept his eyes on Willis; they were bright and angry now. He was trying to see beneath her skin. The room was beginning to feel very stuffy. 'I tell you, I take my hat off to boring little Heather and the way she's managed to ruin my life all by her unimportant little self.' He shifted in his seat, agitated. 'I won't answer questions about Heather. I'm done with that, not guilty, remember? I am sorry someone killed Nicola, but it was pretty inevitable.'

'In what way?'

'People hated her more than me.' He smiled, shook his head. 'They could see she was lying about the McKinney case.'

'Was she?'

'Yes. I will give you this little bit of information now that she has departed from this world. She was in the van with me when I picked up McKinney. She was with me the whole time. There, that's my present to you, now don't forget, you owe me.'

'I owe you nothing. Why did you feel an obligation to her at the time? Why didn't you speak out about her involvement?'

'It didn't make a difference in the end, did it?'

'If you have information that can help us catch this person it will look good on your record.'

'And if I don't?'

'This person may be willing to go to great lengths to keep you in here.'

'I'm not putting a nail in my own coffin just to solve your murder cases.'

'You still have influence on the outside. Yvonne Coombes thought so. I have to presume that you are receiving contraband items such as access to a phone and that you are abusing your privileged time spent on work parties by communicating with criminal individuals. Why does Yvonne Coombes feel threatened by you?'

He lifted his eyebrows, staring back at her, but interest flickered in his eyes – the shifting oceans of sea and sky were colliding and regrouping and he had become very still, very intent on what she was saying. He leaned forward slightly to get closer to her.

Willis nodded and started packing her rucksack. 'You'd better be prepared for the worst. If we find links to you in those graves, you may never get out of here.'

'Don't threaten me.' Douglas jumped forwards a little, his anger uncontained. He was a few inches from Willis's face. She raised her hand and firmly, gently, pushed him back.

'Personal space, remember?' Willis signalled to Kowalski outside that she was ready to leave. 'I will be in to see you soon. By that time I may have some more news about Lambs Farm.'

Douglas turned away and stared at the spot on the wall, a stain.

On the way out Willis wanted to talk to Kowalski.

'It's important that Mr Douglas doesn't get access to anything from the outside, now we are investigating two murders of people he was close to. I want his cell searched for a phone. He's not to go off on any work parties.'

'Douglas is no problem. The governor allows him a fair bit of freedom. He deserves it, he spends all his time helping the others with their legal papers, their letters home.

He also brings in a fair bit of revenue for the prison from the kitchen. This is the governor's shout, not mine and not yours.'

'Okay, I'll put it in writing. He's not to go out unaccompanied. It's dangerous for him at the moment.' Kowalski opened the door for her. She paused before exiting. 'Do we understand one another?'

'We do, but it's our business to look after Jimmy, not the Met's.'

Chapter 27

After Willis had gone, Douglas stood with his back to the cell door and focused on the spot on the wall straight ahead. It was a point of meditation for him. A stain on the wall, a hole. A stain exposed layers of old paint and years of dirt from people who had passed through the cell, lived there for a while, left their lives in the walls, their crimes, their failures, their dead and dying dreams. It was his porthole to a fantasy world. He thought about Heather. Douglas had actually first got Heather to speak to him on a Saturday when she was hurrying to catch the bus into town and she passed him as he stood by his gates. Her face was burning red from the heat of the May sun and the exertion of running for the bus. She had her backpack slowing her down. She was going into town.

'My, you're in a hurry, aren't you?'

She paused by the gateway to the bungalow's field and shaded her eyes to get a better look at who was talking.

'I've seen you at the farm, haven't I?' he said. Douglas's good looks meant he looked twenty-four instead of thirty-four.

Heather nodded. She knew very well who he was. All the stable girls fancied him, but he'd never talked to her before and now was not a good time, as she had to hurry to catch the bus, yet she didn't want to be rude.

He looked at her backpack. 'Where are you going?'

'Town.'

'I'll give you a lift. I'm on my way there now.'

Heather started to shake her head and then looked up the lane. If she missed this bus there would be no more today.

'Thanks.'

He went around the other side of the van and opened the passenger door for her.

'What's your name?'

'Heather.'

He held out his hand, with a smile.

'How do you do?' He took her hand and held on to it, turned it over and looked at it. 'Pretty hands.' He ran the tip of his finger along the inside of her wrist.

She pulled her hand away and rubbed where it tickled.

He stood behind her as she bent to get into the van. She was hot and her T-shirt stuck to her back; it rose up. He saw the dip at the base of her spine and the perfect strip of skin.

The first girl he'd had sex with was fourteen and he was twelve and he tried to do what he saw on the films. She'd laughed at his small cock and he'd hit her. Once he started hitting her he couldn't stop until she managed to fight him off. She'd let him try again and this time he'd managed it and she agreed he wasn't small – when he was erect he was bigger than average. She agreed because he held a knife to her throat.

By that time Douglas was fourteen and had learnt that his pretty looks could fool a lot of people into thinking he was sweeter-natured than he was. Douglas learnt to open doors for women, he learnt to make witty conversation and he learnt to have sex in many more ways than they showed in porno movies because he understood that to really have power over someone you had to make them feel safe first. You had to gain their trust, you had to find out what was in their heart, what was the one thing they wanted in life. And you had to collect people's dreams like a magpie collects shiny things, you had to pretend to give them everything.

Outside, the corridor banged and shouted into life.

'How's it going today, Jimmy?' Officer Kowalski unlocked his cell door. 'What's on the menu today?'

Douglas turned with a smile. 'What do you fancy? Pigeon breast in port and cranberry sauce? Suckling pig with crispy skin to die for?'

'You're making my mouth water.'

'Ha-ha, well, I'm putting together a great Christmas menu, and I'll make sure you get to approve it.'

'You know, Jimmy,' Officer Kowalski looked along the corridor, and then took a step inside the cell, 'I am sorry to hear about your old girlfriend.'

Douglas nodded. 'It was so long ago, but it did make me sad. It wasn't a nice way to be told.'

'I'm sure. Never mind, you've come a long way, Jimmy. I hope you're not worried about that visit from the detective from MIT 17?'

'Not worried at all, why should I be?'

'It's just that I thought I recognised her name and I did some hunting around while she was in here. I have something for you, been doing a little detective work of my own and I can tell you something about Detective Sergeant Ebony Willis. She has things in her closet too. I brought you these articles to read about her and her mother.' He hid the folder in a cookbook. 'Her mother's crimes make you look like a saint and you know what they say, Jimmy? Like mother like daughter.' Kowalski hurried off.

Douglas spent the rest of the day looking at the articles about Willis and her mother. He didn't hold a surgery for the others that day. He sent them away, closed his cell door. He had too much to think about.

He read about Bella, Willis's mother. She would have been his match, he thought, a woman so cold, and she would have been more devious than Nicola and just as cruel. But he wouldn't have been able to control her like he did Nicola. He thought about Nicola's last moments. Had she relished the pain, had she shouted to Jesus to take her to him? Hallelujah! Or had she looked at her blood and wanted to drink it, wanted to watch herself die? Then he thought about Heather; was she back for revenge on him, on all of them? He stared at the spot on the wall again and practised his controlled breathing, inhaling, holding the air in his lungs, expanding his ribcage, feeling the bones stretch and the lungs fill. He practised his meditation, snatching the memory-flashes that made his pulse quicken, made him sweat, made him want to roar, and put them inside a balloon and sent it skyward.

Douglas thought about Willis. He took deep breaths and held on to them, exhaled so slowly, he felt deliriously giddy.

She must have wondered what kind of monster her mother really was. From what he had read, Ebony Willis was the only one who understood what her mother was capable of, who wasn't fooled by her. Did that mean she was capable of truly understanding what made her tick? Strip away the skin and you find what makes the raw flesh twitch.

Chapter 28

Willis got back to Fletcher House and went to find Carter, who was calling a meeting to discuss the events of the day.

'The protection team are spitting blood, by the way, they're blaming us,' said Hector. 'They say we opened the channels to her when we started asking questions about where she was after Millie Stephens was murdered.'

'No way,' said Carter. 'She'd already been moved twice because her identity was leaked.'

'They want us to keep her identity a secret as long as we can until they can carry out an internal investigation,' Hector said.

'I still say both women took some finding,' said Willis.

'Especially Nicola Stone,' said Carter. 'Some kind of leak had to have happened, either within her protection team or within Cedar Court. Hector, what are her team saying now?'

'I had a meet with one of the members of her team who said they are investigating but they say it didn't come from them.'

'They would, though, wouldn't they?' answered Carter.

'Exactly,' said Hector. 'And in the next breath they are admitting they have someone under investigation who might have debt problems, online gambling problems, and might have just offered some information for sale.'

'Ouch, nasty,' said Carter. 'Well, keep us informed on that, push them hard, this is a double murder case and the leak might lead us straight to the killer.'

'I'm on it, sir.'

Willis turned a computer screen around on the desk so that everyone could see; some stood up to get a better look at the screen. She put up photos of both post-mortems.

'The post-mortem was carried out on Nicola Stone,' Willis announced as she handed out the sheet with a diagram of the victim and her injuries. 'The assailant came prepared to inflict those injuries. There was no trace of the knife and it's not the same weapon used to kill Millie Stephens. Both assailants were right-handed, Nicola Stone's killer was five eight to five ten. We don't know whether the same killer was responsible for both deaths, there's not enough evidence to be sure. These murders were different in method, choice of weapon, and location, but they have motive in common: to kill someone who was involved with Jimmy Douglas, a disciple.'

Hector raised his hand to speak. 'It doesn't feel right to link these two murders. Why not kill Millie Stephens in her own home, just like he did Nicola? If it had been me, I would still have chosen to kill her in her own home. It could have been done relatively stress-free.'

'Perhaps they thought her flat was too overlooked,' said Carter. 'Perhaps they are not familiar with the area and looked up Lee Valley Park on a search and decided that it sounded remote.'

'We are looking at car licence plates entering the park

in the previous month,' said Hector. 'Plus people walking on the Rivers and Weirs trail around the park. We are also looking for a match with Finsbury Park CCTV, of which there is a fair amount. I'm feeling lucky with this. I have my officers searching the Internet for any reference to these locations by individuals using the forums.'

'How useful are the forums going to be?' asked Maxwell.

'You'd be surprised,' answered Hector. 'People just ask a small question about the last sighting of Nicola Stone, about Douglas's possible victims, then it snowballs. If the killer is the kind of person who enjoys feeling smarter than everyone else they're going to love joining in the conversation.'

'Have there been any results from house-to-house around Cedar Court?' asked Willis. Blackman wasn't there, she was liaising with the Heather Phillips team. Laptop filled her place.

'Sarge, we are following up on a group of individuals in number seventeen who we haven't been able to get hold of. Community police officers are assisting in tracking these individuals down.'

'What about the neighbour, Roy?' asked Carter.

'Roy has told our Family Liaison Officer that he could have revealed the secret of Nicola Stone's identity to a number of people when he'd had a few glasses of wine,' answered Laptop. 'Except, we know that Roy doesn't go anywhere or see anyone else but those people who come into his flat and they are all connected to Cedar Court, plus, crucially for me, she had to be tricked into opening the door when she knew the kind of people who might be waiting on the other side.'

'If it had something to do with Roy she would have opened it,' said Willis, 'or the church, and the vicar.'

'Exactly ... run background checks on them,' said Carter. 'We have a duty to protect the other disciples, the other people who may be a target for this killer. What do we know about them?'

'We have yet to get statements from Cathy Dwyer or Stephen Perry,' answered Hector.

'That has to be next on the list,' said Carter.

'We're running a trace on Perry's car for plate recognition around all the sites that concern us,' said Hector.

'How did it go with Douglas?' Carter asked Willis.

'He is very highly regarded inside. He has a surgery, almost daily, for helping prisoners with problems. He is known to all of them for his good works in there.'

'Jesus.' Carter shook his head.

'But, as the mask slips,' continued Willis, 'you can tell he hasn't changed. He's in his element in there, so many people to manipulate. He's a very big fish in a small overstocked pond. I have no doubt he must have a phone. I have requested a list of all those work parties and accompanied days out that Douglas has been on in the last two years. I am pretty sure Douglas asks and he gets. He deals in favours, he even tried to say I owed him for information he gave me on Nicola Stone. He said Nicola was fully aware of the abduction of Rachel McKinney and that she was with him when he did it.'

'Too little too late,' said Carter. 'I wonder if she confessed that and other things to the priest at the church she went to?'

'Would he tell us?' asked Maxwell.

'Afraid not,' answered Carter. 'He would be instantly excommunicated.'

'Did he give you anything else?' asked Maxwell.

'He was slightly shocked when I told him about Nicola, but then he calmed and I felt he really didn't care, maybe even saw it as a good thing. After all, when he comes out of there, he is wanting a clean sheet and so far two of his disciples have gone. Two down, four to go, five with Ash,' said Willis.

'Yvonne Coombes should be offered some protection, should be moved,' Maxwell pointed out. 'Surely she's next on the list? Whether the murders are linked or not, we know that Nicola Stone's death is connected with Heather.'

'What did he say about Lambs Farm?' asked Carter.

'He was not expecting it,' Willis answered. 'When I said we were digging up Lambs Farm, it really threw him, for at least a minute. But he is nothing if not shrewd and calculating. He was already pointing the finger at the new killer for all he was accused of in the past. He is angry, frustrated, but even now expecting to come out of there in June next year.'

'I had a meeting with the SIO at the time of Heather's disappearance – that was ex-Superintendent Davidson. It was useful, but it highlighted massive gaps in the inquiry. It showed me that, by putting all their energy in nailing Douglas forensically, they made a big mistake, they underestimated how cunning he is. When Douglas managed to wriggle free, Davidson had nothing left to fall back on and a chance was lost. The only way we can ever get Douglas is by bringing something new to the table. Going forward,' said Carter, 'all the people at risk need contacting: Perry and Dwyer and anyone who was at those parties at the time Heather disappeared. Who has been in trouble with the law since then? Who was on the edge of the disciple circle? We know lots of people saw things that probably shocked them at Hawthorn Farm, at the parties, at the evenings that went on there. Search back through all the statements and get back out interviewing people afresh.'

'Everybody and his brother went to Douglas's parties, half of Chesham,' said Hector, pointing at the sheets of names and addresses that were pinned to the whiteboard. 'That's the list of people who were there the night Heather disappeared. It's just about everyone under the age of fifty who's on the electoral register.'

'Chris, you've been quiet? This is turning into a bigger investigation than we thought, do you need to have more help on this?'

'I would appreciate more researchers and I could do with more space, the maps and charts take up a lot of room.'

'You got it, you can have the end of the inquiry team office, set up there.'

'I would appreciate working with DS Willis on a more regular basis because she is in contact with Douglas as well as the disciples.'

'Sure,' answered Willis, slightly perplexed. 'Obviously all the information I receive gets fed into HOLMES but I will come and chat things through with you on a daily basis, no problem.'

'I believe the killer is on a personal quest here,' said Carter. 'Think of someone who has had their life ruined and has a possible personal connection to Heather, or at least wants us to know this is about the time she went missing, about what happened between this person and Douglas and his disciples. There must be an awful lot of people who had some sort of contact with Douglas and lived to tell the tale, get out there and talk to them, we need to find this killer.'

'If I was looking for revenge on the disciples, Stephen Perry would be high on my list,' said Hector. 'He's been investigated a few times, even ended up in prison – been bankrupt, been done for dealing coke when he was in his early thirties. He's Mr Entrepreneurial – nice house, nice car, fourth wife, six kids. But nothing's stable with him. He teeters near the edge often, he is on the periphery of investigations that involve fraud and gangsters. On Google his name is linked with scams. We are going to need a court order to search his offshore companies, which we're not going to get without good reason. I did look into his credit rating, it's really low right now. He's defaulted on a few loans in the last couple of months and he's been trying to re-mortgage his house but been refused.'

'Where has his money gone?' asked Carter.

'I don't know, I'll keep looking.'

'Who else?'

'Cathy Dwyer,' said Willis. 'We know she changed her name to Bloom, we know she travelled after she left Hawthorn Farm. Perry and Dwyer have a company called Global Escape Travel, GET for short. It's average size with three million turnover. I'm uncovering stuff about them all the time. Gavin Heathcote has been employed by GET, he's down as head of security. I don't know how long he's been back roofing but he's been out of the country for a couple of years.'

'Gavin's been lying to us,' said Carter. 'We'll go and pay him a visit again and to Stephen Perry.'

'Okay, thanks, we'll wrap this up now,' said Willis. 'I know this is a big investigation with two victims and their connection to Douglas, but at the heart of this is a simple concept, this is personal to someone. It's all about them and Douglas and something they want. Is it, where is Heather? Is it, who killed Heather? Or is it someone saying: why was it all about Heather when there are other victims?'

Chapter 29

Gavin Heathcote was even less pleased to see them than last time but he reluctantly came down the scaffolding.

'How are you, Gavin?' asked Carter. The rain had started and Heathcote was battling with a flying tarpaulin as the wind got up.

'Hunky-dory, what do you want?' He glared at Carter and Willis.

'We want to buy you a coffee,' said Carter.

They walked down the street to a workmen's café and sat in the booth at the far end and ordered.

'You had better alter all your routines until we catch the person who killed Nicola and Yvonne,' said Carter. 'They are obviously good at tracking you down and you are quite an easy find.'

'They can try, if they like. I'd like to see them try.'

Carter took a breath and smiled. Willis resisted the urge to roll her eyes.

'Alter your routines; don't tell anyone where you'll be working in advance. Ask your wife to be extra-vigilant if there's anyone hanging about that she doesn't know. If she's worried at all, she should call this number immediately.' Carter handed over the incident room number.

'Have you finished?' Gavin asked, pretending to be bored. 'Was that it, the big talk?'

Willis opened her backpack and took out Gavin's file and her notebook.

'Things have escalated since we last spoke,' said Carter.

'No shit? I heard. Nicola Stone was hated by everyone. Fact.'

'We think the two deaths are connected,' said Carter.

'I've seen the stuff in the papers. I have weirdos waiting to talk to me outside my house, hiding behind my bins, or I did have, they won't try it again,' he grinned. 'Luckily everyone who knows me round here knows I am a fair bloke who does a good day's work. I help little old ladies cross the street, I give a discount to single mums and disableds. People who matter aren't taking any notice of the crap being printed. They've got my back round here and when this blows over, I'm going to have a few words with a few people.'

'It's not going to blow over, Gavin. We have recently uncovered three new gravesites at a place called Lambs Farm, do you know it?'

'Never heard of it.'

'We have already found a connection to one of the disciples in one of the graves. What will we find next, I wonder?' Willis showed him the map and the photos of Lambs Farm.

'It hasn't changed in the last sixteen years,' she said. 'What was buried there then is still there. Will we find links to you there, Gavin?'

He eyeballed Willis. 'No, how many more times?'

'Lambs Farm was one that Douglas used to sell to.'

Gavin's eyes were rolling like an arcade machine as he tried to juggle possible answers in his head to find the right one, to come up with a winning response. 'Where is it exactly? Maps don't mean anything to me.'

'Buckinghamshire.'

'I might have been there. I went all over with Douglas in those days.'

Carter nodded.

'We'll be talking to people who used to go to the parties at the bungalow on Hawthorn Farm, as well as to the other disciples. Do you keep in touch with any of them? Stephen, Cathy?'

'I've seen Stephen sometimes. I did some work for him a few years ago, on his roof.'

'When did you last have contact?'

'Must be a year ago now.'

'Can I check that on your phone?' asked Willis.

'No, you can't. I've got some photos of my cock I wouldn't want you to get too excited about.'

'You're lying to us, Gavin. We know a lot about you, your business, your connection with your bosom pals in the chain gang, Stephen Perry and Cathy Dwyer, and GET, their business. You ran the security for GET.'

'So what?'

'So, you're a liar,' said Carter. 'You like to play with the big boys now and again and you're not one of them. You're just a small-time thug with rich friends who throw you a crust now and again and wouldn't think twice about pressing the eject button on you.'

'Fuck off.'

'Gavin,' Carter picked up his coat and leaned across the table, 'drop the hard man bullshit? I'm talking about protecting your family here.'

'I can protect my family, like I've always done.'

'You're not swanning about in the fucking A-team this time. There'll be no taking the law into your own hands this time, no toting rifles. You leave it to us or I'll take great pleasure in locking you up. We're dusting Nicola's place for prints right now. I hope you find this as funny when the results are in and your fat grubby hands are all over this.'

Carter was still thinking about the look of defiance on Gavin's face as they left him in the café, whilst Willis checked her phone as they got in the car.

'He's been in touch,' said Willis as she read from the screen. 'Stephen Perry doesn't want us coming to his house, he said he'll come into Archway or meet us in a café.'

'Understandable,' said Carter. 'Put in the co-ordinates, we're going there.'

'Nice place,' said Carter as they got out of the car outside Stephen Perry's house in south London. Carter pressed the intercom and showed his badge to the security camera.

'Mr Perry? Detective Chief Inspector Carter, and this is Detective Sergeant Willis. Can we have a word, please?'

The gate opened and Stephen Perry greeted them at the door. He had on black tracksuit bottoms and a grey T-shirt. He lowered his voice as he opened the door just wide enough to talk to them. He had dark blond floppy hair that he had a habit of pushing back all the time.

'I said I would come to the station, I don't want my family alarmed.'

'We were passing, keeping it informal. Can we come in?'

He ushered them into the hall and then into his slightly unused-looking study on the left before closing the door. He offered them a seat in a lounge area that had strategically placed books on uncluttered table tops, a pseudo-leather globe on a brass plinth and photos of his family on the walls, along with memorabilia from boxers and fights going back to Muhammad Ali.

'Wow,' said Carter, 'you have an impressive collection here. Keen boxing supporter, I see?'

'Yes.' Perry gave a forced smile. 'Look, I've had press taking photos of my family. It's not right.'

'We didn't notice them on the way in. But, some things cannot be helped, Mr Perry. I'm sure no one round here knows about your past.'

'They will now. I don't even remember Millie. I mean, I do, of course, but we weren't close. Why are you even here?'

'When we went to Millie's flat the only photos we found there were ones from Hawthorn Farm back in the time that you lived there. Does that say something to you?'

'Not really. What do you expect me to say?'

'It tells us that she thought the comradeship you built up in those days was meant to last. I mean, surely that was what all the tattoo stuff was about, huh? Chained together for ever, through thick and thin. For Millie it was all thin. She never made it like you did.'

'I had my tattoo removed.'

'Why was that?'

'Well, it wasn't something I was particularly proud of.'

'What did it mean to you?' Willis asked.

He shrugged. 'It symbolised a misspent youth.'

'Does that mean you don't have to abide by Douglas's rules any more? Does that mean you're no longer in the chain gang?' Carter asked, still looking at the memorabilia on the walls of the office.

'I was never under any kind of obligation to Douglas, I had nothing to tell the police in 2001 and I don't now.'

'There were a fair few of you who went through that bungalow on Hawthorn Farm, must have been pretty wild,' Carter said, turning back into the room. 'When did you last have contact with Millie?'

'Okay, I want to be honest here, I sometimes used to hear from Millie and, when she was short of money, I'd give her the odd hundred. I felt sorry for her. She went downhill fast.'

'After Douglas was arrested, you mean?'

'Yes, I know she went back home for a while but it didn't work out. Her dad chucked her out. One thing leads to another, doesn't it?'

'What about the rest of you? Where did you go after Douglas was arrested?' Carter was asking the questions whilst Willis studied Stephen's reactions, reading his face for clues.

'For a while Gavin and I hung out, I stayed with him at his place and then I got my own.'

'What were you doing then?'

'What do you mean?'

'Job-wise?'

'Oh, I don't remember, anything I could, I expect. We'd spent six months killing animals and burning them. I didn't have a whole load of useful work experience. I think I skipped off to Tenerife with a mate and started selling timeshare. I found I was good at it. I made my first million and then I tried lots of businesses. Some have been good, some not. I've done okay.'

'That mate, was that Cathy Dwyer?' Willis asked, though she already knew the answer.

'Yes, it was, as a matter of fact.'

Carter set the files he had in his hand down on the table. On the top of it was a photo of Perry from fifteen years previously, a dishevelled, stoned-looking twenty-three-year-old. His cheeks were hollow. He had a smugness about him, even then.

'Do you remember those days?' Carter half-smiled, as he turned the photo round to show Perry.

Perry grimaced. 'Very little, that was the point, wasn't it? Do everything to oblivion?' He looked as if the previous night's drink had just caught up with him. He seemed about to be sick and had begun to sweat profusely.

'When was the last time you had any contact with any of the disciples?' asked Willis.

Perry briefly winced at the reference to his past again and then grew annoyed.

'I have seen a few of them occasionally over the years. We weren't forbidden from contacting one another. We weren't charged with anything relating to Heather Phillips or anyone else. We did nothing wrong.'

'Who have you been in contact with?' Willis accompanied her question with a patient smile. This was supposed to be a friendly visit.

'In the last fifteen years?' He thought about it. Willis was noting down his mannerisms. He was thinking a little too theatrically, his eyes sliding up to his right, an indication of some invention going on. 'I've seen Gavin no more than a couple of times. Cathy and I have worked together sometimes, in the past.'

'Doing what?' asked Carter.

'We have a couple of companies we jointly run.'

'Like Global Escape Travel?'

'That's correct.' He looked a little taken aback that they had investigated his business. 'That is one of them.'

'What are the others?' asked Willis as she poised her pen over her pad.

'I'd rather not say.'

'Why not?' Carter smiled. 'You must be proud of your achievements, I'm sure? Nice house, good area, you have done okay for yourself.'

'Because this has nothing to do with what is going on at the moment, my business affairs are my own.'

'So, will you be meeting up with Douglas when he gets out?' asked Carter. 'Are you looking forward to seeing him again?'

'I don't think so. But, if he's served his sentence, it seems fair to let him live his life any way he wants. Everyone gets a second chance. But I'm not going to be rekindling any relationship in a hurry.'

'He's a good cook, apparently, have you been to The Slammer restaurant at the prison?' asked Carter. 'It's supposed to be very good.'

'Let me think . . . I'd probably remember that, wouldn't I?' He looked pissed off.

Willis was watching him as he sipped water.

Carter continued, 'At the Heather Phillips murder trial, and in the police interviews leading up to that trial, you exercised your right to remain silent. You didn't take the stand against Douglas.'

'I had nothing to say. I still don't. At the end of the day, we know he was capable of a lot of bad things and he's served his time.'

'That didn't bring closure for her family,' said Carter. Perry shrugged and looked away, agitated. 'Did Douglas threaten you?' asked Carter.

'No. Mr Phillips was a pig of a man; everyone knew he beat Heather. There were so many other people that were more likely to have hurt her than Douglas.'

'Were you scared of Douglas?' asked Carter. 'Are you scared of him even now?'

'No.' Perry shook his head and then shrugged. 'Maybe, he had a menace about him. Listen, I was a complete idiot to end up there. I have no idea how it happened. I look back at myself in those days and I feel sorry for myself.'

'How, why?' asked Willis.

'Look at me in the photo, I am innocence on a stick. I mean, I don't think I had enough wits about me to crawl out of there. I was just a mixed-up, drugged-up kid at a crossroads and I happened to take the wrong turn. I was there for six months on and off, that's all.'

'Things have been straightforward for you since then?'

'I've had a few hurdles along the way.'

'You were arrested for domestic violence?'

'My wife, Vanessa, was having mental problems, but she admitted making it all up, self-harming. It was all ridiculous. We are still together. We weathered the storm; fourth time lucky for me.' He smiled.

'Seven years ago you were involved in a scam that saw a lot of people cheated out of their money,' Willis stated.

'I was unlucky in a business venture. It was never my intention to rip anyone off.'

'But you've had more luck with recent ones, what about GET?'

'Yes, that's mine and Cathy's. What is this all about? What has my business got to do with the murders of these women?'

'The murder of two of your fellow disciples, you mean?'

'If you like, yes.'

'We also know that one of the other disciples, Gavin Heathcote, far from being a virtual stranger to you, worked for your company Global Escape Travel, when he did security for some of the villas you let out to holidaymakers amongst other things.'

'Possibly you're right. Cathy would have handled that, she does all the foreign stuff. I prefer to stay here. Why don't you ask her? Can we wrap this up now, I need to get on with my work?' he said.

'Of course, we will be talking to everyone in detail. This is a major inquiry that seems to be getting bigger by the day. It isn't going to go away in a hurry and I'm sure we'll be back to talk again. For now we will need a detailed account of your movements between the seventeenth and the twentieth of last month.'

'I can give you those straight away. I've been working from home in that time. I've walked the dog, gone to the supermarket and that's it. My wife can confirm that.' He called her and once Carter had heard her confirmation of her husband's account of things he continued with his questioning.

'Where do you walk your dog?'

'Anywhere I feel.'

'Do you ever drive up to Lee Valley Park?'

'No, why would I? It's the other side of London.'

Chapter 30

Outside Carter glanced across at Willis once they'd started driving.

'What did you think?' he asked. 'Interesting, wasn't it?'

'Very,' answered Willis, looking at her notes.

'He'd obviously had a skinful last night and he looks like a bully, hard-faced. He has the madness of a megalomaniac about him.'

'I agree, his take on life, on justice, is warped. I don't think he lives in the kind of reality most of us understand. Maybe, all his life he's been used to lying and covering up the truth.'

'His wife sounded like she was used to saying what he wants her to. She didn't have to try too hard to give us an account of his whereabouts for every minute of the day, did she? She looked as if she doesn't stand up to him, or doesn't give a shit any more. She may be worth talking to on her own.'

They were waiting at traffic lights. Carter leaned on the steering wheel, something he did in thinking mode. 'You know what I can't get my head around, Eb? Why do the disciples keep in touch with one another? You'd think they'd want to forget everything that went on in that bungalow. But, they still stick together. The chain still binds them.'

'I'm starving, can we talk and eat?' said Willis.

Carter immediately changed direction and took a detour towards the East End. They went to the Madras Palace on Brick Lane and settled into sharing poppadums and competing for the pots of pickles and chutneys as they rotated on a stand.

'I've been working on a timeline for both their careers and personal lives, let me run it through with you,' said Willis, waiting whilst Carter loaded up his plate. 'Ready?'

'Shoot.' Carter had prepared himself by ordering more beer. They were alone in the restaurant. It was between the people who came to dinner at normal time and the people who came out of the pubs hungry. Willis took out a plastic sleeve from a file in her backpack.

Willis began reading: 'Heather missing in July, come early 2001 they are still in the bungalow until police arrive investigating a young lad from another farm, Darren Slater. He disappeared at the beginning of the foot and mouth crisis, and it threw up a possible link to Douglas, he knew the lad and Darren was seen getting into Douglas's van. In February, Douglas's van was seized, with plenty of links to Heather and to Rachel McKinney. So that's it for Douglas, he is on trial for Heather first, which collapses, and then for Rachel McKinney which is successful. Stephen stays with Gavin and carries on with the slaughtering, as we know, while Cathy leaves for home and then for Tenerife as a holiday rep where she starts selling timeshare and in October that year, 2001, sets up her own company.'

'That's pretty smart.' Carter was piling up curry on his plate. 'The timeshare industry has never had the best of reps.'

'Exactly, and she does well in it, plus she also marries into it; there begins the first of Cathy's marriages. She married a local timeshare magnate who died in a boating accident two years later, knocks himself out on the boom, falls overboard, nobody sees. Cathy inherits some but most of it goes to his kids. Meanwhile Cathy remarries a wealthy American who has clubs all over the world and six months after Stephen is released from prison, he also dies – this time in a car accident. His car plummets off the road in Monaco, Cathy is thrown clear.'

'She's an acrobatic little devil, isn't she?'

'For the next ten years the couple are building businesses together and during that time Stephen has three marriages. One wife died and he's had two divorces. The divorces haven't always cost him, he was paid off a couple of times by wealthy partners. He's currently married to a Swiss heiress but things are not rosy. He was accused of assault by her a couple of years ago, but she dropped the charges. They have two children and he has four from the other marriages.'

'Their lives and their work have been in tandem by the look of it. Makes you wonder why she needs him? She manages well without him,' said Carter, waving to order the bill. 'Or maybe it's more than business?'

'DC Blackman wants a meet later,' said Willis. 'She has information for us. Shall I suggest a pub?'

'Yes, and tell Maxwell to join us. We need to see him off duty. He's far too straight.'

Back in the car Carter took the opportunity to talk about Tucker.

'Tucker is staying around, by the way,' he said as he prepared to drive away.

'Where?'

'At mine for a few days but he's thinking of getting a place here.'

'Really? He never said.'

'Yes, his mate has a solid three months' work on some sets up here and Tucker will help him. I'm sad about you two, sorry to hear it's not going to work out.'

Willis looked at him and realised, for the first time, that was what it was about. Tucker had come up to say goodbye, the look of disappointment she had tried to avoid the night she'd seen him wasn't there, he hadn't even wanted to stay the night. She had a pang of sadness. Their slow and unexciting relationship had kept her from having to look elsewhere. She had thought it was enough for him too.

'Tucker said you're just not interested, which is fair enough. He seems fine about it. He'll bounce back, he's had to do it before when his partner Sally died. I never thought he'd ever get over it but he's had a few hopefuls since then. You were one of them, but really, I think I pushed you into it.'

Willis didn't answer. She was going through their conversations at the restaurant. She'd rushed away. She hadn't really asked him anything about his life. She'd told him about cases and they'd talked about people they both knew.

'He's got his eyes on someone else apparently and I told him you'd be fine about it.'

'About what?'

'Him dating Zoe Blackman?'

She looked across to see if he was joking, but he had the expression she knew very well. It said, you shouldn't have messed him about, people won't hang around trying to scale your walls for ever.

*

Maxwell met them at the pub.

There was music coming from somewhere deep inside the pub. Blackman was checking her phone in the entrance as they got there.

'G and T for me, please,' said Blackman, in answer to Carter's question.

'Coke, thanks,' said Willis.

Carter went to get the drinks with Maxwell whilst Zoe Blackman and Willis found a table.

'How's it going, Zoe?' Willis asked, as she took off her jacket. She avoided eye contact, still unsure of how she felt about Tucker and Blackman.

'Great, what do you think of Chris?' asked Blackman. 'What do you know about his personal life, Eb?'

'Absolutely nothing, but don't worry, Carter will have wheedled all the personal information out of him you'll ever need by the time they get back with the drinks. He's relentless.'

'I would have thought he was your type, Eb?'

'No, too slight for me. I make a rule, never go out with someone who weighs less than me.'

'He doesn't weigh less than you, for God's sake! He has great pecs under his shirt. He definitely works out.'

'You've been out on a couple of dates with Tucker, I hear?'

'How did you know?'

'Carter told me, I told you he always gets to the personal stuff.'

'Yeah, well, I thought it was worth a shot. You know he's moving up here?'

'Supposedly.'

'I think it's already happened. He's been up here a couple

of weeks staying with different people. I met him at the pub one night when he came with Dan.' She glanced across at Carter who was coming back with the drinks.

'I see.'

'I thought you wouldn't mind, Eb? You never talk about being in a relationship. When I've asked you about it, you always say he's nothing to you.'

Willis was a little taken aback. 'I'd never say he was *nothing*.'

'Well, you know what I mean. Look, you say the word and I won't see him again, but so far it seems to be good for both of us. It's just fun. I'm trying not to spend my whole life working and washing kids' clothes. I like having a man in my life who isn't a copper, I'd like to avoid dating another one of those, or another "God" from the gym who has to do everything in front of a mirror.'

'How are your boys?'

'They're lovely, growing up fast. James likes to be called Jay, he's as tall as me now.'

'That's not hard.'

'Yeah, right, we can't all be long leggy giants like you.'

'What are they into?'

'Jay is sporty. He likes his football, basketball, anything with a ball, basically. The younger one, Billy, is the quiet, clever one; he spends too much time playing video games but still manages to come top of the class. Thankfully they both still do pretty much what I say. But then, they haven't hit the dreaded teens yet.'

'I bet you were a wild child?' said Willis.

'God, yes, and now when my boys are driving me mad my mum gives me that smug look and follows it with, "It's payback time". If she says it one more time I'm going to deck her. Seriously, I was a nightmare. I did everything I could to piss her off. My dad would give me anything I asked for. My mum had to rein him in all the time and I got away with murder.' Zoe looked across for a response from Willis but she was absorbed in her phone. 'I've tried the Internet.'

'Oh, yeah?' Willis gave a half-hearted reply whilst answering a text from work. She felt tired tonight. They'd had just a few hours' sleep since Nicola Stone's body had been found and the work didn't seem to be easing off. Now, with the graves at Lambs Farm, the pressure was on and the press would have a field day once they discovered the Douglas connection.

'It wasn't Tinder, it was one of the other ones; you have to view it like a job. It definitely feels like hard work.' Zoe sighed. 'What about you, Eb? Are you seeing anyone at the moment?'

'No. I'm too preoccupied with other things, and I'm not keen on bringing a man back to mine.' Willis was not sure she liked what she was feeling. Her good friend and her ex who she hadn't quite decided was an ex were dating and she wasn't sure she was entirely okay with that.

'Ha ... how many times did you do that anyway?' Blackman teased.

'What do you mean?'

'I mean truthfully, Eb. You told me ages ago that you never let them stay at yours.'

'Well, that may be true. I just like my own bed, my own space. I don't want anyone else in it.'

'What about cuddles? Everyone likes a good cuddle.'

'I'm not that keen. It feels claustrophobic. I don't know.'

'Okay, you don't have to justify it to me – seems perfectly

reasonable.' She smiled. 'I would consider agreeing; I mean, everyone likes to have the whole bed to themselves except ... a sleepy morning shag is my favourite. Actually a shag any time is one of my favourite things.'

'Too much information!'

'Not with Tucker and me, not yet anyway. When are we going to go out again? I haven't had a boogie for ages.'

'The last time was your birthday, I think.' Willis smiled, but she felt hurt even though she knew she had no right to.

'That's way too long, Eb. Let's put it in the diary, get some of the others on board. Meal, club, tequila shots, the whole shebang!'

'Do you promise not to start pole dancing again?' Willis smiled. She knew if she asked that Zoe would drop anything she had going with Tucker, but she wasn't going to do that.

'Absolutely not – where there's a pole, you know I'm going to end up wrapped around it, and I'm taking you with me this time.'

Blackman took a sip of her gin and tonic as Carter set the drinks down. 'Jeesuz ... thanks, this is just what the doctor ordered. You've had a busy day at the site, I hear?'

'Three gravesites, two bodies,' said Maxwell, sitting down opposite. 'But we've found a plastic chest, like the ones you get from the DIY places, and it's clear it was used to stash drugs in. We also found a plastic photo frame with the name Ash carved into it, that was in the new grave they're digging out right now.'

'Ash? The young lad who lived in the van with his mum?' said Blackman.

Carter nodded. 'We are assuming it refers to him, but we can't see the photo any more.'

'So, Zoe, how has it been with the Heather Phillips team? What have you learnt?'

'It's been really good, I think I've got a clear idea about the original investigation now. Shall we work through the suspects at the time?'

'Go for it,' said Carter, already halfway though his pint.

'What about John Phillips, Heather's dad?' asked Blackman. 'I doubt he would have done it himself but could he have hired someone else to do it?'

'Is there any money gone out of his bank?' asked Maxwell. 'That would cost him a few grand at least.'

'We need to get more evidence against him first before we start looking into his bank accounts. The press would have a field day,' said Carter.

'The team don't like John Phillips,' said Blackman. 'He was, and still is, a bully. They say he controlled Heather so much that the only way she could get any privacy in her house was to barricade her bedroom door. They queried the marks on the inside of the door when they first went round to investigate her disappearance. It was Mrs Phillips who told them Heather sometimes barricaded herself in after she'd fallen out with her father but her mother was just as bad; we think she instigated and encouraged the abuse.'

'What were the other lines of inquiry?' asked Maxwell. 'Can you just run through those with us?'

'Of course. They put forward ones about the disciples. They thought there was a lot more they could have told the investigation at the time. They were complicit in other crimes of Douglas's, like selling drugs. They were completely under his power and tuition – it's highly likely they took part in the assaults that went on in the bungalow.

There were some theories that Heather intended to run away with someone too.'

Willis looked up. 'Why did they think she was going to run away with someone else?'

'They interviewed one of her school friends who said that she was.'

'Where is that friend now?'

'They emigrated to Australia and died in a motorbike accident. I have brought along the notes and the statements taken at the time.' She handed them across.

'What were the inquiries at the time, re a person she might be running away with?' asked Willis.

'It wasn't likely to be one of her school friends. It had to be someone she became friendly with at the farm,' answered Blackman.'What did the team find out about what happened to Ash?'

'They got as far as finding his mother had been sectioned and cared for in hospital for a couple of weeks in Southampton and then discharged and there is no trace of either one since,' said Blackman. 'They didn't bother looking any further because neither Ash nor his mum were there at the time Heather disappeared, they had been gone a while according to statements at the time.'

'But he could have come back?' said Willis. 'You have to wonder if he ever made it out of that place alive.'

'He was only sixteen at the time,' said Willis, 'and he and Heather were friends. He had no choice but to socialise because Douglas let him live there on his field.'

'What about Douglas? When are you seeing him again?' asked Maxwell.

'I'll try and see him again tomorrow,' said Willis. 'He'll

have had time to think things over. We've had restrictions placed on his freedoms.'

'What does he seem like when you talk to him?' asked Maxwell. 'What did he say about Lambs Farm and the graves?'

'He was flustered, thoughtful at first, and then he seemed to dismiss it. It almost made him happy. He seems to think this is all going to end up good for him. I really hope he's wrong,' Willis said.

'What about Saul, the blacksmith who lives on the farm lane?' asked Maxwell. 'Douglas mentioned him,' answered Willis, 'but he didn't really throw him into the mix. What have you got on him?'

'Nothing,' answered Blackman. 'The team can't find sufficient motive for him to kill the disciples. But he is selling up. He's a loner. It will be worth checking up on his movements. He was a friend to Heather.'

'Tell me what you have learnt today about Rachel McKinney's grave and at Lambs Farm?' Carter asked Maxwell.

'Well, it depends on whether we find remains that can be directly linked to Douglas, doesn't it? We got close today. I feel we saw some of Douglas's life in those graves. I can't promise you that what I learnt will be worth anything if we don't find a body closely associated with Douglas. We know he was willing to travel anywhere but if he had a special place he brought victims to, it's not going to be hours away. I think three hours max. Rachel McKinney is the nearest we will ever come to a survivor of Douglas's.'

'I don't think she will be able to help us,' said Carter. 'She says she was blindfolded through a lot of it.'

'She must have been moved during that time,' said Maxwell. 'She has to remember something.'

'I don't give up hope on it,' said Willis. 'And there were many people affected by what went on at the bungalow. The disciples brought friends with them when they came to party; they were encouraged to do so.'

'We have made a point of asking people to come forward who haven't felt able before. I'm hopeful people will,' said Carter.

'If Douglas does get out in June, I hope we can fix it to re-arrest him at the gate,' said Willis.

'He must think whatever we find there cannot be traced to him?' said Maxwell. 'Maybe he's right. If so, I'll just have to find another site.'

'Stephen Perry is on my mind a lot,' said Carter. 'Hector is putting together a report on his finances. Perry might want protection and, while I don't blame him, he could afford to hire his own security and he hasn't done so.'

'Has Cathy Dwyer been located yet?' asked Maxwell.

'We know where she lives.' Willis looked at Carter and raised an eyebrow. 'Shall we?'

Carter nodded. 'Time to pay her a visit.'

Chapter 31

When they got back to the car Carter looked across at Willis. 'Do you have an address?'

'I have a London director's address in Canary Wharf, yes.'

Carter looked at his watch. 'I need to ring Cabrina but it'll take too long for me to explain everything. Let me just text her instead.'

'I understand.'

'Actually, no, I'd better ring.' He got back out of the car to make his call. It only took a few minutes and when he got back in, he was smiling.

'All is okay in the world, Eb. My woman still loves me and my son has finally turned a corner and has stopped being a little shit in school.'

'Great, let's go.' She buckled her seatbelt. 'I miss seeing them since you moved further out.'

'I know, it's really hard. Archie keeps asking when you're coming over.'

'So he can practise his rugby tackle on me again?'

'That was funny. I've never seen anyone fall in slow motion and try so hard to stop themselves.'

'He had me around both ankles, plus I didn't want to

fall on him. He just wouldn't let go, it was like having handcuffs on your ankles.'

'Yeah, God, it was funny. I wish I'd had the video running.'

'Can I come out and stay overnight when things get easier?'

'That will be great.'

Carter and Willis parked up in the visitors' car parking space beneath the Arena Vista Tower, one of the high-end, newly built accommodation and leisure blocks in Canary Wharf. The reception desk of white marble and dark bronze was on the left of the foyer. A palatial sweep of steps led up to a glass marble area with lifts and water features.

Carter showed his badge. 'Do you have a Cathy Dwyer living here?'

The concierge shook his head with a smile, as if he hadn't quite understood what Carter had said.

'Okay, let's try an apartment rented by a company called GET?'

'Ah yes, the new complex?'

'Perhaps.' Carter smiled. 'Is there a woman named Cathy Dwyer involved in that?' Willis pulled out a photo of Dwyer, taken from her online company profile.

'This is the woman? This is Ms Cathy Bloom. We don't know her as Dwyer.'

'Okay, does she have a flat here?'

'Yes, it's on the sixth floor, studio 647, but she isn't in, she went out with her colleagues about an hour ago.'

'Where did she go?'

'I think they were intending to go to the Singing Canary

cocktail bar; that's just five minutes' walk around here on the left.'

'Thank you, you mentioned the complex here? Is that happening in this building?'

'Yes, it is. On the top floor.'

'What is it going to be?'

'We don't know anything about it yet; the architects are still working on the plans. It's not opening till next summer.'

'Sounds good, and do you see much of Cathy Bloom?'

'Not really. She doesn't stop and chat. She's always in a hurry.'

'Thank you,' Carter looked at his name badge, 'George, you've been really helpful.'

They walked around towards the bar, as the icy wind blasted off the Thames. There was no mistaking winter had arrived. The vertical village was lit up bright against the black stormy sky. The Singing Canary was a two-storeyed bar in an old tea warehouse, with interesting photographs in black-and-white from the early days of the docks. Old East End memorabilia hung down from the ceiling alongside birdcages housing animated yellow canaries. The walls were bare stone; there was a mix of antique and modern in the furnishings. The place was packed with City types entertaining other City types.

They were greeted by a striking-looking Spanish woman in black. 'Have you booked?'

Carter shook his head and showed his ID.

She smiled nervously and immediately drew closer for privacy. 'My name is Maria, how can I help?'

'We're looking for this woman, she's apparently drinking here. She's called Cathy Bloom? She's with some colleagues?'

Maria looked at it and was obviously wondering what would be the best course of action to please both police and customer and keep her job.

'She's here, but she is with work colleagues having a meeting at the moment. Can I take a message?'

'That's kind, but no, we need a word with her. We won't disturb her long but it is urgent. Take us to her, please.'

The waitress paused, seemed to assimilate the knowledge and then nodded. 'Please follow me.'

She led them up the stairs to the bar area where there was a mix of seating – booths and tables and low-level sofas overlooking the Thames. It was dimly lit with discreet alcoves, and the wall lights were made from birdcages. They followed Maria along to the far end and stopped mid-aisle ten feet from a table of four people, three men and one woman. The woman had her back to them; when she turned to see who was disturbing them, she was instantly recognisable as Cathy Dwyer. On the table was an assortment of tapas and two bottles of wine.

'Please wait here.' Maria went forward to speak to the woman who excused herself amongst a few jokes about the Old Bill coming to arrest her.

'Cathy Dwyer?' asked Carter, as she walked over to him.

'Bloom,' she answered, irritated. 'What is it? I am in the middle of a meeting with colleagues. What is this about?'

'We will try not to keep you long.' Carter smiled. 'Shall we sit here?'

They sat at a free table nearby. Cathy Dwyer sat opposite them, her back to her colleagues on the other table who were taking a keen interest in what was going on. Maria, from the front desk, had been called over to talk with them.

'We are investigating the deaths of Millie Stephens and Nicola Stone,' said Willis.

Cathy Dwyer was dressed in a green silk blouse and a pair of black trousers, with a gold chain belt around her waist. She wore a simple gold chain around her throat that ended in a golden C-shaped moon below her collarbone. Her short blonde hair had honey tones and expensive highlights, in a thick and choppy style with a fringe that swept over one eye. Her green eyes were smouldering. She had the look of someone at the end of a very long day, who knew she still had to look stunning and be at the top of her game but was now relying on low lighting and an extra coating of mascara.

'What has this to do with me?' She watched as Maria passed by.

'Ms Dwyer, we're here to offer protection, to talk about how best for you to stay safe.'

'I don't need protection!'

'You heard the news about Millie and Nicola?' Willis asked.

'Yes, I heard they're dead. Needless to say I'm sorry, but it was a long time ago. It doesn't affect me.'

'We think it does. We believe they were targeted because of their past association with Jimmy Douglas,' said Carter.

Cathy raised her slight shoulder and shrugged. 'Look, how would you even know that? I mean, it was a lifetime ago, why would someone come after us now?'

'We don't know but the killer led us to another site, where we found graves in a field. Does Lambs Farm mean anything to you? It's about half an hour's drive from Hawthorn Farm, do you know it?'

She shook her head and then glared at each detective

with an 'are we done now?' look whilst pushing her fringe away from her eyes. 'I don't have any idea where Lambs Farm is and . . .' Her companions were still turning around and watching the proceedings '. . . look, I'm in the middle of a very important negotiation right now, I need to get back to my clients. I really am very busy.' She turned to her companions to smile and wave and hold up her hand to say five minutes.

'Just a couple more questions,' said Carter. 'Did you ever accompany Jimmy Douglas, in his van, on one of his farm visits?'

'Very rarely, I was usually working or studying. I was doing my A levels at the time.'

'You obviously studied hard, you're doing very well for yourself?'

'Thank you, I get by but I've done it through hard work, not through academics – I completely failed my A levels, but then I was in a strange house with even stranger people, taking a lot of drugs.'

'Congratulations on your achievements in that case. We hear you're involved with the opening of a leisure complex in your block? Is that what this meeting is about?' Carter asked.

'It's too early to say whether it's going to happen. It won't happen at all if I don't get back to my companions. May I?' Cathy Dwyer smiled politely.

'In a minute,' said Willis. 'We need you to be extra-vigilant in the coming days. If this is a vendetta against Jimmy Douglas and all those involved with him, then you're pretty high on the risk scale.'

Carter handed over his card.

She read it out: 'Detective Chief Inspector Dan Carter.

I'll remember that when I'm contemplating who to phone at three in the morning.' Cathy Dwyer smiled, relaxed. 'Look, I know you're just doing your jobs, it's late, I expect you'd much rather be having a beer downstairs than talking to me, so can I set you up with a drink?'

'Nice offer but no thanks.' Carter smiled. 'Look, we don't want to cause problems for you, but there are some more things we need to ask you about. How about you give us an hour of your time tomorrow instead of us taking up your time now. We can come to your apartment, make it simple.'

'Where will you be tomorrow?' asked Willis.

'In board meetings all day.'

'Then we'll leave it to you to phone the number on the card,' said Carter. 'Tell us when you're free to discuss things.'

'Okay, thank you.'

On the way out Carter stopped to chat with Maria at the desk whilst Willis went outside to watch the riverboats and the lights reflecting on the Thames. Every time she looked at the river she couldn't help but think of the bodies that must be at the bottom of it, stuck where there was no current and lodged with the rusty bikes and the silt and the plastic bags.

Willis saw she had a missed call from Tucker, but she waited until she got inside the car before returning it. Carter was still talking to Maria. When Tucker answered she could hear the sound of people in the background.

'Hang on,' he said. 'I'm just going to find a bit of quiet.'

'If you're busy, it doesn't matter, I'm just returning your call, that's all.'

'No, it's okay. It's great. How did your interview go?'

'Okay, thanks, it was useful the stuff you told me, it really was, it felt reassuring to know that you had met him.'

'Good, good. Listen, Eb, I'm sorry if you got the wrong end of the stick about things, about us, I mean. I hope we can always be friends, call on one another. I never wanted to put pressure on you to push forward with something you weren't comfortable with.'

'There was no pressure. I just thought we were okay like that, I suppose. How's it going with Zoe?'

'Shit ... I was going to tell you, but it didn't seem that important. It's just a couple of dates to the cinema and a meal, that's all.'

'She's a friend of mine.'

'I know.'

'It's a bit shoddy.'

'I thought you wouldn't care.'

'I don't. I probably care less now that I know you are the kind of bloke to date my friend without actually breaking up with me. Okay. Well, I have to go now, Scott. I'm interviewing Douglas again tomorrow. I have a lot on my mind.'

'I'm sorry, Eb. I fucked up.'

'No, you didn't. You got it right. Zoe is great; she's a lovely warm human being. Be nice to her, or else! Good luck with everything, Scott.'

'Don't say that.'

'What?'

'That good luck, *arrivederci*, fuck-off shit.'

Carter came out smiling and tucking cards into his wallet as Willis hung up. She felt unsettled by her own harsh words but she didn't want it to show on her face.

'What did you think of Cathy Dwyer?' asked Carter, getting into the driver's seat. 'She definitely wasn't expecting our visit, although she must have known it was likely.'

'Just not at ten at night in a bar around the corner from her home, I guess,' said Willis.

'I think she'll sleep on it and be all sugar and sweetness in the morning. Hopefully by that time we might know more about the other remains in Lambs Farm.'

'What did you find out from the woman at the front of house?' she asked.

'I found out that it was Maria's boss with Dwyer, and that she's in business talks with him and the others at the table. Maria gave me his business card and the card from one of the others.' Carter put the cards from the restaurant on the dashboard and took out his phone as he scanned the cards into his search. 'What do you know about these two companies?' He showed her the phone. 'Accommodation Guru and La Luxe Living, two big companies.'

'Hotels, restaurants?' asked Willis.

Carter nodded. 'I'm sending these over to Hector to get him to work on it by the time we see her tomorrow.'

Chapter 32

The next morning Carter's phone made the particular jingle that meant he had received a text from Willis. He called her as he headed to shower, looking in on Archie on the way.

'Eb? What have you got for me?'

'We have two hits on victim ID. The first victim recovered is Simone Levin, a street worker from Blackpool who went missing in '99. She has no connection to Douglas that we know of, his name was never in the frame for her disappearance. The second victim is a twenty-five-year-old called Anthony Poulson, known as Tony. He was last seen in May 2000 when he was wanted for assaulting his girlfriend. He had been inside for aggravated burglary, arson, and juvenile crimes. Both sets of remains have been taken to a forensic anthropologist to get more information on exactly when they died.'

At twenty to eight, Willis saw Carter parking up and went across to meet him as he left his car in the car park under Fletcher House along with the SOCO vans.

'Did you manage to get any sleep?' asked Carter as she approached.

'Like a baby,' Willis answered.

'Liar.' Carter walked with her to the entrance to Fletcher House, where they passed their IDs through the scanner and entered their department. Carter had called another meeting and Blackman was there this time.

'What about next of kin for Tony Poulson?' Carter asked her when they'd got started.

'He has a sister in Glasgow, she said he left in May in 2000 and she didn't see him again. He came to ask her if he could borrow some money and that was the last she saw of him. She said he was thinking of going across to stay with a friend of his in France but when she didn't hear from him she contacted the friend and was told he'd not been seen there either. She said no one has seen him since.'

'Did he have any connection to the area, or to Lambs Farm, did she know?' asked Willis.

'No. She'd never been that far south herself, and she said her brother never mentioned knowing anyone from the Watford, Chesham area. She'd never heard of Jimmy Douglas or any of the other names from the farm.'

'What about the other graves?' asked Hector.

'More human remains are possible. I had hoped it would be Heather, then it would have been enough, wouldn't it?' said Chris, who looked tired and despondent.

'The female, Simone Levin? What are her team saying?' asked Carter.

'Hers was an isolated incident,' answered Hector. 'No other girls had gone missing from the streets and with no body they just shelved the case. We have new forensic results from Cedar Court – a positive on two partial fingerprints that will at least help to eliminate someone and we have a hair which is not Nicola Stone's. We've pretty much traced everyone from Millie's phone that we can, but as you can imagine there are an awful lot of untraceable numbers on there. We've got officers working their way though the list of party-goers on July twenty-second, still hoping to find someone with a big enough grievance against any of the disciples. DC Blackman is now dealing with the follow-ups.'

Blackman looked at her notes. 'We've interviewed three hundred people so far who attended parties on Douglas's fields and most of them have absolutely nothing to say beyond they had a great time. Even when you tell them there'll be no prosecutions over drug-taking or drug supply relating to that night, we're not looking to prosecute anyone for selling anything they shouldn't, we just want to know if anyone felt they'd been mistreated in the bungalow, or by anyone at that time.'

'Anything promising?' asked Carter.

'If I hear, "if you can remember anything about it, you weren't really there!" one more time, I'm going to stick my foot down the mouth that says it! I did go back to see Millie's father, Don Stephens, again after the fracas with Gavin Heathcote and reports that there had been a big altercation between them; but both men seem to think it was nothing.'

'How is Don Stephens doing?' Carter asked.

'Not well, I would say,' replied Blackman. 'He seems to be drinking a lot. He was out of it when we got there at eleven in the morning. I gave him a little friendly pep talk.'

'How did he take that?' asked Willis.

'He told me to fuck off, which was fair enough. Anyway, I've passed his name on to the Family Liaison Officers, they can deal with him now. He needs some support before he kills himself on one of those machines he mends.'

'How's it going, Chris?' asked Carter. 'What about the possible location for our killer?'

'I have several ideas, I'm just working on them at the moment,' said Maxwell.

'And Willis, you're going back to talk to Douglas again?' said Carter.

'Yes. I'm looking forward to asking him about Tony Poulson. I have two names to put to Douglas, as well as a lot of the other information we're coming up with. This will make him sweat. I have also insisted that he is not allowed out of the prison or to work in the kitchens. He's going to hate that but we need to squeeze him. He has it far too easy in there.'

'Hector, can you find out exactly what happened to Douglas's van for me?' asked Carter. 'This isn't going to be enough on its own unless someone has seen Poulson or Levin with Douglas; even then, we need forensics to back us up really.'

'I'll do my best to try to find out what happened to the van. There may be a record of who bought it at the car auctions, but I'm not promising anything, it's sixteen years ago.'

Later, after they got outside the meeting, Carter steered Willis towards his office for privacy. He wanted them to hit the road that day, to see as many of the disciples as they could, in case they were contacting one another and concocting stories about Tony Poulson. He figured if they did it together they could contain the spread of information. Maxwell had already warned them that there was plenty of speculation about the sight of SOCO vans going into Lambs Farm and they knew from Blackman that there were journalists talking to anyone who ever went to the parties at the bungalow. Some had even come forward with some new photos of Douglas. Carter had ordered her to confiscate all the journalists had with the promise that they'd be given something interesting when they had it. He needed to keep this out of the press as much as possible or they would lose their element of surprise.

Chapter 33

'Yvonne, can we come in please?' Willis called through the letterbox.

'No, please, go away.'

'We're going to need to come in and check that you and Bonny are doing okay.'

They heard her shuffle reluctantly towards the door and unlock the chain. Willis showed her her ID again. Yvonne looked behind her at Carter to make sure they were alone.

'I daren't go out,' she said. 'I'm a prisoner here, me and Bonny. I'm frightened they're going to come for us. Why is it happening now?'

'What are you frightened of?'

She opened the door to them and walked back into the sitting room. Bonny was watching television. 'Being killed, what do you think? I'm sitting in this flat waiting for the knock at the door.'

'We can help you, Yvonne. We can offer you protection, put you and Bonny up in a secure flat.'

'Where is secure? Nicola was supposed to be secure. If they found her, they can find me.'

'Just the immediate team working on this will know

where you are, no one else, I promise you. You're going to be safer there.'

'Yvonne, we have some names to put to you,' said Willis. 'Do you know Simone Levin or Anthony Poulson?' Yvonne shook her head. 'Or a place called Lambs Farm?'

'I never went there.'

'But you've heard of it?'

'I think so.'

Willis showed her the photos of Poulson and Levin and Yvonne started to breathe heavily whilst shaking her head. She started scratching at her hands.

'Do you know them?'

Yvonne paused, looked at Willis, her eyes beginning to brim.

'Come on, Yvonne, now is the time to tell us the truth.'

'But my child? They can come for me any time.'

'You and your child will be safe. We're moving you to a safe house.'

She took a few seconds to chew her fingers and stare at the photo. She looked like she wanted to run.

'I want protection. I don't want to lose my baby. Please, believe me, I never did anything wrong. If I tell you what I know, you have to protect me.'

'We will,' said Carter. He took her silence for agreement and started to caution her.

'No, I'm not telling you this under caution, not yet, not till I'm safe.'

Carter nodded. 'Go ahead.'

'I remember this man.' She tapped on the photo. 'Tony.'

Carter and Willis held their breath as they waited for her to tell them what she knew.

'You promise you'll protect me and Bonny?' Carter nodded. 'I'm telling you, I did nothing wrong.'

'What happened, Yvonne? Tell us,' said Willis.

'It was a Saturday night. Millie wanted me to go with her to the bungalow that night and hang out. Nicola was going to put on a barbecue, we were going to drink some beers.' She looked up from her thoughts. 'They drugged me – put something in my cider, I know it. I was fine one minute then I tried to stand but I couldn't and then the next thing I felt the weight of someone on me. I remember screaming but no noise came out.'

'Do you know who it was?'

'I knew there was more than one. I saw all of them, their faces – Nicola, Stephen and Gav. They were causing me so much pain but I couldn't move.' Yvonne began scratching at her arms that bore the scars of self-harm. Willis held on to her hands to stop her.

'Was Douglas one of the people who assaulted you?'

'Could have been, I passed out, I think, because I don't remember anything more until I came to really early. It wasn't even light.'

'Where were you then?'

'I was in Stephen Perry's room, in his bed.'

'On your own?' asked Willis.

'Yes, I couldn't make it out, what had happened. I felt really crap, everything hurt, I felt sick, my head was pounding. I was bleeding. I remember thinking, shit – I've made a mess in the bed. But another part of me was thinking, it can't be because I'd just finished my period. I was really sore and not just there, my arse was ripped, I could hardly stand, let alone walk. I began thinking I'd been raped. I went into the sitting room, Nicola was there, she was cleaning and

Millie was crying. Cathy was there too, she just kept staring
at me, it was like a dream. It was all really weird. Stephen
walked in from outside, everyone was quiet, no music, no
partying. I looked over in the corner and there was that guy
Tony. His head was twisted to the side. I started screaming.
I remember just standing there looking at him, he was all
distorted, his eyes were open, just staring at me. His mouth
looked like he was screaming at me and I was screaming
back. He had this stuff coming out of his mouth. Nicola
tried to stop me screaming. She shook me and she said to
me: "We had to do it for you. We did it for you. He went
mad, he started hitting out. He attacked you." I looked at
Millie and she just kept crying.

'I was listening to it all, desperately trying to remember,
and I kept getting flashbacks but the person attacking me
wasn't that guy Tony, it was the others. Nicola told me he'd
attacked Millie and Cathy as well. Millie was just crying,
she couldn't look at the head. Cathy didn't say anything.
Stephen was hugging her.

'After a while Douglas came in with Gavin and he said
to me, "We're going to take care of this for you. We are
going to take care of it all. He attacked you, did Nicola tell
you?" I remember just looking at Millie and thinking this
isn't real. Douglas told me Gav could tell me what I did, and
Stephen too. They told me I started having sex with this guy
and he got nasty. They told me he kept hitting me and he
raped me. Douglas had to use all his force to pull him off
me, they said. I remember looking at the body and saying, "I
don't remember it." Then Douglas told me we were off our
faces and when I said we had to call the police he said, "And
tell them what? It was self-defence? They're never going to
believe you. Look, this man is just no one, he's a nothing,

he's not worth you worrying about. You'll both get life sentences for it and he's just worth nothing. We have a place we can take him, no one will find him. We are prepared to do it for you." I remember looking at Stephen and Gavin and they couldn't even look me in the eyes. Millie looked at me and just shook her head. Nicola came and hugged us both and Douglas said, "I was trying to pull him off you, me and Stephen, and you were forcing his head back, I don't know who actually caused it, but we all share it; we're all in this together, the chain keeps us safe. We're stronger than any chain, no one breaks it, we're all in this together."

'I went and sat on the toilet and I still couldn't understand what was happening. I heard Ash talking to Douglas and then the sound of the van starting up. I think they must have moved the body then, it was just beginning to get light. Nicola said she had to look after Elle, Ash's mum, and she'd give her a bath. She asked me to run it and we all helped wash her. It was unreal. We pretended like nothing had happened. When Jimmy came back Nicola did our tattoos. It took all day and I remember thinking, oh God, please let me go, let me go home, and Millie was walking around in a daze but every time she started crying again Nicola or Douglas would just start telling her we should be grateful, and we were, in an odd way.

'After the tattoos we sat around drinking beer, while Nicola lit the fire pit and burned Tony's clothes. We stood around and watched. Jimmy took me home in his van; we didn't speak all the way. He stopped to let me throw up, that was all. As he dropped me off he told me not to worry about a thing, it was all taken care of and only the boys knew where the body went. That way they shared in our guilt. We all shared it, that's what he said. I went to bed and stayed there till the next morning. I kept trying to remember what had happened. I kept getting flashbacks; I remembered looking across and seeing this weird shape, like some kind of weird-shaped animal, and then I realised it was Douglas riding on someone, fucking someone from behind. Cathy was there somehow too but I just couldn't get it clear in my mind. Millie and I never spoke about it again. The tattoo was a reminder to us that we'd done something with the others, something terrible.'

'Even though she counted you as a good friend, you never discussed what had happened to you in the bungalow?' asked Carter.

Yvonne started rolling another cigarette from the dust at the bottom of the tobacco pouch. 'No, we never did. I've never been violent in my life. I've self-harmed, but, no matter how off my face I've got, I've never hit anyone. I didn't kill him, and I don't think it was him that did all that to me.'

'What happened back at the farm afterwards?'

'It settled down, we never heard a word about Tony, no one came looking for him and we spent more and more time at the bungalow, or Millie did anyway. I made excuses, but it was always a threat they held over me and Millie. I mean, Cathy didn't seem to be the same as us, she was Douglas's favourite. She wasn't the same type of girl as us. She had it easy in life – she chose to rebel. Millie was from a hard-working, single-parent family. I was out of the care system but Cathy stuck her nose and her head in the air and she wasn't like us. Thinking about it now, she was just like Jimmy Douglas.'

'Pack up just a few things for you and Bonny,' said Carter. 'Whatever else you need, we'll provide.'

'I need to get my methadone.'

'We'll send someone to get that for you,' said Carter. 'We'll take you to a secure place and I want you to put this down in a statement.'

Once outside, Carter looked at his watch. 'Let's go see Hawthorn Farm.'

Yvonne stood in her sitting room and listened to the sirens wail from outside, with a feeling of fear that she hadn't had for years. She had an overwhelming urge to ring the people who had mattered most to her in all the world, at one time; the people she had chained herself to.

Chapter 34

'Tucker is moving into a flat, did you know?' asked Carter as they walked across the street to the car.

'Zoe told me. I'm surprised, I thought he loved living in Devon?'

'He's keeping his flat there, renting it out. I guess he realises he was never going to make inspector.'

'I didn't know he even wanted to?'

'No, nor did I, if I'm honest. I thought he'd bumble on into retirement instead of which he's turning into a man who makes video sets for a living and is moving about all over the place.'

Willis was looking at the ground as she walked, nodding. Carter stopped her gently, touching her arm.

'It's nothing serious with Zoe, you know that, don't you? It's you he loves.'

'It's not love. It's never been love. It was friendship and a bit more, but never love.'

'Whoa! Rein it in, Tonto, I don't mean to push any buttons.'

'How can it be love if it doesn't last?'

'Because things need upkeep. Tucker said to me you never told him your feelings about anything. You never said what made you happy, what made you sad? Christ, Eb, why do you make it so difficult for yourself? I tell you what I'm going to do, I'm going to write a manual for prospective dates: "What is Ebony Willis really like?" By the time you ever get to the point of deciding *someone* is for you it'll be too late to have kids.'

'I don't want kids.'

'We all say that, and then bingo! You'll be waddling around talking about how you can't stop peeing every few minutes and how uncomfortable you're getting.'

'Never.'

'Not never, Eb, for Christ's sake. Come on, give me a hug.'

'No, I don't want one.'

'Not for you, you silly bugger, I need one.'

Ebony reluctantly gave way and allowed him to hug her briefly before shrugging him off.

'Okay, Eb, Tucker is hanging about today, you going to meet him?'

'Maybe. I just have had other things on my mind.'

'Eb, as weird as it sounds to you, everyone who's married or in a relationship in this department has to manage the two sides in their life. You have to make time for a life outside the force. Tucker is a good guy.'

'Christ, you'll be offering a dowry next.' She smiled, embarrassed. 'I've been in touch with him, we're cool.'

'Good, because I was seriously thinking of upping my offer from one goat to three.'

'Way too rash.' She grinned as they got into the car.

Forty minutes later they were close to their destination. 'It's near now,' said Willis, who had the map over her lap.

'Straight ahead for a mile then we take a right onto the private farm lane.'

'There's the sign for Hawthorn Farm,' said Carter. 'It says it's a glamping site and a farm shop.' He indicated, ready to turn off the main road to Chesham.

'Yes, I saw the website,' said Willis. 'The bungalow is still there, it's a holiday let now. This is all Hawthorn farmland, all the way from the main road.'

They passed fields on either side of the lane and woodland areas, before coming level with the bungalow on the right. It had been given the name Rose Cottage but it hadn't really grown into its pretty title; it was still a basic agricultural bungalow but now it was painted pink and the gravel driveway had plant pots on it.

'Can we stop here a minute? asked Willis. 'It looks empty.' She had the original investigation photos on her lap, including the search of the bungalow.

Carter parked at the gate. They got out of the car and opened the gate, as quietly as possible. There was only the sound of the birds and the squirrels' chatter. A concrete path led to the front door of the cottage, its name hanging on a wooden plank from the porch that was a recent add-on. They walked around the outside, past a frosted-glass window on the road side of the bungalow, round to the patio at the back which had a barbecue and patio furniture under wraps. The garden was fenced off from the field in which it was built by a low picket fence and a gate. The field was flat, the hedges high at its perimeter.

'I must admit, it's a great site for a party,' said Carter. Willis was nodding, her eyes taking in the scene.

'According to statements, this was the field Ash and his

mum lived in.' Willis looked behind her at the sliding patio doors. 'This place has a few tales to tell.'

'Unless you're thinking of renting the bungalow, I'll thank you to get off my property.' A man approached from the lane wearing Wellingtons and a blue checked shirt, his hair curly, pale auburn, thin, balding on the top.

'Mr Truscott?'

'Yes?'

Willis showed her badge. 'We'd like to ask you a couple of questions, please.'

'What is it you want to know? I've had press around already today, they've been phoning for interviews. I told them this farm is not the same one as Douglas used to live on.'

'Good try, but it is, isn't it?' said Carter. 'And this is the bungalow he used to rent?'

Willis had moved to the far side of the patio and climbed on top of an upturned plant pot as she looked at the skyline for three hundred and sixty degrees.

'We have a different name now and we don't keep horses any more, or any animals since 2001. This is called Rose Cottage.'

'Even so, we have some questions to ask you about the people who lived in this bungalow in 2000.' Truscott started groaning and moving away. 'From a personal perspective, I think you have a great place here,' said Carter. 'The girlfriend is always looking for venues for our wedding day, when it comes around.'

'I do weddings in the field opposite the car park, you can pitch your own tent here or hire a tepee or a cabin. I'm building a pool this winter.'

'Mr Truscott, whose is that house I can see over to the left?' asked Willis.

'That's the farrier's place, he's called Saul. Lives on his own, been the farrier in this area as long as I can remember. Doesn't like company; he's moving away soon, retiring back home, he says.'

'Where's home?' asked Willis.

'Wales somewhere.'

'Has he lived there long?' she asked.

'Long time, he bought the place in the eighties.' Truscott turned back to talk to Carter. 'He asked me if I wanted to buy it, but it's no good to me without planning permission, and I'd never get it. Shame, you could have a big wedding party in those fields.'

'Are those his fields, on that side of the lane?'

'Yes, he has three more. A hundred and twenty acres or thereabouts. What do you want to talk to me about? I'm a busy man.'

'Can we go to your farm and talk? I'd like to get a look at the pool you're building.'

Willis avoided smiling at Carter's not so cunning ploy. They got back into the car and sat for a couple of minutes. Truscott took the shortcut back across the field, the way he'd come. Willis was looking through the statements, balancing the file on her lap.

'Did the farrier Saul feature in the original investigation?' asked Carter.

'He made a statement but he wasn't thought to be a threat. He'd no previous and no problems before.'

'Has he ever been married?'

'He lost his wife and daughter in a hit and run – drunken driver accident in North Wales, that was in eighty-one. He moved here shortly after. He's in his sixties now, I suppose being a blacksmith is really physical work.'

'Do you want to check him out?' asked Carter.

'While we're here, I think we should.'

Truscott was opening the gates when they got there. There was a big sign on them welcoming people and a list of rules concerning pets and children's behaviour.

'Park over there,' he said, pointing out a visitors' car park to their left, beside the main farmhouse, which was a simple grey stone building with over-fussy plaques and farm memorabilia and an old tractor for the children to play on. To the right was a building with 'Farm Shop' written on the door and a reception centre. Building work was going on beyond that, to the sound of jackhammers and drills. And a digger was scooping out the hole for the pool.

'Come inside. By next season folks can go into the reception centre and be greeted, get their chalet keys. Then this house will be for rent too.'

'Where will you go?'

'I haven't decided yet. Not far.'

'Do you live here at the moment?' asked Willis.

'Yes, me and the wife and one kid.'

Truscott took off his Wellingtons in the porch as they entered the farmhouse and moved into a parlour area with leaflets and a guest book.

'Mr Truscott, you mentioned the press have been in touch?'

'About Millie and Nicola, yes. They are talking about revenge. I told them it has nothing to do with me. I told them they must mean somewhere else.'

'We'd appreciate it if you wait to talk with others about this, as we are investigating it at the moment,' said Carter.

He held up his hands. 'No problem. You can count on my discretion.'

'That won't put them off for long. I'm surprised they haven't found a way in here?'

'Well, I have considered hiring some security but I don't see why I should need to, it was never anything to do with me. I lost my niece, I'll have them remember.' Carter nodded and smiled.

'Mr Truscott, can we show you some photos and see if you can tell us who's in them, please.' Willis handed them over one by one. They had come from Millie's flat.

'I know these,' he pointed out Gavin Heathcote, Yvonne and Cathy, 'and I know him, that's Stephen Perry.'

'When was the last time you saw any of these people?' asked Willis, taking out her notepad.

'I used to see Millie with her father Don sometimes, but not for a long time. People told me she was on the streets, working as a prostitute in Hackney.'

'Who told you that?' Carter asked.

'Must have been Gavin, he is the only one I see regularly. He still works in the area. I see his van about sometimes when I'm out and about. Gavin also said Don Stephens was looking to sell his business and move away from the area because Millie has become a nuisance, always wanting money.'

'Gavin seems to know a lot about Millie and her family?'

'I suppose so, he and Millie were close and I think him and Don have had words. Nothing serious, mind. Don't be telling him I'm stirring up trouble when there is none. Poor old Don, he's going to be devastated. As much as he's a hard man, he loved that girl. She was all he had left. It wasn't his fault how she turned out, it was Douglas's, he twisted that young girl. I saw it happen before my eyes, although there was nothing I could have done.'

'It seems like many people were affected by the things that went on here on your farm,' said Willis.

'Not to do with this farm, it was all about Douglas.' Truscott turned away and busied himself sorting out some leaflets on the side table.

'Before this incident, has anyone contacted you about anything to do with Heather's disappearance in the last year?'

'No. Is this what it's all about? Heather? Is that why Millie was killed? Doesn't make sense, why now?'

'We are not sure yet,' answered Carter, 'but we have evidence to suggest that the person who killed Millie might have been somehow affected by things that went on with Douglas and with his disciples. Things that went on here, in other words.'

'Jesus Christ, when will it ever end? If this gets out, people won't want to come here.'

'Rest assured, Mr Truscott, we are going to keep this low-key. We also don't want another witch hunt.'

'I regret ever letting Douglas and his girlfriend live there, but we can't turn back time, can we?' said Truscott, shaking his head mournfully.

'At the time, you had quite a good relationship with Douglas and his girlfriend, didn't you?' said Willis, looking up from her note-taking.

'They were good tenants. Douglas did me favours from time to time. I can't lie. It seemed to be ideal. But if only I'd seen through them.'

'And Nicola Stone was one of the reasons you let them rent the bungalow, wasn't she?' asked Willis. Truscott looked at her with a hint of embarrassment. As they were talking, a woman in her late twenties came to lean on the door, listening in. She was Asian and wearing a denim mini skirt with a plain T-shirt.

Truscott addressed her. 'Go and keep your eye on the workmen, and keep your nose out of my business.'

'Hello, excuse me, who are you?' asked Willis, taking a step between the young woman and Truscott.

'My wife,' Truscott answered for her. 'Melody.'

The woman nodded before she obediently moved away.

'Have you been married long?' asked Willis, after she had gone.

'Too long.' He shook his head. 'I picked her out from a catalogue. I should have sent her home before the year was up but things were going so well till then, I didn't bother. I regret it now. Should have traded her in for a new one, got my money back. But now I have a child.' He looked at Willis. 'I am only joking, don't write that down.' Willis carried on writing it word for word.

'What about the others who worked here? Cathy Dwyer and Stephen Perry?'

'Stephen didn't work for me, he was a lazy useless toff who lorded it over everyone, but Douglas kept him on because it amused him. Cathy Dwyer was a weird girl, looked like a Goth, always blacked-out eyes and I never saw her smile. The others, I have never seen them since the day I kicked them all out. Since the day they chose to say nothing to help my Heather.'

'You were close to Heather, weren't you?'

'I was; she was like my daughter.'

'But her dad just lived down the road, didn't he?'

'He wasn't much of a father. I could see a lot of potential in that girl. All he saw was trouble. That's why I said she was working when she wasn't. I thought she deserved a night away from him. He was a tyrant.'

'Do you think he hit her?'

'Think? I know he hit her. We all saw the marks on her. My sister should have protected her but she couldn't protect herself.'

'Did you ever report him?'

'No, but I should have.'

'Mr Truscott, when Heather disappeared on the Saturday night, where were you?'

'I've been through this a hundred times. There was a party going on at the bungalow, in the two fields by the main road that they rented from me. I saw Heather and Cathy earlier on in the evening, before the party started; I was checking the log store at the back of the bungalow. I knew there was a lot of people due to come that night, a big party was planned. When those parties went on, they always used a lot of my logs, so I was making sure they had enough.'

'That was generous of you,' said Carter.

'Five pound a bag and I provided fire pits, couldn't chance them setting fire to the grass.'

'Why did you allow them on your land at all?'

'It wasn't my land, Douglas rented it.'

'But you could have said no parties.'

'I didn't see the harm in it.'

'Who was at the bungalow at the time you saw Heather and Cathy?' asked Willis.

'Nicola, Yvonne, maybe Gavin. There was a lot going on with setting up the stage and organising the ticket collection.'

'What did Heather and Cathy say to you?'

'Nothing. Look, you know I lied for Heather, she asked me to. She said she wanted to go to the party and I felt sorry for her. I agreed to ask her parents if she could help me with the animals. I didn't know she intended running away.'

'Did you see her again after that?'

'I may have seen her later in the yard, I can't be sure. I had a couple of ciders that evening.'

'After Heather disappeared that night, did Douglas voice his opinion as to what might have happened?'

'No, not to me anyways.'

'When did you next see Douglas?'

'Later the next day. He wasn't looking his best; he had a big cut on his head, said he staggered into a tree at the party and then woke up in a field. I didn't imagine it was anything to do with Heather.'

'When was that you saw him?'

'I saw him about three in the afternoon. I asked him straight away if he'd seen Heather and he said he hadn't. I was beginning to worry by then. I told her parents I'd send her back by eleven that morning and I thought she had gone by herself until John called me to shout down the phone at me.'

'What happened in the months after Heather left?'

'We were waiting to hear from her, the family was, I mean.'

'What about Douglas and the others at the bungalow?'

'It all seemed to settle down for a while. Most of us felt happy for Heather, she had got away. We never once dreamt she was dead.'

'Did the parties continue?'

'No, they didn't. I was thinking Douglas was getting ready to move on. He seemed to spend more time away than ever and then after Christmas the foot and mouth epidemic started and a farm near us got affected and that was the end of all our animals. Douglas was a knackerman, he had his qualifications. He was allowed to slaughter animals and people were ringing day and night to look for people to do it. He took Gavin and Stephen with him and they went all over the place killing animals, helping with the burning afterwards.'

'Mr Truscott, do you recognise this man?' Willis showed him the photo of Tony Poulson.

'Never seen him before in my life.'

Willis gave him a card. 'Mr Truscott, can you please contact us straight away if anything comes to you about that time, or if you hear anything you think we should know.'

'We estimate he was killed in May 2000,' said Carter, pointing at the photo in Willis's hand. 'His body was buried at a farm Douglas used to visit.'

'Jesus! It's a wonder we all weren't murdered. He can't be coming out of prison, surely?'

'We would have to have new evidence to put him on trial,' said Carter. 'So if you think of anything, please ring.'

They got back into the car and watched Truscott return to berating the builders. His wife was standing nearby, a lonely figure watching them leave. They drove on down the lane towards the Phillipses' old house. Willis took out the plan of Hawthorn Farm. Whilst she unfolded it, Carter was going over something in his mind.

'What did you see from the plant pot?'

'That the farrier gets a good view of the rear of the bungalow.'

'What was his statement at the time?'

Willis pulled out the farrier's statement. 'He didn't go to

the party, never did. He said he made a check on his fields the next day to see if there was anything he should pick up, or chuck out. He had sometimes had people sleeping there in tents before. He said he usually just politely asked them to move once they'd woken up.'

'What time did he check his fields?' Carter asked.

'At eleven the next morning.'

'It couldn't have been in the farrier's field that Douglas woke up then. We'll go and talk to him again.'

They pulled up at the crossroads opposite a large cottage with an extension and a new-looking conservatory and a well-kept garden to the front, with a low stone wall running next to the road. Smoke rose from the chimney.

'This is where Heather Phillips lived at the time of her disappearance,' Willis said.

'What do you think of the parents' file?'

'I need to go and talk to them in person.'

'I agree.'

'Was this the kind of abuse that leads to killing a child? Or was it out-of-control, heavy-handed discipline?'

'It was definitely abuse.'

'Why didn't Davidson look into it more? He just calls it stern, calls it physical discipline. Why didn't he look into it more?'

'Because he set his sights on Douglas and had tunnel vision. He didn't want his team getting distracted by child abuse claims.'

'No matter what happened, we know the father showed little emotion at Douglas's trial. I can understand why they moved away,' said Willis. 'They would have been looking up this lane every day, for the rest of their lives, waiting for Heather to come walking down it and you'd never be allowed to forget. Maybe also wishing they'd treated her better. Let's talk to the farrier.'

They drove up a narrow lane and parked up at the top of a driveway. There was no sign of life when they knocked at the door.

'Saul,' Carter shouted through the letterbox and got no reply.

Back in the car, Willis looked up the address for the Phillipses. 'They live about forty minutes from here,' said Willis. 'We have time. They deserve to be kept up to date now, and they will be getting it from the press already.'

Chapter 35

There was only one photo of Heather on the wall above the fireplace. There was another photo of a man with two small boys dressed in Disney outfits.

'Are these your grandchildren, Mrs Phillips?' asked Willis.

'Yes, my son Oliver's children. That was a few years ago – they're big boys now.' Her voice was monotone.

'Do they live close to here?' asked Willis.

'Yes.'

'Do you see them often?'

'No,' John Phillips answered.

'I expect they call you for babysitting, school concerts?' said Carter. They had accepted Mrs Phillips' offer of tea and were sitting in her kitchen. 'I know I always rely on my mum to help with my little boy.'

'No, we don't get asked.'

'Oh, what a shame.'

'And this is Heather?' Willis went across to the dresser.

'Yes,' Mrs Phillips answered without looking at the photo. 'Taken just a few weeks before she disappeared.'

'Have you found her, is that why you're here?' John asked curtly, coldly. The atmosphere was very strained.

'We wanted to talk to you both about something that has happened recently, it's connected to Heather's case,' said Carter. 'Nicola Stone was murdered, as was Millie Stephens, who worked at the farm.'

'We heard it on the news,' said John. 'I can't say I was sorry. Why has no one ever been found guilty of Heather's murder? Why don't we have a body to bury?'

Mrs Phillips was getting upset, her head already shaking in small involuntary movements.

'When will you find her? When?' he asked.

'We will never stop looking for the truth,' said Carter. 'I know that it's upsetting to reopen these wounds but there is always hope when it comes back into the public eye.'

John Phillips' face was ashen and deep-set vertical lines aged him more than his seventy-nine years. 'Where has Nicola Stone been all this time, that's what I want to know?' he asked.

Willis answered, 'After she served her sentence she was given a new identity and was living in north London when she was found and killed.'

'Huh! It makes me sick – my tax going to keep that woman alive. Well, good luck to whoever did it. I feel nothing but hate towards that woman. She knew something about my daughter's disappearance. She knew and she never said. None of them did. And why was that woman allowed to have a life of anonymity? How is all that allowed when my wife and I will forever be known as the missing girl's parents and people will always whisper behind our backs. They still think one of us did it!'

'I am so sorry for everything you've been through,' said Carter, 'but the state has a duty to protect people. I under-stand how you feel though.'

John Phillips let out a snort of incredulity as he dismissed Carter's words with a grunt of disdain. 'As if it isn't bad enough, what happened to us, to lose our daughter and not even know what happened to her, and now she becomes somehow wrapped up in that evil woman's death?'

Carter was nodding earnestly. 'We have never stopped looking, and we won't.'

'I'll be long dead by then, for Christ's sake!'

Willis was startled by the noise that came from Eileen Phillips as she started sobbing.

'It's been confirmed today, I am not expected to make it to spring. I am dying and I would like to be buried with my daughter.'

John Phillips sighed, closed his eyes for a few seconds and then began talking, reluctantly pushing his thoughts and words out. 'Trevor told us a bunch of lies, everyone did. Eileen found the note while I was gone. God knows what was in Heather's mind. I had no idea from one day to the next – all her secrets. I didn't feel I knew her at all.' He rubbed his face with his hands and took deep breaths whilst he sat back in the chair. He looked drawn and ill. There was a pause, when both Carter and Willis questioned whether they should stop interviewing John Phillips because he looked ready to collapse, but Carter persisted.

'When you went looking for Heather at the farm the next day, what did you find?'

'A bunch of people lying about, still drunk, taking God knows what. Dossers! That's what they were,' he said angrily. 'All my brother-in-law cared about was making money and having his women on tap! He should never have let them in, I blame him for my daughter's disappearance.'

'Did you have a conversation with Douglas that day?'

John shook his head. 'Mr Phillips, did you see Saul the farrier the next day?' asked Carter.

'I don't know. Saul is a good man. Don't cast aspersions about him, he was quiet, lived alone, he did no harm. He bought Murphy from Trevor after Heather left and he looked after the old fella.'

'But you didn't see him when you went to look for Heather?' Carter persisted.

'No, I didn't.'

'Didn't you think that was odd?'

'I did, a little. There was still all the rubbish in the fields and there was livestock in there and normally Saul would have seen to that but maybe he was ill.' John Phillips looked down at his hands. 'I don't know, you're confusing me now.'

'Did you notice if his van was there?' Carter asked.

'I did not.'

'You must have thought you should ask him if he'd seen Heather?'

'Of course.'

'And did you?' Carter was pushing so hard.

'I was so caught up in rowing with Trevor about his lies that I didn't think to speak to Saul. I wanted Trevor to sort it – his fault – he should make amends.'

Carter paused before he asked, 'When you look back on your relationship with your daughter, Heather, what do you think about it?'

'Nothing,' answered John. 'I did my best. She was wilful and wild and if she didn't like the way she was treated she should have stuck up for herself.'

'Mrs Phillips, maybe this is the time to make sure everything said is said, and nothing is left forever unknown. Is there anything you want to tell us about the disappearance of Heather?'

Mrs Phillips stared at her husband before she turned to Carter and Willis. 'We've told you the truth, we loved our daughter, it wasn't us who did her any harm. Now get out.'

'Okay, I apologise for upsetting you.' Carter held up his hands. 'I just want to understand what happened here; so many people say she was beaten by you, John, is that true?'

'I took my belt to her when she deserved it. Running away, sneaking out, she came to a bad end, and that's what happens to girls like that: wilful and arrogant. I did my best with her.'

Willis shook her head. 'Poor Heather.'

That night Willis went home and lay on her bed in the house she shared with her friend Tina. Willis had the top bedroom, on her own on that landing. She had never consciously decorated her room; it didn't occur to her to transform it into anything other than a sleeping and working place. Tina sometimes had other ideas and a chair or a new cushion might appear. The things that Willis valued about the room and the house were its position away from others in the house, its London plane trees outside the window and the fact that she could run to the park in eight minutes and then her mind could go anywhere it liked. Willis sometimes needed that. She had grown up with pain and insecurity, she still had some healing left to do. Running, making time to face her past, helped that. Her phone beeped and she saw that it was a text from Tucker.

You up? Want to talk? x

Willis turned her phone face down and put it beside her bed. She had a busy morning ahead.

Chapter 36

Saturday 22 July 2000

The day of the party Cathy spent the afternoon working with Heather, helping the kids in the pony club, whilst they tried to make their bored ponies work a little harder. Now as they untacked the ponies, wiping them down and leaving them tied up in the fresh air to cool off as the last of the kids had gone home, Cathy was thinking about Heather. The more she studied her, the more she could finally see what all the fuss was about. Douglas had such an obsession with the young girl. Cathy noticed how Heather was changing daily. She remembered what that was like; it was a wonderfully bewildering time when the clitoris announced its existence. Cathy remembered squeezing her legs together really tight when she lay in bed and feeling the wonderful ache in her sex, the compulsion to touch herself, to touch other girls, to tickle their knickers or touch their breasts. The sticky fingers and the ache for something but you didn't know what.

Cathy looked at Heather as she groomed Murphy, wiping the saddle sweat from him and washing him down with the hose on his legs to cool him off. *She must have felt it as she sat on Murphy, felt the pressure like a vibrator, the tease of the touch and release*, thought Cathy. Heather had so much to learn about her own body. She could be a teacher for Heather, she was only three years older. Heather was so ready for it.

Heather looked across at her curiously, catching Cathy staring. Cathy blew her a kiss and she laughed, embarrassed.

Cathy understood how it would be a magnificent thing to give Heather to Douglas, to present her. Nicola couldn't give Heather to him, neither could Yvonne, Heather wasn't sure about them, but Cathy knew she could. Heather trusted her.

'Christ, I've had enough for one day. I need a beer,' said Cathy. 'What time is it, Heather?' Cathy came to sit next to her on the hay bales as she finished washing Murphy's legs.

'Nearly seven,' answered Heather, looking at her watch.

'Fuck – you'd better run, Heather, you're gonna be late!'

'No, it's okay. I'm allowed to stay and help my uncle with the animals tonight. My dad said I could.' She smiled, triumphant.

'What? Jesus, how come he agreed?'

'My exams are over, I've been trying hard to keep on his good side the last couple of weeks, so he said yes.'

'That's incredible. My exams are finished too. Come on, we'll have a celebration drink at the party tonight, it's going to be a great one. It's going to be the best we've ever had.'

Heather sat down on the bales and stretched out her legs as she tucked her hands under her thighs and looked sideways at Cathy, smiling.

'What is it, Heather? Tell me?' She shook Heather's arm and made her giggle.

'Nothing.'

'Go on, Heather, just do it, I can see you want to, fuck it!

You haven't heard from Ash, have you? Forget him, there'll be loads of boys at the party. Gavin's going, aren't you?' She shouted across as he was walking past.

Gavin put down his barrow and pumped his palms in the air. 'Saturday night, whoop whoop.'

'Gavin, come here.' Cathy beckoned them across. 'I was trying to persuade Heather to come. It's going to be sick, isn't it, Gav?'

Gavin grinned at Heather. 'It's going to get messy.'

Cathy giggled and Gavin went back to his chores.

'I can't come, I'm sorry. I am really helping my uncle tonight. He's worried about the livestock.'

'Okay, then I'll walk up the lane with you and we can just call in at the bungalow, see who's about?'

Heather agreed.

As they approached the bungalow Truscott came from the back of the building and Nicola appeared naked in one of the windows, grinning. Truscott pretended he hadn't seen her when he caught sight of the girls and Murphy.

'I'm just checking on the log store. Don't want to run out of logs,' he said, shuffling off. They watched him jog back towards the farm.

'Dirty old git,' observed Cathy. She knew Heather didn't like to say that about her uncle; coming to the farm to ride Murphy and hang about was a lifesaver for her, even though he had wandering hands.

Nicola came to the front door wearing just a dressing gown. 'Heather! How lovely to see you. Come in, leave Murphy tied up, he'll be fine. Come on, Heather, about time we had you round here for a drink.'

'I can't come in right now, thanks.' Heather smiled nervously. 'I might come by later.'

'Heather is going to be staying around tonight,' said Cathy. 'She has permission to stay over at the farmhouse and we're both celebrating finishing our exams.'

'Oh, Heather, I'm so pleased for you.' Nicola came out and gave her a hug and held on tightly to her. 'You don't want to sleep at the farmhouse, Truscott will be creeping into your bedroom. You come and stay here where you'll be safe. We'll look after you, won't we, Cathy?'

Cathy started giggling. 'Yeah, tonight's going to be incredible.'

Nicola smoothed Heather's hair and held her face in her hands. 'My beautiful Heather, we have loads of people coming. There's a DJ too, loads of people will be jamming. We're having a hog roast. I can find you something to wear, just come for an hour or two. Come in now and we'll do our nails and drink a few shots. You can borrow some of my clothes. I'll dress you. I can dress both of you!'

Cathy looked at Heather. 'Take Murphy back now and then come straight back.' Heather looked undecided.

'Look, I'm going back inside,' said Nicola, 'you come in when you're ready. I need to go for a shower. See you later, Heather.'

After Nicola had gone back inside, Cathy looked at Heather. 'Please, Heather, come back here and I promise it will be fine. You can sleep here in the bungalow and I'll look after you.'

Heather nodded. 'I'll think about it, Cathy, anyway, I can sleep in the field with Murphy. It's baking tonight, I'll be fine, I'll put down a rug, don't worry about me.'

'What's the big deal? A drink together, to *celebrate*!'

Heather laughed. 'I'll come for a while later on.'

Cathy went inside the bungalow. Nicola was in the bathroom, she had run a bath. She helped Cathy undress.

'You get in first,' said Nicola, and Douglas came into the bathroom and sat watching Nicola wash Cathy.

'Is Heather going to join us?' Douglas watched as Nicola squeezed a warm soapy sponge over Cathy's shoulders. Nicola was naked; her body was white as alabaster, her ginger hair and milky complexion didn't lend itself to tanning. Her nipples were pink, her breasts small, but heavy. Her shoulders were narrow and her waist tiny but her bottom was voluptuous. The bathroom was steamy hot.

'God, no, Heather is still a virgin,' answered Cathy.

'She can stay a virgin,' said Nicola, 'it's just a massage. Just a little feminine love-in, that's all. Heather is not going home tonight, Jimmy, isn't that good?'

'She says she'll sleep in the field with Murphy,' said Cathy. 'That's her idea of heaven, but she has no idea what heaven actually feels like.'

Douglas stood and opened a cupboard and pulled down a bottle of raspberry vodka. 'This is my own special brew and it's just for girls I'm in love with.'

Cathy giggled. Nicola leaned back and opened her mouth as Douglas poured the liquid into it. It dribbled over her chin and she leaned over Cathy and passed it into her mouth.

'Heather is going to have some night, then?' said Douglas.

Cathy smiled. 'Heather is going to have the most special night of her life.'

Heather looked back as she walked away with Murphy and saw Nicola watching her from the window. She looked at her watch; it was seven-thirty. She had a long evening ahead. She took Murphy back to the yard to get his supper and then she walked him up to the field where they would spend the evening. As they got into the field she felt for the letter in her pocket. She had instructions. Ash said she was to wait for him, he had got a car, and he was going to pick her up on Saul's side of the main road, two fields up from Saul's house and well away from the lane. She was to go there at twelve, when the party would be in full swing and there would be so many people at the party no one would notice her. Saul had not asked what was in the letter but, when she'd asked him, he'd promised to look after Murphy for her if she wasn't around for a while.

'Where are you going?' he'd asked, unfazed by what she said and the fact he knew she was going to run away.

'I don't know yet. I'm going with a friend, I'll be okay.'

'You call me if you're not. I'll look after Murphy until I see you again.'

Heather had reached up and kissed his cheek.

Heather watched the evening grow steadily dim as she sat on the grass listening to the party and the music. She sat so still that rabbits came out and looked at her. A badger scurried past. Murphy carried on chewing the grass. The party had a glow around it, there were sparks from the fire. There was laughter and the sounds of guitars warming up and there was a magic in the summer air that made Heather feel sick with excitement.

At ten o'clock the party was packed and the music was thumping under the summer skies. Murphy never strayed far. He wandered around near her, sometimes coming to nuzzle her as she whispered to him. She saw the people arrive, their cars parked up in the lane and down the main road around the approach to the lane, although most people had come out on foot. It was the warmest night so far, it was sweltering and Heather had forgotten to bring any water. She stood, her bottom numb from sitting, her throat dry, and she walked back across the field. Heather heard the phone ringing in Saul's cottage as she passed. Back at the farm the phone rang there also but nobody answered it.

As Heather entered the gate to the bungalow, Nicola put the phone down and came out of the front door. The party was all around. The lane was full of people.

'Heather, you came!' Nicola was happy to see her and took her by the hand, Cathy hugged her.

'Come with me!' Cathy led her by the hand into the bungalow and through to the sitting room. The patio doors were wide open, the party was everywhere. The rooms were full of people Heather didn't know. Cathy took her into the bathroom and opened the cupboard where Douglas kept the vodka. 'Here.' Cathy handed her a glass. 'I saved this for you, just in case you came, and here.' Cathy dipped her hand into a plastic container hidden in the cupboard and pulled out a wrapped bag of sugar lumps. 'You can be my little pony for the night, come on, pony, eat your sugar lump.'

Heather stared at it; she didn't like the look of it much. Cathy made a sad face. 'You have to drink it and take your sugar lump. Here, like a good little horsey.' She stretched out her hand flat on which sat the cube of sugar laced with LSD. Heather giggled nervously as she ate it off Cathy's palm.

Heather tasted the sweet vodka as Cathy led her out onto the patio where Gavin was smoking a spliff. He handed it to Heather who shook her head. He grinned at Cathy.

'Heather and I are going to party,' Cathy said. 'We are celebrating, aren't we, Heather? Drink up.' She poured more drink into Heather's tumbler. 'Come on, Heather, let's go and see who's here and have a dance, see if we can find you a good-looking boy.' She led her by the hand out to the field and Heather felt her heart start racing as she danced and drank. She looked at her watch and realised she couldn't focus on it. She put down her drink. 'I need some water,' she said, walking back towards the bungalow and feeling like the ground was moving beneath her feet. Gavin stopped her and spun her round and she fell down. Stephen hoisted her to her feet again and helped her to walk into the bungalow. She went into the kitchen and Nicola poured her a glass of water as she kept asking her how she was feeling.

'Are you flying yet? Can you see all the colours?'

Heather nodded, staring at Nicola's face and seeing every freckle on her face, every eyelash around her eyes. She reached up to touch her skin. Nicola started laughing.

'Heather!' Heather heard her name and turned and realised the whole world had become distorted. She couldn't make out the small man coming towards her until she realised it was her uncle. She started laughing and couldn't stop.

'What time is it, Uncle?'

'It's past your bedtime. It's nearly twelve.'

Heather looked at the room closing in on her, she looked at her hands that had grown large and kept waving in her face and she felt Nicola's arms around her waist and she tried hard to push her away.

'What's wrong with her?' Truscott was talking, and he looked so funny when he talked that Heather wanted to die laughing but inside her chest, her heart was thumping fast like a trapped moth at a bright window, and something was telling her to run. She ran past them and out onto the lane. It was dark now, the colours from the party were everywhere around her, swirling and moving and distorting beneath her feet as she climbed over the gate into Saul's field. She tried to run but her legs bent and wobbled and she fell, so she crawled. The field came alive with scampering animals as the grass tried to swallow her beneath her hands and bats whizzed past overhead. She heard people calling her name. She didn't dare move. Heather crouched like a baby rabbit in the grass. Her chest burned. The ground was pulsating and the grass was pushing up between her fingers and her knees as though she was sinking.

She couldn't see Murphy but she saw lights on the main road that seemed as far as the horizon now. She knew she had to get through to the other field to get there. The car headlights were shining like two bright eyes. Heather heard her name called again as someone came towards her, wading through the field like a giant. She propelled her body forward and she ran like a darting hare. She saw the grass turn black beneath her feet like the deepest ocean and fish rose to snap at her legs. She ran until she stopped dead. Murphy was standing with a man. The lights from the car were off now. There was just the night and the stars and as she walked towards him Murphy stared at her. The man beckoned her to him. Murphy opened his mouth and sighed the word, 'Run'.

Chapter 37

The next morning, Carter left before seven to miss traffic. He'd only been home for a few hours. Normally he wouldn't have bothered, he'd have been like Willis who often slept at her desk. He knew his partner Cabrina was feeling his absence though – the move to Barnet was proving to be a drain on them all. Cabrina spent her time working with her business partner Gemma, putting together their sports and fashion range. Now they had moved out to Barnet she also had a lot more travelling to do every day and she had to make sure she got home in time to pick up Archie from school. He wasn't settling in too well. He was missing his nursery friends and being disruptive again, the teachers said. He was having tests for behavioural problems and special needs.

He found Willis as he was parking up and walking into Fletcher House. She had come out to get some sunlight and was jogging on the spot.

'Did you get any sleep?' asked Carter.

'Yeah, an hour or two.'

Carter followed Willis back inside the building, which had no reception, just an entry pad that needed a code and then the choice of stairs or the lift.

Cathy Dwyer had agreed to see Willis and Carter in a meeting room at her apartment block at twelve. It was the standard long table, sparsely furnished kind of room with blue décor and a great view of the Thames. Carter and Willis had spent the morning preparing. Hector had compiled a report on the companies Dwyer owned or jointly owned with Perry.

Dwyer had power-dressed in a dark trouser suit and cream silk blouse. She wore a few simple items of jewellery, including an expensive watch. Only the dullness of her eyes gave her tiredness away, the rest was a mask of perfection and calm.

'Can I order you something to drink?' she asked.

'No, we're fine, thanks.' Willis had already poured them out some water.

Dwyer sat down. 'Firstly I need to apologise if I was a little startled by your arrival the other evening and therefore a little curt. I am not normally so, it's just you caught me at the end of an exhausting evening trying to close a deal.'

'It's understandable, it must have been a shock,' answered Carter, as he drew up a chair and sat opposite Dwyer and next to Willis, who had a small pile of documents on the table in front of her. 'Did you manage to close your deal?'

'I hope so, thank you.'

'And this is the company that you run with Stephen Perry?'

'I run it, mostly. Stephen and I have been working together for a few years.'

'Almost since you started out in timeshare?'

'Yes, that's right. You've been doing your research. We've set up a few companies in that time, not all of them successful, but on the whole, we've done okay.'

'You must have, your new venture is with some heavy-weights in the business, isn't it? The colleagues you were meeting two nights ago are big players?'

Dwyer didn't answer as she sighed and drummed her long black nails on the table.

Carter continued, 'It seems strange to us that you continue to be friends and business partners with Stephen Perry, in the light of what happened in the Douglas days. Is it because you still feel a special bond with the other disciples?'

A frown flashed across her forehead and then was gone. 'There's no bond, and I find the whole sensational use of the word "disciple" faintly ridiculous. The press invented it, Douglas never said it.'

'Douglas still calls you his disciples,' said Willis.

Cathy looked at her and smiled. 'Does he? How strange. I have a working relationship with Stephen and I have seen Gavin a few times over the years,' she replied. 'It's hardly a bond with my fellow disciples.'

'Did you see much of Millie as well?' asked Willis.

Dwyer shook her head. 'No, I didn't stay in touch with her. I had no idea how low she had sunk. I would have tried to help, if I'd have known.'

'Didn't Gavin or Stephen tell you?'

'They didn't mention it. Why would they?'

'Because they saw her sometimes, they both said they gave her money.'

'Well, I didn't.'

'What about Yvonne? Do you ever see her?' Willis continued her questioning.

'Absolutely not.'

'We have names now for some of the people we have

unearthed at Lambs Farm.' Willis stood up and went around the table to show her the photos of them. 'Simone Levin and Tony Poulson. Do you know these people?'

'No, I don't. I've never seen them before today.'

There was a pause as Willis grabbed a chair and brought it to sit at right angles to Cathy Dwyer, so close their knees were almost touching. Cathy Dwyer looked uncomfortably at Willis.

'Thing is, Cathy, we know that's not true. This man is Tony. You remember, Glasgow accent? Hitchhiker? There on the first barbecue of the season at the bungalow?'

'I don't know what you're talking about and I want a lawyer if you're going to accuse me of something so ridiculous.'

Willis sat back in her chair. Carter took out more photos from the envelope and pushed one across of the plastic chest from the grave. Willis picked it up and held it in front of Cathy Dwyer.

'Drugs were very much part of the time in the bungalow, weren't they? Douglas was the supplier for all the locals, there's no denying that, it was common knowledge. You all helped sell them, didn't you? Was this one of your stashes?'

'Sorry, this all means nothing to me.'

'Do you remember Ash?'

'I vaguely remember he was a boy at the farm.'

'Another disciple. In fact he was the last disciple; he got his tattoo the same day as you, after a night of significant suffering. But it wasn't your suffering and it wasn't any of the disciples', it was Tony's.'

'I don't know what you're talking about. I thought this was a meeting to talk about my safety?'

'It is, but first we have to have an idea who, from those

days, might be back now looking for revenge? Someone wanted us to discover the bodies at Lambs Farm; they led us there. Someone murdered Millie Stephens and Nicola Stone and wrote the name "Heather" on the wall above Nicola's body. They must have been there, with you, with the others, at that time?'

'So many people came and went there. It could be anybody. Well, let me clarify, any lunatic. If this is all about Heather then I really can't help. I don't know what happened to her. She was a sweet girl with problems at home.'

'We have your original statement here, from the time Heather went missing. Do you want me to read it?' Willis opened her file.

'If you want to, but it's a long time ago.'

'I can summarise,' said Willis. 'No comment. That's all you said, all the way through. It was your answer to every question.'

'That's because I knew nothing then and I still know nothing about Heather's disappearance.'

'Nicola Stone and Millie were killed,' said Carter. 'Whatever information they had may have passed on to this killer. Who knows what people say in their dying moments when they are under stress?'

'You're barking up the wrong tree. I didn't know then, and I don't know now. The killer won't be coming for me because I am innocent. All I did was get a stupid tattoo, which I had removed that first year, and I got stoned a lot and slept with dubious-looking people. I also happened to be in the same place as a schoolgirl who went missing.'

'Not just Heather. Rachel McKinney was held for five days, Darren Slater, a young lad from a farm in Essex, was last seen getting into Douglas's van. There is still so much to answer for,' said Willis. 'Your name is connected with Tony Poulson's. We believe you were there in the bungalow when he died.'

'I wasn't.'

Carter started to pack up the file. Willis stood and came back around the desk.

'The press will find out who you are soon,' said Carter.

'Thanks for the heads-up.' Cathy glared at Carter. 'Any other pearls of wisdom? Can I go now? I have a lunch engagement and some more businessmen to entertain. Right now, I am more concerned about not being killed financially than anything else.'

Chapter 38

It was 3.50 p.m. and Willis was twenty minutes into her second interview with Jimmy Douglas. He sat, resting his forearms on the table in front of him. Officer Kowalski stood outside the door. They were in an interview room as she had requested. She reminded him that he was still under caution.

'I am no longer allowed to work in the kitchen, why is that? Necessary precautions, I was told, what does that even mean?' he asked.

Willis stared back at him. 'It means that it isn't safe for you to be anywhere where the public may have access to you.'

He laughed sarcastically. 'What's the deal, Ebony?'

'Address me as Detective or Willis or both, but not by my Christian name. We are not friends. We found human remains at Lambs Farm and there are still graves to be analysed.' She put Simone Levin's photo on the table in front of him. 'Do you recognise this woman?'

He picked up the photo and looked closely at it for several minutes. 'I have never seen a woman who looked like that.'

She slid the photo of Tony Poulson across. 'What about

him?' She watched Douglas carefully. Now, with the information from Yvonne, she knew he couldn't deny having met him, at least.

'Never seen him before.'

'I think you have met him. Is there anything you wish to tell me now about the death of either Simone Levin or Tony Poulson, or their burial at Lambs Farm?'

'No.'

'So, you didn't pick Tony up when he was hitching, you didn't bring him back to the bungalow on Hawthorn Farm?'

'I don't recall it.'

'Really? Someone else does. Someone recalls it very well. They also remember you leaving in the early morning to go and bury Tony's body.'

'They must be lying because I don't know what you're talking about. Who is this person?'

She shook her head and showed him the photo of the plastic chest and the photo frame with the name 'Ash' carved into it. 'Do you recognise these things?'

'I know the name Ash, he was a lad who lived in the field with his mother. Maybe this is starting to make more sense then. Ash must have some knowledge of this Tony and the woman. Have you asked him?'

'Where would I find him?'

'He left to look after his mother. I always thought it was him who took Heather. They planned to run away together.'

'Did you see him at that time?'

'I can't remember. Probably. It was a big party, there were people I hadn't seen in ages. The whole area seemed to come together in my fields. Ash could have been there, definitely. He and Heather were always planning things together, plotting against the others. I told that to Davidson but he wouldn't listen to me.'

'Perhaps because Heather's blood was found in the frame of your van door.'

'Luckily the judge had the sense to throw that out, inadmissible evidence.'

Willis watched Douglas closely. He had a sparkle of amusement in his eyes. He was enjoying the way the interview was going so far. Willis regretted showing him the photo of the chest and the frame.

'We are starting searches on ten of the farms that you might know.'

Willis turned the list to face him and showed him a map, which included the whereabouts of each farm. Douglas picked it up and studied it. Willis had worked on the list with Chris; they had put all his ideas together and this was the result. Douglas put the list down and looked at her.

'You're going to be a long time digging up all those fields.'

'Not really,' she lied. 'We're going to get a large team on it. We are re-interviewing everyone from that time. You were famous for selling drugs at your parties. The plastic chests where you hid your stash of drugs were mentioned by several people in their statements after the party. You obviously weren't as careful as you thought you were. People are now adding to their statements.'

He flared up. 'This has nothing to do with me. The person who killed Nicola, this is their history, not mine, these are their crimes, their victims' bodies being dug up, their drugs stash, not mine. You find this killer and you will have answers to crimes from the past as well as the present. Who knows, you might even find Heather.'

'Then help us.'

'You want me to tell you the things I learnt about people back then? You want me to tell you who I think was capable then and now?'

'That's correct.'

'What do I get for that?'

'Your co-operation will be mentioned when you come up for release next year and your kitchen duties will be reinstated.'

'And assurances that nothing I say can incriminate me?'

'I can't give you that; you know I can't. If you tell me something that I can use against you, I will use it.'

'Your priority is always to put me on trial again.'

'Not right now. My priority at this moment is to stop this murderer. They are making it plain they know you. You must know them. I have a list of people that I would like to go through and photographs for you to look at.'

'Wait . . .' He held up his hand to pause the proceedings. 'First I feel we have to get to know one another better. I have to know whether I can trust you. I have to know who you are. You have to know who I am. I want to share some moments with you.'

Willis wasn't prepared for it. She was staring at him and getting no hint what was behind the frigid stare.

'I was sent to a children's home where I was abused,' said Douglas. 'What was it like for you?' he asked, and then Willis realised he knew her history. She knew straight away it was the prison officer Kowalski who had provided it. Anyone who wanted to could look up her history, the story of her mad mother, they could all know that about her, but they didn't know the half of it. No one did. She was reeling, but she was determined not to show it. She took a few seconds to answer.

'My life has nothing to do with you.'

'But my life has everything to do with you? You have the power to stop my release. You have the power to extend my sentence. You hold my life in your hands and you come here to ask for my help – well, I want something in return. I want empathy. I want humanity.' He stretched towards her across the table. 'I want a little fucking give and take here.' He sat back and smiled as he held up his hands by way of apology. 'Excuse my French. For every question I answer about someone, I want something back from you. All the things I read about you just skim the surface, don't they? The truth is something we never share with anyone, isn't it, Ebony? Well, you want me to tell you things I've never told anyone, you have to trade.'

Willis knew she couldn't walk away from this interview with nothing. She was confident she could take it so far and no further, and a part of her said, the more you hang on to these things in the past, the more power they have over you.

'Tell me, in the children's home,' Douglas began, 'did you find yourself dreading the nights? Did people come creeping into your bed and smother you to keep you quiet?'

'No, my times in the children's homes were happy. Tell me about Nicola.' Willis took out a selection of the photos from the farm and pointed to the one of Nicola with her Indian-print skirt on, where she was holding a bottle of beer and standing over the barbecue.

'Do you remember it being taken?'

'No, I remember the skirt, what was beneath it, her fat juicy rump that had such a lot of rebound to it.' His eyes came back to focus on Willis. 'Who would hate her that much, you mean? My lovely Nicola was not the prettiest of women, nor the smartest, but she could curl her tongue around me in ways that you wouldn't believe. Her tongue could reach so far into my anus she could tickle my pancreas with it.' He laughed. 'When I met her she was looking for someone to learn from.'

'Is that how you saw yourself, as a teacher?'

'No, not really, she didn't need a teacher; she needed a vehicle for her imagination to turn it into reality. She found me, I didn't find her.'

'Did you teach her that? To make her fantasies into realities?'

'Some of them. But Nicola had a secret side to her that she didn't show, even to me. I am not the monster you think I am. I was only ever the person who put food on the table for a bunch of waifs and strays who were yet to find their way in the world. They came for nurturing. They came to be fed when they'd been rejected elsewhere.'

'Drugs and sex, pain, isn't nurturing.'

'If that's what they wanted, needed in life to grow, then yes it is.'

'It was quite a unique set-up at the farm, wasn't it?'

'Yes, people came and went, took what they wanted from it, and left.'

'Not everyone had a good experience. Not everyone came out feeling loved, did they?'

'They did at the time. It's all right them coming back sixteen years later and saying, "I didn't really enjoy that fifth orgasm, I want to make a complaint!" Now it's my turn. Who was your best friend when you were in the home?'

'Micky.'

'A boy? That doesn't surprise me, you would have been an awkward-looking child. Even now your eyes are too large for your face, your mouth too wide, not pretty enough for the girls to fuss over. I was beautiful. I was raped every night until I learnt to get in their minds, learnt what made them tick.'

'Children are abused no matter what their rating on the prettiness scale. It's a terrible fact and I feel sad that happened to you. I count myself very lucky that the homes I stayed in were good homes and I did not suffer abuse.'

'No, because all your abuse went on at home, didn't it? Did your mother farm you out to her boyfriends? Dress you up *real pretty* and make you perform for them?'

'Tell me about Nicola's life at Hawthorn Farm.'

'Answer me.'

'My mother was mentally ill and she didn't understand boundaries.'

'Ha ha, very well-rehearsed. How many times have you gone through that in your head?' He mimicked her, '*She didn't understand boundaries ...*'

Willis stared at him. He wiped his face and tried not to smirk.

'I didn't control the people who lived in or worked at Hawthorn Farm; in many ways I was just as lost as them.'

'You were much older than them, more than ten years older. Some of them were teenagers. How can someone *end up* somewhere like Hawthorn Farm, when they're just a teenager? I believe you and Nicola did your best to draw them in.'

'Of course we did! It was one big party. It was great fun.' He sighed and sat smiling for a few seconds, then he leaned towards Willis, across the table, his forearms resting, his eyes sparkling. 'It was all Nicola. She was the instigator of everything.'

'The rape of Rachel McKinney?'

'She knew about it.'

'Who else was involved?'

'I am not telling you any more.'

'Why, because the other people involved are still living? The rest of your disciples?'

'No comment.'

'You were quite a team, weren't you, you and your disciples?'

'Whatever! You really want to believe we were like some kind of perfect storm, then go ahead.' Douglas looked at her for a few seconds, then laughed. 'I love the idea of it, grabbing at everyone as I thunder through – a human tornado. But, Ebony, you make a fundamental mistake here; you underestimate those who stood waiting, arms outstretched, willing the tornado to hit, begging me to choose them. They were all ready to explode on their own, burst into fire, self-combust. Don't credit me with so much power or hold over those innocent young lives; they had sought me out just as Nicola did, they had been looking for me and they just wanted a place to incubate, to flower, to blossom and that I gave them. I fed them and sheltered them and I worked to put food in their mouths but I didn't breed them, create them or change them. They came to me, remember . . .'

'Not always. They didn't always come to you. Rachel McKinney didn't come to you to blossom. Your sole aim was to destroy her.'

'She tried to destroy me! Look where I landed up. The truth is that some people mean less in life than others. Some people are just vehicles for others. I was a vehicle for Rachel McKinney.' He paused for a second, his expression blank, and then exploded in a squeal of laughter. 'Talk to me about Micky.'

'I never saw him again after they sent me back to live with my mother.'

'What is your last memory of him?'

'An outing to the beach, the hot sand, playing for hours, jumping the waves.'

'What did it feel like?'

'The best day of my life.'

'Because it was, wasn't it? It still is?'

'Yes.'

'The hot sand? Did you desire Micky?'

'We were only young. I loved him like a brother.'

'Except you had no idea what it was like to love someone like a brother because your mother was abusive to you?'

'Yes.'

'And she was the only family you knew?'

'I lived with foster parents at one time and I was very happy there. They taught me the value of belonging to a family. My mother took me away from them, I was forced to go back to her.'

'Bravo.' He started slow-clapping.

'I want to look at the others in the photo, tell me about them.'

'Millie was a sweet little girl. She was lost. She loved cuddles and getting drunk.'

'Nicola and Millie were very close, weren't they?'

'They were in the beginning. She put her faith in Nicola but Nicola grew bored of her. She was always trying to find favour with Nicola. There was some friction between them sometimes. Like mother and daughter.'

'Why do you think someone would have targeted Millie for revenge?'

'I don't know.'

'And what about Cathy Dwyer, what do you remember about her?'

'I hardly remember her at all. Gavin and I were close then. What's happened to him?'

'He has a roofing company.' Willis thought Douglas probably knew that and he was toying with her.

'I remember the most important thing about Gavin was that he loved killing. The foot and mouth was like Gavin's idea of heaven. It was lambing time and all night we had to stay and help the farmers. Lambing, sometimes thirty a day. It was unreal – birthing, pulling the baby lambs as they slid from their mother's uterus, clearing their throats to hear their first bleat. We shot the mothers but the lambs were too small for that, the bullet would pass straight through, too risky, so we bashed their brains in or we stunned them and slit their throats or we did both. We killed hundreds of animals, a thousand, easily, probably more. Birthing one second, killing the next, again and again, all day long. We had to dig a hole with the tractor and bucket. The hole was forty feet long. Some of them were only dazed when they were thrown on the pile, covered in petrol, burned in the pit. Most of the animals were healthy but the farmers couldn't move them, they couldn't get food for them, they couldn't be sold for meat. Over ten million animals were slaughtered in the UK, most of them healthy. There was no need, foot and mouth was around all my life in the country, no other place in the world slaughtered all these animals for nothing. We didn't even eat them. It was the biggest barbecue I will ever see.' He paused, looked up at Willis and for the first time she saw something like emotion in his eyes. Then it disappeared. 'Have you ever made the most exquisite meal from the lowly offal?' he asked. 'You know: livers, hearts, brains, balls, that kind of thing?'

Willis stared straight ahead. 'I can make them dance, sing like opera,' continued Douglas, smiling. 'I can create a masterpiece with a pair of kidneys, something out of this world, like you've never tasted.' Willis watched Douglas perform. His eyes were sludge-green, so dark they were almost black, with a floating brightness like a mirror on them, as he seemed to be reliving a taste in his mouth that made his lips wet, made his jaw slide, made his Adam's apple shift up and down his neck as he salivated. There was a pulse ticking in his bald head. 'Crispy salty skin, with enough fat to make it spit, is my favourite. To think, when I first started with my love of the countryside I was a knackerman and at the end, I went back to it.'

'Gavin Heathcote said you made a game of killing the animals, made a competition out of it?'

Douglas frowned, irritated that someone might have stolen his thunder. 'Gavin is an ignoramus, incapable of expressing feelings of any kind, just grunting answers. He just understands the basest of human needs. Tell me about your childhood. How did your mother make you dress? Did she say things like, "Nothing pretty for you, no dolls to play with, no ballet lessons"? I see by your face that wasn't it at all, I couldn't be more wrong. My dear, I am learning so much about your face, the minutest change means something momentous, doesn't it? Your eyes stare out at me and behind them is panic. You don't like remembering, do you? She dressed you as a whore, didn't she? She made you walk in front of her down the street, she put make-up on your face and she begged people to find her child attractive so that they might fuck her, fall for her, is that right? You know how it is, Ebony, you endure such a lot as a child and you take it and you take it and you bear the scars internally and the outside ones heal but they always leave a mark and they leave a memory, a switch which someone can flick and you're suddenly back there, in that room, in the hallway, or in that bed, and there is no way to escape and you tell your body to believe it's somewhere else and it does, just enough for you to survive, but it stores that hate, that terror, in its core. People like you and me survived for a reason, we are the damaged, the scarred, but we are the absorbers of pain and humiliation, degradation. We understand on a different level than all those around us.'

'Many people have survived abuse.'

'Yes, but how many of them go on to make a mark in life? People are one of these things: the wick, the gunpowder, the mountain to be moved or the seam of gold waiting to be found. Which are you, Ebony?'

'Tell me about Cathy Dwyer.' She showed him the photo of Cathy and Yvonne from the farm.

'I ask again, which are you?'

'The mountain.'

'That's where you're wrong. I hardly remember Cathy, I told you that.'

'She is now in business with Stephen Perry. I presume you know that?'

'Ah, Posh Boy.' Douglas thought for a few seconds and chuckled. 'I remember how he suffered under Nicola's control.' He mimicked a woman's voice, '"You will do as you're told. On your knees!" Nicola loved dominating him, teasing him, and he loved the humiliation of squashing his cock inside a chastity belt. She made him wear it for a week sometimes, teased him by masturbating in front of him, whipping him for getting an erection when she unlocked it.' He waited for a reaction from Willis but didn't get one.

'Ah,' he sighed, 'there was a lot of fun in the bungalow, a lot of laughter. People found themselves in there. You wouldn't understand that because you refuse to embrace who you are. You block out whole bits of your past instead of immersing yourself in them and seeing where they lead. You're afraid to feel anything.' His eyes went hard and accusing, tarmac with a green tint, and then softened to the colour of ferns in a dark wood.

'You haven't asked me about Yvonne?' He stared at her and she went to speak but he jumped in first. 'So, if it isn't one of my disciples killing the others, then it must be some-one from Heather's past, mustn't it? Her father is probably too old now but he could pay, couldn't he? I could pay in here to have someone killed. Money buys you anything in the prison system.'

'Like information on the detective interviewing you?'

'I didn't have to pay for that. What about Truscott? Did he ever lay his grubby hands on Heather? Probably. But would there be any reason to kill my disciples now? Probably not. Saul, the farrier, the curly-haired Welsh blacksmith, he was a voyeur. I saw him watching us. Saul loved Heather. He wanted her and he wasn't around the next day, after the party. He didn't come and find me to moan about the people in his field as usual. I didn't see him for two days. Where did he go? If someone thinks getting to my disciples is a way to get to me, they're wrong. You don't hurt me by killing my disciples. Help yourself! They mean nothing to me.' He shook his head then smiled. 'You sit across from me unmoved, you are a rare human being, Ebony. You cannot keep feelings suppressed for ever. You must have inherited some of the devil in your genes, you need to embrace it.' He laughed.

'You don't know me.'

'I know what you betray. I know what you most fear. You are afraid you're like your mother. You won't have children because of it. You're afraid you'll treat them like your mother treated you. That some primeval force inside you, the sharing of a monster's DNA, will come out and there's nothing you can do about it. You're still a frightened little child inside, aren't you? I can taste your fear in the air. I can smell it on your skin.'

She heard his voice rise and fall with the soft musicality of an Irish love poem but what he said was venomous.

'I know what you are scared of, that you're not normal . . . not able to aspire to the normal things that others want: love, for one. Well, you are right. Some of us will never walk the middle path. You are one of them. Be grateful.'

'I don't accept anything you say. I am not defined by who my mother was. I can and do care very deeply for several people in my life.'

'The more you silently scream, the more pain will come. Are you capable of truly caring for someone?'

Willis realised she was holding her breath as his voice softened and his eyes sparkled like sunshine on the deep ocean when the cloud clears and turns everything blue. He had the look of a smiling Buddha that hides a rattlesnake behind his back.

Chapter 39

Carter was in a meeting with Bowie.

'The killer led us to five graves at Lambs Farm, three of which contain human remains. So far we have exhumed the bodies of Simone Levin and Tony Poulson; the other grave is being exhumed now. There was also a plastic chest recovered from the site.'

'Okay. So, what we are sure about is that the person killing now was involved in both these deaths back then?'

'The killer knew about them; he led us to them but we don't know how much they were involved beyond knowing where they were buried. We did find a reference to one of the disciples though, the sixteen-year-old called Ash, in one of the graves. I'm not convinced he would have thrown that in himself. Douglas was pretty smart at the time. We know Douglas took in young, impressionable people and took them under his wing. They went to the farms with him and they lived in his house, but we don't know how much more they were involved. He was all about control. He could have planted evidence with just this in mind.'

'What actual connection is there to Douglas in those graves?'

'None at the moment.'

'Dan, that's where I'm coming unstuck when I have to go back and justify all this to those above me. They're questioning what this investigation is really about? I know the country would not forgive us if we uncover grave after grave and don't have evidence to charge anyone. Those bodies can wait there until someone somewhere comes up with enough evidence for us to start new proceedings and launch new investigations into the deaths. Maybe this investigation will lead to that, and I really hope so, but at the moment, I'm not able to give you authority to carry on with any more LiDAR searches without absolute proof this will lead to a conviction of the person who killed Nicola Stone and Millie Stephens.'

'Okay, got you, I'll keep working on it.'

'We need to find the person who is out there killing right now first, then we can go after Douglas. When we get cold hard facts and find some people who haven't been completely fucked up by what happened to them in the bungalow to come forward with absolute proof that puts Douglas in the frame for murdering someone, then we'll request funding and open a new inquiry against him.'

'Okay, I understand.'

'We know he's really smart. We know he uses people. We could have a hundred bodies dug up and still have no link to Douglas that we can be sure will hold up in court, because, you can bet anything, if it's not watertight, he *will* get off. This person wants us to make this all about Heather Phillips, but it ain't happening, Dan. This is not about her. Right here, right now, this is about someone killing people who should have been safe. Yes, Nicola Stone probably blabbed and caused a breach of security but she'd done her time and she was entitled to live out the rest of her life without being killed in her own home. Forget Heather, we're not playing by this killer's rules. Forget Heather and find him.'

'Yeah, I understand.' Carter was squirming in his seat. But he had to stay and listen as long as the boss wanted to talk.

'Leave the investigation into Heather Phillips to her team and the other victims from Lambs Farm to their missing persons teams around the UK. Of course, if you find her, the directive from the top will change overnight, and we'll be heroes.' He smiled.

'Yeah ... absolutely.' Carter smiled ruefully. 'Chris Maxwell, the profiler, is going to be mortified that we have to pull the plug. He and Willis have compiled a shortlist of farms that we *were* going to examine next. Maxwell believes Heather will be on one of those farms; he is certain.'

'Well,' Bowie said with a sigh, 'I have to toe the line. Stop looking all over the countryside, concentrate on what you've already found. We know Douglas didn't kill Nicola Stone or Millie Stephens, concentrate on finding out who did and hold a press conference tomorrow so we can make it clear what we're doing. Let's shut the press down from all their questions abut Douglas and his disciples. Keep questions afterwards to a minimum. Do not start entering into conversations with journalists. The term witch hunt is being bandied around.'

'Okay, I've got it.'

At just gone eight, Carter caught Willis coming in as he left Bowie's office.

'How was it?' She didn't reply straight away so Carter

jumped in with, 'Come on, I need a coffee, and you must be desperate for a break.'

Tina was in the kitchen when they got there. They took their drinks across to a table so they could speak privately.

'He knows about my mother,' said Willis as they sat down.

'Shit! How?'

'I suppose it is easy enough to research,' answered Willis, 'but I'm pretty sure he's a little too friendly with his guard. He was pretty pleased with himself when I talked to him on the way out. I'll raise my concerns with the governor. Douglas has always been good at wrapping people around his finger.'

'Did he say anything about Tony Poulson or Darren Slater?'

'Nothing, but he's worried.'

'What does he want?'

'He wants to trust, he says. But really he hopes to use me, to have me on his side. He's collecting information about me so that he can find out where we are in the investigation and maybe what his next move should be to get what he wants. I am sure he sees these new murders as an opportunity to clear his name, or at least he feels confident that he will still be getting out. Something about all this is making him smile. He sees a way of shifting all the blame onto someone else. Whoever is committing these murders is walking straight into Douglas's trap, except, when I showed him the list of farms next on our list to be looked at, he definitely studied them hard, long and hard. It changed his attitude. He wants us to find this killer now. He didn't like it when I showed him the farms Chris and I have on the shortlist.'

'Yeah, well, we'll have to put it on hold. We have to stop searching farms, someone at the top is taking offence at us going after Douglas. What does he say about his disciples?'

'He was dismissive of all of them.'

'Douglas didn't put chains on people's wrists to then watch them walk away. What does he say about Heather?'

'He is irritated one minute that he's defined by the disappearance of a fifteen-year-old girl, but then he praises her the next, as if she eluded him.'

'You feel you made progress?'

'I don't know, but I'm pretty sure Douglas will feel he did.'

'Sandford has left a message,' said Willis as she checked her phone. 'He's started excavating the last grave at Lambs Farm.'

'Okay, good. But if it's not her, we have to call it quits.' Willis looked up at the sound of a familiar voice. Tina was talking to someone and it was Tucker.

Willis frowned at Carter.

'It's been a long time since I came in here,' said Tucker. 'I thought I'd see if the coffee in the café was as bad as I remember.' He winked at Tina.

'Cheeky bugger. Go and sit down, I'll bring it over.' Tucker walked across to the others.

'Sorry,' Carter leaned across the table and whispered. 'I forgot to tell you Tucker was coming in. I was supposed to meet him upstairs an hour ago.' Carter looked apologetically at Tucker. 'Sorry, mate,' he said, 'I got caught up with the boss, had a bit of a roasting, Bowie fashion. I meant to call you.'

'Bowie style? More of a light toasting then?'

'I've been told to leave any more digging up the

countryside for a later date,' said Carter, as Tucker sat next to Willis, across from him. 'I've been told to concentrate on what we have. Seems like people at the top don't want this to become another Douglas witch hunt until we have absolute certainty of a conviction against him.'

Willis stirred two sugars into her tea. She'd only just started drinking the stuff but it was a step up from cola.

'We can open up investigations into Tony Poulson and Simone Levin though, can't we?' said Willis. 'Plus, the likelihood of there actually being many more bodies buried around the countryside is pretty high. We can't just walk away.'

'Not walking away, handing it over,' said Carter. 'Sorry, Eb, no more helicopters for a while. The bodies aren't going anywhere, Bowie was right about that. They can stay where they are, and be preserved in the ground, until we get the go-ahead to start looking for them. We can't be running around like headless chickens; we need to focus and find our killer.'

'What about Douglas, Eb? How's it going?' asked Tucker.

'It's going okay. He seems to have access to outside information that he shouldn't have, like my past history.'

'Really? I suppose that was always on the cards. It's out there, isn't it?' Tucker glanced across at her with a sympathetic shrug. 'You can handle it.'

She nodded. 'Yeah, I had to run with it.' She paused. 'Did you ever interview Yvonne Coombes in 2000?'

'Yes. Yvonne said nothing. I mean, she looked like a rabbit in the headlights the whole time.'

'We've had an account from her of the time Tony Poulson was murdered in the bungalow,' said Carter. 'She didn't see it but she saw the body the next morning and she was made to take some of the responsibility for his death.'

'She didn't mention all this before.'

'She was scared of reprisals, still is. Plus it looks like it's taken her years of chewing over what happened that night to realise she was probably raped, assaulted, by the others in a violent drug-fuelled orgy. She's been quiet about it all these years but she's scared now, scared that someone's coming for revenge on her and the others. We're moving her to a safe house and she's going to make a statement about Tony Poulson to us.'

Tucker raised an eyebrow. 'Really? If I was her I'd stay quiet.'

Carter nodded and sighed. 'I know, but we have to start somewhere and no one else is coming forward with any information we can use. I won't allow her to be charged. We won't have sufficient evidence. I'm not going to make her life worse. But we will move her to a safe place until this killer is caught.'

'What about Stephen Perry or Cathy Dwyer back in 2001?' Willis looked sideways at Tucker. 'Gavin Heathcote? Also did you look into what happened to Ash?'

'Yes, yes and yes. I was on the Heather Phillips missing persons investigation, so everything I did concentrated on that,' answered Tucker.

'What did you think of Cathy Dwyer at the time?' asked Carter. 'Willis and I have made her acquaintance.'

'How did it go with Cathy Dwyer?' asked Tucker.

'No comment,' Willis quipped. 'Same as the others, they're all sticking to their original stories. We need to find more witnesses, it must be possible to get people to open up after all this time.'

'What is she like now?' asked Tucker.

'She's bright, very capable, confident in business.

She doesn't appear to be the least bit fazed by her past,' answered Willis.

'Then she's naive,' said Tucker.

'Yep, we can agree on that,' said Carter. 'Perry and her seem to be very much part of one another's lives, business and personal. What do you remember about her?'

'What stands out in my mind about Cathy Dwyer from that time was that she was brimming over with arrogance and provocation. She was using sex like a weapon. She was smart but burning up inside with the desire to be someone else. She came from a pretty ordinary background, her parents were middle class, she just wanted to rebel and she did it in style. She was really fond of Douglas. They were very similar types.'

'Was she with Stephen Perry at that time?' asked Willis.

'Yes, but she was pretty much obsessed with and closest to Douglas. I remember when I interviewed her again after Douglas was charged with Heather's murder, she just kept talking about the sex she'd had with him and she said "no comment" to anything else. She just sat there smiling, they all did. They all had this idiotic arrogance that they could get away with anything, and they pretty much did. Perhaps she still does.'

'Cathy Dwyer has become quite a high-flying company director. She and Stephen Perry have these dubious business ventures. But she's much tougher than him.'

'I heard he was in prison in Spain for a while.'

'Yes, cocaine smuggling,' said Carter.

'Perry seems to have a harder job holding on to his money than Dwyer does,' said Willis. 'She has a few expensive properties around the place, Perry is struggling to re-mortgage his house at the moment.'

'And Gavin Heathcote?' asked Tucker.

'He has his own roofing company,' said Willis. 'He's a thug.'

'No change there then,' said Tucker. 'The lifestyle at the bungalow really suited him, it was all sex and drugs. He was never going to admit to anything although I did get the feeling he wasn't so much nasty as greedy and lacking in any feelings. I couldn't get him to say a bad word against Douglas or anyone else. I think, if you asked him now, he'd probably say he had the best time of his life in the bungalow, all the drugs and the parties and the sex.'

'One thing we did find out from Dwyer is that she is messing with some big underworld bosses,' said Willis. 'Hector's been looking into them. She's going into business with some crime bosses on a new venture which I'm sure Hector will find out all he can about.'

'Will you see Douglas again, Eb?' asked Tucker.

'If we have reason to, then I will. If we don't come up with any more evidence against him then I won't. I get the feeling I'm giving away too much at the moment and getting nothing back. I feel worried about the way things have gone with him. I feel I've walked into his trap.'

'No you haven't. It's not over yet,' said Carter. 'Tucker, you want to come up and meet Chris Maxwell? He's going to appreciate meeting someone from the original team.'

'Yes, I've got a few days hanging about, I'm at your disposal.'

'Where are you going after that?' asked Willis.

'I've got a couple of weeks' work in France, building a house. I'm looking forward to it. Should be fun.'

'Excuse me,' said Willis, a little abruptly, 'I need to get back to work.'

'Eb?' interrupted Carter. 'You coming for a quick bite to eat with me and Tucker? Cabrina will be there too, we finally got a babysitter.'

Willis looked at Tucker and then shook her head. 'Not tonight, thanks though.'

'Come and see her for ten minutes.'

'Of course.'

Cabrina came tottering along the pavement towards them.

'Eb? Oh my God, I have so missed you. Hug!'

Willis was laughing and shaking her head. It was a wonder to her how Cabrina managed not only to walk but jog towards her in heels that were basically stilts. Still, when they hugged, Cabrina, even in heels, came up only to Willis's shoulder.

'Please say you're coming with us for dinner and I don't have to try and look interested in what these blokes are saying?'

'I won't tonight, but I'll come and stay soon, when you have room.'

'You mean our lodger? He's just temporary. You're permanent.' Cabrina drew back from the hug and looked at Ebony. Reading the look on her face she squeezed her arms as she nodded and said, 'Understood, don't wait too long though, hon, promise? Archie misses you too.'

Yvonne Coombes set Bonny down in front of the television and sat at the kitchen table listening to her daughter answering the television in toddler-speak as she rolled one cigarette after the other. She picked up her phone every other minute and stared at the screen. She went to stand in the doorway and watch the little girl who was chuckling away at the screen, which made her feel calm. Bonny was all that mattered to her.

She went outside in the corridor and knocked at the door of the neighbour across and down the hall, the woman who looked after Bonny for her when she was at her cleaning job.

'Will you take Bonny for me for a few days, Beverly?'

'How long for?' Beverly was retired and had no grand-children of her own but she knew that Yvonne took advantage of that sometimes. However, it was hard for Beverly to say no when she adored Bonny.

'Just a few days, maybe a week. I'll ring you.'

The woman nodded but she looked worried. 'What's the matter?'

'Nothing. Just don't tell anyone you have Bonny. Don't tell anyone you saw me.'

Chapter 40

Willis got back upstairs to the inquiry team office before Tucker and Carter. Maxwell had taken over a corner of it for his maps and charts. She went to sit on the desk nearby. She had a lot of work to get through.

'Has Yvonne been moved?' asked Chris, as he saw her there.

'Not yet, but it's in hand,' said Willis.

Tucker and Carter walked into the office, Carter glancing at all Chris's things spread out and on the walls. 'You're getting cramped in here too, Chris,' he said. 'You and Willis need your own floor.'

Maxwell smiled at Willis. Tucker stepped forward to shake his hand and introduce himself.

'The pupil is overtaking the master,' Maxwell said. 'Ebony has a fantastic brain for all of it and a way of looking at the facts that make them much more three-dimensional.'

'I think I should stick to facts and figures and stay out of Douglas's way from now on,' said Willis.

'Did you learn anything new?' asked Maxwell.

'I've made notes,' she answered. 'I'm going to look through those tonight and listen to the tape and then I hope I'll be able to take it in better.'

Maxwell smiled encouragingly.

'Did Eb tell you about my meeting with the boss?' Carter asked him.

'I was just getting around to it when you walked in,' said Willis. 'I'll let you be the bringer of bad news.'

'I'm afraid we have been warned off more searches of farmland and told to concentrate on what we have already,' said Carter. 'Apparently people in power want us to leave any vendetta, or witch hunt, against Douglas, and concentrate on finding the killer of Millie Stephens and Nicola Stone. But don't worry, your work won't go to waste. And, if we find Heather, everything changes. She could be in that last grave on Lambs Farm.'

'What kind of people are they who want it to stop?' asked Maxwell, not really getting it.

'Knobs. Big ones who have even bigger ones above them, and if you look hard enough you'll probably come across a bit of corruption as well,' added Tucker. 'But I couldn't possibly comment on that.'

Maxwell was staring at him. There was an awkward silence and then Maxwell addressed Carter. 'So we are being reined back?'

'Yes, afraid so. At this moment in time,' said Carter, 'all this has to do with, is the person who killed in this last month. This has nothing to do with Douglas physically. How can it be, when he's inside? The killer has to be someone on the edge of the group at Hawthorn Farm, someone who was missed first time around. That's why we thought you might like to meet Tucker here. He was part of the original investigation. He met everyone back in 2000.'

'I'm happy to help in any way I can,' said Tucker, looking around at all Chris's work on the boards and spread out on the table. 'God knows I remember Davidson concentrated so hard on nailing Douglas he didn't even consider whether there was a possibility it was someone else. So we think this new killer could be someone I once interviewed?'

'When we know who the last body in the ground is, we can narrow down the possible suspects from Douglas's acquaintances,' said Willis, 'and all the people who came to the parties. We might have to hand it all over to the relevant investigation teams, but it doesn't mean we have to completely stop working on it. We find Heather in that grave, fingers crossed, then we're back on track.'

Maxwell turned away despondently.

'Chris, the dig has started now,' said Carter. 'Do you want to head down there in the morning?'

'Perhaps, thank you.'

Carter looked at his watch. 'Come on, Tucker, I can only spare a couple of hours, we're going to be on the night shift here. Eh? Don't tell me you're not hungry. Chris, what about you, fancy joining us for a pizza? You can meet the missus. My son isn't here, thank goodness.'

'You missed meeting Carter's crazy feral son,' said Willis to Maxwell. 'He's a lovable little devil.'

'He loves *you*, that's for sure.' Tucker smiled. 'It's all about how strong Ebony is, how fast you can run. He's all about being like Ebony when he grows up. You should be very proud of the relationship you have with him.'

'Nonsense, it's just that I put him in his place!' Willis said, embarrassed, and picked up some documents to read.

'Yeah, right. It's okay to admit you're fond of him, you know?' Tucker laughed.

Willis looked at Carter. 'I'm okay. I have a ton of work to get through; thanks for the invite though.'

'And I do too,' said Chris. 'Especially now I have to change my approach to this, but thanks for the offer. Nice to have met you, Tucker.'

'And you, I'm sure we'll meet again.' Tucker shook his hand extra hard. 'That's if you don't mind me hanging about?'

Chris winced from the handshake. 'Not at all.'

After Carter and Tucker left for dinner Willis went back up to tidy her desk and finish writing up her report. She was restless now. Chris hadn't done much for the last forty minutes. Willis had seen him standing despondently staring at his maps.

'Hey, Chris, what if I give you a lift home? I need to get out of here for half an hour.'

'Thank you. I would like that; I'm having a hard job concentrating.'

They drove to King's Cross and sat outside his building.

'See you tomorrow then,' Maxwell said, unclipping his belt. 'I would invite you up but it's a bit of a mess.'

'Don't worry, I need to get back. But, Chris, I don't want you to give up hope with this Douglas inquiry. When the time comes, we'll have done such a lot of groundwork – we'll be ready to fly with it.'

He nodded, but he looked crushed as she watched him walk away.

Willis was back at her desk when she got a call from Blackman.

'Zoe, what is it?'

'Yvonne Coombes? I went around there to pick her up and she's gone. Her, the baby, both gone.'

*

Chris Maxwell didn't stay long in his flat after Willis dropped him, as he was restless and needed to think things over. There were things he had hoped to do that weren't going to happen now and he had to get his head around what to do about it. But, at one in the morning, he headed back to his flat. It was in what was loosely termed luxury student accommodation. Slightly better than a small noisy room, he had a bigger less noisy room and a passable bathroom. There was an entry phone to get inside the building, free Wi-Fi and a small café bar in the basement. He liked it because people came and went all the time. Every week there were different faces in the hallway, mainly foreigners, coming to the UK for a week or two. Chris had been living there for a month now. He could afford the rent, just about. He only had himself to pay for now, he just had to get himself sorted, tie up the loose ends in his life.

He opened his flat door and slipped quickly inside and took his jacket off. He was sore and aching. He took out some codeine from a packet he had on the bar and swallowed two with a gulp of wine. He switched on his laptop and waited for it to charge up before he signed into Skype and called the number he wanted. He sat, glass in hand, and waited. On the third ring a woman's voice answered and then her face came into view. She was a woman in her eighties.

'Hello, Chris, how are you? We've been worried.'

'No need to worry, Gran. I'm fine, just getting on with work.'

'That's good.' She was staring at him intently. 'I'm glad you're okay. You look thin. Is that a bandage on your arm?'

'No, it isn't, don't worry about me. How's Mum doing?'

'I told her you would call tonight and she wants to talk to you.'

'Mum?' Chris smiled into the webcam and he saw his mother's face appear. She tried to speak but she started crying.

'Don't cry, Mum, please. I have things to do here but I'll be back soon.'

His gran's face came into view. 'Don't worry, Chris, you do what you have to do. It's been a long time on your mind. I can cope here for another couple of months.'

'Thank you, Gran.'

His mother irritably pushed his gran aside. 'My son,' she said accusingly. 'My beautiful Ash, come back to me.'

Chapter 41

Carter and Willis had been waiting at their desks all night for news of Yvonne but there was none. Now the phone company had called to say her mobile had been traced and had travelled in the back of a bin lorry on the weekly clean-up. It had now been crushed, along with anyone who might have been in there. Blackman had gone down to take a statement from the refuse collectors and the tip had been notified that everything must halt until they found out if Yvonne had been with her phone inside the lorry.

Hector had spent the night gathering and looking at what CCTV footage he could get hold of at that hour, and he now showed it to Willis and Carter at Willis's desk. Maxwell wasn't in yet.

'Here she is in her parka coat, crossing over Seven Sisters Road on her way into the underground station at Finsbury Park. She has her hood up but from your earlier identification of her, the shoes are the same, as is the bag she's carrying.'

'Where has she left Bonny?'

'We don't have the CCTV from outside her flat yet. We pick her up here first. She could have left her anywhere on these few roads.'

'She loves that child more than anything. She left her with a neighbour when she went for her cleaning job, so we should check that again,' said Willis. 'I don't understand why she ran? She must have been so scared. She must have thought that was a safer option than being put into one of our safe houses. We need to get hold of her phone record if we don't find her in the next few hours.'

'The refuse collection route is along York Way, past Caledonian Road station. She could have got off there, I'm just waiting to look at that.'

'All we can do is keep looking for her and send someone back to talk to all the neighbours again.'

'Where's Maxwell?' asked Carter, looking over at the empty desk in the corner of the office. 'We should hear from Sandford soon. I want to hold off the press conference until we know who it is in the last grave at Lambs Farm. I thought Chris would want to be here for that?'

'Sandford's on the line,' said Willis. 'DNA results are in, it's Darren Slater, the missing lad from Essex.'

'Jesus, one more piece in the Douglas puzzle. Does Sandford say there's anything else in the grave?'

'He says there is nothing in there that he can see so far, but the soil is being lifted and sifted. I'll get in touch with the team investigating his disappearance and tell them the good news. At least his family will have answers.'

Carter went across to talk to Hector who had set up a desk in the inquiry team office, along with everyone else.

'Did you find out what business Dwyer has with the men we saw her with in the Singing Canary bar?' asked Carter.

'Plenty,' Hector answered. 'The company she and Perry own has formed a new one with the owner of the Singing

Canary, Alex Ramirez. The new company is called "GET Enterprises". They are rumoured to have taken up leases on six restaurants that will open from summer next year. Sounds interesting, doesn't it? Even more so when you hear their theme for it and what it's going to be called. How does "Skin on Bone" grab you?'

'It doesn't really.'

'It may do, when you read the blurb,' continued Hector. 'It's billed as an "all new eating experience" and a themed restaurant chain with an ex-convict as its chef.'

'No way. How has he managed to set this up from prison?'

Willis walked over to join in the conversation. 'I can tell you how. I've looked into all the work parties he's been on and checked with the restaurants' guest lists. He's been meeting Dwyer and Perry at these places. We know he has phones in there. We know he does favours for other prisoners in return for phones, SIM cards, letters out. If these restaurants are for Douglas then it would mean they must have needed big money to put this together.'

'How much are we talking?' asked Carter. 'What's the cost to buy a lease and refurb, to get everything in place, per restaurant?'

'In the locations they've chosen, anything from half a million, minimum; in some cases in excess of two million if it's central London, and we know two of them are.'

'No wonder Stephen Perry is broke, they must have had to put money in themselves to get this deal,' said Carter.

'Is anyone linking them to Douglas?' asked Willis. 'Have the press started asking questions?'

'Not yet,' answered Hector.

'So they've secured backers willing to put the money in

and wait at least a year before they begin to see profits,'
said Carter. 'Probably two years?'

'This is a massive deal for relatively small players like
Perry and Dwyer,' Hector agreed.

'And if it goes wrong?' said Willis. 'And if it's financed
by crime bosses? There will be nowhere to hide.'

'It seems like Cathy Dwyer is definitely the mover and
shaker in this partnership,' said Hector. 'I think she's a very
busy woman right now. Juggling lots of balls in the air.'

'If the criminal underworld are laundering their money
through Douglas's restaurants then they will not want
anything standing in their way,' said Willis.

'We bring in one, we watch the other one. Bring Perry in.
Phone Maxwell and see where he is,' said Carter.

'I'm here,' Maxwell said as he walked in. 'Sorry, I
overslept.'

'Lucky you. We have news about Lambs Farm – Willis
will fill you in while I go and chat things through with our
press officer, Janice,' said Carter as he left the office and
went into his own for some privacy.

'You okay?' Willis asked Maxwell. 'You look like you've
had less sleep than me. Do you want to grab a coffee?'

'No, you're very kind, but I'm okay, really. Please tell me
about what Sandford has found.'

An hour later, at eleven, Carter was waiting to address the
press-packed room with Willis sitting at his side and Bowie
watching from the sidelines. Maxwell was listening from
the corridor outside. The room was packed full of waiting
journalists and press photographers. Janice stood at the
back. They had discussed the things that they needed to
get across. The police were under attack for messing up the

Heather Phillips investigation first time around. Heather fever had gripped the nation again but now her name was added to those of the others and everything, from lack of sympathy for prostitutes to Darren's gay lifestyle, were firing people up to accuse the police of failing to protect the vulnerable, the people who didn't quite fit into society.

Bowie had asked him to draw a line under the Douglas links now. Darren Slater's team would be taking over. If there was any way they could find new evidence to link to Douglas they would, but there appeared to be nothing in the grave and the only link so far, in any of the graves, was to Ash.

As the journalists finished settling into their spots, Carter stood ready to speak.

'We have concluded the digging out at Lambs Farm, and we have uncovered the remains of three people: Simone Levin, Tony Poulson and, this morning, Darren Slater. Those unexplained deaths, along with the murders of Millie Stephens and Nicola Stone, are presenting us with a huge challenge which we are meeting, but please be patient, this was never going to be easy.' He took a drink of water and glanced down at Willis. She had notes in front of her that Janice had made into bullet-points for Carter, in case he got lost. She pointed a finger to the next paragraph for him.

'With reference to the murder of Nicola Stone,' he said, 'the Independent Police Complaints Commission are going to be investigating the circumstances around any leaking of information about her whereabouts. We are appealing for anyone who knew Millie, known locally as Felicity, and anyone who has information about the day, the nineteenth of September, when she was last seen, to come forward. We don't believe Millie would have gone into Lee Valley Park with someone she didn't know. We also don't believe that Nicola Stone would have opened the door to someone she didn't know or trust in some way. Therefore, we believe the deaths might have direct links to the past and to the women's time with Jimmy Douglas when he rented the bungalow at Hawthorn Farm.' A hush descended on the room. 'Jimmy Douglas has had links to these people; we know that, but not their deaths, necessarily. The investigations into these deaths are ongoing and involves the co-operation of several forces across the country and relevant teams who have been dealing with the individual missing persons investigations.'

'Is Douglas going to get away with it again?' asked someone from the back of the room as the questions started coming. 'Darren Slater was seen getting into his van,' the man continued. 'Wasn't Douglas questioned about his disappearance by the police?'

'Yes, I believe so,' answered Carter. 'He was questioned but no evidence or DNA linking him to Darren was found at the time.'

'At the time, yes, but what about now? Can you re-test?' asked another journalist.

'Unfortunately the van that Douglas owned was sold off at auction when the case was closed. As I said, we need all the public's help on this we can get. We are in the early stages of this new investigation but we are confident it will lead to the conviction of whoever is responsible for these murders.'

'What about Yvonne Coombes? Where is she, do you know?'

'I cannot comment on that at present.'

'Is someone picking off the disciples? Is this some kind of revenge because they never told the truth back in 2000?'

'Perhaps . . .' Carter stopped and almost glanced Bowie's way, but caught himself before he did. 'Some of the disciples still refuse to tell the truth about what happened to Heather Phillips or any of the others who disappeared after having some connection to Jimmy Douglas. The chain of silence that binds some of Douglas's disciples still exists. If they told the truth, we would be further ahead than we are.' There was a commotion in the room.

'Are you saying you believe Cathy Dwyer, Stephen Perry and Gavin Heathcote are still covering for Douglas?' a journalist asked from the back. Janice walked forwards along the edge of the room with the intent of bringing the conference to an end.

'That's right,' answered Carter, 'we need the public to come forward now. We want people to tell the truth about the parties they went to at Douglas's bungalow on Hawthorn Farm. After sixteen years we finally need people to stand up and tell the truth.' Janice hovered at the edge of the stage but one glance from Willis told her to stay there.

The camera flashes went berserk.

'Do you think that Jimmy Douglas's release from prison next year will be reconsidered?'

'Let's say, it's in the balance.' Carter ended the conference. Bowie stormed out ahead of him and waited in the corridor. When Carter caught up with him he took him out of earshot.

'What the fuck were you thinking? Why didn't you clear this with me before you shot your mouth off in front of the world's press? It's me that has to calm the commissioner down. For fuck's sake, Dan! You'd better be absolutely sure of everything you said in there because I am now just as culpable as you. They are going to haul me over the coals for this. I'm no stranger to getting my arse scorched but this had better be worth it.'

'We think it is. Yvonne Coombes has gone missing. She may have been killed, she may just be alive. Perhaps they have plans to keep her from testifying or even make her take the fall. Perry and Dwyer are putting together some new deal and I saw them with the Marbella Mafia. This could lead straight back to Douglas. This could be all about clearing a path for Douglas when he gets out. I want to put pressure on them, force them out in the open. I want to make them feel vulnerable.'

Chapter 42

Cathy Dwyer finished watching the press conference live on the TV and stood on the balcony of her apartment, resting her elbows on the tops of the green-tinted Perspex panels.

'What the fuck is going on?' she breathed into the phone as she dragged on her cigarette and turned her face from the biting wind. 'Did you see the news?'

'I saw it. What can they do?' Perry answered. 'The police are bluffing. Douglas will make it right. But we need to stop talking with one another.'

'You think he can fix everything and he can't. I'm out here alone, facing the Mafia, and they will have seen that report and so will all their lawyers and money men and I'm sure they're going to want these problems sorted. There's no plan B here, Stephen.'

'Maybe, but Douglas has a touch of the Midas about him. They won't risk it, they'll do what they have to do, put pressure on where it's best put. They need him and he needs us. This is their thing. They will work it out, don't worry. Have you talked with Gavin?'

'Gavin only answers to you or Douglas, it doesn't matter what I say to him, he just grunts at me and carries on with previous orders. He's made a mess of things. We need him to disappear for a while.'

'He's all right, he'll stay in the background.'

'It cannot fail,' Dwyer said.

'It won't.'

'I hope not. We should have just stuck to what we know, Stephen, don't you think?'

'You okay?' Perry asked.

'I feel like a very small piranha in a big pool of great whites. We might think we're the big dogs but we have nothing on these guys. It's okay for you, you sit at home and toast your feet by the wood burner and I have to face these guys day in, day out, on site. They are keeping me on a short leash. I feel I'm on my own with this. They're frightened we're going to run with their money and now they will have heard this on the news. They know who we are.'

'That was always part of the attraction for them, we are the disciples. We will be part of the entertainment value. Just keep selling it to them. Set up a meet with them for later today and I'll be there by your side, as always. You're never on your own. I'm just here at the end of the phone. This is all going to be worth it and then you and I are headed for some beach somewhere; how does that sound?'

Cathy Dwyer calmed, as she always did when she spoke with Stephen. She smiled, drew on her cigarette and stared at the Thames and the riverboats. The seagulls were gathering inland ahead of the approaching storms and the air was charged with thunder and lightning.

Cathy went back inside her apartment and closed the sliding door. The apartment was every shade of pale wood, white walls and beige leather settees, blonde on blonde. She went into the bathroom and looked into the mirror.

She hadn't changed, none of them had changed. Stephen was still the same lost little boy inside who preferred to give his life to others to dictate and Cathy could lead him anywhere. He was driven by his need to keep looking for himself through the eyes of others.

She looked at herself in the mirror and saw the same person she'd always seen since she met Douglas; before that day she hadn't existed. Before that day she was just boring Cathy with a boring life. Douglas pushed her right to the edge and held her there dangling. He made her look at a world that was so close to death and so exhilarating that nothing could ever feel the same; he took her breath away.

She picked up her keys and opened the door of the apartment and walked straight into a fist in her sternum, knocking her backwards. She was picked up by her arm as she scrabbled to stand and walk and was half-carried, half-dragged towards the sliding balcony doors.

'Wait, wait, what are you doing? Get out!'

No one answered. She looked at the man she'd never seen before, who was dark-skinned and wearing a black tracksuit. She caught a glimpse of another man standing by the front door; she knew him. She heard the balcony doors open and the icy wind hit her as she felt her body lifted in the air as if she weighed nothing and then she felt the grip on her wrists. She was dangling in mid-air. She looked up at the man holding her.

'What do you want? I can give it. We can talk.'

He grinned at her as the other man came to look down at her over the balcony. It was the owner of Singing Canary, Alex Ramirez.

'We just wanted to have a little chat, if you have time?'

'What do you want? This is no way to treat me. I am a business partner.'

'This is the way we do business. My backers are getting nervous, which makes me nervous, and when I get nervous I drop things.' The man holding her let go of one arm and she swung in mid-air, buffeted by the gust of wind.

She looked up at the man holding her. 'I know how to sort this.'

Douglas had watched the press conference from the recreation room and went back to his cell, escorted by Kowalski, who stepped inside with him.

'Are you worried, Jimmy?'

Douglas stared at the spot on the wall, wishing the guard would go, but he breathed in slowly, held it, released slowly and tried to keep his mind clear. He was beyond angry. He was about to rip someone's face off but he couldn't show it. He felt betrayed and he felt under threat. He turned around and smiled.

'I have faith in my friends. Can I get a little "me" time this lunchtime?'

'Of course, go to the chapel, I'll make sure it's empty for you. You won't be disturbed. Give me half an hour to fix it, one o'clock okay?'

Douglas turned back to the stain. 'Good, thank you, and another request. I believe I have some information for Detective Sergeant Willis. I need to see her as soon as possible.'

Willis and Blackman went to bring Perry in for questioning. On the way Blackman wanted to get something off her chest.

'It didn't work out with me and Tucker. It never got off the ground. I'm just not his type.'

'I'm sorry.'

'No, don't be silly … it was a mistake anyway, from start to finish. I should have asked you first. I mean, asked if you were properly finished.'

'I would have said yes because we are.'

'But I would have seen by your face that you were lying. Tucker is in love with you, in his own quiet, non-assuming way, he's burning up, Eb. I think you underestimate what an exciting guy he really is. You just need to make him feel relaxed and …'

'You sound like you found hidden depths in him that I could never find.' Willis looked across at Blackman, wide-eyed.

'That's because he doesn't fancy me. He gets withdrawn around you. Just make him feel like you are willing to take the risk. It's a big risk for him too, you know. He's loved and lost. He has a lot to lose.'

They parked up across from Perry's house and went up to the entrance together. Willis pressed the intercom and showed her badge to Vanessa Perry via the security camera.

'I would prefer it if you didn't come here, as I said last time,' said Perry as he opened the door to them.

'Exactly, we've come to give you a lift into the station, Mr Perry,' said Willis. 'We'd like to ask you some questions about the death of Tony Poulson.'

'I need to call my solicitor.'

'You can do that on the way.'

Chapter 43

When Willis got back from locking up Perry, she found Tucker working with Maxwell on possible locations for Yvonne Coombes in the inquiry team office, which was crammed with detectives assigned to the case.

'How did Perry react?' asked Carter.

'He wasn't pleased, I think he would have preferred some notice,' she smiled. 'We'll leave him a few hours.'

'I've just heard,' announced Blackman. 'Someone went round to Yvonne's neighbours, and you were right, Eb, Bonny is there with the neighbour and we are happy that it's safe for her to be left there for now. This woman is used to looking after her. Good news about the bin lorry as well, Yvonne can't have been in it, it's been verified that the weight of the lorry load wasn't enough for there to have been someone in there. Now we just need to find her alive.'

'So where is she?' Willis looked towards Maxwell, who seemed to be happier now his maps and charts were spreading even further over the tables. 'Wherever she is, she's without her phone and her kid and she must be desperate.'

'No one would nick the phone and just chuck it in the bin,' said Carter. 'She's in trouble. Have we tried looking where she usually scores? She could have gone back to the streets on Finsbury Park?'

'I don't think so,' said Blackman. 'We have officers actively looking for her.'

Hector stood up from his seat and called them over to look at his screen. 'This is what our analysts have found from looking at the CCTV,' he said. 'This is twelve last night. There's someone following Yvonne. It's a man wearing a big coat, so it's impossible to see his build, but definitely between five eight and five ten. We'll keep looking.'

'It could be Gavin,' said Willis as she stared at the frozen image on the screen. 'But it's too hard to call.'

'Put him under surveillance straight away,' said Carter.

Maxwell had stopped working to turn and listen to the conversation.

'If he took her then he would have brought her to somewhere Douglas and him used to go,' he said. 'To the lockup, the second location, where Rachel McKinney must have been taken.'

'Find me it, Chris,' said Carter. 'Keep looking for it; and Tucker, give him a hand.'

'Will do.'

'Douglas wants to see me today,' said Willis after taking a call.

'Don't go,' said Maxwell, and the office fell silent as his voice came out plaintive, pleading.

'Why not?' asked Tucker.

'You can't trust him,' said Maxwell. 'He will have seen the press conference. Just leave him to stew in it. I mean ... it's not worth the risk, one more murder is nothing to him if he senses he's not going to get out of there.'

'It's okay, Chris, I'll be okay. How are you getting on with the possible second sites?'

'Yes, good.' He turned away, embarrassed, and Tucker nodded reassuringly at Willis in an 'I've got this' way. Willis smiled back gratefully.

'We are looking at all the notes again, listening to the dictation notes too. I am missing something, I'm sure,' said Maxwell. 'I wish we could talk to Rachel McKinney? She is the only survivor of the second site, she must have been there for all the days she was missing?'

'She's refused to speak,' said Willis. 'She's got her life back, she doesn't want us taking it away again.'

Yvonne Coombes opened her eyes and reached up to touch her throbbing head. Her hands were tied at the wrist and she rubbed the edge of her thumbs along a sticky-feeling cut. She remembered the first blow of the hammer, turning her head as it came towards her, she didn't remember the second. Her left eye would not open; it was stuck together with blood. She tried rubbing it with the heel of her hand and gradually worked it free. She was hoping that, with both eyes open, she might be able to see something, but she couldn't. She leaned back and her shoulders touched the bars of a cage. She moved her hands to one side and stretched out her fingers and felt plastic beneath her bottom. She reached forwards, stretched out her hands and felt the bars all around her and above.

Her eyes could still see only darkness or she was blind from the hammer attack. She tried listening very hard and heard a scratching on the roof above her, a scratching on metal. Was she in a lorry? She could hear nothing else, no one talking, no sound of traffic, just the scratching on the roof. She smelt a musty scent of old meat, the scent of something long since dead in a airless place.

Chapter 44

Willis drove to Wandsworth Prison and checked in with Officer Kowalski. She watched him look through her bag before she said, 'Do you like your job?'

'I do, as a matter of fact. I get on pretty well with the prisoners and we do a good job here; it's rewarding.'

'A lot of stuff gets into prisons that shouldn't, doesn't it?'

'Yes, I'm afraid so, but we try and keep it to a minimum. It's the drugs we are most concerned about.'

'We know that Douglas has access to phones in here.'

'I can't comment on that.' He finished examining her backpack.

'I hope you search Douglas's cell as thoroughly as you searched my bag?'

'Of course.' He was watching her, trying to guess what she was going to say next.

'That's reassuring.' She nodded slowly, thoughtfully. 'We know that when he was on work parties, accompanied by you, he was left to his own devices and during that time he met his disciples. Maybe he wasn't even left to his own devices, maybe you helped organise it?' He stared at her with loathing. 'Is your job going to be paying for your mortgage when you and your fiancée get married?' He didn't reply. 'Jimmy Douglas is the master of getting into people's heads and finding out their desires, what did he promise you?' asked Willis.

'I don't know what you're talking about. Did you want to see Mr Douglas today?'

'Did he promise you a cut in something he was planning when he got out?'

'Of course not. You have something on me then make a formal complaint.'

Willis nodded. 'I will. I hope you understand the gravity of the evidence stacking up against you? I hope it's been worth it. He's played you for a fool.'

Willis sat opposite Douglas in the interview room and looked him over. He seemed stressed. His face was saggy, his eyes puffy, the colour of shifting mud. She couldn't tell what he was thinking.

'What did you want to see me about?' Willis asked as she laid out her notebook and tape recorder on the desk. She saw Douglas's eyes linger for two seconds on the pencil she had brought with her and picked it up in her hands.

'I saw you at the press conference. You were sitting next to Detective Chief Inspector Dan Carter. I saw it and you know what I thought? I thought that nice girl has set her heart on betraying me and that made me sad, after all the things we've shared.'

'I have told you a lot about my life, but got nothing relevant in return. I have found out that three of your disciples are in business together. Cathy Dwyer is in charge, Stephen Perry is her emotional crutch and Gavin Heathcote is the strong arm. We have traced all your visits to work placements and discovered that you met the new associates that

Cathy and Stephen are in business with; you met them a year ago. You have phones, we know that. You have been communicating all this time with your disciples. We have all we need to keep you in here.'

'Are you threatening me?'

'No, just stating facts. You should have come out quietly and stayed low but you wanted to come out to a fanfare, didn't you? You wanted people to know that you had come out of prison bigger and better than ever? The world is different outside now. You think you can make your deals with criminal bosses and scheme away and it will be okay but you weren't discreet enough. Cathy and Stephen weren't clever enough. Gavin wasn't bright enough, why? Because they were all taught by you and you just can't make it on the outside now. We are never going to stop looking for your victims.'

'What are you waiting for then, charge me!'

'Yvonne Coombes has gone missing. If you know who took her you need to tell us now.'

'I don't know where Yvonne is.'

'Did you order someone to kill her?'

'How could I possibly have done that from in here?'

'Easily. We know the deal you have struck with the Mafia. We know that Perry and Dwyer and you are going into the restaurant business – or rather you hope to, but from where I'm sitting, it doesn't look likely to happen. After all, we now have Stephen Perry in custody and we will be charging him with his part in the death and the disposal of Tony Poulson's body, possibly the others as well.'

'Was Yvonne's testimony going to form the basis of your allegations?'

Willis stared at him and realised he knew it was Yvonne

who had made a statement to the police. 'No, not Yvonne,' Willis lied. 'We have people coming forward every hour, since the press conference. People realise you're in danger of getting away with it again. They don't want you to get out. They don't want you to get rich on the back of themed restaurants. We now have full permission from the people in charge to really look for evidence against you. It's not proving too difficult. If you know where Yvonne is, tell me and I can help you still.'

'How?'

'By saying you co-operated.'

'No. DC Willis, you are an abomination of a woman. You will have nothing but sadness in your life because you deserve nothing more. You have crossed me. You'd better keep looking behind you now because I will be there.'

Chapter 45

When Willis got back to Fletcher House she went straight over to talk to Maxwell and Tucker.

'You were right, Chris, he knows where Yvonne is, I'm sure. How well are you doing with the search?'

'We need to narrow it down. We can't possibly check every field on every farm, it will take us a month. Yvonne Coombes won't have a month.'

'Eb, can we go and talk to Rachel McKinney?' asked Tucker.

'If we ring her, she will say no,' said Willis. She looked across at Carter who was checking something on Hector's desk.

He nodded. 'Chris, you and Willis go.'

Maxwell shook his head. 'I'm better off staying here, Tucker knows what we need to know and so does Ebony. I trust them to go.'

'Is your mum in?'

A young girl had answered the door of Rachel McKinney's flat in Lewisham. It was the ground floor of a converted Victorian terrace.

The girl turned and shouted into the hallway, 'Mummy, someone at the door!'

'Rachel McKinney?' Willis showed her badge to the woman as she approached. 'This is my colleague, DC Tucker.'

'Yes, hello, what is it you want?'

Rachel McKinney had hair streaked with purple and grey, and piercings in her nose and eyebrow. Her look was of one who had been an addict once, her face mottled and her skin dull, but her eyes were bright and light brown. She was petite, no more than five foot. She wore black leggings and a sloppy jumper, and the Indian bracelets around her wrists jangled as she walked. The scars from Douglas were still evident on her face and arms and what was visible of her chest. There were straight lines, square angles, missing rectangles of skin and flesh. She'd had plastic surgery in the few years after it happened but nothing could completely heal where he had partially skinned her, removing areas of flesh. Fingers on her right hand were missing; they had been burned so badly that the surgeons had fused two together to enable her to hold a pen. She had stated that she did not remember the attack. She remembered getting in the van and she remembered the walk to the gravesite.

'We wanted to talk to you about what's been on the news recently. You must have seen it?'

They followed her into the lounge where she ushered her daughter into another room.

'Get out of your uniform now, Vivi, and you can play on the iPad until I say it's time to stop, okay?'

The daughter nodded with all the enthusiasm and angelic compliance of a girl who was so happy she was about to burst.

Rachel showed Carter and Willis into the kitchen, a large space, big enough for a table.

'What is it you want to see me about? I've been following the media about the case. I saw your press conference.'

'A woman has been kidnapped and we believe she might be being held at a place Jimmy Douglas will have once known. Please, Rachel, have you thought any more about trying to remember where he held you?'

'I've thought of nothing else, but it doesn't mean I can help you.'

'Rachel, can we just take ten minutes of your time and ask you a few questions?' Tucker asked.

She looked at Tucker. 'Do I know you?'

'I was around the last time, working on the Heather Phillips case, but I was a lot younger then. I remember talking to you. Your scars have healed well.'

She nodded and stared at him until her memory slotted him into place. 'I do remember you, it's funny how at really awful times you remember people's kindness. You were kind to me, I felt you understood what I was going through.'

'You've done really well for yourself, you're a great role model for Vivi. Did you ever manage to finish your law degree?' asked Tucker.

'God, no, that seems like a different life back then. I suppose I am still dealing with some aspects of the law; I'm working for the rape crisis charity locally.'

'It's a great charity,' said Willis.

'Unfortunately the need seems to be growing,' McKinney answered.

'How are things for you now?' asked Tucker.

'Things are good, thanks. I still need a bit of help now and again when I get low.'

'Rachel, it's great to see you doing so well, and we appreciate you seeing us today,' said Tucker. 'We've come to talk to you about what happened to you in 2000. You've heard about the deaths of Nicola Stone and Millie Stephens, and about the graves at Lambs Farm, on the TV earlier today.'

'That's right, yeah. I don't know what I felt really. Violence of any kind, against anyone, is wrong. I kept thinking how frightened they must have been. Nicola Stone was vilified. I mean, the public never forgave her but really, what she did wasn't the worst thing.'

'She doesn't deserve your sympathy,' said Willis. 'She was with Douglas at the time you were abducted, she knew all about it. She was involved.'

Rachel hesitated and frowned. 'How do you know that?'

'I've talked to him,' said Willis.

She shook her head slowly, as if the movement would help this new information to settle in her mind. 'Okay, well, she is dead and I am alive and I have to live every day in a positive space.'

'You should be very proud of yourself, you've survived such a lot.' Tucker smiled at her.

'Yes. I listen to survivors every day and I realise we have a common thread that joins all of us; it's that we thought somehow we could have prevented it. Wrong place, wrong time, random choice of victim.'

'Sorry, but Douglas didn't choose you randomly,' Willis said. 'You fitted a type, an age, a build, not necessarily a scx, as hc is biscxual, but there was something about you that made him choose you. You must never think you could have prevented it, because you couldn't have. They were waiting for you on that road.'

Tucker stared at Willis, wondering what she thought

she was doing. He interrupted. 'Rachel, someone, one of Douglas's own disciples who was raped and abused by Douglas and the others, and who witnessed the murder of one of these people found at Lambs Farm, has gone missing. We believe she may be dead already, but there is a slim chance she might be alive, that they might be waiting to see what's going to happen with the case. They may be intending to put pressure on her to change her story. At the trial you were unable to give details,' Tucker persevered.

'I was barely able to breathe, to carry on living; I did my best.'

'I know, I completely understand. But, and I know this is a big ask and one that you may not be able to help us with, but, do you think that now you would be able to give us more information about what happened to you and where you might have been held in those five days? Do you remember there being other people there?' he asked.

'I knew there were other people there in the beginning, when I first came around, but memories are like nightmares, I don't know what's real and what's not. I don't want to know. I can help others because I understand exactly what they are going through but I still cannot heal myself. Many survivors choose to fully face the facts of what happened to them, we all have coping mechanisms. I can't afford to risk it now – I might lose everything, my sanity, for a start. My daughter depends on me.' She shook her head emphatically. 'I cannot revisit those memories. It wouldn't do me any good.'

'I understand,' said Tucker.

'Listen to me,' Willis reached across the table, 'we know that this is a terrible thing we're asking you to do, but we are in terrible times. A woman with a two-year-old child is missing, abducted, she may have been taken where you were held. Please, Rachel, please help us to find her.'

Rachel sat motionless, staring down at her hands. Minutes passed, and the only sound was that of the kitchen clock ticking in the background. Then she nodded.

Willis got out her notebook and waited, poised.

'At first I remember thinking I must be blind. I couldn't see anything; it was completely dark. It was completely quiet, except sometimes there was a squeaking as if a branch was touching the outside wall. Sometimes something hopped over the roof and I would lift my head to listen.' Rachel McKinney kept her eyes closed and a frown crept across her forehead. She looked as if she was in pain, beads of sweat started gathering at the sides of her face. The scars on her arms were becoming livid.

'The top of the cage was just a few inches above my head. I knew it was a cage, my hands were bound together at the wrists.' Rachel instinctively drew her hands together as she talked. 'When I first saw Douglas the light came streaming in and I realised where I was, in a container in a garage, a lockup of some kind. Every day he came to take me out of the crate. Then he'd put me back in and leave me there until the next day. The last day he hoisted me out of the crate as usual and I remember I was trying to beg him. I was gagged and I was filthy dirty, sitting in my own excrement. He usually hosed me down inside but this day he took me outside and made me stand just beneath a small tree and he hosed me down there. My body was stinging so badly like it was on fire. Douglas ordered me to lift my arms and I tried, they were so heavy, and he came across to me and held them above my head and then poured the water down over my face and body and it was a relief. The cold helped with the pain and when I opened my eyes I saw that I was next to an old cattle shelter at the top of a field. There were no crops in it; it wasn't lush grass, it was barren.

'I looked across at the fields in the valley opposite and there were trees there, tall straight cedar trees at the top of the field. There were five of them at the top of a small steep field.'

Willis realised that Rachel was describing a scene that she already had in her mind, but in reverse, it was one Maxwell had previously described.

'There is a barn, an industrial unit in the distance, possibly a cowshed. It is remote but surrounded with small, remote fields. Woodland in sight. Above me, five tall cedar trees.'

Chapter 46

'It's called Margery Farm,' said Willis as she explained to Carter what they had found. 'The farmer is called Jon Cole. He's been there for twenty-five years, so he must know what's on the land.'

'It makes sense Douglas didn't dirty his own back yard,' said Carter.

'That's right, he wasn't someone that Douglas delivered to,' answered Willis.

They sat with maps spread out and satellite photos of the area around Jones's farm.

'This is it. Margery Farm.' Maxwell nodded. He was quiet, thoughtful.

'You okay?' said Carter. 'You might have cracked it. We might find something of Heather in there as well?'

He nodded. 'This has to be our last chance, I think?'

'If this is Douglas's second site, we will find evidence in there, don't you worry. We'll have enough to keep him inside for life. We'll go into my office and ring Mr Cole now.'

Willis put her phone on speaker so that Carter, Bowie and Tucker, who had all crowded in, could listen to it. The farmer answered almost immediately and she explained why she had called. He remembered someone called Heathcote asking if he could buy some land from him.

'That was in 1999? And what did Mr Heathcote say he wanted it for?'

Everyone in the office stayed quiet and listened to his reply:

'He had a container of belongings and we aren't supposed to put stuff like that on the fields but, seeing as I wasn't going to use it, and I already had old machinery and a rusty old cowshed there, I said yes. I'm not going to get in trouble, am I? Stony Field was never much use for anything.'

'No, it's okay. Can you tell me, Mr Cole, has anyone been up to the field recently?'

'I can't be sure, I haven't been up there myself for six months. I thought I did see some tyre marks leading from the road up the back lane, but I can't be sure. I was just thinking then, I don't think anyone's been there for years. I thought Heathcote must be dead, although he was only a young fella, good-looking lad.'

'Can you describe him to me?'

'He had a slight Irish accent; he was dark-haired, green eyes, nice way about him. Do you want me to take a look and see if anyone's been there?'

'No, stay away from it please, and keep this conversation to yourself for now. We are going to need to come up and see for ourselves.'

Willis came off the phone.

'That's definitely a description of Douglas, back in the day,' said Tucker. 'That was never Gavin. He was always heavy-set with a strong cockney accent.'

'Agreed,' said Carter.

*

'Maxwell, you happy with that?' Carter asked as he informed the rest of the team what they'd found out about the field lockup in Somerset. 'We go down there now and take a look. But we go prepared.' Carter had been in to see Bowie to get clearance for what they needed to do. He'd called a meeting as soon as he'd got the green light.

Maxwell nodded. 'I'd like to come with you, please.'

'Okay.' Carter looked at him curiously. ' If you're sure, I have no objections. Where is Heathcote right now?' Carter turned to ask Hector.

'Surveillance lost him in town, but he was picked up by a camera on the motorway an hour ago. He's headed in the right direction. He could be on his way there.'

'Then we go down to Margery Farm armed,' said Carter, 'and we get down there as fast as we can. We'll go by road, not helicopter, we run the risk of being spotted too soon otherwise. But we'll have the helicopter on standby and a firearms unit waiting at the end of the lane where it meets the main road.'

'Hector, you are licensed, aren't you?' Hector nodded. 'So am I,' said Carter. 'Willis, I need you to stay and run things from here. Maxwell, you will need a vest and protection. We leave within the hour. I want to talk to Stephen Perry first.'

Willis sat next to Carter, opposite Perry and the representative from the highly acclaimed criminal law firm Sutton and Sons. Jeremy Sutton was one of the sons. Maxwell was monitoring the video in the adjoining room.

After they had dispensed with the introductions and the caution, Carter thanked Stephen Perry for coming in.

'Did I have a choice?' He sat back in his chair and tried to look relaxed, in his jeans and a blue shirt, with a gingham pattern on the inside of the collar. He was neat and clean-shaven. His hair had been styled recently, cut longer on the top, and left naturally choppy and wavy.

'You can leave at any time, Mr Perry,' Carter added.

'Let's make this quick then.'

'You've had time to talk to your solicitor, Mr Sutton?'

'Yes, he's advised me to say nothing but "no comment" but I don't have anything to hide and as long as I feel I can help, I will, especially if it speeds things up.' He smiled at his solicitor.

Willis spread out the photos of Tony Poulson, Simone Levin and Darren Slater on the desk.

'Remember them?'

'No, I don't know these people.'

'Let me specifically check if you remember seeing this man.' Willis pushed the photo of Poulson around to show him as she took away the others.

'I've never seen him before.'

'We know he was a hitchhiker Jimmy Douglas picked up and brought back, remember him now?'

Perry shook his head, 'Jimmy brought a lot of people to the bungalow and we had a lot of parties, there were strangers in and out all the time.'

'It was in May 2000, one of the first barbecues, and it was the night before three new disciples got their tattoos,' said Carter. 'He had a strong Glaswegian accent, ring a bell now?'

Perry was shaking his head but it was clear from his expression that his mind was reeling.

'What did getting the tattoo mean to you, Mr Perry?' asked Carter. 'Must have been a big thing?'

'It meant nothing,' answered Perry, glancing across to his

solicitor who was looking as if he was about to intervene. Perry shook his head as if to say he intended to carry on. 'It meant Jimmy Douglas was making us feel special, a bunch of lonely kids who didn't fit in anywhere. I'm guessing that's what it meant.'

'We heard it was a big deal when you got your tattoos, that something serious had happened between you all? So something went on that Saturday night, 20 May 2000, that meant that three people earned their tattoos,' said Blackman. 'What happened?'

'Nothing happened. Listen, I can't answer anything more than I know.'

'Did you ever know about the holes dug on farmers' land, where drugs were stashed?' asked Carter.

'No.'

'Mr Perry, can we just return to the subject of Tony Poulson for a moment?' said Carter. 'Apparently Tony Poulson was killed in the bungalow that night or in the early hours of Sunday morning. His body was then driven in Douglas's van to Lambs Farm and placed in a grave that probably had been used for storing drugs in a chest like this . . .' Willis showed him the photo of the plastic chest and gave its exhibit number to be recorded. 'This was uncovered in one of the five graves we found at Lambs Farm,' continued Carter. 'We know Douglas was famous for his drugs. Famous for hiding them in chests and some people have come forward to tell us they knew he hid them on farmers' land.'

Perry shook his head. 'It's news to me.'

Carter smiled as he sat back and watched Perry becoming ever more uncomfortable.

'Someone's also told us that you were one of the people who helped bury him. For the tape, Mr Perry is shaking his head. 'Do you deny helping to conceal Tony Poulson's body at Lambs Farm?'

'Of course.' Perry's face was beginning to twitch. 'I've never seen this man.' He glanced across at his lawyer, then back at Carter. 'This is absolutely madness. I have no idea who he is, or the other ones, and I certainly didn't see anyone murdered. That's just not possible.'

'Tell us how someone became one of Douglas's disciples?' Carter prompted. 'You specifically? How did you become one?'

'I don't know. I lived in the bungalow, so I suppose I was just there.'

'But he didn't just tattoo everybody, did he?' said Willis. 'You had to be someone like Ash who had done something pretty awful. Someone like you? What do you think he liked about you?'

'I can't speak for him, but I think he could have a conversation with me. I had a lot to say about a lot of things in those days; we used to talk about history, politics, I read a lot, he liked that.'

'Clever?'

'I suppose it was just my upbringing. Private education sets a minimum standard which tends to be higher than average.'

'Mr Perry, we understand that in order to become a disciple you had to be part of something that bound you together, that you had to experience something together,' said Willis.

'I don't remember that. What is the obsession with Douglas and becoming a disciple?'

Carter asked, 'You told us about the sexual assaults when we spoke to you last time, at your house, didn't you? The ones Nicola and Yvonne used to carry out?'

'I may have mentioned that there was a lot of sex in the bungalow.'

'If someone is restricted against their will and forced to take part in a sexual act, that's considered an act of violence. They would have seemed like violent attacks to other people,' said Willis.

'Look, I don't know, I was just there and it all happened, I didn't pass judgement at the time.'

'Do you think your boundaries were blurred by Douglas and your time in the bungalow?' asked Carter.

Willis added, 'Did things just escalate into something bigger all the time?'

'And before you knew it,' Carter said, leaning across the table to get as near to Perry as he was allowed, 'there was Tony Poulson's body lying in the corner of the sitting room at the bungalow?'

'I don't know what you're talking about.'

The lawyer sat forward. 'I insist we stop the interview now for me to talk with my client. We are not prepared for this line of questioning. Charge him or let him go.'

'We will be holding him for questioning and to decide if charges will be brought. Mr Perry, before we let you go back to your cell, we would like to ask you about a place called Margery Farm – have you heard of it?'

'No, I haven't.'

'We believe it is where Jimmy Douglas kept a container that he used to cage, torture and kill people in. We have had a first-hand account from Rachel McKinney and we have now traced that container. Before we open it, would you like to tell us anything you know about it?'

Perry shook his head.

Chapter 47

After Carter, Maxwell and Hector had left, Willis and Tucker sat together at the desk where Maxwell's maps were laid out and talked strategy together. They had to decide on the best route in and keep radio contact with the team so that they could help by changing the route at the last minute, if needed. Whilst they worked on it, Willis got a text from Tina to say that Cabrina and Archie were in the canteen and they were waiting for Carter. Willis went down to see them.

As soon as he saw her, Archie ran at Willis and the two began a wrestling match until Willis managed to bear-hug him into submission. She held him in a tight grip whilst she talked to Cabrina.

'I won't be able to control your son much longer.' Willis laughed. 'Imagine when he's thirteen, he'll be throwing me through windows!' She growled in his ear. 'That day may come ... but it is not this day!'

She let him go and mussed his hair. He had soft black curls from his mum's Cypriot side of the family and big brown eyes. He was short for six.

'Sorry, Cab,' said Willis, 'Dan got called out on an operation, it could be a long one.'

'Typical ... What are you up to?' she asked Willis.

'I wish I could hang around with you two,' replied Willis, 'but I'm in the middle of something big. Got to go. I'll tell Dan you were looking for him. See you soon, wild boy,' she teased Archie, and he went to attack her again as she skipped away.

Willis took the stairs two at a time as she went back upstairs. Tucker shook his head and smiled at her expression.

'Don't worry, you didn't miss anything.'

'Good.' She sat down next to him.

'Why do you think Chris Maxwell wanted to go to Somerset?' Tucker asked her. 'He doesn't look like an action man to me.'

'He was gutted when we had to stop the search for Heather; he seems to be a one-man crusade in his search for her. This may be the last chance we'll get to search for her for a long while. Thanks for being so nice to him, by the way. I know he's a bit of an odd bod.'

'He's really weird.'

'Yeah, I know, but he can't help it and I understand how he feels about some things, he's so pent-up.'

'Excuse me?' Tucker turned to her and shook his head in disbelief. 'Did I hear you right? You're opening up to me a little bit there, be careful.'

She rolled her eyes and went back to looking at the maps.

'Eb?' Tucker stayed focused on her.

'Yes?'

'Will you take some time after this inquiry is over and come out to France to visit me?'

She stared at him. She had never really looked at the colour of his eyes before; they were the colour of the sky in the early morning, the kind of morning that makes you feel good about life. Before she realised what she was doing she was nodding her head and saying yes.

Archie was fast asleep as Cabrina drove them home from having had tea without Dan. Tina had made a massive fuss of them, and her mind was on other things, when the blinking of the petrol gauge brought her back to earth. She spotted the garage up ahead and pulled in. When she'd finished filling the tank she queued up to pay. There was just one man on the till so Cabrina had to wait, and whilst she did her mind wandered back to Tucker and Willis. She had hoped it would work between them. Tucker was one of those men that just needed someone to push him and Ebony hadn't wanted to do it but Cabrina still held out hope.

'Any fuel?'

She'd finally got to the front of the queue.

'Number Four.'

The stern-faced assistant whose name badge read Raj looked over Cabrina's shoulder and said, 'Red Nissan?'

'Yes, that's correct.'

'You left your back passenger door wide open.'

Cabrina couldn't breathe as she looked out to her car to see the passenger door she knew had been shut now gaping wide open. She raced out of the shop and past the petrol pumps till she got back to the car but Archie was gone.

Willis, Tucker and Zoe were there within fifteen minutes. They pulled up on the forecourt. The garage was now cordoned off and other officers had arrived before them.

'Where's Dan? He should be here.' Cabrina rushed forward when she saw them.

'He's not in London, Cabrina,' said Tucker. 'We'll let him know as soon as we can.'

Willis hugged her. 'It's all right, Cab, stay calm. What happened?'

'I went in to pay for the fuel and he must have got out of the car.'

'Did anyone see him get out?' Tucker asked.

'No. But I should have locked him in; I just hate doing that, in case there's a fire. My God, Eb, please find him. Why would he just wander off like that?'

'Just stay here, Cabrina. I need to go and talk to the man in the office,' said Willis. 'Zoe, stay with her.'

Tucker was already walking towards the kiosk. Inside it were two other detectives from MIT 19. One of them was Kev Baldwin. They all shared the same canteen and went to the pub together. Willis knew him well.

'Kev?' she said, joining the others at the counter, watching the CCTV footage.

'Here you can see, this is her car, this red one,' said Kev, pointing at the screen. 'That's hers, and you see the van behind?'

'How long had this white Transit van been there?' Willis asked Raj behind the counter.

'That van had come in straight after the red car, but not for fuel. I thought the driver was waiting to use the vacuum or putting air in his tyres, but he didn't use it, he just left.'

'And the registration number of that van?' Tucker asked.

'We've already rung that in,' said Baldwin. 'We have patrol cars all over this area looking for it now, we're on this. We were here within minutes of him going missing. Allowing for the fact that there was a queue at the tills, it was probably seven minutes before. We'll get him back, I'm positive.'

'Any more cameras to get a look at who was driving the van?' asked Tucker.

'No, I'm sorry,' replied Raj, 'not on the vacuum station, just on the fuel and he didn't get any fuel. He never came inside the kiosk.'

Baldwin took a call on his radio. 'The van's been found abandoned half a mile from here,' he said. 'No one's inside. I'm so sorry.'

'We are done in here,' said Willis.

'This wasn't opportunistic. Archie was targeted,' said Tucker. 'We need to get back and co-ordinate the search from Fletcher House. If this is an abduction we have to be ready for their call.'

Willis nodded but her heart was telling her there would be no call. She knew what they wanted already. They got back outside and walked across to Cabrina who was shaking her head as she watched the two detectives come towards her.

'I'm not leaving here, Eb, it's all my fault, isn't it? I didn't lock him in? It's all my fault.'

Willis held Cabrina tight. 'No, it isn't your fault. They targeted you and Archie, there was nothing you could have done.'

'I can't leave here, what if he comes back?'

'He's been taken, Cabrina, he's not going to be walking back in here. We need to go and find him. Zoe will stay by your side and Tucker and I will find him.'

'Tell Dan to find Archie, you promise me? You promise?'

Willis nodded. Tucker hugged Cabrina and told her not to worry.

'Zoe, take Cabrina and drive her car to her home please,' said Willis. 'Take a statement from her, any tiny details she can remember about who she might have seen driving behind her, parked near her – anything.'

Zoe nodded and led a trembling Cabrina away.

Tucker and Willis walked back across to the petrol station office. Baldwin came off his radio as Willis opened the door.

'We've already had confirmation,' said Baldwin. 'The van was bought a few hours ago on eBay. We're looking into it now, the new owner's name on the logbook is a false one. I'm sorry. This was obviously planned. No one will rest at MIT 19 until we find him, you know that?'

Willis nodded. 'We're going to have to work together on this. I'm not trusting anyone else with this, my friend's son's life is at stake. Within a couple of hours Archie could be dead, could be on a boat to Europe or could be back at his mother's side. Everything we do now will determine that. Okay, Kev?'

'I understand. You tell me what you need me to do. We'll work together.'

'I need every port, every station alerted,' said Willis. 'Every boot of every car checked on every ferry that leaves here. I need cupboards ripped out and floorboards pulled up, I cannot have Archie leaving this country, otherwise that's the last we'll see of him.'

'Understood,' said Baldwin. 'What's this really about, Eb? Tucker?'

Willis looked at the phone in her hand. 'It's about Douglas.' She showed them the phone and a text message that consisted only of an icon of a face with rivers of tears coming from the eyes.

Chapter 48

'Should we send someone around to talk to the farmer?' Hector asked, as they pulled in down a back road to Margery Farm. Inside the car was Stephanie Davies, who was in charge of an elite firearms team.

Carter took out his binoculars and got on top of the jeep to look above the hedge.

'I can't see the container but I can see a cowshed and old farm machines. I think I can see the back of a van. I think Heathcote could be here.'

'We've had confirmation that his van came off the road at the last junction. We have to assume it's him,' said Davies.

'It looks from the satellite picture as if the container is tucked in beside the cowshed,' said Maxwell. He had a box full of printed images of the site and Ordnance Survey maps.

'How do you want to approach it?' asked Davies. 'You know the people concerned here, you tell me what way is best to come out of this with no loss of life.'

'I know we're not going to be able to risk a show of force,' answered Carter. 'If he feels like it, Heathcote will kill Yvonne.'

'Okay,' said Davies. 'Then we go in there, from the

bottom of the field, and work our way upwards, a softly-softly approach. At the same time we have people ready at the main exit via the farm and the way across the other fields. I will radio in now. We have a camera drone ready to go up, do you want to use it?'

'I think we should,' answered Carter, 'as long as it's high enough that he can't hear it.'

'I agree,' answered Davies. 'Just remember if we need back-up it will take seven minutes for it to reach us.'

Whilst Davies was relaying the instructions to her team, Carter got a call on his phone.

'What is it, Eb?'

'Yeah, Dan, something major has happened here. Archie's been taken, abducted in a slick operation when Cabrina stopped for petrol. The van was traced straight away, just been bought and was dumped nearby. We're pretty certain it's Douglas and his disciples ...' Willis paused when Carter didn't answer or even try to inter-rupt, '... so, what I'm saying is, I'm on this, Tucker's on it, everyone from MIT 17 and MIT 19 is on this and Bowie is running it. We will get him back, Dan. Dan?'

Carter needed a moment. He couldn't believe this was happening but at the same time he knew he couldn't lose his head. He was stuck where he was with no choice but to see their plan through. And in any case he knew if anyone would find Archie, Willis would. He pushed back the feel-ings of panic and fury that threatened to throw him off balance.

'I heard you, Eb. If it can't be me there, then you are the next best thing for Archie. You think with your head, not with your heart. The heart is never going to win in a fight with Douglas or his disciples. If the worst thing happens, and Archie is dying when you get there, you tell him how much I love him. Okay?' His voice faltered slightly despite his attempts to keep his emotions under control.

'You know I will.'

Davies was out of the vehicle. When Carter finished the call he walked away to clear his head for a few minutes before he came back and filled her in.

'They've taken my son. He's been abducted and Willis is sure that it was ordered by Douglas, carried out by his disciples. The Mafia must be putting on the squeeze.'

'It shows you how desperate they are for us to back off,' said Hector. 'What do you want from us, Dan?'

'There is nothing we can do but what we came here to do and that's get Yvonne back alive. I have faith in my team. Willis loves Archie like her own, which is why they chose him, why Douglas ordered it. I am the closest thing to family Willis has. She will do what she has to do.'

'I am sorry,' said Maxwell. 'I pushed for this to go further.'

Carter shook his head. 'Don't be sorry for being good at your job, Chris. Now, let's get this done.'

Davies nodded. 'We go in twos here,' she said. 'Two of us get back into the vehicle and drive it and block off the escape route on the lane and walk on foot to the entrance to Stony Field. The other two join my team and make their way up the field. Carter, your call?'

'I'll take Hector with me.' Carter left Maxwell with Davies, and got back into the car with Hector.

'Remember,' said Davies, leaning in at the window, 'you wait for our signal before you go in at the entrance to the field. We must have a good view, we are climbing uphill, we need to get halfway up the field to get a good shot.'

'Understood.'

Carter and Hector drove to the top of the lane, and set their car across the road, blocking it. Carter radioed in that they were about to start walking. They strode silently up the lane, along the side of the hedge. As the hedge came to an end they could see the gate to Stony Field. The old cattle shed was roofless and falling down, but the container was there, its top just visible through a break in the hedge. It was grey and solid with bracken growing around its edges – it was being absorbed by nature.

'We're on our way,' said Davies.

'We have the gate in our sights. I can see Heathcote's van.'

'Count to fifty, then go, not before,' said Davies.

Carter stopped and looked at Hector. From inside the container they could hear noises. He unfastened his holster and Hector did the same. A chain was looped around the gate, but it wasn't locked. They walked past Gavin's van and pushed the gate a little to step just inside. Carter looked down the field and saw a glimpse of movement as Stephanie Davies and her colleagues made their way up the field towards them.

Back at Fletcher House a missing child took priority over everything else.

'I am going to be the SIO,' said Bowie, as he addressed them all in the inquiry team office. 'We will be running this operation with MIT 19. I am overall in charge of the four units in this building and I exercise my rights to oversee this. I don't care what it costs. Get everything we have into the air and look for him. Who do you think would have done this?' he asked Willis.

'It was ordered by Douglas,' said Willis. 'Cathy Dwyer more than likely carried it out. We know she's trying to placate her backers. She may not have had their help in abducting Archie but she will be able to call on it if she needs it and then we won't see Archie again. We have to get him now while she may be thinking what to do.'

'Has Cabrina received a call for ransom?'

'No,' answered Willis. 'I don't think we will hear from them. They want us to get out there and tell the world's press the case is done with and that Douglas is coming out, that we have others facing charges. They won't care who we have to fit up, they just want their restaurants to open. It's all about money. We should consider putting out a statement if we don't find him in the first twenty-four hours,' Willis went on, unable to look at Tucker whilst she said the words. 'It should say that the investigation into Douglas and the new graves at Lambs Farm is being called off, just to give us time.'

'No,' said Bowie, 'we can't do that; you know we can't. They will roast us for that and we can't play by the Mafia's rules or by Douglas's. We are not Mafia-owned and we can't save Archie by those means. He lives or dies by our ability to find him.'

Laptop read his report on intelligence so far. 'We know this van was a newly bought fifteen-year-old Transit van and we have not been able to get a lot of information on the owners. However, the CCTV has been analysed, and it's believed that the person driving it in the picture could be Cathy Dwyer. We are still collecting CCTV footage from various locations during the afternoon, still hoping to get better images of the van.'

'All press communication is on lockdown,' said Bowie. 'We don't want this discussed outside these walls.'

'Perry must know the plans,' said Willis. Bowie was nodding.

First chance he got Tucker took Willis to one side. 'Nice try, Eb, not like you to want to pervert the course of justice?'

'I want Archie back, any way we can get him. If the Mafia step in to take the heat off Perry they can get Archie on any yacht in any small harbour in the UK and that will be it.'

'It's not going to happen,' Tucker said, reaching out to squeeze Willis's hand.

Blackman walked into the room. 'How's Cabrina?' asked Willis.

'She's holding up. I left someone with her.'

Willis moved to talk to Laptop. 'Do we have a list of the leases they have bought up for the new restaurants?'

'We do, they're all around the capital. Let me find that for you.' Laptop leafed through a file and removed the printout.

'Have we any leads on Dwyer's whereabouts?' asked Willis. 'Has the surveillance team kept on them?'

'The concierge in Arena Vista Tower says she was last seen when she left there earlier today. He said she'd had a visit from two men shortly before. There'd been reports of a woman seen dangling from the floor that she lives on, but Cathy Dwyer denied it, apparently, laughed it off. She wasn't seen after she went into the club in Shoreditch. We sent someone in there to look around. It seems there is another exit and Cathy Dwyer had gone.'

'That gives her plenty of time to liaise with the people who bought the van and pick up Cabrina's car from outside here after she came back from the pizza place. I'm going in to ask Perry if he knows anything about the abduction plans, or Margery Farm. Are you free to assist Tucker?'

'Definitely,' Laptop replied.

Jeremy Sutton QC was in position next to Stephen Perry. Stephen had spent the last few hours in the cells, which was never pleasant – it was impossible to ignore the smell of those who had gone before and a hard bed with minimum cover was lacking the comfort he was used to. Perry was therefore angry and he glared straight at them.

'Mr Perry, there have been some developments, as I expect Mr Sutton has made you aware of.'

'A police officer's son is missing, he told me, but what that has to do with me I don't know. I've been in here. Charge me or let me go.'

'We are searching for a little boy,' said Tucker.

'Good luck, I hope you find him,' said Perry. 'I would never be involved in something as low as kidnapping a child.'

'Mr Perry,' said Willis, 'the van the boy was abducted in was bought by someone working for the company that you and Cathy Dwyer jointly own and, since that time, we have been unable to locate Ms Dwyer. Do you know where she would be?'

'Ridiculous. Obviously there is no connection with GET and the van. Whoever you've hired to try and set us up is an amateur at best.'

'You know what your new associates are capable of?' asked Tucker.

'I'm not answering that. No comment, these are suppositions, what ifs. I wouldn't have thought you had time to waste on such things.'

'We know you are in business with Alex Ramirez and others,' said Willis. 'You set up GET Enterprises in order to start your empire with Douglas and his restaurants.'

'So what?'

'While Mr Ramirez has a legitimate face here in the UK,' Willis continued, 'he also has Mafia connections abroad and the two people I saw Cathy Dwyer with in his bar were well-known crime bosses.'

'We don't know anything of that. We are in the hospitality business, not on the set of *The Godfather*,' he scoffed.

'We're not going to fall for that, Mr Perry,' said Willis. 'You are anything but naive. You've spent time in prison yourself for running cocaine for these types of guys, don't tell me you haven't taken their money to set you and Douglas up?'

'No comment.'

Willis opened her phone and turned to show Perry the screen displaying the crying emoji.

'Douglas sent me this. Do you think Cathy Dwyer is under so much pressure, out there on her own, that she's made bad decisions without you? If she's kidnapped the boy then she's not going to come out of this well, and neither will you if you don't co-operate. This is your time to open up, Mr Perry. We are on the way to finding Archie and, when we do, anyone involved in this will be charged and can expect a lengthy sentence. Gavin Heathcote is being tracked down as we speak. We believe he is holding Yvonne Coombes at a location that you may be familiar with. It's a field on Margery Farm.'

Willis could see him chewing things over in his head.

'Please take some time to discuss with your legal team,' she said. 'Interview terminated.'

Willis left him talking to his lawyer. Outside she and Tucker talked it through.

'Have you heard from Douglas again?' Tucker asked.

'No, we need to get on the road and find Dwyer.'

Laptop came in with some information. 'Cathy Dwyer's gone back to her flat.'

'Alone?' asked Willis.

'Yes,' he answered.

'Okay, I'm going down there to talk to her. You coming, Tucker?'

They left Fletcher House and got into a pool car and headed down to Canary Wharf. As they passed through Whitechapel Tucker got a call. Cathy Dwyer had left the building.

Chapter 49

Carter and Hector stood just inside Stony Field and listened. As he looked down the field Carter caught a glimpse of Maxwell's face looking up from cover. Carter glanced back and nodded at Hector, who had his gun drawn.

Walking a few paces in they could see the side of the container to their left. Looking down the field, Carter could see the black uniforms fanning out and making their way up towards them. As he and Hector got level with the container they noticed the chain on the ground and that the door was slightly open. They heard the turning of a crank handle from inside the container.

Carter raised his hand and signalled to Davies that they'd be going in on the count of five. She acknowledged her understanding and was ready for him to start.

Carter began counting down and then saw Maxwell running up the hill towards them. He saw Davies get to her feet to try to stop him but she couldn't. He was a solitary figure running straight for the entrance to the container. Carter instinctively went forward first and slipped between the plastic sheets at the entrance to the container and before he had chance to adjust his eyes to the dark, the blast from a shotgun threw him backwards and he grappled to stay upright. He held on to the plastic curtain as Hector pulled him backwards out of the line of fire just as Maxwell ran straight into it. Three shotgun bullets pierced his neck and grazed the side of his skull. One made a hole in the artery in his thigh as he was blown backwards off his feet at the same time as Davies and her team stormed inside.

Carter crawled across to Maxwell, who was semi-conscious, his thigh pumping out blood with every heartbeat. Hector was trying to stop it at the same time as he was trying to save Carter's life.

'She's headed towards the Isle of Dogs,' said Laptop into the radio, after talking to support in the air.

'Okay,' answered Tucker, 'we'll head straight there now.'

'When you get there, follow the cranes, they're working on a large five-storey building there, it's nearby.'

'Okay.'

They drove in and around the building site and towards the newest construction. They saw Dwyer's car opposite the site entrance and the *GET Enterprises* sign.

Willis and Tucker parked up, went across to the building site manager and showed him their badges.

'What is this about? What are you here for? We don't have a problem normally with thieving. You're going to have to move your car, you're blocking the road there. How's that red car meant to get out?'

'Do you know who owns that car?' Tucker pointed to the black Range Rover.

'Ms Bloom. She's just come back. She's not stopping though, she told me to make sure no one did what you've just done.'

'Was she alone?'

'She's got a child with her. I saw him earlier, he was sleeping then. It's her nephew. She took him to her office.'

'And where is that?' asked Willis.

'Head towards your right, go to the back of the big building under construction there and you'll see three blue containers. Hers is the middle one. You'll need hard hats and there are unstable areas.'

The place was full of men working and machines. They were having to shout over the booms and wails they emitted.

'Have you got a plan we can take?' asked Willis.

'Yes, sure, it hasn't got the internal structure in there, but it gives you an idea of where everything is going to be.'

As she was talking to the site manager, Tucker touched Willis's arm and she looked up to catch sight of Cathy Dwyer passing along the first floor of the concrete structures on the main building with Archie in her arms.

'She must have seen us,' said Tucker.

They split up as they ran across the site towards her, and Tucker signalled he was going to go around the far side of the building. Willis strapped on her hard hat and started climbing. Inside the concrete shell of the building there were just the cement floors and the open windows. Willis looked around her and listened for any noise above the banging and thumping of machines. She heard Tucker shout and she ran across the floor to the far end, up the ladder to the next level and up again until she heard him shouting at someone. Willis alighted on the top floor and found Tucker bleeding, lying on the ground, stabbed in the neck. She ran towards him.

'Stay still, Scott.' Willis radioed in for help as she took off her coat and wrapped the sleeve tightly around his neck.

The side of his neck was an open wound and he had stab wounds in his shoulder and arm.

'She has Archie.' He pointed to the next section along.

Willis ran across and climbed over the concrete divisions, ducking under scaffolding as she searched on each level and clung to the side of the building. Builders stopped work to watch and one by one the machines became idle. The cranes were the only contraptions still working, their operators unaware of the drama unfolding beneath them.

'Let him go.' Willis stopped and watched as Cathy Dwyer stood at the edge of the scaffolding railing. She held Archie under one arm. He was waking up, looking around him, trying to understand. He called out, 'Ebony?'

'Yes, Archie, stay still, it's okay.' Willis switched her gaze to Cathy. 'Let him go. You have a lot of mitigating circumstances, believe me, you will get a deal. You are a victim of Douglas's, like so many others.'

Archie began to wriggle and Dwyer gripped him tighter.

'I won't get a deal. I know about deals. I made a deal with the Mafia that Douglas was coming out and we would be opening all these restaurants and now that's all falling apart. It's all screwed. They will kill me. If I'm going, I'm going out in style. People will remember who I am. I'll be the woman who jumped off the new complex on the Isle of Dogs with a small boy, a policeman's child. He will be famous and so will I.'

With no words, just by holding his gaze, Willis was telling Archie to focus on her, not to be frightened, not to panic. He was staring at her. Out of the corner of her eye she saw Tucker coming. He was stooped over, holding his neck, dripping blood. He was slowly making his way towards Dwyer and Archie.

'We'll give you protection if you testify about those times in the bungalow, tell us what really happened?' Willis watched Tucker but his progress was so slow. He was unsteady on his feet and she could barely stand to look at him. It was taking a supreme effort for him to stay upright.

'If I told you what I know about the things I saw, the things I did, that others did, you'd never let me out again. I'm finished, whichever way you look at it.'

Willis kept her main focus on Archie. His black hair was flying around his face but he didn't cry, he didn't waver. Dwyer stepped nearer to the edge of the scaffolding and below them they heard the shouts of the men bellowing up for them to get back. They heard the scream of police cars coming and a helicopter approaching.

Dwyer pulled Archie closer to her as the helicopter hovered overhead, glancing down over the scaffolding and then back at Willis. Momentarily distracted by the chaos of the scene she didn't see Scott Tucker launch himself forward. It all happened so fast that she barely fought him as he wrenched Archie from her. Tucker released the boy and Archie ran towards Willis, who caught him in a tight embrace. She buried her head in his dark curly hair, feeling relief for a second before she looked up to see Tucker staring at her. A knife was sticking out of his chest. For a moment time froze until, to her horror, Tucker and Cathy Dwyer fell over the side of the building.

Chapter 50

Douglas stared at the spot on the wall that had been his portal to the outside world and he filled his lungs with breath as he practised his Tai Chi. He moved his hands in circles, like the wheels of a train, and tried to block out the banging doors in the corridor outside. He practised his controlled breathing – inhaling, holding the air in his lungs, expanding his ribcage. He felt the bones stretch, the lungs push against his ribs. He practised his meditation, snatching the flashes of anger as they popped into his brain and putting them inside red balloons and sending them skyward. He stood with his back to the door. He had had all the details worked out. The colour of the napkins, the quality of the cloth, the way they felt to the touch, the crisp, clean folds. The cutlery, the crockery, the layout of the tables. But now, the visions in his mind were becoming contaminated.

He focused on a spot on the wall straight ahead. It was a point of irritation for him; a spot of dirt that wouldn't go away, no matter how hard he scrubbed it. The scrubbing only made it worse, it spread it, it removed some of the paint and left it looking much worse. He took a few steps towards it until it was level with his eyes and he stared straight into it as he'd never done before. The layers of old paint, the years of dirt from people who had passed through the cell, lived there for a while, left their lives in the walls, their crimes, their failures, dead and dying dreams in the wall.

He looked at the calendar, which he'd turned forwards to June. The picture of the sea, so still, the sand so white. In June he was getting out. But why did he feel the sand slipping between his toes, being sucked down the cracks in the cell floor? Why did the sunny picture make him sweat on such a cold day? It was the horrible realisation that he might never feel the cool water between his toes. It had taken him years to control his anger and to harness his thoughts. Douglas breathed, held the breath and as he let it go he released another balloon that burst, showering his world with blood. The old anger inside him made him want to open his mouth so wide that his jaw cracked either side of his head. He wanted to scream, roar, bellow in fury, so loud that it burst the eardrums of all who heard it and in their silent agony he could walk through the corridors, the walls, pass through the prison doors and slaughter everyone who dared to look at him.

Douglas clapped his hand silently in front of his face as he stood in front of the hole in the wall. He turned to wave at the calendar with the girl who looked like Heather in the photo.

'Officer Kowalski?' Douglas called out and the officer came to talk to him through the grille.

'Sorry about all your troubles, Douglas. I hear you'll be back on trial, you'll have to leave here, go back to high security.'

'Please step in here a moment, I have something of great importance to tell you.'

As Kowalski turned to close the door behind him, checking quickly that none of his colleagues was watching, Douglas picked up a boning knife he'd stolen from the kitchen. He looked across at the calendar and the month of June and he could no longer see it for the blood.

Yvonne Coombes pushed Bonny on the swing in the park. It was early June now and the weather was lovely. Willis was standing next to her.

'I know it's hard having to live in secret like this but it won't be long now, and you and Bonny will be on your way to a new life in Australia. You've done such a great job, you're clean now, and you're going to have a great new start – a new life, new identity.' Willis tried to say it with a smile but her heart was still solid with grief. She watched Bonny swing her legs and she could tell Yvonne was worn out by all the court appearances, all the questions. They were all worn out. 'Just five more minutes,' said Willis. 'We'd better get you back inside.'

The last eight months had been taken up with the unfolding investigation into all the lost people that Douglas had kept in the lockup. Perry was trying to put as much blame on others as he could, but he was still facing a life sentence. Heathcote would get the same.

Chris Maxwell's body was cremated and sent home to his family. Willis had been one of those to go into his room in King's Cross. The photos of Chris and his mother and the articles about Douglas and Heather and the trial were all over the walls. There was a full account there, in Chris's hand, of his life and about how he had never meant to kill Nicola. He had just wanted to ask her some questions. Mainly, it was all about his regrets over Heather.

Willis had been moved by one particular page of his writing, which said:

'The night Heather disappeared I phoned everywhere and only Nicola answered. She promised she'd tell Heather I couldn't make it; my mum had had a stroke and I missed the ferry to England. Then I heard Heather was missing, presumed dead, and Douglas was on trial. I waited all these years to hear that someone had found her body, that Douglas would never come out of prison and I would never have to tell what I saw and did, but it never happened and I knew, if I didn't make it happen, then Heather would never get justice. I have done terrible things. I will never be a person who can live a normal life and enjoy the things others do. I carry the weight of all my crimes on me. Tony's face haunts me every day. Over the years I have contemplated suicide many times and I know I am forever damaged by what I did with Douglas. But, I found friendship in the last week and I have some feelings of pride that my work might help to keep Douglas inside prison and may even find Heather one day.'

He'd been right under their noses all of that time and it unsettled Willis to know that they hadn't picked up on it at all. She'd liked him but he had been troubled. He'd committed murder. But he'd died trying to get justice for those who had suffered at Douglas's hands. Willis didn't know how to feel about Chris Maxwell, or Ash as they now knew him to be. Maybe she never would.

Chapter 51

Saul the farrier had built his house with the kitchen and the living room on the first floor, bedrooms underneath. It gave him a lovely view over the gently rolling hillside. He was glad the Phillips family had moved away; he had watched Heather since the day she was brought home from the hospital, listened to her baby cries and his heart had broken for her. From his kitchen he could see both the side and front of the Phillipses' house and the patio of the bungalow. He could see into the farmyard. He'd often talked to Heather, letting her ride Murphy around his fields that he'd left as meadow, or loaned to Truscott for the sheep to graze. He put up some jumps sometimes – just planks over barrels, no more than two feet high. Murphy was too old to be put through more than that but he still loved jumping. At the start of the foot and mouth all the animals in the fields had to be destroyed, except the horses. They didn't get the disease but they couldn't be moved, they couldn't even be walked down the lane. Food was hard to come by for them. Generations of sheep, which Saul could call by name, were slaughtered. Then came the slaughter of the horses. Truscott decided they were no longer viable. Saul was glad he had saved Murphy. He'd bought him from

Truscott in the September after Heather disappeared. He'd looked after him and built him a shelter in Forge Field, next to his house, so he could watch him from his sitting room and could imagine Heather still there.

He was there the day they burned Ash's van. He saw the black acrid smoke billow upwards and he saw Ash running. By the time Ash reached the van Douglas and Nicola were standing back and watching it burn.

'Sorry,' said Douglas, 'I had to do it, it was just a stinking pile of shite in the end.'

'You shouldn't have done it,' said Ash, 'that was my home. My mum's stuff is in there.'

'I pulled out what looked usable, there's a pile of shit over there.' Douglas pointed to some clothes on the grass. 'You can live with us.'

Douglas and Nicola walked away, arm-in-arm. Nicola turned back and grinned at Ash. Ash stood back as the flames ripped through his home.

Truscott came running across the field shouting. 'Get back! Get away, it could explode.'

Douglas called over, 'We took out the gas cylinder, there's nothing going to explode. It's just a pile of junk – you told me to get rid of it.'

'Even so . . .' Truscott looked guilty.

Nicola and Douglas had sat down on the patio at the back of the bungalow and opened beers. Nicola was rocking on the chair. Truscott marched across to talk to them. Nicola looked across at Ash. He was picking up what he wanted from the clothes and the belongings and putting them in a rucksack.

He walked onto the lane and down it, past the road,

keeping out of sight of the bungalow before stopping outside Heather's house, up at the end of the field that bordered the farm. He stood and waited for what seemed like forever, as the hours passed until she saw him from her bedroom window. She slipped outside and ran up to hug him as they crouched and whispered in the hedgerow.

'I saw the fire, was that your van?'

'Yes. I have nothing left here of mine now,' said Ash.

'We still have each other. Nothing and no one else matters.'

'I'm leaving now, Heather, it's not safe for me here.' They hugged one another. 'Don't trust anyone here, Heather, believe me, none of them are our friends. They are getting madder every day in the bungalow. I've done things I can't get out of my mind, things I can't forget. Terrible things. I don't know who I am any more. But I'm going to meet with my gran and we'll make a plan about Mum and I'll write to you as soon as I can.'

'Write to Saul's.'

'Yes, okay. I'll address it to Murphy. Oh God, Heather, I'm sorry.'

'Don't be sorry. Just come and get me and we'll be fine, you and me. Don't forget me, promise?' Heather pleaded.

'I could never forget you.' He hugged her. 'You are the best thing that ever happened to me. I'm going to be waiting, every day. I will get word to you, don't worry. I'll get it all organised and get my mum sorted, then it'll be just us.'

She nodded but her eyes were full of panic.

'I have to get my mum to a safe place, you understand, don't you, Heather? There's something so bad about Jimmy and Nicola, and the others; you never know what they're thinking. They don't care about anyone. Don't ever trust them, promise? Remember that when I'm not here.'

'I will, I promise. I've been saving to get away. I have money for us to live for a while,' she said.

'That's good, we'll need to just hide away until your birthday, then it will be legal for us to be together. They can't force you to return home after September.'

Heather came to see Saul the day after the van had been burned down and Ash had left. Saul had seen him go.

'Is everything all right, Heather?'

She hesitated, nodded and then smiled.

'Saul, can I ask you a favour? Can I get things sent to your home instead of mine? Like letters?'

'Sure, you'd better address it with your initials in brackets by my name, otherwise the postman will probably take it to your house.'

'Thanks, Saul; it will be addressed to Murphy.'

Midnight, Saturday 22 July 2000

Saul watched Heather as she left for the party at ten that hot evening. He lost her in the crowds of people and the lights and music and he was about to climb over the gate and see what had happened to her, when he saw her come running out of the bungalow. She climbed the gate to Forge Field and he saw her fall to the ground several times as she ran across it. He strode after her, calling to her, trying to catch her up, but she just kept running from him. He looked back and saw Nicola and the others hovering at the gate before they turned back to the party. He saw Douglas leave and walk past the gate as he walked away from the party and down the lane. Then he saw Douglas's van pull

up at the entrance to his field, by the main road, where Saul
parked his blacksmith's van to stop any gypsies trying to get
into his field. He saw the lights for a few seconds and then
they were gone. Next he heard a door being opened and
he heard the sound of the back of the van being opened.
He heard Murphy blow through his nostrils as he ate the
grass and heard him start moving. Saul hid and watched
as Douglas stepped up beside Murphy; he had a length of
material in his hand, he had it curled in his fist behind his
back. He watched Heather run again, wobbly on her feet,
and he watched her stop dead in her tracks. Murphy looked
at her and seemed to sigh loudly. Heather turned to run
but Douglas grabbed her and picked her off her feet. He
smothered her mouth with the blanket and in seconds he
had her in the back of the van until Saul stepped up out of
the darkness and brought his hammer down onto Douglas's
head. With great care, he picked Heather up and carried
her to the front seat of his blacksmith's van and strapped
her in and drove.

Chapter 52

Saul had finished packing up his house. The place was sold. He headed up to Wales on a bright June morning, driving into the heart of the Brecon Beacons and parking up outside a stone farmhouse. Getting out of the car he stretched his weary bones and went across to an ancient old horse who had watched him arrive with interest and walked across to greet him at the fence.

'He never forgets you.' A woman appeared from the cottage with two children who ran over to welcome Saul. The woman was dark-haired and dark-eyed with a beauty reminiscent of an Italian Renaissance painting.

She walked across to greet him with a carrot in her hand for the horse.

'Here you go, Murphy.' She smiled at Saul, kissed him on his cheek. 'It's good to have you home. Ewan is just out tending the sheep, the flock is growing all the time. I'm milking them now to make cheese, it'll be great to have help.'

'Are you happy, Heather?'

She smiled and nodded. 'I'm happy.'

Carter was waiting in the car for Willis after she finished talking to Yvonne. 'Is she going to be all right, Eb? She's having to go through a lot, and the rehousing programme in Oz means she has to be clean: no drugs.'

'She knows. She's finding it all tough, but I know she can do it.'

'What about you? I've hardly seen you out since Tucker died.'

'It's the case. It's just a long one, it's all-consuming.'

He looked across at Willis and she nodded, but at the same time as she smiled she started crying. He hugged her.

'You'll be okay, Eb. You'll be okay. You need a little bit of TLC and you need a break from all this sadness. Tina says you sit in your room and won't talk about Tucker.'

'I don't know what to say. I miss him. I wish things were different, I regret things, and what good is that now he's dead?'

'There's nothing you could have done about it. You couldn't have stopped him dying.'

'I know that.' Willis stared out at the blue early-morning sky and sighed.

'Things move on, you have to be grateful for the one life we get, Eb. Don't ever regret. You give everything you have to give and more, I know that. We're having a celebration in the pub tonight and you're coming. Tina's bringing you.'

'What's it in aid of?'

'Cabrina and I have set a date. You're going to be my best man.'

She knew what he was doing, he was trying to show her that life moves on. They'd both been through hell with this case and she'd realised too late what Tucker had meant to her. But Carter was right, she couldn't change things and she had to move forward. And what better way than being there for Carter on what was meant to be the happiest day of his life.

She took a deep breath and smiled.

'Count me in.'

Acknowledgements

This book took a lot of putting together and I need to thank Dave Willis for giving up his time to work through the plot with me, as well as Aengus Little, for all things Crime Scene related.

I need to thank John Jacobs and Chris Maxwell for their invaluable help with the technical stuff and all my family and friends who deserve a big thank-you for listening to my murderous ideas time-and-time again. I can still hear my mum saying: 'when are you going to write something light and funny?!' No time soon, Mum, I'm afraid; I'm having far too much fun.

Special thanks go to Becky Long at 'Visage'; and Norma, Noreen, Della at 'True Colours' – all invaluable sounding posts for me.

Many thanks go to my editor Jo Dickinson and to the team at Simon & Schuster who helped me make this the best book possible. Your hard work is much appreciated. And thanks to the agent who saw me through to this stage in my career and who I will be eternally grateful to – Darley Anderson.